The **Skorpion** Directive

The **Skorpion** Directive

david **stone**

G. P. PUTNAM'S SONS • NEW YORK

PUTNAM

G. P. PUTNAM'S SONS
Publishers Since 1838
Published by the Penguin Group
Penguin Group (USA) Inc., 375 Hudson Street, New York, New York 10014,
USA • Penguin Group (Canada), 90 Eglinton Avenue East, Suite 700,
Toronto, Ontario M4P 2Y3, Canada (a division of Pearson Penguin
Canada Inc.) • Penguin Books Ltd, 80 Strand, London WC2R 0RL,
England • Penguin Ireland, 25 St Stephen's Green, Dublin 2, Ireland
(a division of Penguin Books Ltd) • Penguin Group (Australia),
250 Camberwell Road, Camberwell, Victoria 3124, Australia (a division
of Pearson Australia Group Pty Ltd) • Penguin Books India Pvt Ltd,
11 Community Centre, Panchsheel Park, New Delhi–110 017, India •
Penguin Group (NZ), 67 Apollo Drive, Rosedale, North Shore 0632,
New Zealand (a division of Pearson New Zealand Ltd) •
Penguin Books (South Africa) (Pty) Ltd,
24 Sturdee Avenue, Rosebank, Johannesburg 2196, South Africa

Penguin Books Ltd, Registered Offices: 80 Strand, London WC2R 0RL, England

Grateful acknowledgment is made to reprint
the image on p. 333: 2009 Google
Image Copyright GeoEye
Imagery Date: June 25, 2009
33'36'30.00 N/ 7'37'59.19 W

Library of Congress Cataloging-in-Publication Data

Stone, David, date.
The skorpion directive/ David Stone.
p.   cm.
Summary: After a close friend is murdered, Micah Dalton is on the hunt for vengeance.
ISBN 978-0-399-15632-8
1. Dalton, Micah (Fictitious character)—Fiction.   2. Intelligence
officers—Fiction.   I. Title.
PR9199.3.S833S37   2010   2009051555
813'.54—dc22

Printed in the United States of America
1   3   5   7   9   10   8   6   4   2

BOOK DESIGN BY AMANDA DEWEY

for **Catherine Stone**

And in memory of

**RSM Ted Adair,
Governor General's Horse Guards:**

"I am not unwell . . ."

My sincere thanks to Chris Pepe, my very patient editor,
Barney Karpfinger, my very patient agent, and to
Inge de Taye, Cathy Jacques, Debbie Fowler, Barbara Wojdat

A scorpion and a crocodile reached the edge of a broad, swift-running river, and both paused a moment on the bank. The scorpion, who could not swim, asked the crocodile to carry him across it. The crocodile was reluctant, fearing that once they had set out upon the river the scorpion would sting him. The scorpion replied that if he were to sting the crocodile in the middle of the river, he would die as well.

The crocodile considered this, and then consented to carry the scorpion across the river. But when they reached the middle of the rushing river, the scorpion coiled and stung the crocodile many times.

Dying, the crocodile cursed the scorpion for his malice, but the scorpion answered that the crocodile knew what kind of creature he was when he agreed to carry him across the river and the crocodile should not be amazed when a scorpion behaves like a scorpion. The river, wiser than either, killed them both.

—Traditional, possibly from Egypt

Vienna

Micah Dalton, riding a crowded escalator up into the cold blue light of the Schottentor trolley station, was instantly spotted by a member of the *Überwachungs-Dienst*, in this case a twenty-eight-year-old cut-crystal blonde named Lasha Seigel. Seigel had been assigned the *trigger* position, the trigger being the most likely member of the Overwatch Service to have First Contact with the target.

HumInt obtained by the Cousins—they would not reveal the source—indicated that Dalton was likely to surface at the Schottentor subway stop at some point in the early evening of this day. Seigel had therefore taken up her trigger post at daybreak, in a vacant office on the fifth floor of the Volksbank, on the far side of Währinger Strasse, and had remained there ever since, fixed, alone, without relief, mainly because her boss, Rolf Jägermeier, was a *Pfennigfuchseres Arschloch*, a blunt Teutonic curse that, when sounded out, needs no translation. The rest of the "box" team would commence *der Aufzug*—the lift, the active mobile surveillance operation—as soon as Seigel established First Contact. Which, to her credit, she managed to do three seconds after Dalton cleared the escalator exit. In another two seconds she had a digital camera with a thousand-millimeter lens zeroed in on Dalton's face. And as soon as she had it focused, down in his lizard brain, Micah Dalton sensed . . . *something*. Nothing as specific as a surveillance lens, or the adrenalized young woman behind it. Just a sudden and skin-crawling sense of unease. In his current state, this was not surprising.

He had not slept for two days, and his weary mind was far away in London, recalling the murder of an Uzbek courier on an escalator very much like this one. He became aware that his pulse rate was also climbing, but thinking about the Uzbek's murder could be the cause of that as well, since Dalton had been the murderer.

The Agency had gone to no end of trouble to recruit this Uzbek, whose family was supposed to have a direct connection with the largest al-Qaeda unit in Tashkent, and they were not at all pleased to learn that he had already been doubled by the Albanians, or at least that's what Dalton had been told, by Tony Crane, the head of the CIA's London Station. Dalton, whose time in the Fifth Special Forces had given him some intimate and bloody contact with the Albanians, didn't think they had enough tradecraft to double a decaf mocha latte.

No matter. According to Tony Crane, the inconvenient Uzbek needed his ticket punched. Crane was a languid blond-haired Back Bay princeling with a perma-tan, a history degree from Oxford, and a Harvard Yard drawl. His only firsthand experience of incoming fire was facing a forehand smash on a clay court. Nevertheless, Crane labored, with some success, at least among the young and gullible on the staff, to create the impression that he and sudden death had been roommates at Choate. Crane wanted "the hit" done in a *memorable* way, "so those *fucking* Albanians would get the *fucking* point."

Crane's XO, Stennis Corso, known as Pinky behind his back, a round, seal-like little man with tiny pink ears and bright pink cheeks and soft pink hands that were always raw from too much scrubbing—no one at London Station cared to know why—had a hopelessly mad crush on Dalton at the time, so Dalton got the assignment as a kind of burnt offering from Pinky, whose private passion for Dalton had tented Pinky's hand-sewn Quaker bedspread for over two years.

Dalton resented the assignment bitterly: he didn't mind a necessary combat killing, but he deeply despised murder. Nevertheless, he had stayed on the Uzbek for a couple of weeks, realizing pretty early on that, for a double agent supposedly steeped in guile, the fragile old man had the situational awareness of a mollusk.

On the day marked for what Crane liked to call "the hit"—the Friday of the Victoria Day weekend, a three-day holiday in London—Dalton had stalked him for hours, checking for countersurveillance, waiting for his moment, which, as these moments often do, presented itself on an escalator, in this case the one inside the Marylebone tube station. He could still see the old man's tweed coat, draped over his narrow bony shoulders like a shawl, his yellow-gray hair, damp with sweat, his left hand shoved deep into his coat pocket, a few inches of his spine showing above a grimy white shirt collar, as he rode the escalator up into the rush-hour clamor of a London afternoon, his right hand, clawlike, gripping the worn rubber rail. The Uzbek was deep inside himself, curled up inside his thoughts like a cat in a closet.

In the final seconds of his life the old man, perhaps sensing Dalton closing in, turned sharply, his blue lips tight, his cheekbones jutting out, his milky eyes widening. Dalton showed his teeth in what he quite mistakenly imagined to be a disarming smile and put four subsonic .22s into the old man's lungs, the man's shocked breath a short, sharp puff of peppermint and whisky straight into Dalton's face.

The chuffing crackle of the Ruger, the silenced muzzle pressed hard up against the man's woolen vest, was no louder than a dry cough, barely heard above the shuffling din of the crowds, the roar of the subway, and the *rattle-clank-rattle* of the ancient cast-iron escalator. Four in the lungs looks a lot like a fainting spell to anyone passing by, and everyone did just that.

The Uzbek's clothes reeked of Turkish tobacco. His teeth were too large and unnaturally white, like little slabs of plastic, the gums a lurid pink. Baltic work, very likely. Dalton had seen enough of that sort of Stalinist dentistry in the blackened mouths of bloated corpses all over Kosovo.

He caught the man's body as it fell, holding the Uzbek up, pasting a worried look on his sharp-planed, cold-eyed face for the benefit of the other people on the escalator, all of whom glanced quickly away, avoiding involvement of any kind, flowing easily around the two of them like water over stones.

Dalton dead-walked him to a nearby bench, kneeling down in front of him as if he were offering roadside assistance, keeping his pale blue eyes fixed on the man's face. Dalton was ashamed of feeling not much of anything as he watched him struggle for one more breath, watched his cheeks blooming pink, and then fading slowly to gray.

The Uzbek, his coal-black magpie eyes fixed on Dalton's, had said something with his final breath, a prayer, a curse, a question, but Dalton spoke no Uzbek, and the man did not try to say it again in English, so although they were quite close together, locked in this obscene intimacy, the old courier died alone.

When the Marylebone crowds thinned out Dalton set the Uzbek gently back on the bench, put a copy of *The Times* on his lap, and arranged him into a plausible counterfeit of sleep. Then he stood up, tucking the Ruger into a copy of *Hello* magazine with the skull face of Victoria Beckham scowling from the cover, and walked out of the tube station and into the crowds on Harewood Row, under a hazy twilight sky filled with blue and gold light, an evening, as it happened, very much like this evening in Vienna five years later.

Lasha Seigel, in the office on the fifth floor of the Volksbank, tightened the focus of her lens and clicked another digital shot of Dalton pausing at the top of the escalator, time-marked it, and hit SEND.

This time Dalton felt a second and much stronger ripple of unease. Something about this evening in Old Vienna was . . . not right. He paused for a moment, looking to his left to glance at a poster advertising a Senegalese rapper-poet named Goebe.

Galan's mark, the *tell*—a slash of blue marker on the lower left-hand corner—was there, as required by the protocols. Its presence stated that, in Galan's professional view, it was safe to go forward to the contact point. Of course, Dalton had been told that kind of thing many times before, and sometimes it had even been true.

The fact that his meeting was with Issadore Galan, an ex-Mossad agent now running the *agenzia di spionaggo* for the Carabinieri in Venice, made it important to push his luck. Galan disliked face-to-face meetings and avoided them unless he had something to say that could not be safely said in any other way.

Dalton pulled in a breath, let it out slowly. If Galan had made a tradecraft error here in Vienna—as unlikely as that was—there was only one way to confirm it.

He paused for a moment, gathering himself, taking in the city.

Vienna, like most aging harlots, was at her best in the twilight: Baroque façades lined the Ring District, richly detailed five- and six-story wedding cakes in pink and cream stone, coffer-roofed, every available inch of wall surface covered in gilded nymphs, onyx satyrs, alabaster cherubs, copper putti, bronze Valkyries, winged stallions with nostrils flaring—all of this *Dream of Ossian* imagery overlooking a maze of streets packed with earnest little Austrian eco cars bustling up and down the avenues under a glittering web of trolley wires, like fat white rabbits, late, too late, for a very important date.

It had rained hard most of the day, clearing around seven, turning the Viennese sky into a luminous California sunset. The Ring smelled of wet stone, early-spring mosses, diesel fumes, and, floating on the misty air from a student café across the *Strasse,* the biting tang of fresh dark coffee.

In this threshold moment, Lasha Seigel took one last chance to pull in tight on the target, filling her lens with the glowing image of a taut, muscular man, narrow-hipped but broad at the shoulders, a little less than six feet, with longish blond hair, a slightly cruel face made of angles and edges, deep-set eyes hooded by the downlight. He was too well dressed to be a student or a tourist, in a long blue overcoat over navy slacks, a blue V-neck sweater, a scarf of pale gold silk, expensive black wingtips.

Her heart rate rose perceptibly as she studied Dalton's uncompromising face in the lens. Back at the Office, during their final Tactical Briefing, trying to drive home just how dangerous this target was, the unit chief, Nenia Faschi, had told them that the Serbian Mafia, who had tangled with the target several times last year, were calling him the *Krokodil.* Seigel had to admit he had that . . . *look.* The voice of Rolf Jägermeier, in his Mobile 2 unit in front of the Regina Hotel, came up in her earpiece. Jägermeier had seen the transmitted image from her digital camera, checked it with a file photo in his laptop.

Ja. Das ist Dalton. Gehen Sie in die Strasse, mit dem Aufzug.

Yes. That's Dalton. Get down on the street with the Lift Team.

Double-clicking her throat mike to let Jägermeier know she had heard and would comply, Seigel noticed that the Viennese, a wary people, were giving this *Krokodil* a certain space. She packed up her gear, stopping at the door to see that she had left no traces, and slipped out into the deserted hallway, heading for the stairs, thinking, as she came hurriedly down the darkened hall, *He can't lose us in the Ring. Too many buildings, too much street light.*

Across the *Strasse,* Dalton was thinking exactly the same thing: this was bad ground for a covert meeting. Too brightly lit, too many rooflines, too many long walled-in blocks, and no room at all to maneuver. *A cattle chute to the slaughterhouse*, Dalton's CQB instructor at Fort Campbell would have said. Exposed, lines of fire from every angle, fully in enfilade, no chance to get to cover. It must have been hellish to fight in the streets of Vienna during the war, although the Panzers and the Stukas would have been a great help.

There was a broad open space to his right—Sigmund Freud Park, looking threadbare and tired after a hard Austrian winter—and, on the far side of the park, he could see the floodlit yellow hulk of the Regina Hotel. To the left of the Regina, the twin spires of the Votivkirche glittered like silver spikes against the fading glow of the evening sky. A red-and-cream trolley rumbled past on steel tracks, heavy as a Tiger tank, shaking the ground under his feet. A young blond woman in faded jeans and a mud-brown ski vest popped out of a door in the Volksbank Building across the street, clearly in a hurry. She glanced in his direction, seemed to flinch away, and then she jerked her head around sharply, turning north on Währinger Strasse, lugging her camo-colored backpack, melting quickly into the street crowds. That jumpy glance, and her body language as she headed away from him, that was all it took.

His vague ripples of unease hardened into a near certainty. He made the professional decision to assume he was under surveillance. It was the only safe thing to do. But surveillance by whom?

Possibly the KGB.

He had, just a few weeks ago, exposed a KGB mole buried deep inside the U.S. Army, in the process decimating a KGB network in Istanbul and Kerch, so the KGB had no reason to love Dalton. And these days the KGB—who had changed their official name to the FSB in 1991 but who were still thought of as the KGB by every opposing agency—were thick on the ground in Vienna, now that over two hundred thousand Chechen refugees had made their way here.

Or it could be the Serbs and Croats, who had declared a vendetta against him ever since he had run a small but extremely brutal private

war against the Serbian Mafia in Venice. Another contender would
be the Singaporean SID, whom Dalton had managed to piss off quite
spectacularly only a few months ago.

Whoever it was, the Austrians were old hands at the spy game, and
neither the KGB nor any other foreign security service would be allowed to run a surveillance operation without the permission, and
perhaps the assistance, of the OSE, the *Österreichische Spionage Abwehr
Einheit*. Austria had an official policy of neutrality—had ever since
1955—but that didn't mean that allowances could not be made when
it served the state.

Dalton had met, and respected, Austrian special forces soldiers
doing UN work in Bosnia and Kosovo, and Galan had once told him
the Austrians had a detachment in permanent position on the Golan
Heights. The Austrians had a more muscular definition of "neutrality" than the Swiss, and lately they had been taking "advice" from the
KGB about their Chechen refugee problem.

It wasn't out of the question that they had also been taking "advice" from the KGB about a troublesome CIA officer named Micah
Dalton. Well, there was only one reliable way to find the answers to all
these questions, and that was to draw these unknown watchers out.

To do that, he had to move.

So he moved.

CLASSIFIED UMBRA EYES DIAL
INTERNAL AUDIT COMMITTEE
File 92r: DALTON, MICAH
Service ID: REDACTED

Preliminary logs from BDS/WEIN have been entered as STET.
Committee concurs with BDS After-Action Report assessment that
DALTON detected the OSE Surveillance Team almost immediately
after reaching the exit of the Schottentor station and that DALTON
then commenced aggressive CS in an attempt to draw out and
identify the members of the OSE/UD team assigned to contain
and monitor him.

*There are conflicting reports concerning the reasons for the establishment
of an OSE Overwatch operation on DALTON, although preliminary
investigation suggests that it was done on behalf of an OGO (Other
Governmental Organization) the identity of which must at some point
be made part of this record.*

*The purpose of Dalton's visit to Vienna is unknown as of this writing,
but it is a matter of record that he was traveling undeclared and in a
private capacity, and was in no way charged with legitimate Agency
matters, which, in view of the subsequent deaths and injuries that took
place, allows for the argument to be made that there can be no official*

Agency liability for the actions of a private American citizen abroad.
PARTIAL/INTERIM/ report continues.

MARIAH VALE/OD/DD/EXECUTIVE SECRETARIAT

Dalton walked slowly north along Währinger Strasse, crossing into the edge of Sigmund Freud Park, making a long lazy loop through the area, scanning the darker places, watching the people around him, checking out the cars and buses, the dim forms of people half seen in the evening shadows. Since the assumption was that he was already being watched, there was no reason to be tricksy about his countersurveillance tactics, no point ducking into alleyways or changing direction sharply, trying to force a watcher to react, to look sharply away, to suddenly find the window of a closed shop utterly fascinating. He wasn't interested in losing these watchers; he wanted to isolate and identify them, establish the size, shape, and professionalism of the unit.

Nor was it worth trying to convince these people—whoever they were—that he wasn't worth watching; that decision had obviously already been made. He had to assume there'd be a box team on the street already, probably at least eight people, more likely twelve.

One person would have the Eye—have Dalton in direct line of sight. Usually this person would be behind him, on foot, probably no farther back than thirty yards. There'd be a backup watcher another twenty yards behind the Eye, ready to overtake and step into the Eye position if the first watcher felt he was closing up too tight or if Dalton did anything that might compromise the Eye. And there'd be a *third* watcher across the street, moving in the same direction as he was, probably one of those ordinary-looking people over there who were already level with Dalton right now.

The Eye would be in radio contact with the mobile units—very likely unremarkable sedans—always with four doors, since the "box team" members would be constantly switching in and out of the mobile units to prevent the target from seeing too many familiar faces.

Everyone else would maintain radio silence. If Dalton turned right or left on a side street, the Eye would walk straight through the intersection, letting the backup watcher take over as the Eye while the third watcher across the street would close in and take up the second position. The first Eye would either be cycled back to a mobile unit or redeployed in the third position, across the street from and level with Dalton. All of this movement would be fed constantly to the control officer in one of the mobile units.

Control would have a grid map of the city. The Brits, who had refined this kind of ad hoc street scramble into an art, called it a Spot Map. Control would track the reports coming in from the Eye, maneuvering the outlying box team to keep every alley and side street covered, switching agents in and out, pulling some back, closing in new ones, singles, pairs, breaking them up, mixing and matching as they moved, always at least three watchers keeping the target, Dalton, in the line of sight. A skilled team could do this sort of thing all day and all night, and no civilian would ever detect the operation. But there *were* things to see for those who knew how to look.

For one thing, none of the watchers, if properly trained, would ever make eye contact with the target. Which meant that if the blonde coming out of the Volksbank were part of a surveillance unit, they had some training issues to deal with. Generally, by elimination, anyone passing him on the street who *did* give him a direct glance could be disregarded.

The entire unit would also have *gone gray*, nobody would be wearing standout clothing—no reds, no blacks, no flashy jewelry. Green, gray, brown—mud colors—would be the choice. Since they all spent so much time walking, they tended to wear comfortable shoes—sneakers, rubber-soled slippers, hiking boots. They'd also be carrying bags, and wearing coats and sporting hats that could be taken off to alter their appearance—clothing baggy enough to hide radios and cameras.

They'd have tics, even the best of them: touching ears or wrists where their mikes would be, rearranging uncomfortable belts and straps holding their radio gear. Some of the newer ones would have that happy-sappy aimless look—no clear focus, too obviously trying to look casual—"loitering with intent," his instructor at Camp Peary had called it—instead of walking with the oblivious self-absorption that quite often allows experienced agents to get very close to the target without being sensed.

Dalton looked for all of these indicators as he came slowly north past the park, checking, assessing, rejecting, rechecking, looking at the streetscape and the crowds through any reflective surface, stopping now and then, as if he were uncertain where he was going, very aware of any change in the rhythm of the pedestrian traffic around him, his breathing steady and calm, keeping his adrenaline under control.

Twenty-five minutes later he had reached the intersection of Währinger Strasse and Rooseveltplatz, and he was reasonably certain that the rusted gray four-door Audi with the tinted windows parked near the cab stand in front of the Regina Hotel was part of the surveillance unit, as was the rat-brown Opel idling in front of Charlie P's Irish Pub. He picked that one out when a traffic cop ticketed a car doing exactly the same thing a half a block away while completely ignoring the Opel.

And he suspected that the young woman in a dull-green peasant head scarf, sitting in the trolley that had just rumbled past him, was the edgy blond goddess with the backpack who he had seen coming out of the Volksbank across from the Schottentor trolley station.

There was a couple across the street, on the far side of Roosevelt-platz, sitting on the low pillared fence that ran around a grotesque red stone pile. Dalton had seen the woman standing at the bike stand in Sigmund Freud Park, quite alone, supposedly trying to unlock one of those bright yellow rent-a-bikes from the automated lock-stand. Now the same girl, in a different jacket, was necking with a tall, bald young man in a leather car coat and jeans and a pair of unlaced hiking boots made of what looked to be dried cow pies.

Finally, the rather splendid young woman standing a yard behind him at the traffic light, fiddling with a cigarette and paying him no attention whatsoever, had spent most of his long walkabout through the park and up Währinger Strasse at a steady fifty feet back, keeping pace with him almost exactly.

The traffic light was a long one. Just to raise her hackles a bit, Dalton took out a pack of his ridiculous Sobranie Cocktails—long gold-tipped cigarettes in a range of colors from turquoise to rose pink to canary yellow—selected a blue one, turned around and said, *"Bitte, Fräulein. Haben Sie ein Feuerzeug?"*

The woman flinched very little, smoothly recovered. She looked a bit royal, and was quite handsome in that damn-your-eyes-*my*-family's-in-Debrett's style that made him think of Mandy Pownall. Slender, an aurora of wild auburn hair, strong bones, and dark, intelligent eyes. Her pale cheeks bloomed a bit as she fumbled in her purse, an Hermès, but by the time she offered him her heavy silver Art Deco lighter with an insignia inlaid in ebony she had a fine cool smile in place, although in her eyes there was a faint flicker of fear. Dalton lit his Sobranie, studying the insignia as he did so—VRM—waved the cloud away, smiled, and handed the lighter back to her, saying, *"Vorzüglich, Fräulein. Wie Sie sind."*

Exquisite, Fräulein.

As are you.

She held his look for a moment, quite steadily. The light changed.

She smiled carefully, and turned to walk on in front of him. Dalton stayed where he was. As spectacular as she was—far too showy for any halfway competent box team—he had no doubt that she was the Eye. And now she would have to cross over Rooseveltplatz ahead of him, forfeiting her position to her backup. In order to indicate that she had to surrender the Eye, she would either give the couple across the street some visual indication—they were still locked in a pretty convincing embrace—or she would call it in to her Control.

There was a spherical and hairless little man, carrying a Burberry raincoat, standing at a phone kiosk about a hundred feet back, apparently absorbed in a vigorous debate with someone on the other end of the line. He would be the second watcher. And in a moment, if she handed off, he would become the Eye.

Halfway across the broad avenue, her back rigid and her shoulders a little too straight, she reached up to brush a strand of fine hair away from her left ear, holding her hand there for just a moment. Dalton saw a tiny black rectangle against the white skin of her wrist, a microphone. She had just called it in.

She reached the far side of Rooseveltplatz and disappeared into a crowd of students without a backward glance. On the far corner, the couple was breaking apart—one last air kiss—the boy trudging off toward the Pension Franz, dragging his bootlaces, his hands shoved deep into his pockets, and the girl on her cell phone.

As he watched her, something off to his left in the middle distance caught his eye. The head-scarf girl who had gone by in the trolley— the blonde he had first seen leaving the Volksbank—walked out from under the arched entrance of the Regina Hotel and got into the gray four-door Audi, which immediately pulled away.

On the far side of the street, the girl with the cell had ended her call and was now walking in the same direction as he was. Behind him, the round fat man had put on his Burberry raincoat, opened an unnecessary umbrella, and was now following Dalton at the regulation fifty feet.

There you go, thought Dalton. *We have now officially confirmed the surveillance. Isn't that just peachy.*

Now what?

CLASSIFIED UMBRA EYES DIAL
INTERNAL AUDIT COMMITTEE
File 92r: DALTON, MICAH
Service ID: REDACTED

Within hours of the events of (REDACTED) BDS Incident Unit conducted NEGID Field Interviews with OSE/UD Aufzug Unit Commander Rolf Jägermeier as well as civilian employees of Regina Hotel and were able to assemble a detailed narrative of DALTON's movements and decisions as they related to the events that subsequently took place. These interview transcripts have been entered into Audit Committee logs as STET.

As well, NSA extractions of DALTON's BlackBerry usage in the relevant time frame have been provided through the Inter-Agency Enforcement Agreement. These have also been entered into the Audit Committee logs.

Report segments follow.
PARTIAL/INTERIM/ report continues.

MARIAH VALE/OD/DD/EXECUTIVE SECRETARIAT

Now? thought Dalton.

Now it was time for a drink, as Porter Naumann would say.

Dalton crossed Rooseveltplatz, heading for the lobby of the Regina Hotel, for a couple of reasons. First, it would rattle his watchers, who were probably using the hotel's lobby washrooms for pee breaks. At least, the head-scarf girl certainly was. Second, there was a pretty good cigar bar in the hotel, with a range of excellent scotch, and he intended to sit down there for a while and think this thing through. His meeting with Issadore Galan was only another block north on Währinger Strasse, at the Pension Franz, but Dalton had no intention of dragging this chain of watchers into Galan's territory.

The Audi four-door was nowhere to be seen by the time he reached the cab stand outside the Regina. He pushed open the double glass doors and walked into the ornate lobby, nodding to the gray counterman, in his gray suit, who returned his greeting with a gray smile and a perfunctory *Guten Abend, mein Herr.*

The cigar bar was on the left, on the far side of a wall of wonderfully indecent satyrs and nymphs frolicking in a gravity-free pink marble Arcadia. There was no one around in the lobby other than a couple of comatose bellmen, apparently tricked out as extras in *The Merry Widow.* There was no one working in the newsstand and no one loitering about the lobby trying to look invisible.

He figured Control would settle for having all the hotel exits covered rather than risk putting a watcher inside, where Dalton could get a closer look. This also told him that there was probably no electronic gear zeroed in on him, that the surveillance team's mission was to track, monitor, and contain him, not to gather signals intelligence. He sat down at the far corner of the long bar—also quite deserted, the global recession having its effect even here in Vienna—got his back up against a wall, established a clear sight line to the lobby entrance, and ordered up a Laphroaig—doubled, no ice—from a stiff-necked old crowbar behind the counter who looked exactly like C. Aubrey

Smith, right down to the craggy bloodhound face and the huge white handlebar mustache.

The man had a miniature medal pinned to the left-hand lapel of his red mess jacket, a navy-blue-and-red swallowtail pennant with a gold iron cross, and over the cross the inscription 1WDK 1944–1947. Dalton recognized it as the breast badge of the First Warsaw Cavalry Division. He saw Dalton looking at it, said nothing, but gave him a short, comprehending smile, which Dalton returned with genuine respect. While the old Hussar—a brass tag over his breast pocket had his name, CESAR—was hunting down some Laphroiag, Dalton considered his situation, which boiled down to a simple question:

Why me?

Dalton's current MOS, his operational designation, was Cleaner, an Agency "fixer," working out of Clandestine Services, based in London Station, and at least nominally run by Tony Crane. Dalton's tactical AO was Europe, Greece, the Balkans, and until recently he had been operating out of Venice. His drink arrived in a large crystal glass as heavy as a hand grenade. Dalton thanked Cesar. Cesar nodded, giving Dalton a moment of morose regard and apparently finding him marginally acceptable before turning away to shuffle massively down to the other end of the bar, where he began to polish some heavy hotel silver.

Dalton went back to his situational analysis. He was usually assigned to fix, repair, or otherwise pressure-wash away the sticky residue of an endless variety of cluster fucks and self-inflicted disasters generated by field officers or their agents in place, all of whom were prone to nervous collapse, envy, greed, paranoia, delusions of adequacy, conniptions, hissy fits, the vapors, the marthambles, as well as most of the standard vices and—Dalton had to give them credit—a few stunningly original ones as well, the most memorable of which had involved live goldfish.

Dalton did not run networks, did not attempt to construct or tend a trapline, made no brush contacts, serviced no drop boxes, recruited no sources, ran no covert agents, solicited no HumInt in other people's backyards: in short, he did none of the back-channel double-dealing dirty work that so often irritated the living hell out of in-country agencies. That kind of covert HumInt stunt was usually the responsibility of whatever station chief happened to be on the scene. His professional life had been pretty well summed up many years back by Warren Zevon, in his song lyric "Send lawyers, guns and money / The shit has hit the fan," except that Dalton was no lawyer.

So why all the attention?

He checked his watch—a little after nine in the evening. It would be midafternoon in D.C. He punched in a few numbers, waited, hit the company access code, waited some more for the encryption to kick in . . . And then he heard, with some surprise, the voice of Sally Fordyce, once Jack Stallworth's senior assistant and now, after Stallworth's death, apparently back on Fourth Floor West at Langley.

"DeeDee's office. Is that really you, Micah?"

"Sally? You're back at Clandestine?"

"I am. The new man's new guy likes me."

The "new man" was the new President. The "new guy" was Clay Pearson, an ex–Navy JAG officer who had served in the White House under Carter and emerged from the second-most-calamitous presidency in modern history with his career actually enhanced, which meant he was part cobra and part mongoose.

Clay Pearson was the man chosen by the new President to replace Deacon Cather, Dalton's aging mentor and the former DD of Clandestine, now forced to the sidelines with an honorary title as Adviser Pro Tem to DD Clandestine.

Pearson, an African-American, was tall, lean, cool, calm, as steely smooth as the kiss of a guillotine, with a throaty baritone purr, a ready smile, and a great memory for the faces and family connections of anyone with even the faintest chance of becoming useful, one fine June day, to the lovely and talented Clay Pearson.

He was, however, no friend at all to covert operations, which were messy and vulgar and occasionally violent escapades, heavily freighted with political risk, and Clay Pearson, as a Carter man, strongly disapproved of political risk.

It was generally believed by the permanently paranoid CIA staffers that Pearson was in the DD Clandestine post with orders to assign blame, to view with righteous alarm, and generally to hound and afflict any hapless bastard who had actually been of some tactical use in the War on Terror. Which, by the way, according to the new administration, was henceforth to be known as the "Expression of Strong Disapproval of Man-Caused Disasters."

"The new guy *likes* you? Doesn't he know you were a Marine?"

"He's regular Navy. A squid. They never take the corps seriously. Squiddies think we're knuckle-dragging mouth breathers who eat our dead."

"And you're not?"

"I see you're in Vienna. At number 15 Rooseveltplatz, wherever that is."

"It's the Regina Hotel. I'm at the long bar."

"And, pray tell, *why* are you in Vienna? The duty roster has you in Bonn, I think, babysitting an Albanian stringer with a bad case of the yips? No?"

"I was, up until yesterday. His wife left him for another woman. After thirty-four years of marriage. I sat up with him for three days and nights. We told each other outrageous lies and drank several bottles of Cherry Heering. Have you ever had Cherry Heering?"

"Sounds like a stripper. What's it like?"

"It's exactly like Bonn."

"Gad. That awful?"

"Yes. Only with cherries."

"The stringer all right? Got over his case of the yips?"

"Yeah. Eventually. Made a pass at me on day three."

"How did you handle that?"

"With my usual style and grace."

"Oh my. He's dead, then, is he?"

"Sally, can you do me a favor?"

"I live to serve."

"I think I may have developed a following here in Vienna."

"What? You mean surveillance?"

"Yes. Very persistent. Skills only adequate. And not a small outfit. At least eight, maybe twelve people. Foot. Mobile. High-quality gear. Is there any Company-connected reason why I should be getting this sort of attention?"

Sally paused, thinking about the phone lines and the general air of impending doom that was pervading the CIA these days

"You're thinking of the Black Mariah, are you?"

This was a reference to Mariah Vale, until a few weeks ago the chief of the Audit Committee, now promoted to the Executive Secretariat.

"Yes. I know they boosted her upstairs after her little triumph with the mole, and now I hear she's on a head-hunting mission."

"Yes. She seems to think the President's slogan about HOPE stands for 'Heads on Pikes Everywhere.' But your head has not come up on a pike yet, at least officially, and I'd know it if it had. My guy doesn't allow poaching, and you're still on his roster. I mean, that's not to say he wouldn't carve out your googlies with an ice-cream scoop if she wanted him to. But Vale would have to clear it with him first, go through the channels, and she hasn't."

"You'd know?"

"Micah. Sweetheart. This is the CIA, not the IRS. Nobody here can keep a secret. Just ask *The New York Times*."

"So I can assume these people don't work for us?"

"Yes. For now. But let me see what else I can find out. Can you tell me why you're in Vienna? Maybe it's relevant?"

"I'm seeing an old friend."

"Dear God. Not that Cora Vasari creature? I thought her family stashed her away in a castle in Crete and barred you from the gates?"

"It's a villa in Anacapri, as far as I know. And yes, they have. But Cora's no 'creature.'"

"I know. I know. Mandy Pownall told me all about her. Mandy loathes her, root and branch, mainly because Mandy has plans for you herself. Anyway, I'm just heating you up. You haven't said why you're in Vienna. Or who you're there to meet."

"I don't like to say it in the clear."

"You're not in the clear. This line is shielded."

"Well, keep it to yourself, but I'm meeting Issadore Galan. Galan's got a problem, a nasty one. I need to meet him, take care of it."

"Okay. No need to get more specific. Good luck with him. In the meantime, I don't think whoever is on you is any friend of ours. So you be careful. Lots of people don't like you very much. Especially those Cagey Bees. They're all over Vienna too, horrible nasty little bugs. And you can't trust the Austrians either. Hitler was an Austrian. So was Henry Kissinger."

"Hitler was a Bavarian, but I hear you. Bye, Sally."

He rung off, set the machine down, thought it over for a moment, and then picked it up again, hit BROWSER, and pulled up a restricted CIA search engine. Cesar, polishing his silver and looking in the mirror behind the bar, studied the young American's rocky face for a time and then put his head down and went back to his work.

ALTHOUGH Rolf Jägermeier was indeed a *Pfennigfuchseres Arschloch*, he was also a seasoned street operator, and it had been his bitter experience to lose more than one target inside a hotel. A sallow, boneless man with a wide dish-shaped face made morose by years spent disapproving of everything placed in front of it, he had sat slumped down behind the wheel of the gray Audi, fretting and biting his nails for two hours, while the target—who was *really* beginning to grind on Jagermeir's nerves—sat at the long bar inside the Regina Hotel, quietly drinking serial scotches and, as far as his watchers could tell from their occasional furtive sashays through the lobby, playing games on his *dämliches* BlackBerry.

In the meantime, Jägermeier had multiple agents out and about in the streets, cooling their heels, wandering aimlessly around the Ring District or sitting in cafés buying themselves Löwenbräus and Weiner Schnitzels on his ticket, and all of this dead-end farrago at double time and a half for excessive overtime.

And then there was Veronika Miklas, the aristocratic little bitch, who had gotten herself so completely burned at the intersection of Währinger Strasse and Rooseveltplatz—she lit his *verfluchte Zigarette*, can you believe it?—so there was no point paying her overtime to hang about the perimeter with nothing useful to do. At least he could do something about *her*, which was to cut her loose and send her home. And he was really looking forward to doing it.

He'd get that stiff-necked little *Kokain-Kopf* under his heel and grind her into a stain. When he got through with her, she'd be in a mobile unit on her way back to her artsy little flat in Heiligenstadt, sniveling into a hankie, with her tiny ears pinned back and burning cherry bright. So something to savor, at least. But how was he supposed to justify all of this killer overtime to necrotizing fasciitis, his *Spitzname* for Nenia Faschi, their section chief?

Reluctantly, after some more nail biting and fretting, Jägermeier decided to confirm Dalton's status again, this time sending in Jürgen Stodt, the tall, bald kid Dalton had observed necking with a girl at the intersection of Rooseveltplatz and Währinger Strasse.

Stodt now wore a shapeless cloth shooting cap—backward, of

course—and a very nice Burberry overcoat to hide his baggy jeans. Dalton would have recognized him anyway—the cow-pie boots alone would have been enough—and he tried hard not to laugh out loud as the kid moonwalked slowly by the entrance to the bar, trailing his ragged laces, looking maniacally interested in a rack of tourist magazines.

Stodt sent Jägermeier a couple of clicks on his wrist mike to confirm that the target was still there and then continued his lace-dragging, boot-schlumping progress through the lobby and out the exit that led onto the grounds of the Votivkirche.

As soon as Stodt had pushed through the heavy glass doors, Dalton got up from the bar, laying down a fat sheaf of euros. He smiled at the old Hussar, who gave him a sharp salute, his long, sad face cracking into a sideways grin for just a moment.

"Sie haben ihn eingeschläfert, glaube ich, mein Herr."

Dalton considered the old man for a long, taut moment.

"You think I have put *whom* to sleep, Cesar?"

Cesar looked down at the velvet cloth in his hands, moved it in a small circle to clear away a nonexistent speck, and then looked back at Dalton, his face suddenly quite stern.

"Die Überwachungs-Dienst. The bloody OSE."

"Really," said Dalton, showing his teeth in a sideways smile. "And why do you say that?"

Cesar shrugged, raised a shaggy white brow.

"Die gottverdamten Sozialisten. They are always in and out of here. They use the washrooms, pissing all over the walls, fucking Bolsheviks. They never pay the attendant. They hang around in the lobby, scratching their arses and picking their noses, and bringing down the tone. Their street boss is a penny-pinching arsehole named Rolf Jägermeier. Squats at *my* bar, taking up two stools. Drinks *kaltes Wasser* and stuffs *gesalzene Nüsse* down his face. Never the smile, never the tip bigger than Stalin's pizzle. You are *amerikanischer Soldat?"*

Dalton considered lying but decided against it.

"What gave me away?"

Cesar touched the Warsaw Cavalry pin on his lapel.

"You knew this. What it means. Did not have to ask. And you carry yourself like a soldier. May I ask what unit you are with?"

"I started out with the Fifth Special Forces at Fort Campbell in Kentucky. Since then I have . . . diversified."

That got a broad smile, with more than a little of the Cossack in it. "Why are the Socialists interested in you? Are you spy?"

Dalton smiled, this time more convincingly.

"If I were spy, I would deny it."

"And if you were not . . ."

"I would of course deny it."

Cesar's seamed face cracked into a predatory grin.

"*Ja.* I would deny it too. I do not wish to be . . . *unverschämt?* Impertinent?"

"Please. Be my guest."

"On your honor as a soldier, do you mean to bring harm to any civilians here in Wien? To do any violence or damage to innocents?"

"In no way. I'm here to meet a friend. And then quietly go."

Cesar said nothing for a full minute. Dalton felt his appraisal. It was not unlike standing in front of an open furnace.

"*Gut. Ich glaube Ihnen.* I believe you. Do you wish to shake off these Socialist *Welpen?*"

"It would be . . . useful."

Cesar nodded, his face hardening.

"There is a subcellar hallway that leads to the Votivkirche—"

"There is? Why?"

Cesar shrugged, turned his palms upward.

"This is an old hotel. In the time of *Der Kalte Krieg*—even before—in Wein there are always tunnels. In the old days, for lovers and thieves and Hungarians. Later, for the Bolshies and the Nazis and the black market. Wein is a raddled old whore, but she still keeps her secrets. Do you love your very expensive coat?"

Dalton turned around, looked down at his long blue overcoat.

"I have sincerely enjoyed having it."

"You will have to leave it."

"Done. I thank you. Is there anything I can do . . . ?"

Cesar stiffened, his cheeks darkening.

"Are you offering me *money*?"

MIDNIGHT, and the tiny pink ears that were burning cherry bright did not belong to Veronika Miklas. Jägermeier had suffered through a very disagreeable confrontation with Veronika, who had set him down hard when, after making a couple of snide references to her previous relationship with "recreational chemistry"—a sore point—he started to criticize her *professional* skills, she finally reminding him, at the end of a short, sharp encounter conducted on her part with the kind of subzero ferocity that her class had once used to put the peasantry in its place, that her great-grandfather, Wilhelm Miklas, had been the President Doctor of Austria, and had, on March 11, 1938, single-handedly faced down Seyss-Inquart and all his Hitlerite flunkies, thank you very much, you nasty little *Schneckengewinde*.

The interview ended in his complete rout—she had called him a nasty little worm, and he had actually apologized to her—and now, perhaps as an indirect result, Jägermeier found that he really—no, *really*—had to pee.

He decided to do a press check on the target, while he was at it, dragging his numb butt and aching back out of the miasmic funk of his own methane-rich atmospherics. The Audi was also his personal service car, and he spent more time in it than he did at home in his lonely bed. Jägermeier hauled himself across the steps of the Votivkirche and into the lobby of the Regina, slouching, if not toward Bethlehem, then toward the men's washroom hidden behind a row of fake linden trees.

As he passed the entrance to the bar, he glanced sideways just long enough to see that the target was still there—the lazy son of a bitch— sitting with his back to the door now, hunched over what Jägermeier presumed was that damned BlackBerry, his girly-man blond hair splayed out across the collar of his coat and glowing in the down- light. *What a* tanzender Junge *he is*, thought Jägermeier, with a curl of his thick red lips. Krokodil! *Hah! The only people who have to fear this* Krokodil *are in the Vienna Boys Choir.*

SADLY for Rolf Jagermeir's career prospects, the *tanzender Junge*— the dancing boy—was actually slightly more than two miles north- northwest of the Regina Hotel, sitting on a bench in a small park at the intersection of Heiligenstadter Strasse and Barawitzkag, watching the main entrance to a dreary, slab-sided concrete block of Bolshevik Bauhaus called, appropriately, the Wohnungen Arbeitnehmer Hafen— Workers' Haven Apartments.

The blond-haired person currently sitting at the long bar back at the Regina, wearing Dalton's Zegna topcoat, secretly enjoying Dalton's scent—a mix of Balkan Sobranie cigarettes and some sort of spicy lemon-scented cologne—and idly fingering the pockets, which were stuffed with euros, was the old Hussar's niece, Steffi, who had been dragooned into service in exchange for a pocketful of ready cash and the grim admiration of her terrifying grand- uncle Cesar.

Dalton had already done a series of routine checks to see if there was still any kind of surveillance on him. He was reasonably certain there was not, and that there was no security guard in the building.

He had only been there for little over an hour, and he was prepared to spend the night, but a few minutes later a familiar rat-brown Opel pulled up at the curb outside the entrance to the Workers' Haven. There was some sort of brief exchange of hugs with the driver, who, his face caught in a shaft of dim light, looked to be the round fat man with the umbrella he had last seen in Sigmund Freud Park.

In a moment the passenger door popped open, and the Girl With the Silver Lighter got out onto the sidewalk, looking weary and wrung out as she waved the Opel off, and then turned to trudge up the walkway to the entrance doors. Dalton, moving soundlessly across the lawn, reached her just as she put her hand on the chrome bar, saying, as softly and as nonthreateningly as he could, "*Vorzüglich, Fräulein.*"

Her response was immediate—a lithe twist of her body, the leading edge of her left hand bladed and taut, a white blur striking at the front of Dalton's throat. Had she got this very professional strike home, it could have, very likely would have, crushed his larynx, and his short but memorable career would have ended with his slowly choking to death on the scruffy lawn of a workers' housing project in the suburbs of Vienna. However, she did not get it home. Dalton caught the blow in his left hand, turning the palm strike into a rolling armlock and pressing her up against the glass door, doing as little harm as he could manage, saying, in English, "Please, Miss Miklas, I'm not here to hurt you. Please."

She struggled a moment longer—in her mind, all she could hear was a single word repeating: *Krokodil! Krokodil! Krokodil!*—but he was immensely strong, and she forced herself to be still.

Her moment would come, now or later.

"But you *are* hurting me, Mr. Dalton."

Dalton held her a moment, doing a quick and only mildly indecent weapons check and finding a pager, a cell phone—both of which he turned off—and a small Heckler & Koch P7 in a leather holster tucked into the small of her back.

He pulled it free and stepped back, holding the weapon muzzle down, trying—and failing—to look as harmless as possible. Veronika Miklas straightened her clothes, her face a little pink, pushed her hair back with both hands, and stood facing him. The fear was there, but so was the iron. She stared at him in silence for a moment.

"The bloody damned lighter, I suppose?"

Dalton nodded, his face creasing in a commiserating smile.

"Yes. I was surprised they really were *your* initials."

Miklas sighed, and a tremor ran through her body. When she reached up to touch the side of her check—she bruised easily—Dalton could see that her fingers were vibrating.

"A gift from my mother. Initials alone are not enough."

"No. It was a place to start. It narrowed the range. I have access to an Agency database that lists all the civil servants in Austria, along with their parent agencies, except for the OSE. I searched for those initials in the tax lists for civil employees. Your name stood out—"

"Because of my great-grandfather?"

"Yes. A famous name. There's a website, and your picture is there, as one of the authors of a paper about the Anschluss."

Her face lost some of its hardness.

"A brave man, a terrible time for Austria. And so, here you are. What the hell do you want?"

Dalton looked around the street and then back at her.

"A few minutes of your time. Some answers."

She shivered again but rode it down.

"Listen, Blondie. I am not going *anywhere* with you. And *you* are not coming inside with me. You may use my pistol if you wish, but here I stay. So just shoot me, and that is the end of it."

"I understand that. And you're right. Never let anybody move you or get you into a car or box you up in a flat. I wouldn't either. The thing is, I have no intention of harming you in any way. Look, Miss Miklas, it's not a bad night. It's stopped raining. There's a little park across the street, a little bench. Have a cigarette with me."

She hesitated, and Dalton thought she might break and run, but she did not. Instead, she gave him a sardonic sideways smile.

"One of your *Regenbogen Zigaretten*?"

Dalton smiled back, fighting his strong desire to fall down where he stood and sleep for two days.

"Yes. My rainbow cigarettes. As many as you want."

She gave it some thought.

Finally, the curiosity of the confident young woman won out over professional caution. On the other hand, if Dalton had been a squat toadlike homunculus, she'd have given him the back of her hand, thirty seconds of the Full Jägermeier, and, if the opening was offered, a quick knee to the nuptials.

"Okay. Sure. Why not?"

They walked across the deserted street, she some distance away and with her hands at her sides, he reflexively scanning the roofs and darkened windows, the overarching trees and the parked cars that lined the street.

They reached a wrought-iron bench, sheltered by a stand of oaks and lindens. She sat at one end and he as far away from her as he could manage at the other. In the uneasy silence he offered her a choice from his Sobranie Cocktails. She took a blue one. She lit it with the heavy silver lighter. And then, after staring down at it for a while and going inside herself, she leaned over to light his cigarette, studying his face in the glow of the flame.

"You have a scar on your right cheekbone. It looks like a dueling scar. It is recent. How did you get it?"

Dalton reached up, touched it briefly, seeing the muzzle flash in the shadow of the boat, hearing the sound of it bouncing off the old stone walls that loomed over the icy little canal in Venice.

"Shaving accident."

She smiled then, retracting her claws a bit.

"Liar. Such a liar. They are calling you *Krokodil*—the crocodile—at the office. How can you smoke such silly little cigarettes if you are this terrible *Krokodil?*"

Dalton inhaled, leaning back into the bench, crossing one leg over the other. He was cold and missed his Zegna. He hoped Cesar's niece was enjoying it, which of course she was.

"A good friend of mine used to smoke them. His name was Porter Naumann. He would have liked you. He admired steel.

"*Would* have liked me? He is dead?"

"Yes. He was killed in Cortona, almost a year ago."

"A shaving accident?" she said, teasing him a little.

Dalton smiled, shook his head, said nothing, took another pull at his cigarette. So did she. And they sat there for a while in what was turning into a strangely companionable moment of calm and stillness.

The clouds had passed over hours ago. The Viennese night was calm and clear, the glow of the city touching the tops of the higher trees and the steeple of a little church a block north. Where they were was cool, quiet, sheltered.

"You are odd kind of spy," she said finally, exhaling a cloud of smoke and watching it turning in a tiny shaft from the streetlamp, cutting through the leaves.

"I'm not really a spy," he said, smiling into the dark. "At the Agency, they call people like us Cleaners. Basically, I'm a fixer. I don't run any agents, don't recruit. Let's just say that when things go wrong on the operational side, I come in and try to fix them."

She laughed at that—a short sharp bark and a puff of smoke.

"In your files they say that last year, in Montenegro, you 'fixed' a Serbian Mafia boss named Branco Gospic, after you also 'fixed' two Serbs who tried to mug you in Venice. Then last winter, again in Venice, you 'fixed' another Serbian mafioso named Mirko Belajic, along with four of his men, one of whom you are said to have killed by snapping his neck with your bare hands. I know these gangster Serbs. They are the most dangerous men in Eastern Europe. And then in Istanbul, not so long ago, you 'fixed' several KGB officers, and chased the rest of them all the way across the Black Sea to Kerch. That's a lot of 'fixing' for one man."

"You're pretty well informed on the subject."

"Yes. We have good relations with the British. You are known to them, especially in London. So you are just hired killer, then?"

Dalton stubbed out the cigarette on the arm of the bench and put the gold-tipped butt in the pocket of his trousers. He took out another—blue and gold. Veronika lit it for him, watching the glow of the flame reflected in his eyes, seeing the haggard look on his rough-cut face.

"No. I do what is needed. The OSE does the same."

There was nothing to say to that.

This was Vienna, after all, and there was no city in Europe with a murkier history in the covert world.

"I know you want to get some rest, Miss Miklas—"

"You've had your hands all over me. I think you can call me Veronika. I will call you Micah."

"Thank you, Veronika. I'm hoping you can help me with something."

She turned and looked directly at him for a while, considering his gaunt face and his obvious exhaustion, feeling a conflict in her heart between official reserve and what she had to admit was a strong sensual pull. With his long blond hair, his pale blue eyes, his scarred and weathered Viking face, he appealed to the Old Norse in her blood.

He radiated a blend of latent menace, weary intelligence, even a very dry sense of humor, but underneath that . . . sadness.

Perhaps even a deep grief.

She found that she wanted to know how he came to be the way he was. In spite of the apparent glamour of her work with the *Überwachungs-Dienst*, the pay was poor, her boss, as has been noted, was a nasty little *Schneckengewinde*, and the work itself was—she smiled to herself as she thought this—*literally* pedestrian.

Dalton, on the other hand . . . *interested* her.

"I think I know why you're here. You want to know why we Austrians are putting the *Überwachungs-Dienst* on you."

"Yes. That's right."

"When we look at your file, do you not think any country you visit would be crazy *not* to put surveillance on you?"

"Excellent point. Let's debate that later."

"No. We will debate it now, Micah, if you wish for my help."

Dalton said nothing, which Veronika rightly took for assent.

"*My* question is, why do you care?"

"Why do I care? I'm under surveillance by a unit of a government that's supposed to be strongly aligned with the U.S. Austria's in NATO. We have reciprocal intelligence agreements—"

Veronika laughed and waved that away in a cloud of smoke.

"Hah. So go through channels. Register an official complaint. Write a strong note of protest to *The New York Times*. Instead, you come right at us, like a shark in shallow water. You are worried about something more than a protocol breach. What is it?"

Dalton pulled on his cigarette, exhaled in a sigh, let the question hang in the shaft of light along with the smoke. Veronika, who seemed to know something about Chinese silence, did not feel compelled to yield the game. Instead, she waited him out.

"Okay," he said, resigning himself to it. "A friend—a professional—got in touch with me about a week ago. He said it was vital we meet.

That he needed to talk face-to-face. This guy's a pro. He doesn't get the vapors. He doesn't spook. If he needs a personal contact, he has to have a damned solid reason."

"Okay. I guess you're not going to tell me what you think the reason might be?"

"No. Not because I won't. Because I haven't a bloody clue."

"Fine. That's fair. But you assume his reasons are . . . serious?"

"With this guy, a better word would be *grave*."

She worked that through.

"I see. So when you come up out of the subway and you find you are being watched—"

"In this business, paranoids tend to have a higher survival rate. If I were just here for a walkabout and a schnitzel, I'd have said okay, it's a routine exercise. A CIA officer arrives in Vienna, he's undeclared, he's got a reputation for trouble, so the locals want to show the flag, teach him some manners. That's fine. Every agency does that."

"But you add in your . . . friend. With his *grave* reasons?"

He looked at her then, a brief sideways glance, but she felt the edge in it, the carefully calibrated aggression.

"Then it's *personal*. You have to react immediately. No hesitation. You go straight back at them, find them, fix them, burn them down if you have to, you get inside their decision cycle . . ."

She nodded.

"Keep the opposition, whoever they are, off balance?"

"Yes. That's how it works. That's how it's done."

She fell into silence again. He could hear her breathing, and caught a scent of her perfume under the smoke.

"Yes. That is how it is."

She lit a second cigarette, then held it, twirling it between her fingers. The little red glow at the tip left a fiery streak in the darkness as she moved the cigarette to her lips, inhaled, released it slowly.

"Yes. I see all this. So. It is not us who initiated the *Aufzug*."

"You're sure?"

She gave him a look. Half of it was sardonic. The rest of it had some body heat in it, which surprised him.

"Every file we open has . . . *Nomenklatur*."

"A coded notation indicating the project history?"

"Yes."

"And you have this code, this *Nomenklatur*?"

She inhaled the last of her blue Sobranie, stubbed it out beside her on the bench, and handed him the butt with a wry smile.

"Yes. I have it. It's up in my flat."

"Will you bring it down to me?"

She sighed, got to her feet, and looked down at him, the light of the streetlamp putting a golden aura around her hair.

"First, I'd like my pistol back. And the cell and the pager."

Dalton hesitated, tugged the pistol out, the cell, her pager, handed them over to her. She hefted the H&K pistol and gave him a broad conspiratorial smile.

"You've unloaded it."

Dalton smiled back at her.

"And your own pistol?"

"I'm not stupid enough to wander around Vienna with an illegal weapon. It's back in my car."

"And where is your car?"

"At the Westbahnhof, in the Auto-Park."

"Okay. We will look at this file together."

"Do I wait here?"

"No. This is not a business for out-of-doors. You will come up to my apartment. Maybe we will find out how dangerous you really are."

CLASSIFIED UMBRA EYES DIAL
INTERNAL AUDIT COMMITTEE
File 92r: DALTON, MICAH
Service ID: REDACTED

Dalton's encrypted BlackBerry, with its embedded Agency GPS Locator activated, was shut down at 12:29 a.m. local time. At shutdown, the GPS indicator was showing his location as 48/14/40 N and 16/21/37 E, the intersection of Eduard Ponzi Strasse and Barawitzkag, the location of the MIKLAS flat.

BDS reconstruction has Dalton entering the flat owned by MIKLAS, VERONIKA, at approximately 12:34 a.m. local time. The security service monitoring her home alarm system logged in her usual DISARM/REARM code entered into the control box within two minutes after the DOOR OPEN tone had been detected. MIKLAS, VERONIKA, also had a pager and a cell phone, her cell phone showing the identical LONGS and LATS. Both of these devices had been shut down twenty-five minutes earlier.

It is not yet known whether force was being used on MIKLAS, VERONIKA, to compel her cooperation. Her security service had supplied her with an ALERT code that could be punched in instead of her HOME code, at which time the local police would be notified. This

ALERT code was not entered, but the absence of compulsion or intimidation cannot be assumed. In view of DALTON's history, this office asserts that compulsion was very likely present, although some subsequent events undermined this inference.
PARTIAL/INTERIM/ report continues.

MARIAH VALE/OD/DD/EXECUTIVE SECRETARIAT

Her flat was spare but stylish—creamy white walls and a red oak hardwood floor, a large living room, with some very fine pieces of richly carved mahogany that looked expensive and old. *Inherited from her family*, thought Dalton as he waited in the hallway while Veronika punched in a code on her security alarm. If she was entering a HELP code, he'd find out soon enough. There was a wall of windows framed by cream-colored sheers, a narrow stone-walled balcony visible through the drapes, and above one of the brocaded couches was a row of very strong and quite shameless female nudes in black-and-white, spotlit by a row of tiny halogens in a ceiling bar. They were of Veronika herself, he realized, feeling a ripple of blood heat in his chest and throat.

She was full bodied, well toned, and the poses, although charged with erotic power, were restrained and graceful. The effect was elegant and sensual. He wondered who had taken them. A lover maybe?

Beyond the living area there was a large antique dining-room table, covered with camera gear, and beside it a laptop computer, open and glowing. A tiny galley kitchen, simple, white, with a few more photos over a red aluminum breakfast table.

On the other side of the living room, through an open doorway, an oversized mahogany four-poster with a plush indigo silk comforter on it took up most of a tiny navy blue room with gilt crown molding, the space softly lit in deep amber by an Art Nouveau bedside lamp. The flat smelled of a spicy perfume—sandalwood?—and cigarettes and black coffee. He felt another wave of weariness come over him, closing his eyes for a moment. He may actually have fallen asleep where he stood. When he opened his eyes again, Veronika had changed out of her street clothes and was standing in front of him, barefoot, in faded jeans and a scarlet V-neck sweater. Her expression was direct, penetrating, as if she were marking him down for her memory book.

"You're dead on your feet. How long since you have slept?"

"Too long."

"What were you doing? 'Fixing' another problem?"

"No. I was in Bonn, babysitting a suicidal agent. He talked at me for three days and nights and made me drink something called Cherry Heering."

"Oh God. Cherry-flavored cough syrup. Poor thing. Go into the bathroom—it's through the bedroom—and splash some cold water on your face. Have a shower, if you like. There are towels in the cabinet under the sink. I will make some coffee. How do you like it?"

"Black. Strong and black," he said, heading for the bathroom. When he came back out, showered, shaved—he'd taken liberties with her razor—back in his clothes and feeling much more human, the dimly lit flat was filled with the rich scent of coffee brewing. Veronika was sitting at the dining-room table, staring down at her computer screen, frowning slightly as she ran her cursor through some pages of text. She lifted her hand, waved her fingers at him.

"There are cups on the shelf over the sink. Can you pour me one too? And may I have another one of your silly cigarettes?"

Dalton brought her a cup, pulled up a chair beside her, fishing out his Sobranies and offering her the open box. She studied them as if they were a selection of Viennese chocolates, the side of her face filled with a glow from the monitor. Her hair fell down around her face in a cascade of auburn light.

"You're not at all like an American," she said, taking a turquoise one and turning it in her fingertips. Dalton's heart sank a little, and he braced himself for one of those tedious lectures traveling Americans were always getting on the Evil Empire.

"No? Tell me, Veronika, what's an American like?"

She looked up at him sharply, her topaz eyes widening.

"Oh no! No you don't! Not from me. No bigoted lectures on the Ugly Americans from a Miklas. Remember? I wrote a treatise on the Anschluss. I know very well what happened to the Jews of Vienna when the Germans came. They took everything they could carry and they raped and shot and burned what they could not carry. Hitler hated Vienna because he was such a miserable failure here between the wars. So he got even with the Viennese. Then the Allies came, and Austria was divided into four—like Berlin—and they gave Vienna to the goddamned Russians, who were no better than the Nazis. So my family fled to Salzburg, which was in the American Zone, and the Amis were kind to us, and we were safe there. And after the war the only things the Americans left behind were a lot of babies and their young men dead in graves all over Europe. My family came back to Vienna after the Soviets got out. And now the Soviets are crawling in again, like roaches."

"The KGB?"

"Yes. Only now they're the FSB. Same brutes under a different hat. They say they are here to help us with the Chechens, but they do much more than that. We—the Overwatch—we have to work with them sometimes. They put their hairy hands on the younger girls. And that worm Jägermeier, he does *nothing*—"

She stopped abruptly and took a puff of her cigarette.

"Anyway, you will not hear me say anything about Americans. I only meant that, like me, you smoke too much, and I think you drink too much. You are a young man, but your eyes are old. And we are always hearing that you Americans are so obsessed with your health and staying fit and eating right because you want to love—I mean *live*—you want to *live* forever."

She shrugged, smiled at him. Not far from him now, close enough for him to catch her scent and feel her breathing on his cheek. A little sadness of her own showing around the edges of her lips and in her eyes. Then she pulled away, seeming to shake herself out of a drifting dream.

"Well, yes . . . Anyway, the *Nomenklatur*?"

"Yes," he said, making his own effort to pull himself together.

She swiveled in the chair, tapping the screen of the laptop.

"See this? This is sort of our work order for your surveillance. It's in German. But these numbers here, in the upper left corner . . . ?"

Dalton looked, saw a series of letters and numbers:

```
UDamt4-OSE-fall: auswärtig: 53W87923>KS:NF:VERWANDTSCHAFT
```

"Most of this is pretty simple. The first letters stand for us, *Überwachungs-Dienst*. I belong to 'amt' 4, office number 4. You know what OSE stands for, and 'fall' means 'case.' Now, this part is something you hardly ever see. *'Auswärtig'* means 'foreign.' I have no idea why that's in here. The numbers and letters refer to the region we'll be working in. 'Fifty-three W' means central Wein, Vienna—specifically, the Ring District—and then the file is '87923.' That's how we bill it to whoever it is we're contracted out to. We work more or less on assignment, sometimes for the national police, sometimes the Army, even for the tax people. The OSE rents us out, in a way, so we don't always know why we're following the target, you see. Now, this part . . . The little arrowhead, means a cooperating agency that helped us locate you. 'KS' means the 'Cousins.' That's Interpol. 'NF' stands for 'Nenia Faschi,' my über-boss. She runs amt 4, and her initials indicate that she is the supervising officer for this file. This is the part I don't get. *Verwandtschaft.'* It means 'related.' Like a family."

"You've never seen it before?"

"No. I was going to run a search on it in the *Abteilung*—the OSE department-code registry, but I'm afraid if I do that—"

"Your bosses will know, and you'll have to explain why you were doing it in the middle of the night. So don't do it. Can you print this page out?"

"Yes," she said, punching a button on the keyboard. A printer on a chair beside her began to zip out a single-spaced sheet. When it was done, she handed it to Dalton, and he considered the word:

VERWANDTSCHAFT

"The *family*? You've *never* seen this reference before? Could it mean something like a related agency? Don't you call Interpol the Cousins?"

Veronika shook her head, watching his face.

"That's an in-house term. We'd never use that in an official record. We always use the Agency's official designation—mainly to protect ourselves if whoever they are decide they want to deny using us."

Dalton shook his head, trying to clear it. His mind was clouded, and he was having trouble seeing the screen.

She sat back in the chair, reached out and closed the lid down on the laptop.

"Micah, look at you. You can hardly sit up."

He looked up at her. With the laptop closed, her face was lit only by the amber glow from the lamp.

"I can't seem to think straight. Maybe some more coffee."

"Then you will be wide awake and stupid. Then what?"

He sat up straighter, looked around the room as if were surprised to find himself here.

"Look, I really have to go. Your boss finds out I was here—"

He stood up, looked down at her, weaving slightly.

"And where will you go?"

"Remember? I left a car at the Westbahnhof train station."

"The trolleys are shut down. You will walk five kilometers?"

"Okay. I'll find a local pensione."

She stood up, faced him.

"No. You will sleep here," she said, her tone final.

He looked over, a little longingly, at the big brocaded couch under the row of black-and-white nudes.

"Just a couple of hours? If you have a blanket."

She reached up and touched the bullet scar on his right cheekbone with her fingertip, traced a line down to the corner of his mouth, ran her hand around his neck and pulled him close enough to breathe him in, to smell her own shampoo in his damp hair.

"Are you scarred *everywhere*, Micah?" she asked softly.

"Yes," he said, with a slight smile. "I've been told I look like a battle map of Antietam."

"You are horrible to look at, then, if you are naked?"

"Yes. Hideous."

She kissed him very lightly on the corner of his mouth.

"Then we will turn off the lights."

DALTON, waking abruptly, stared up into the blackness above him, his heart pounding in his chest. Beside him Veronika was deep in sleep, one arm on his chest, her hand resting on his pectoral muscle, her cheek on his shoulder, her body pressed up against him, her left leg lying across his belly. In the east, on the far side of the Danube, the sky was showing a faint milky light, but in the city it was fully dark. Vienna was—here in the northern suburbs anyway—as black and silent as a crypt.

Dalton lay there in the night, his eyes open, feeling her slow, steady breathing and the frantic hammering of his heart in his chest. He looked at the window, where heavy silk drapes kept the room in darkness. A warm yellow light, almost too faint to register on his retinas, was showing around the edges of the drapes, the glow from the streetlamp just outside her window, which was why she had such heavy drapes in the first place. The interior of the flat was black and utterly still. In a moment, he realized what had awakened him.

The refrigerator in her kitchen was old and tired. The compressor wheezed and rattled and rumbled and groaned when it wasn't clicking off and on. But all that had stopped. He looked to his left, and saw that the moon-faced clock on the night table was dark. The power was out.

If the power had gone out, why was the streetlamp still on?

Of course. A separate system.

If the power had gone out, would her security box have switched over to battery power?

And, if it had, wouldn't it be beeping?

He had a similar system in his hotel room in Venice, and it always beeped when the power was off. Another kind of system? A different setting on the same system?

Maybe.

Maybe not.

Get up and see.

He gently eased Veronika's arm off his chest. She stirred, said something in German he could not understand, rolled over and burrowed into her pillow, went right back to sleep. He slipped out of the bed and stood in the room, his heart rate slowing as he forced himself to be still, to *listen*.

The skin on his neck and along his shoulders was cold and crawling.

The blackness seemed to press against his eyes. In his throat, an artery was throbbing. His personal sidearm, a SIG-Sauer P226, was in a locked compartment in the trunk of his Mercedes, and the Mercedes was in the Auto-Park at the Westbahnhof.

Veronika's H&K pistol.

Where the hell had she put it?

He had no idea. An unforgivable lapse of tradecraft, and being dead-bone tired was no excuse. Maybe it was in her night table.

He pulled on his slacks, came around the end of the bed, keeping his left hand on the bedroom wall, his eyes slowly adjusting. The door to her bedroom was wide open, a blacker rectangle in the dark.

He was reaching for the night table when he heard a faint noise. It came from the living room and sounded like someone swallowing, someone with a dry throat. There was someone in the outer room.

He got the drawer open. No pistol.

He waited a moment, letting his eyes adjust, and then stepped soundlessly out into the dining area. Here, the light from the street-lamp cast a glow through the curtains.

There was a shape standing in the entrance hall, a large man in a sweater, jeans, gloved hands, with no face at all, just two narrow slits where his eyes should have been and two ovals where his nostrils gaped open, like the snout of a pig, and a slash of a mouth. A mask?

The man closed in, blindingly fast, a ripple of blurred motion as he rushed at Dalton, and he went into the air—literally—and aimed a vicious kick-boxing strike at Dalton's head.

Dalton blocked the blow, staggering under the force of it, and caught the man's leg by the ankle, shifting his weight to deliver a blade kick to the man's exposed groin. And once again the man seemed to turn to smoke and water, literally spinning in midair, a blurring motion in the half-light. There was a blur to Dalton's left, and something rock hard struck the side of Dalton's head. He reeled back, half stunned, his vision blurring. But instead of closing in for the kill, the man dropped into a crouch and backed farther away into the living area, his eye slits fixed on Dalton's face.

There he set himself in a defensive stance, clearly waiting for Dalton to reengage as if this were some sort of formal martial-arts contest. Dalton took a breath, shook his head and shoulders, and began to move toward the man. At that moment, Dalton sensed a quick movement behind him. Turning his head, he saw a small gray shape running toward the bedroom. A second man, going for Veronika. Dalton took two steps after him, a very bad idea. Somehow the man—Dalton had tagged him "Smoke"—covered the distance between them in a blur and delivered three rapid knuckle strikes, two to Dalton's right kidney and one to the back of his skull. Dalton's head nearly came off his neck, and a red fog clouded his vision. Fighting a wave of nausea and vertigo, he went down on one knee, rolled onto his left hip, and did an ankle-level leg sweep that knocked the big man's feet out from under him.

The man went down hard, slamming onto his back. Dalton was on him, three rapid strikes, twice to the throat and vicious knuckles into the man's left eye. Smoke grunted in pain, his breath chuffing out. From the bedroom came an agonized shriek, cut suddenly short. Smoke arched his body violently—he was unbelievably strong—smashed a knee into the side of Dalton's head, broke free, rolled away, was up on one knee and starting to rise. Dalton stepped in fast and kicked him in the face, giving it everything he had. Smoke's head snapped back, and blood flew from his open mouth. He rocked backward under the force of the kick, turned it into a shoulder roll, and vaulted to his feet again, as lithe as a panther, his feet wide apart, his body half turned, poised, rooted, ready. In the light Dalton could see the man's misshapen mouth open, revealing strong white teeth, covered in blood. The man was trying to *smile*.

The . . . thing . . . The fucking Orc . . . was actually *smiling* at Dalton, his scarred lips twisting into a grimace.

"Come on, Slick," he said, in English, a Slavic accent, the words slurring, his voice strained and hoarse. "You fight like fucking girl."

The only thing on Dalton's mind was Veronika. This man had to go down now. Smoke did a head fake to Dalton's right, a rippling blur as he pivoted into another kick strike at Dalton's head. It literally brushed Dalton's left ear as he dodged backward. The man landed on the balls of his feet, feinted right, cut left, and abruptly broke off the fight.

He turned his back, raced to the balcony, butted the door open, vaulted the rail, and dropped soundlessly into the night.

Dalton spun around and headed for the bedroom, his heart a cold stone in his chest. The room was black, but he heard rapid breathing coming from the bathroom. And something else too. A high-pitched, whistling sound.

"Veronika?"

Her voice, coming from the bathroom:

"Micah. In here."

Dalton jumped over the bed, got to the bathroom door. A match flared, and he saw Veronika in its glow lighting a candle on the edge of the bath. She was naked, her breasts and belly, her right hand and forearm all sheeted in blood. On the floor in front of her lay the second man, a razor-edged leaf-bladed punching knife on the bath mat beside him. The man was on his back, writhing and making a barely audible keening sound, like a teakettle whistling. His legs were kicking convulsively, and a wet stain was spreading over the crotch of his jeans.

He had both of his hands up to his face. They were gripping the plastic handle of something that had been shoved very deep into the socket of his left eye. The handle had a long coiled electric cord attached to it. It took Dalton a moment or two to realize what it was. A curling iron.

Dalton stepped around the man on the floor, went to Veronika, knelt, looked at her hands, her body, afraid of what he would find.

"Did he cut you?"

"No," she said. "It's all his blood. I heard something thumping. I thought it was dream. I couldn't feel you. Then I knew it wasn't a dream. I keep the pistol in the bathroom, like a panic room. I am thinking I would lock the door, get the pistol. He was too fast, right on my back. He kicked the door open. I reached for whatever, caught that, and went at him. I could not see him, but I could smell him. It punched into his eye. I hope I kill him."

Dalton looked at the man, writhing and gasping on the mat.

"I think you have. It just hasn't gotten through to him yet. They cut your power off. Do you know where the switch is?"

"There's a panel in the janitor's closet, at the top of the stairs."

"Where's the pistol?"

She reached into the cabinet, pulled it out from under the towels.

"Can you handle him?" he said.

She nodded, doing an automatic press check to see if there was a round in the chamber. Then she leveled it at the man on the floor. Her hand wasn't shaking at all, and the look on her face was a killing look.

"I'll be back."

A minute passed.

Veronika watched the ugly little man suffering in utter horror, the reality of what she had done sinking in.

Then her bedroom light came on, and Dalton was back at the door, with her bathrobe in his hands.

He switched on the bathroom light, covered her, held her for a moment. They stood and watched the man's agony. The keening sound he had been making slowed, finally stopped, and now there was just the thump and rustle of his boots on the floor and his ragged breathing, shallow, gurgling and rasping in his throat.

Dalton knelt down, pulled the man's bloody hands off the butt of the curling iron. White skin, a black growth of beard, in his gasping mouth a row of tiny yellow teeth. His body, although badly formed, with signs of chronic malnutrition, was bony and hard as a tree root. His one open eye was a shiny black pebble. His lips were turning blue, and his mouth was filling up with blood. Sensing Dalton nearby, he reached out and grabbed him by the hand, his bony fingers sinking into Dalton's skin. His lips moved, but only a whisper came out

"Haldokló?"

"He asks if he is dying," said Veronika. "Is he dying?"

"Yes," said Dalton. "What language is it?"

"I think it's Hungarian."

"Can you ask him who sent him?"

"Ki küldött?"

The man jerked at the sound of her question and then became still. Only the slow throbbing of a vein in his forehead indicated that he was still alive. Dalton touched the end of the plastic handle, held it for a time, feeling the pulse of the man's brain in the handle.

"Mi a neved?" said Veronika. "I ask him what his name is."

The bloody mouth opened.

"Kurva. Tisztatalan."

"He says I am whore. And unclean. I think he is Muslim."

Dalton picked up one end of the electric cord, handed it to Veronika.

"Plug it in."

Veronika, realizing what Dalton was proposing, shook her head, her eyes widening. Dalton got up and did it for her. After a few moments, a wisp of smoke began to curl up around the handle of the rod protruding from the man's bloody eye socket.

The smoke was acrid and reeked of scorching flesh, burning brains, human fat cooking off. His chest began to shudder, and his mouth opened in a rictus of pain, but no sound came out other than a dry croak. Dalton leaned down and spoke into the man's ear, words that Veronika could not hear, a silky whisper. The man began to shake uncontrollably. Dalton sat back on his heels and watched the man for a time, his face set and cold.

"What's your name?" he barked at the man. "Tell me, and it stops."

The man found his voice.

"Yusef. *Akhmediar,* Yusef."

Dalton looked at Veronika, pointed to the cable. Veronika unplugged it, her face paper white, her expression full of horror.

"Who sent you?"

Yusef shook his head, his jaw tightening.

Dalton reached for the plug again. Yusef must have sensed the motion because he tried to speak.

"*Ut . . . a . . . zók. Uta . . . zók.*"

"What is he saying?"

"I don't know. The Wanderer? The Traveler? The Tramp?"

Yusef's chest shuddered twice, and then he stopped breathing. Dalton reached out and touched the handle. The man was dead.

Dalton stood up, his legs shaking a little. A row of bullet wounds that looked like cigarette burns rode up the left side of his chest. He had a surgical scar on the lower part of his abdomen, about sixteen inches long, and still a little red-looking. Veronika looked at Dalton, taking him in. He was, in a way, terrible to look at, just as he had said, his flesh was like a cave pictograph telling of ancient battles.

"You said something I couldn't hear. And then he starts to talk. What did you say?"

"I said that that he was Muslim, that he was dying, and that if he did not speak I'd soak his corpse in pig's blood and bury him with a dead dog to keep him company. It would mean he'd be defiled and could not enter Paradise."

"God. Such people, the Muslims. Are you all right?"

"There were two. That's why I couldn't help you."

"I know. I could hear."

He didn't say what was in growing his mind, that the point of the attack was to kill *her*. Yusef had waited until the bigger man, the fighter, had drawn Dalton out of the bedroom. The fighter had held back, even when Dalton was dazed and vulnerable. It was a fight Dalton could easily have lost. The man was good, maybe better than Dalton. But he suspected that Veronika was the real target.

"Where is the other one? Is he dead?"

"No. He jumped. From your balcony."

"I'm on the fifth floor. Maybe he died."

Dalton doubted it. Fighting him had been like getting caught in a printing press. The guy was six feet at least, much heavier than Dalton, and one hell of a lot stronger. Frighteningly fit. At the end of the fight, Smoke hadn't even been breathing hard.

Broad and squat, but he moved like a duelist, on the balls of his feet. Stunningly quick. As elusive as smoke and water. And tough as a steel-toed boot. Dalton might as well have been punching an engine block.

Smoke.

A pit fighter, perhaps, but very well trained. Special Forces training? His style was mixed, some Thai, some Spetsnaz handiwork, and a few Delta Force tricks that Dalton had almost forgotten.

And that face.

That ruined face, literally featureless, two slit eyes and an ugly stump of a nose, bald, blue-veined skin as shiny as plastic, and totally earless. And the voice, harsh, guttural, as if the vocal cords had been scorched. Burned.

Smoke had been in a fire, a very bad one, his features melted, burned away. Skin grafts, surgery, whatever had been done for him had not been done very well. Smoke was a walking horror.

A fifty-foot drop onto a lawn would not kill something like that. Dalton wasn't sure what would.

Maybe an RPG.

"I don't think he's dead, Veronika. I think we'll see him again. Let's get you into the shower. I think they bypassed the alarm, but your neighbors will have called the police."

She shook her head.

"They're turning this building into a co-op. That's why there's a big scrap bin out at the back. Renovations. They forced out most of the renters. There is only one other family on this floor, the Zuckermans, and they're in Tel Aviv. The building is made of concrete. I don't think anybody heard anything. And, if they did, they'd mind their own business. They're old. They remember the Russians. Old Viennese do not call the police when they hear things in the night."

"We'll have to go."

"*We?*"

"Yes, Veronika. You can't stay here."

"Why?"

"Because I think Yusef was here to kill you."

"Why do you think that?"

Dalton laid it out for her, how Smoke had held back, keeping Dalton busy, while Yusef had slipped past him and gone after her. When he was done, her eyes were full of a liquid light, and her skin was as pale as new snow. He took her in his arms and held on to her for a time. Gradually her breathing steadied.

"Now what? What do we do now?"

"You take a shower. I'll clean up the place and dump Yusef in the bin. Then we get the hell out of Dodge."

She looked up at him, puzzled, and managed a smile.

"Dodge? What is 'get . . . out of Dodge'?"

Dalton smiled grimly, and bent down to pick up what was left of Yusef, rolling him into the bloody mat, hoisting his skinny corpse easily, draping it over a shoulder.

"I mean, we're leaving. Leaving Vienna. Leaving now."

. . .

THEY cleaned up the flat as well as they could. Dalton carried Yusef's body down the fire escape, dumping it into the construction bin at the bottom of the yard and burying it in a mounded heap of discarded shingles. When he got back up to Veronika's flat to clean himself up, she was dressed and holding a small black leather bag.

She looked shaken, confused, frightened, resolute, and very sad. Dalton, who was feeling a few of the same emotions, and a couple of different ones—guilt and anger being the strongest—thought she was feeling exactly the way she should be feeling.

She had a small Volkswagen Jetta parked in the lot, a little black bullet with racing tires and a tuned exhaust. She eased it out of the lane, and they headed south through the deserted streets. In a few minutes they were on the Gürtel, and only a short distance from Mariahilfer Strasse. Dalton, in the passenger seat, scanned the streets and the skyline, and the road behind them, looking for a sign of surveillance. Unless they were a lot better than Jagermeir's team, he was reasonably certain that they were not being followed.

As they turned south on Mariahilfer Strasse, entering the maze of office clutter and antique housing that ringed the Westbahnhof, the sky in the east was full of a fiery orange light, and a huge flock of ravens was wheeling and spinning in the sunrise, their glossy black wings glinting with gold and copper flashes. Veronika, who had been, in the main, silent as she worked her way through the center of Vienna, finally found a way into the heart of her concerns.

"Why *me*, Micah? Why are those men after me?"

Dalton looked at the side of her face, lit by a shaft of rising sun as they cleared an intersection before plunging back into the shadowed canyons of the Ring District. Her skin was white, and her hands on the leather wheel of the Jetta were white with the force of her grip.

What the hell have I gotten this woman into?

"I have a theory."

"Please share. Before my hair bursts into flames."

"How would it look to your people, to the OSE, if you were to be found dead in your flat this morning? The first thing they'd do would be to look into what you were working on. Your unit, I mean. And your unit was working on me. I'd be the first person they'd want to see."

"But what about you? If I am killed, wouldn't you stay around to sort it out? Explain it to the . . ."

Her voice trailed into silence.

"You said you've seen my files," said Dalton. "See how it looks? I cut you out of the unit, followed you home, dragged you inside, forced you to show me your computer, and next morning you're dead. Once they saw that, they wouldn't see anything else. I'd be in Lödesburg Sink, wrapped in heavy chains, talking to a prosecutor from the ICC. The U.S. doesn't recognize the International Criminal Court, so the ICC would have a dream come true, an undeclared CIA agent who murdered an Austrian OSE agent on their turf."

From the look on her face, cold and fixed, it was clear that Veronika found this statement uncongenial.

"So. You would leave me there? Dead?"

"I like to pay my debts in person, Veronika. To stay out of a holding cell and go after these people? Yes, I would have."

That created a difficult silence for a while.

The barnlike hulk of the Westbahnhof was looming over the slate roofs of Mariahstadt. Traffic was beginning to build. A blue-and-white police car flashed past them, its klaxon wailing. Dalton wanted out of this Jetta soon. Very damned soon. Veronika had worked her way through the following chill and surfaced again, her face a little stonier.

But she still had that iron.

"What about Yusef's body? What would they make of that?"

"An accomplice. People see what they want to see. And even if I were gone, the police could still connect me to you. Remember, I did an Internet search on you last night?"

"But wasn't that on a secured CIA link?"

Nothing seemed to change on Dalton's face, but now he looked like a death mask.

"Yes. It was. It was an Agency BlackBerry. Encrypted. There's no way that anyone outside the Agency could have tracked my search string."

"Unless someone cracked the encryption."

"Not likely."

"But possible?"

"Yes."

"Was . . . is your BlackBerry GPS-equipped?"

"Yes. If it's on, its location would be identifiable, but only to the Monitors at the National Security Agency in Maryland."

"Is the GPS locator also encrypted?"

"Yes. Heavily."

"Who would be capable of cracking an encrypted CIA BlackBerry?"

Dalton thought about it.

"The Brits, I think. Maybe the Chinese . . ."

Dalton did not name the third possibility, the Mossad, but it was at the forefront of his mind for a number of reasons.

As it turned out, he wasn't alone.

They reached the entrance to the Auto-Park. Veronika pulled up across the street from a towering concrete labyrinth of open floors, each level packed with cars.

Dalton was looking at the cameras over the automated gates. And thinking about the time stamps on parking receipts.

And that blue-and-white police car.

"When does that construction bin at your apartment get emptied?"

"Whenever it's full. About once a month. How full was it?"

"Less than half."

"That will give us time. Unless this day gets a lot hotter. Then he'll make his presence felt pretty soon. In the meantime, we—"

"That's my point, Veronika. It isn't going to be 'we.' Where's the closest police station?"

Her answer was short and sharp. And suspicious.

"There is a transit police kiosk inside the station entrance."

"Good. Let's go," he said, cracking the passenger door.

"To the *Polizei*? Why? You said—"

"Not me. You. I'll see you to the entrance, watch until you get to the transit station. Tell them everything. *Everything.* Nothing has happened up until now that compromises you in any way. Tell them I turned up at your flat last night, that I forced you inside. Tell them why. The truth, all of it, about the *Nomenklatur*, about the word *Verwandtschaft*—whatever that means—the whole thing. Hold nothing back. Get them to take you into protective custody. Maybe you can get your boss to tell you what *Verwandtschaft* actually referred to. You can say I forced you to drive me to the train station—"

"Sure. And perhaps I can tell them that I submitted to rape just so I could get a sample of your DNA. Maybe they'll even give me a raise."

This was said with such a bitter edge to it that it stopped Dalton for a moment. Her face was closing down fast, but Dalton cut across her and drove the argument home.

"Look, Veronika, if the idea was to frame me with your killing, it's not going to work very well if you're not actually dead, is it? This isn't your fight. You walk away right now—"

"Not my fight? I killed a man last night. In my own home. And if I leave now, what happens to you?"

"It's two hundred and eighty miles to Venice. I have friends—"

"Really? Like the man who puts the mark on that poster? That said everything was safe? *Friends* like that? Who else knew that you'd be coming up out of the Schottentor station? And *when?*"

There wasn't any other answer to that. Dalton had been visiting that prospect for several hours and wasn't enjoying the view at all.

"No one. He was the only one."

"The Cousins do not tell us who gave them the information about you. We both know Interpol doesn't do anything but pass on data to real agencies. They're just a clearinghouse."

"Yes."

"So he—whoever this *friend* is—it's possible he's the source that Interpol was covering for. He's the one who put that *tell* on the poster and led you right into the trap. He wanted you watched so he could set you up somehow—"

Dalton put up some fences just to see if she could clear them.

"There's no way he could have known about my contact with you, about the lighter. None of that was predictable—"

"No. But *you* are. You said it yourself. If you're under attack, the first thing you do is turn right around and go straight at them. The shark-in-shallow-water. If your friend knew *you*, he'd know that he could depend on you to—what do you say in English—percolate?"

"Escalate."

"Right, and isn't that what you *would* do. Every single time?"

Veronika moved closer, leaned into her argument, her scent around him and her topaz eyes fixed on his.

"If he has access somehow—we don't know how—to your Black-Berry, then he knows you searched for the name of a unit member—me—and he knows where you are because of the GPS, so he sends in a team to kill me. Micah, listen, no one else *could* have. He's the one behind all this. You had a fallback meet, didn't you? I mean, everyone does. Where was it?"

"Leopoldsberg. At ten this morning."

"Are you going to go?"

Galan. Issadore Galan.

Dalton could hear his laugh, a dry, creaking rasp. The voice of the Joshua tree. He could see his yellow skin, wrinkled and old beyond his years, and his eyes, the eyes of a crow, piercing black, full of sharp wit and cold intelligence. All these features were crowded into the center of a round, bald skull. Then there were the misshapen, claw-like hands, broken with hammers by the Jordanians, his body crippled after that. The stoic grace and resignation with which he bore these marks they had left on him, the things they had done in the months they had had him, things so terrible that when they finally dumped him, bound and naked, out in the Negev and then he later saw himself in the window glass of the Israeli Army medical unit, he quit the Mossad. And he never went back to his wife and family in Tel Aviv.

Galan went to Venice, to put some sort of life together in history's first Jewish ghetto, and eventually became the spymaster for Allessio Brancati, the chief of the Venetian Carabinieri. Both men had been Dalton's allies in his private vendetta against the Serbian Mafia. He owed those two men his life. Galan would not—could not—have betrayed Dalton. There must be another answer.

"I *know* this man, Veronika."

"I see. And does *everybody* love you, Micah?"

Dalton's face changed, hardened, like concrete setting. This was too close to his core. Much too close. He had been married once, to a lovely woman named Laura, and they had had a little girl. And now they were both dead. Veronika saw the effect of her question.

"I'm sorry. I think that went where I did not mean it to go. What I mean is, have you perhaps become . . . *inconvenient?*"

Dalton didn't immediately answer. But into his covert world, "change we can believe in" had come with a vengeance. The CIA was under heavy fire from the left wing for what it had done—or had not done—in the aftermath of September 11th and the wars that followed. There seemed to be a special venom reserved for any Agency officer who had ever terrified a terrorist, and there was to be no mercy granted even for officially sanctioned actions taken by field officers working under unbearable pressure in the aftermath of an unprecedented attack on the nation.

A Special Prosecutor had been appointed, plea bargains were being cut, old friendships broken, loyalty and trust betrayed, long-standing but informal covenants between domestic and foreign agencies shattered. A miasma of fear floated in the corridors, the halls were full of informants, Iagos and Savonarolas listened at the keyholes and monitored the phones. The morale of the operational sectors had plummeted to abyssal levels. The flow of useful HumInt had dried to a trickle. Very few CIA officers, especially those with families, were willing to do—or to authorize—anything aggressive out in the field.

Most of them were riding their desks, shuffling paper and keeping their heads down, waiting for the Great Eye to pass over and find another victim, *any* victim. The Big Chill had settled over the American intelligence community, drawing the amused contempt of America's allies and greatly comforting her enemies. And if there was a list on a desk somewhere, the name of Micah Dalton had to be in the top one hundred.

Inconvenient.

Just like the old Uzbek.

Veronika reached out and touched the side of his face. Her fingertips were cold, but his skin was warm. He did not react. He was staring straight ahead, his thoughts clearly in another place. The traffic was building up, and she could see a couple of foot patrolmen walking slowly along the walk, sipping coffee from paper cups, talking.

Dalton was right, of course. Veronika knew that she should get out of the car now and walk into the train station and tell Dalton's version of the story to the transit police. They'd believe her. Relations with the CIA Station Chief in Vienna would be severed for a while, and the OSE would be theatrically outraged. The papers would hear of it—an "international incident." And of course she would never again be assigned to Overwatch because she's notorious. On the other hand, Nenia Faschi would eat Rolf Jägermeier alive for letting this happen to her. But Veronika could, eventually, manage some kind of normal life. And of course the *Krokodil* would be gone forever.

It was the sensible thing to do.

The *Austrian* thing to do.

"Galan," said Dalton.

"I'm sorry?"

"Issadore Galan. That's the name of the man we're talking about. He's an Israeli, used to work for the Mossad, left them to live in Venice. He runs the *agenzia di spionaggo* for the Carabinieri."

"Issadore Galan. He's a Jew?"

Dalton gave her a quick, hard look, but she didn't feel it. She was staring out the window, her attention on something else.

"You remember what Yusef said just before he died? You asked him who sent him. He used the term *utazók*. It means 'wanderer,' Micah. But I think in Hungarian it's slang for 'Hebrew.' Hebrew actually means 'wanderer' or 'homeless.'"

Dalton looked over at her.

"Okay. That's enough. I think I know where he is."

"Then we should go and ask him a few rude questions. I can help you. I will call in to work and take some days off. They won't find Yusef for a month. If ever. I have contacts in the OSE, contacts all over Europe. I can get access to the databases, this Smoke person. There would be paper on a man like that, with such terrible scars. I can drive—I can. What do you people say? 'Scratch your back'?"

In spite of his black mood, Dalton had to smile at that.

"*Watch* my back, and you already have. No. You have a life here, Veronika. A good one. Much better than mine. Go back to it."

He was thinking, but did not say, *People around me die.*

Veronika leaned over and gave him a kiss, a very fine one. The two patrol cops grinned as they passed by, their muffled voices carrying through the window glass. Dalton felt the kiss with varying degrees of intensity everywhere in his body. So did Veronika.

She pulled back, touched his cheek again.

"Maybe I don't like my life that much."

LEOPOLDSBERG, a Catholic cathedral-fortress about three miles northwest of Vienna, was a limestone monolith perched on top of what they like to call mountains in that part of Austria. The Danube, not actually blue, ran in a broad, lazy curve around its base before straightening out, splitting in two, and running like a divided high-way right down the middle of Vienna. The view from the stone ter-race on the south side, a memorial to the war dead, took in the entire city, from the industrial regions in the east to the dense masses of pink stone buildings in the Ring District. Low green hills and tilled farmlands rose up almost to the forward glacis of the cathedral. At this time in the spring, everything was green and growing, and the old city glowed with a rose light under a pale yellow sun.

They were in Dalton's ancient Mercedes-Benz, a squared-off and gleaming black tank with a black-leather-and-rosewood interior, that Dalton had inherited from Porter Naumann, along with his town house in Wilton Row and his hotel suite in Venice.

It was a wildly impractical car, too damned big for most European towns. Getting it through a chicane was like riding a rhino down a wet clay bank. Every time he filled it up, he got a thank-you note from the Sultan of Brunei. It had the carbon footprint of a five-alarm fire in a rubber tire plant, but it was as hard to stop as a heart attack. Dalton could drive it through a brick wall. And the engine block had once taken three 7.62 rounds without missing a stroke. Try that with a Smart car sometime.

Veronika, when she had first seen it, said all of the same things about it that everyone else did—the Austrians being an earnest and eco-minded people—but by the time they were coming up the long curving drive that led to the parking lot, she wanted to give up her flat and move in. The car had international plates—Dalton always kept a couple of valid sets in a hideaway under the trunk—and today he was using a set linked to an actual consulting firm in Marseille, where he had a freelance stringer who'd cover for him on any official check. And Europe was jam-packed with old black Mercedes-Benzes. So, all things considered, including the black-tinted windows, it was a good ride.

It was about nine in the morning. The parking lot was full, and the café-restaurant was crowded with people. Hundreds of mangy back-packers and overstuffed tourists were milling about the grounds.

Veronika wheeled the Benz slowly up and down the ranks of parked cars while Dalton scanned the plates and looked for anyone in the crowds around the cathedral steps who was paying a little too much attention to them. But no one was.

It was just another sunny Viennese morning, God was in his Heaven, and all was right with the local tourist trade. An ice-cream truck had set up shop in one corner of the cobblestoned park, under the shelter of a twenty-foot stone wall, and a platoon of little kids in matching uniforms—blue and white—was lining up for ice cream and chocolate sauce. The sun was growing in strength, and parasols were popping up here and there above the crowds like flowers in a summer garden. From the far side of the cathedral—Dalton assumed it was from the terrace—a string quartet was playing, of course, *Tales from the Vienna Woods.*

There was no sign at all of Issadore Galan.

Dalton was early, of course, but Galan always arrived at a meet about an hour before just to check out the terrain. They came around the last bend and rolled up beside a short row of vehicles: a large green maintenance van, a small blue Audi, a silver Opel Meriva, and a mud-brown 1986 Saab sedan with rusted fenders, sagging shocks, and bald tires. It looked empty.

Dalton, watching the Saab carefully, asked Veronika to keep rolling and park the Benz a few rows away. She found a slot two rows beyond, managed to back the tank into it without scratching the paintwork, and shut the Benz down.

"Was that his car?" she asked. "The Saab?"

"Yes," he said, pulling his SIG out of the lockdown under the glove compartment.

"Aren't we sort of out in the open here?"

"Can't be helped. You know what to do?"

"Yes," she said, patting the little H&K on the seat beside her. "If you're hurt or killed or taken, I drive like hell to the nearest police station and tell them everything. If anybody tries to stop me, I run them down or I shoot them with this. Or both. And, yes, it's loaded."

Dalton gave her a smile, and a kiss on the lips in case it was his last, shoved the SIG into his belt under his navy V-neck, pulled the gold silk scarf around his neck, and climbed out of the car, patting the hood as he closed the door.

The sun was strong on the back of his neck as he walked through the car ranks, and he studied every face in the crowds around him as carefully as he studied every car and truck he passed and the walls of the cathedral-fortress that overlooked the parking lot. Down in his lizard brain, whatever lived there was sleeping soundly. He did not feel that he was being watched. Not even by Issadore Galan.

But now he was quite certain that Galan was here.

Dalton reached the Saab.

It was parked at the rear of the lot, hard up against a low stone wall, more or less in the corner farthest away from the cathedral itself. The Saab just sat there, forlorn, squat, as ugly as the man himself, covered in dust, looking as if it had been there since the war.

Dalton ran a fingertip through the dust, lifted it up. The dust was not from this parking lot. It was greasy brown and smelled of diesel, sewage, and seaweed. The scent reminded him of Venice in the summer. He came around to the driver's side, wiped some dust off the glass. The interior of the Saab was clean, nothing on the seats, nothing on the floorboards. The ashtray, which Galan usually kept stuffed to overflowing with crushed-out Gitane butts, was empty.

The interior looked as if it had been recently vacuumed, which was very unlike Galan, who treated the backseat like a Dumpster and could not be persuaded to clean the vehicle until he couldn't see out the back window. Dalton dropped to a knee, leaned down, and checked the underbody carefully. No wires. No explosives taped to the exhaust. His heart heavy and a tight feeling in his chest, he walked around to the rear of the car and stood for a time looking down at the trunk lid.

The dust lay thick on it and had not been disturbed at all. If there was anything in the trunk, it had been there for a while.

He looked across the roofs of the other cars, saw the big square Benz fifty feet away rising above the rounded little eco-cars like a bull in a rabbit hutch. The sun was on his face. The sky was a perfect sky blue, as was only right, and the air was full of the scent of spring flowers and strong Austrian coffee. He was young and healthy, and his unreliable libido was in working order again after a very long hiatus. It was a good day to die.

He reached down, grabbed the trunk handle, braced himself, and jerked it upward. The trunk lock popped as it always did, which was useful since Galan was always leaving his keys inside.

Dalton let his breath out slowly, relieved to find that he was still in one piece. He held the lid for a moment, leaning down to look for a detonator, a wire, a trigger mechanism of any kind, although anything clever would have gone off as soon as he popped the lock.

There was no wire. But in the narrow gap he could see brown burlap sacking stained with something dark. And now the stench hit him, drove him backward, his eyes watering. As he stepped back, his hand came off the trunk lid, and it rose slowly on its springs, opening up like the lid of a coffin.

Crowded—no, stuffed—stuffed into the trunk like a load of dirty laundry was a large man-shaped bundle wrapped in burlap soaked with dried blood.

Dalton reached down, got his fingers into the fabric, and ripped it away. It was stiff with blood and shredded as it came off Galan's body. Dalton stood for a time looking down at what had been done to Galan. A cursory glance told him that almost everything that the Jordanians had *not* done to Galan these new people finally had. Based on the bleeding and the bruising and the dried blood pooled in his empty eye sockets and around his exposed intestines and the obscenity of his genitals, it had been done while he was still alive.

Well, they would, wouldn't they?

I mean, otherwise, what's the fucking point?

No man could have endured this without, in the end, telling them everything—anything—they wanted to know. In a way, it was a kind of relief to Dalton. Galan had not turned against him, and whatever he had revealed in those last terrible moments of his life had been torn from him by utterly vile men who were going to die as soon as Dalton could find them. But Galan had not betrayed him.

Inevitably, he had told—whoever did this—everything about the meeting. The Schottentor trolley station. The *tell*. It didn't explain the access to his BlackBerry and GPS, but it explained a lot.

How long had they had him?

A week at least, since Dalton had gotten Galan's request for a meeting over a week ago and had come as soon as the Albanian hysteric in Bonn had stopped threatening to kill himself. It was hard to say how long Galan had been dead without a detailed examination, but the state of decomposition and the lack of rigor mortis suggested an outer limit of twenty-four hours, perhaps less.

He looked at Galan's left hand. There was something driven through his wrist, something metal. It was a large slot-headed wood screw. They had actually screwed his wrists into his hip bones just to amuse themselves. The Jew had been crucified on the skeleton of his own body.

For no reason at all other than Yusef, Dalton thought of Muslims. Compared to the ingenious torturers of the New Caliphate, Torquemada was an acupuncturist, as had been vividly demonstrated on the bodies of several American soldiers captured alive in Iraq. There were odd indentations like gouges in Galan's skin just under his fingertips. The nails were bloody and filled with decaying flesh. Dalton brushed at the marks, and a thin scale of dried blood flaked off.

Scored into the skin of Galan's left hip were two odd marks. Dalton cleaned the surface of Galan's hip and stretched the skin out.

8 B

He looked at the gouges for a moment, thinking of what it must have cost Galan to do something like that, done under conditions of unspeakable agony in the certain expectation of his own death and with the faint hope that perhaps after his body was found, Dalton would see the marks and know what they meant. A final act of defiance—and faith—from a good man and a fine friend. Dalton, his eyes burning a bit, sighed heavily and then stood up again.

There was a tube of paper, rolled up tight and stuck in Galan's bloody mouth. Dalton took it out slowly. It was dry, without bloodstains, and looked . . . fresh.

He unrolled it.

The Yid died begging Slick it was big fun we all had him he squeal like girl when he get fucked but you probably already know that anyway we just getting started fucking with <u>you</u> Slick
we see you real soon

Your old friend

Ps—you got five minutes from when you open trunk so you better run but don't worry if you die we still do that Miklas whore same like we do the Yid

Dalton read the last words, shoved the letter deep into his pocket, slammed the trunk lid, raced around to the front of the Saab and wrenched the hood open. The starter wires were still there. He spent a precious thirty seconds trying to find the device and gave it up. He figured he had—*hoped* he had—at least two minutes.

He tugged out his BlackBerry, turned it on. In the Monitor's Room at Crypto City, his indicator code flashed on, and the Activation Notice, along with the GPS coordinates and the brief voice packet that followed, was digitally tagged and logged for the Requesting Agent. Working with one hand on the ignition wires, he thumbed out Veronika's number and held it to his ear. *Answer! Answer! Answer!*

"Micah, what—?"

"The Saab's wired. I've triggered it. I've got to get it away from these crowds. Come after me, but *not close*. Hear me! Not close—"

"But Micah, you'll be—"

"No time, Veronika. No talk. Just *move!*"

He clicked off, dropped the BlackBerry into his pocket. He heard the Benz growl to life, heard the engine snarling and the huge Pirellis shriek on the cobbles. If the Saab blew up now, at least Veronika would be shielded inside the Benz. Someone in the crowd shouted a complaint at her—*Fucking Nazi*—and Dalton got the wires loose. His chest was cased in ice, his heartbeat was redlining, and he wanted nothing more than to turn and run away. But all he could see was the lineup of little kids at the ice-cream wagon. Ninety seconds. He got a crackle out of the wires. The engine coughed, started up, died. Another spark, and he tugged on the throttle cable at the same time. The Saab started up. A cylinder misfiring made the engine rock and rattle. He slammed the lid, ran to the driver's door. *Locked!* He looked around, saw a piece of rock lying on the ground, picked it up, stepped back, and threw it through the side window.

Heads turned at the sound of shattering glass. He was behind the wheel and slamming the Saab into gear as the shards were still hitting the cobblestones. He drove the pedal down, and the old wreck jerked forward.

He wrenched the wheel right, feeling the back end sliding. Straightening it out, he headed for the gate up a narrow lane that ran alongside the containment wall. Maybe he had sixty seconds. In his peripheral vision, he could see uniforms running toward him. He honked the horn at a fat man in cargo pants and Birkenstocks and a T-shirt that said DIVERS DO IT DEEPER, got the finger for his trouble. Someone was blowing a shrill whistle at him, someone was shouting in German, a stentorian official blare, "Halt!" He jinked the Saab left, cleared a bovine family licking cones. Someone was backing out of a slot right into his path. He accelerated, slammed into the rear taillight of the car, a Benz, silver. He scraped past it. There was the gate. A car was pulling into it. He floored the Saab, hearing the old motor grinding and the pistons chattering. He managed to get the Saab through the gate with an inch to spare, cutting off the incoming car, another outraged horn blast in his left ear as he sideswiped it. He looked for Veronika. He must have beaten her out of the yard— *Please don't get too close to me*. He checked his rearview mirror, and there was the Benz a hundred feet behind him, as he jolted and bounced down the curve away from the cathedral. Now he was on a tree-shaded lane. He had no more time. No one was near him. He jerked the wheel to the left and punched through the hedgerow and right into a ditch by the side of the road. The Saab hit hard, the windshield cracked, and the engine abruptly died.

He rolled out of the Saab, slightly dazed, and heard Veronika calling his name. He scrambled out of the ditch. The Benz was right there, idling in the lane. He could hear a police klaxon sounding from the cathedral parking lot. Then he was in the Benz, and Veronika floored the accelerator.

They were a hundred feet away when the shock wave hit. The Benz rocked on its shocks. Dalton looked back, saw a pillar of fire and a column of smoke rising in a lazy spiral above the trees and into the blue sky. There was a gold-and-copper light inside the black funnel, and it made him think—insanely—of the crows they had seen near the Westbahnhof station wheeling in the rising light.

He checked the lane behind them. No one was following them. An exploding Saab tends to distract the chase.

Veronika got them onto the southbound S9, powered it onto the river road. The Danube flowed at their left, and Vienna filled up the screen. The big car moved fast, but in a zone of cast-iron silence. Even the sound of the tires on the blacktop was a distant hum, soothing and rhythmic. The outside world could have been a travelogue playing on a screen. They sat there for a time, listening to each other breathe.

"Are you all right?" asked Veronika, her voice a little tight.

"I am. Are you?"

"I'm okay."

"Is your cell still on?"

"Yes."

"Better turn it off. And your pager. We're going dark."

He tugged his BlackBerry out and was about to shut it down and take out the battery when he saw an e-mail notice on the screen. It was from Sally Fordyce. He clicked on it:

> micah i must have hit a trip wire when I checked surveillance on you this is my last e-mail they're taking my cell phone and putting me in lockdown remember what I said about HOPE
>
> what is going on in this country?
>
> be safe trust no one
>
> semper fi
>
> sally

He read the message twice and then shut the BlackBerry off, flipped it over, and took out the battery, just to be certain.

"Micah, what is going on? What was the e-mail?"

"From Sally Fordyce, an old friend at Langley. She just got arrested for trying to help me."

"Jesus and Mary. I don't understand any of this."

Dalton pulled the paper out of his pocket, unrolled it, and held it out for her to read. She glanced down, scanned it quickly.

And then again more carefully.

He took it back.

Nothing was said for some time.

"I guess you're staying with me after all," he said finally. "I don't trust anybody else to keep these people off you."

"I would anyway. I told you that. And I think after this I may not have a job to go back to. There were security cameras in the parking lot. They would have seen me with you."

She was right about that. He had seen the cameras outside the Westbahnhof as well, and they were low enough to see her kiss him.

She was in it now, one way or another. And even if she left, it would drive him crazy just worrying about what might be happening to her. Last year he had made the mistake of leaving Cora Vasari's safety in the hands of a Carabinieri protection unit. She had been shot and badly wounded by a Serbian assassin in Florence a week later. *People around me die.*

But not this one.

"Something else to think about, Veronika . . ."

"Yes?"

"This guy, in the note, he names you."

She frowned at that as she worked it through.

"But we only met a few hours ago. How could he know?"

"Great question. Also, the note's fresh. It was stuck in Galan's mouth only a little while before we got there. Galan's blood was already dry. It had to be put there sometime this morning. There were security cameras in the lot. Are you allowed to park overnight there?"

"No. They lock the gates at ten p.m. They open automatically around dawn, I think. There are no guards on duty at night. They come on at eight in the morning. But there are signs. Your car would be towed."

"The people we're up against, they would have known that. So it had to have been driven there this morning. Based on the note, by people who knew your name. Somewhere there's security video of the Saab arriving at Leopoldsberg. Video of the driver. Any idea of how we could get that?"

"It would have been easy a while ago. As a member of the Overwatch, I could easily requisition the security videos."

"Do you have anyone on the inside who might do it for you?"

She said nothing for a time, staring out at the autobahn. They were passing a string of river barges towed by a fat little red tugboat with blue flowers painted on its funnel. A little blond boy on the foredeck, shirtless, was waving cheerfully at them as they blew by. Veronika, deep inside her thoughts, waved back at him anyway.

"Maybe . . . Jürgen Stodt."

"Who's he?"

She looked unhappy but managed to get it out.

"For a time . . . we were together. Last year. He works with me on the Overwatch. You saw him last night? Tall, skinny, he shaves his head now . . ."

"Wears big floppy hiking boots? Leaves the laces undone?"

"Yes. That's him."

Dalton didn't say what he thought of Jürgen Stodt's street skills, but if he'd managed to get more out of Veronika Miklas than the back of her hand he was better than he looked.

"Could you trust him?"

Veronika shrugged her shoulders, her cheeks reddening.

"He's a big, floppy puppy. He makes those . . floppy puppy eyes . . . at me still. He's really very sweet. Yes. He would do it."

"Would he keep his mouth shut?"

"Jürgen? Goodness no. He'd wet himself and roll over on his back as soon as somebody raised his voice. He's afraid of everyone, and especially Nenia Faschi. But would that matter if he could get the video first?"

Dalton shook his head.

"No. It wouldn't. How would you get in touch with him?"

She patted her laptop.

"He's addicted to his Treo. Never shuts it off. Day and night. We could find an Internet café, I could send him a message, check for a reply at the next café down the road? Could they—whoever *they* are—trace that?"

"Yes. But that video's worth the risk."

They cruised on for a time, passing through downtown Vienna

and on out into the lowlands. The land was emerald green and rolling, dotted with white-walled farmhouses and the silvery spikes of church steeples.

"These are very bad people, Micah. Do you have any idea who *they* are? He says 'your old friend.' Is it someone you know?"

"I know a lot of people who don't like me very much. Only a very few of them are capable of getting an edge on a man like Galan and then doing what they did to him."

"Your friend Galan. He was there?"

"Yes. In the trunk."

"Oh, Micah . . . I'm so sorry. Was it very bad?"

Dalton told her a little. Not much. It was enough. They were passing through the middle of Vienna, lost in the morning traffic stream. There was no obvious pursuit. No choppers in the air.

In the far north behind him he could see a pillar of smoke rising into the sky above the green dome of Leopoldsberg: Issadore Galan's funeral pyre.

"You said only a few people could—how you say—*get an edge* on Galan? What does this mean?"

"It means outmaneuver and defeat him. And there were very few men who could do that. There was a freelancer named Kiki Lujac. He used to work for Branco Gospic, and then he went into business with the KGB. He might do something like this. But this note—Lujac was fluent in English, well-educated, polished—he would never write a note like this. Besides, he would have taken pictures of the process and then put them on the Net. That was his . . . trademark."

"We don't know that he hasn't. Where is he now?"

"Nobody knows. He was seen in Garrison, upper New York State, last winter. The FBI and NSA security people tore up the eastern seaboard looking for him, but they never got him."

"Is there anyone else?"

"There was an old Comanche I ran into a while back. He'd have loved this kind of thing. But he's dead now."

"You're sure?"

Dalton thought but did not say, *Pretty sure, Veronika, since I put a couple of .357s into his face, hacked his head off with a hatchet, stuck it in a beer cooler with some dry ice, and FedEx'd it to a state trooper in Butte.*

"Yeah, I'm pretty sure."

"Anyone else?"

"Yes. A few. But this thing . . . it feels . . . Muslim."

"Do you mean al-Qaeda."

"No. Not their style. Too . . . byzantine. They like to blow up discos and incinerate office workers. This is more like the Chechens. Or the Albanians. Or the Serbs."

"Slick. That name. Didn't the man, the one you called Smoke, didn't he call you Slick?"

"Yes. And he had an accent, sounded Balkan, maybe Russian. Lots of Muslims in the Balkans. And Yusef was definitely Muslim."

"Have you ever operated against al-Qaeda?"

"Not since I joined the Agency. Before that, yes. With the Special Forces. In the Horn of Africa, Afghanistan. Waziristan. The Army had me in Kosovo and Bosnia for a while, before I got on with the Cleaners, and there was a heavy Muslim factor in that sector, although when I was there we were fighting to *protect* them from outfits like the Serb Skorpions. Maybe this Smoke guy was someone I knew. His fighting style was hard-core Special Forces. I think he might even be Spetsnaz. But if we had ever locked horns, it was sure as hell before he got all burned up. You see this Smoke guy now, you're never going to forget him."

Blood-red veins.

Pale green light.

Once again, something deep in the well of his memory, something dark, began to rise, a shapeless, cloudy horror full of blood-red veins, wrapped in pale green light.

He waited for the memory to declare itself, but instead it sank back again, clouded over, and was gone.

Veronika glanced over at Dalton and then back at the highway rolling toward them. Beyond Vienna, as you go south and west, the land grows craggy and begins a gradual climb toward the Alps and the mountain passes that lead down into Italy. Far in the southwest, the sun was glinting off a row of white shark's teeth: spring snow in the high passes.

"So your friend did not betray you?" she said in a soft voice after a long silence.

"No," said Dalton. "He didn't."

"What will we do now?"

"We try to get to Venice. It's what Galan wanted me to do."

"Did you set that up before . . . all this?"

"No. He left me a message."

"How?"

Dalton told her.

"Merciful Christ."

"You think so? That hasn't been my experience."

"What do those marks have to do with Venice?"

"Galan has rooms in Cannaregio, on the Fondamenta degli Ormesini, across from the Tempio Israelitico, in the old Jewish quarter."

"The Ghetto?"

"Yes. He has a flat on the top floor of a little villa, with a terrace overlooking the canal. The number of his flat is 8B."

CLASSIFIED UMBRA EYES DIAL
INTERNAL AUDIT COMMITTEE
File 92r: DALTON, MICAH
Service ID: REDACTED

Security cameras outside the Westbahnhof station Auto-Park in Vienna confirm that DALTON and MIKLAS arrived there at 0821 hours and that it appeared from their actions that some sort of physical intimacy had taken place, which is common in hostage situations if rape is a component.

Although the main security camera at Leopoldsberg malfunctioned, peripheral cameras confirm that DALTON and MIKLAS were next seen in the parking lot of the castle at 0917 hours, just prior to the explosion of a brown Saab.

In the confusion of the blast, which killed one and injured two police officers, the authorities lost track of the pair, and their current location or direction remains unknown.

MOSSAD confirms that the body found in the trunk of the Saab was that of GALAN, ISSADORE—a former MOSSAD agent currently in the employ of the Italian Carabinieri in Venice. BDS officers from the Vienna station have been dispatched to Venice to interview the local officials.

As GALAN, ISSADORE, was an Israeli citizen, The MOSSAD have expressed a desire to assist us in our inquiries into this matter. As a courtesy and at the request of the Consulate, we have notified the MOSSAD of DALTON's last known GPS coordinates, as well as a description of his vehicle.

Actions considered at this time/date after consultation with Commander PEARSON, DD of Clandestine Services, and his Adviser Pro Tem, D. CATHER, former DD of Clandestine, with the DNI in attendance, include but are not limited to the possibility of an official Joint Task Force Liaison with elements of the FBI, the BDS, and the Justice Department, under the aegis of the Audit Committee's Official Mandate: (op cit: Presidential Finding F2391).

No conclusion has as yet been reached, pending final decisions from POTUS/DNI.

LEGAL IMPLICATIONS:

The Secretariat, having consulted with General Counsel Dir/CIA Justice and DNI, takes note that new POTUS Intelligence ROE Policy mandates that, since all subsequent events that occurred in the early hours of the following morning had their predicate cause in DALTON's aggressive response to the possibility of surveillance by Parties Unknown to him, Presidential Finding F2391 requires that legal responsibility for these outcomes must devolve upon DALTON and not upon this Agency or the U.S. Government, since DALTON was not acting in any official capacity as a CIA employee but as a private citizen.

CONCLUSION:

We bear <u>no legal responsibility for and offer no protection to</u> *DALTON, MICAH, in this matter. This is the* <u>official position</u> *of the United States Government and as such will be communicated to the relevant authorities in Vienna, the UN, Tel Aviv, INTERPOL, and the ICC officials in Bonn. No statement will be issued to the media or the press concerning this matter until it has been resolved by the investigating authorities or by external events.*

MARIAH VALE/OD/DD/EXECUTIVE SECRETARIAT

Fort Meade, Maryland

Nikki Turrin saw the navy blue Crown Victoria parked outside her town house as soon as she got off the Odenton transit bus. It was idling, like a whale in a lagoon, in the dappled shadows under the Civil War–era oaks that lined Caisson Street. Sunlight shimmered in a golden veil through the leaves and pooled on the walks and lawns where the kids were playing. A sprinkler was hissing away in the gardens in front of her place, sending a jet of diamond sparkles through the sunlight as it circled.

As she came down the walkway she checked out the plate: U.S GOV-ERNMENT. The windows of the car were heavily tinted, but she could vaguely discern the shapes of two men inside, one in the back and another up front behind the wheel.

The presence of an official vehicle outside her town house wasn't particularly surprising to Nikki Turrin, since she was on the staff of the Assistant Director of Research and Analysis at the National Security Agency, an ex–Marine colonel named Hank Brocius. Nikki, an auburn-haired odalisque in the classic Italian style, kept her eyes on the rear door of the Crown Vic as she came up to her steps, shifting her briefcase to her left hand and, just as a precaution, freeing her right hand in case she needed the hammerless SIG she kept in a nylon holster at her waist.

The rear door cracked just as she put her right foot on the stairs, opened up wide, hinges creaking, revealing a very elderly white male, lanky and rail thin, with age spots on his hands and face. Deacon Cather, the Gray Eminence of Clandestine Services.

She knew him from his photograph on Hank Brocius's office wall. The pair had served for a time together in the same AO in Central America, Cather with the CIA and Brocius with the Marines. She herself had had a glancing contact with him during a terrorist incident at the Port of Chicago the previous fall. Cather, never aglow with health, looked like a cadaver: bony, sunken features, hooded eyes, sallow, jaundiced-looking skin stretched too tight over prominent cheekbones, teeth like yellow tombstones in bright red gums, withered, age-spotted hands, twisted and arthritic.

But his eyes were clear, alert, and seemed to radiate an icy light, as if all the fading forces of his aging body were being concentrated in his look. A subtle, cold-blooded reptile with a very long memory, he held most of the secrets of the Cold War in the stony labyrinths of his mind. And although he had recently been shunted out of Clandestine Services by the new administration, he still wore power as easily as he wore his navy blue pinstripe, his pristine white shirt, and the gold-and-ochre tie with its hieroglyphic pattern that was his signature accessory.

"Miss Turrin," he said in a raspy whisper, "may I impose for just a moment . . . ?"

Nikki felt a momentary chill and found herself at a loss for words. The intelligence community was full of stories about Cather and his sudden appearances, impromptu and unexpected encounters where people who got invited to share a moment with him in a car quite frequently never came back to their offices or to their homes and families.

"Of course, Mr. Cather," she said, resisting the temptation to throw her briefcase at him and bolt for her town house door.

He developed out of the car slowly like a wolf spider coming out of a drain, straightening up with an obvious effort, smiling his terrible rictus of a smile at her with as friendly an air as a man with his reputation could manage.

"Thank you, Miss Turrin. It's a lovely afternoon. Perhaps you would do an old man the honor of a stroll along the avenue?"

Towering over her like a rusted derrick, he extended his left arm in a ghastly parody of chivalry. Nikki took it, feeling the forearm bone like a dry twig under the material of his suit jacket. They walked along together, arms linked, as Cather's driver slowly eased the Crown Vic to a crawl, keeping pace with them, its motor growling and muttering like an unhappy guard dog.

Nikki saw another blue Crown Vic parked a block up, facing their way, the shadows of two men visible in the tinted glass. Cather's CIA security detail.

"You have a good eye," said Cather, following her glance. "I hope you can tolerate the melodrama. I think they're convinced I'm going to defect, God bless their paranoid little hearts. Let us choose to ignore them."

Nikki looked up at him, at the side of his face. He was staring ahead, his eyes on the sidewalk in front of him, but there was an air of sadness around him, sadness and something else.

He looked . . . worried. Troubled.

"We never actually met, did we?" he said after a few moments. "I know we spoke on the phone during the . . . events . . . in Chicago last fall. Of course, Mandy Pownall was familiar with you, I recall, and her description of you—she compared you to Isabella Rossellini— seems to have been quite accurate. Compliments from a woman as formidable as Mandy Pownall are rather rare. I'm very glad that Hank has you around. He's well, is he?"

"Yes, sir. He's on leave right now."

"Is he? I suppose even a Marine needs a break now and then. He's had a difficult time recently, I know."

"His wife left him, sir. Because of the scarring."

Brocius had been badly burned in an IED explosion in Iraq, trying to get the fifty gunner out of a flaming Humvee.

"I'm aware. Not at all *Semper Fi*, was she?"

Did he know that Nikki and Hank Brocius had been lovers up until quite recently? Did he know that the AD of RA's "leave" was being spent up in Garrison, New York, helping in ways Nikki did not care to contemplate a former lover named Briony Keating put her life back together after her son, a naval corpsman stationed in Crete, had been kidnapped and murdered by the KGB?

Of course he knows.

"No, sir. She sort of broke his heart, actually."

A few more steps. Cather, in a heavy silence, stalking like a heron, clearly enjoying the leafy avenue, the green lawns, the row of red brick, federal-style town houses, the children playing in the shady street, the Rockwellian perfection of it.

An illusion, but how beautiful it was.

"I'm imposing my wearisome presence upon you, Miss Turrin, for a reason, I'm afraid. A matter of some subtlety."

"Yes, sir. I'm here to do whatever I can for the service."

"I know that, Miss Turrin. You've been an extraordinary help in a number of areas not usually addressed by an NSA officer. Your unofficial mission to Trieste, and, in the winter, that business in Santorini and Istanbul. That is why I am here, as you may have already inferred. I've given this matter some careful consideration. Before I present my case, allow me to lay before you a few preliminary observations in order to harmonize our viewpoints. As an initial predicate, you're familiar, I'm sure, with the recent changes that have taken place at Clandestine Services?"

Nikki handled that one as if it were a Fabergé egg.

"Only what has been circulated, Mr. Cather. I know that a Commander Pearson has taken over as Deputy Director."

Cather seemed to find her tact grimly amusing.

"And that I've been . . . marginalized? Rendered an operational nullity?"

"People who know your record, Mr. Cather, would never make the mistake of regarding you as 'an operational nullity.'"

He looked down at her, his yellow face cracking into planes and deltas, his eyes hardening into chilly blue stones.

"But the *intent* is there, my child," he said, squeezing her arm between his ribs and his forearm. "The doors are already closing as I come down the halls . . . Old friends and colleagues grow noncommittal. Communications go unanswered. The fog of irrelevance rises up around my barren desk. Well, let us not indulge in self-pity. None of this is unexpected, Miss Turrin . . . I have observed our great nation for many decades, from a position of power and influence. Change has come upon us again, as it must. America, I suppose all democracies are vulnerable in this way, although it seems to be a singularly American weakness. Our nation tends to *lurch*, to stagger drunkenly, from left to right, as if afflicted with an inner-ear problem. De Tocqueville predicted this, suggesting that it was a flaw woven into the very fabric of democracies. He appears to have been correct. We lunge at extreme positions of thought and ideology as if they were lampposts to lean on. We abandon the ancient Persian House of Pahlavi and blithely embrace the far greater evil of the Ayatollahs. We ignored the growing threat of Islamic terror in the early eighties, dreaming our isolationist dreams. In the late nineties, as the threat grew and grew, we indulged ourselves in the political persecution of a President for silly sexual follies that would have paled beside the saturnalian debaucheries of those Kennedy boys, creating as we did so a bitter divide in the House and Senate that continues to cripple us to this day. We slept on, until, in our folly—and, as a senior member of the intelligence services, I bear great responsibility for this disaster—we awoke to the horrors of September eleventh . . ."

He seemed to falter here, going inward, as if seeing that day in all its obscenity and horror playing once again in his memory. They went on in silence, Cather's face creased in regret and remorse. After a while, he recovered, began again.

"And then, for reasons that seemed sufficient at the time, we plunged into the jagged canyons of Afghanistan. We quickly disposed of the Taliban. As a result, our hubris fully in play, we conjured up an elective war in which we crushed the armed forces of Iraq in three weeks and then spent the next six years snatching defeat from the jaws of victory. So here we are today. The cycle repeats. We pursue our enemies in their gathering multitudes with neither judgment nor sustained commitment, wavering—in a metronomic, biannual regularity that greatly comforts our enemies—with every shift in Congress and at the White House."

"We're still in Afghanistan, sir. The NSA is still doing its work. The armed services are fully engaged and profoundly dedicated to the safety of this country. Perhaps you're just . . . weary, sir. Perhaps you've seen too much."

"Perhaps . . . perhaps. I'm an old man, arriving at the end of my long hallway lined with delusions, failures, crimes. Here, at the end of my life, I have come to realize that the only reliable law is the Law of Unintended Consequences. This new administration, for the most part, is neither stupid nor blindly partisan, although some of the younger staffers at the White House seem to think it clever to act like junkyard dogs, as if political combat were the same as actual combat. But, then, when the young Turks in *any* new government aren't prating to their elders, they're preening in their shaving mirrors. They all share the same delusions of adequacy. The previous administration persuaded itself that it had the power to impose a kind of Junior League Republicanism on murderous tribal theocracies. The new one imagines that it can impose the asinine Marcusian sophistries of Noam Chomsky and the Harvard Faculty of Humanities on the people of America, as if Socialism had not already been tried many times before only to collapse in ruins, frequently very bloody ruins. And God only knows what sort of grotesque ideological calliope the next army of enthusiasts will ride in on, horns blatting and banners ablaze. My consolation is that I'll probably not be around when the wheels fall off once again."

The last was said in a fading whisper, and they went on for a time in silence. Nikki could feel a tremble in the old man's arm, and a sheen of perspiration had come out on his sallow cheeks. But she felt compelled to wait him out and not to insult an old Cold Warrior with her concerns about his health. They reached a corner, and Cather hesitated at the crosswalk, looking off toward a small parkette sheltering under an ancient stand of live oaks.

"Look," he said. "There's shade there. Do you mind if we . . . What did Stonewall Jackson say . . . ?"

"'Let us cross over the river and rest under the shade of the trees'?" said Nikki softly.

Cather turned and beamed down on her, his cold eyes softening. "You give me heart, young woman. Let us do that."

By the time they reached a little wooden bench, his cheeks were quite damp, and the tremor in his forearm had spread to the rest of his skeletal frame. Nikki got him seated, looking over her shoulder at the Crown Vic, which had pulled up by the curb. Then a tinny radio voice came out of Cather's pocket, a slow Southern drawl, but packed with affection and worry.

"You okay, boss? You need anything?"

Cather didn't bother pulling out the walkie-talkie, content to wave a bony hand at his driver in a dismissive gesture and then patting the bench beside him. Nikki sat down close to him, aware of the fever heat coming off Cather's body.

He was not at all *okay*.

Cather took a folded linen handkerchief out of his suit jacket, dabbed his cheeks, refolded it carefully, and put it away.

"Stop looking at me like that, girl. I'm not going to keel over and die on you."

Nikki smiled.

"Am I looking at you *like that*, sir?"

"Yes. I'm getting it a lot lately. As if I were being fitted for a shroud."

"In my case, would that be the Shroud of *Turrin*?"

His response was alarming. He put his head back, closed his eyes, the tendons on his neck stood out, his mouth opened slightly, his body seemed to undergo a series of short, sharp contractions, and he began to emit a number of dry croaks. After a moment she realized that he was laughing. He looked like a pterodactyl swallowing a frog. He did this for a while longer, she endured it. He subsided, and patted the back of her hand.

"Very good, child. I like a girl with sass. My wife was very much a girl with sass. Dear Eleanor. How I miss her . . . Well, the afternoon is fleeting, and I have not yet begun to make my position plain. You'll forgive me for enjoying the company of a beautiful young woman for a while."

Nikki, whose father and mother had moved back to Friuli a year ago, was surprised to find that she was actually enjoying the company of this legendary old spy.

"Not at all. I'm quite happy to sit with you, sir."

He gave her a look with some warning in it.

"Don't misjudge me, Nikki . . . May I call you Nikki?"

"Please."

"Don't mistake me for a kindly old uncle. I've sent many young people every bit as bright and beautiful as you off to die ugly and ultimately futile deaths in terrible places, often in the service of policies that turned out to be either venal or idiotic. I may be doing that again right now."

A pause while he gathered his thoughts. The second Crown Victoria had taken up a position on the far side of the street, and two squared-off crew cuts in baggy suits were walking under the trees a few yards away, the crackle of their radios a tinny insectile chittering in the pollen-thick haze of late afternoon.

"So I come, by my usual roundabout way, to the crux of the matter, Nikki. At this point, it is only fair to caution you that I am about to reveal some classified matters to you and that your continued attention from this point on will imply an acceptance of the consequences of privileged information."

Here he fixed her with his pale blue eyes.

"Shall I go on?"

Stop now, she was thinking to herself. *He is not a kindly old uncle. Say thanks so much, but I think not, and slowly back away.*

For reasons she was never able to explain to herself afterward, she did not say or do this. Cather waited another beat, took her silence for assent, and went on.

"I've spoken of how America seems to *lurch*. We are in the midst of such a period now. We, the intelligence community, have become the object of scorn on the part of the new powers. This has happened before—the Church commission, the Clinton years. I need not retail all this for you since you know the history as well as I do. But this *scorn*, this taste for . . . I believe the phrase in vogue is *truth commissions* . . . as if the average senator would not recoil from the truth as a vampire recoils from the crucifix. And now we have another of these pestilential 'Special Prosecutors.' My lawyer informs me that I can expect to be subpoenaed later this year for acts carried out by members of Clandestine Services under my watch. All of this is having a terrible effect on our rank-and-file officers. I refer here to my department, but I'm sure these threats of retroactive prosecution for acts carried out on the instructions of previous Presidents must be having the same effect at the NSA."

"Not to the same extent, since we're not an operational arm. I do think this is partly the reason why my boss has taken a leave. He found the idea of retroactive prosecutions . . ."

Here she searched for a phrase that would tactfully convey the force of Hank Brocius's fury at the idea, which was literally volcanic and involved the use of phrases such as 'gutless peacenik scumbags' and 'hippy-dippy, draft-dodging Bolsheviks.'"

Finally she settled on this: "He found them a bit . . . galling, sir."

"'Galling,'" said Cather, who knew the man better than she did. "Yes, Hank would find this *galling*, as do I. In the name of self-righteousness and moral preening, the new powers seem ready to destroy the morale—the operational *fire*—of the intelligence community, and they may succeed. I'm using up most of what little power that remains to me in various attempts to protect my most vulnerable men and women, which includes all seventeen people in my Cleaners Unit. Well, now we come to it."

Cather stopped again, giving Nikki a searching look as if to reaffirm the trust he was about to place in her and her acceptance of the consequences.

Nikki remained silent. He went on.

"Nikki, I believe you're familiar with one of my Cleaners, a young man, an ex–Special Forces captain, named Micah Dalton?"

"Yes, sir. He was active in Chicago. And it was in connection with an inquiry of his that I went to Santorini and Istanbul last winter."

"Yes, I'm aware of that. This is partly why I am here tugging on your sleeve this afternoon. And what is your professional opinion of this young man?"

"I think," she said, stiffening, "that he's one of the best field operators America has. He's intelligent, he has courage—"

Cather held up a hand.

"I concur, although he can also be . . . spectacular. His methods lack a sense of proportion. He's given to vendetta—"

"So's my whole family, sir. We're Italians."

"Yes, I understand. Personally, I think the unreasoned pursuit of vendetta can be detrimental to the overarching mission of the intelligence branch . . . But your point is well taken. You'd be sorry, then, to hear that he has been thrown to the Mossad?"

"'Thrown'?"

"Yes. Quite literally. Here, I have something for you."

He opened his palm. Resting in it was a small Sony Micro Vault. He offered it to her. She took it, looking into his eyes and seeing something there beside disease and disillusionment.

Cather was burning with anger.

"This device contains a highly classified document. In it, a woman named Mariah Vale . . . Perhaps you know of her?"

"Yes, sir," she said, keeping her expression blank. "Hank Brocius speaks of her often."

Cather showed his teeth.

"I would imagine he does. Miss Vale is now effectively in the position of Grand Inquisitor for the CIA, with the de facto support of the new administration. I know she acts in what she believes to be the best interests of the nation, but she is quite unsuited to sit in judgment upon operational issues. She is far too . . . fastidious. In her soul, she is convinced that if America really were a kinder, gentler place, the nation would have no enemies abroad and no dissent at home. In her view, we invite, through our aggression and arrogance, the hiss and enmity of the world. So she has set out to scour the CIA, to rid it—by any means available—of 'rogue agents' and 'opportunistic sadists,' thereby saving the Agency and the nation's honor. As an illustration of her tactics, the document contained in this flash drive is Miss Vale's summary of events that took place in Vienna over the last few hours. It will not surprise you that the events were . . . spectacular . . . and that our Mr. Dalton was right in the middle of it."

"Vienna? There was a terrorist bombing in Vienna, wasn't there? I saw something about it on Intelinet."

"It's being described as such, yes. The reality is rather less clear. A brown Saab blew up close to Leopoldsberg. The narrative in the device will lay out Miss Vale's official view for you. I will simply sketch in the outlines. As I understand it, Dalton was on an assignment in Bonn and that he had been contacted by—or had initiated a contact with—an Israeli named Issadore Galan, retired Mossad, now in the employ of the Carabinieri in Venice. We believe, but do not *know*, that a meeting was arranged, to take place in the city of Vienna. Dalton arrived in Vienna two days ago. Our inference is that the meeting with Galan was to be conducted on what we have all come to describe as Moscow Rules, a term of art for which we may thank Mr. Le Carré. You are familiar with this sort of defensive tradecraft, I'm sure?"

He didn't wait for an answer, going on to describe, in a general way, the events of the evening: Dalton's realization that he was being watched, his isolation of Veronika Miklas. Nikki listened with a tightening throat, sensing that something irrevocable had happened and that perhaps this time Dalton had simply gone too far. Cather rolled onward, his voice gathering power as the narrative developed, his frustration clear.

"At this point, the story becomes rather murky. According to the preliminary report prepared by Mariah Vale—you have a complete version in this device—there was some sort of confrontation at Miss Miklas's flat in the suburbs of Vienna. The body of a man named Yusef Akhmediar, a Hungarian Muslim who was known to the OSE—I gather he was some sort of freelance footpad who did a variety of unclean things for whatever agency wished to keep its shirt cuffs tidy . . . In any case, his body was discovered—I'm told it declared itself in the heat of the morning—dumped in a large bin at the back of Miss Miklas's apartment building. You will not be squeamish if I tell you that he had been killed by the rather innovative method of having an electric curling iron thrust through his left eye and deep into his brain. There is some forensic evidence that he did not die at once, and that his passing was facilitated to a degree by having the electric current turned on, which quite literally cooked his brains."

"Spectacular," she said, with a grimace.

Cather nodded.

"Quite in the Dalton style, yes. Setting that aside, the pair—for we are now to consider Miss Miklas to be a willing accomplice—were next seen the following morning at Leopoldsberg, a hilltop cathedral-fortress close by the curve of the Danube in the northern suburbs of Vienna. Here the picture becomes even cloudier. From what I have been able to gather, the main camera was out of commission that morning, perhaps intentionally disabled, but other cameras mounted on a nearby retaining wall show a series of images: Dalton's vehicle, a large black Benz, driven by Miss Miklas with Dalton in the passenger seat, cruises slowly past an old brown Saab and parks in a slot a few rows away."

"Are people allowed to park overnight? In that lot?"

"A good question. I do not know the answer to that."

"Is there any video of the Saab arriving? The time?"

"As I understand it, we have all the *available* video, with the exception of the central camera, which, as I mentioned, has somehow 'malfunctioned.' To continue, Dalton gets out, approaches the Saab, seems to examine it, and then goes around to the rear, where he opens the trunk. The camera does not allow us a view of what he saw there, but it occupied him for over two minutes. He pulls something from the trunk—a thin white tube—examines it, and now events move rather quickly. He slams the trunk, runs around to the driver's door, and then to the front, where he opens the hood. He makes a call on his cell phone. He then manages to get the engine running. He breaks a window, jumps behind the wheel, maneuvers the Saab through the crowds, drives it for some distance down the lane, and now he is out of sight of the security cameras. A police car sets off in pursuit of what they viewed as a car theft. They reach a curve in the road, and their vehicle is enveloped in a large explosion, originating from the Saab, which Dalton had parked in a ditch by the side of the road."

Nikki began to speak, but Cather lifted a palm.

"Allow me to tell the tale, my dear, and then I would greatly value your analysis. The blast radius is very large. The driver is killed, and two others are severely burned. The brown Saab is totally engulfed in flames. Subsequent inquiries establish that the Benz is also missing, having left the parking area shortly after Dalton drove the Saab through the gates. Firefighters arrive. The fires are quelled. The Saab is examined. A body is found in the trunk, which dental records establish as being the charred remains of Issadore Galan. Issadore Galan was the registered owner of the Saab. How would you address this scenario?"

Nikki gave it some thought.

"First of all, who was watching Dalton and why?"

"Excellent question. He was being observed by a unit of the OSE known as the Overwatch Service. They state that the request to have Dalton monitored came from Interpol and was authorized by the OSE as part of a reciprocal intelligence-gathering agreement the Austrians signed several years ago."

"Has anyone asked Interpol why they wanted Dalton monitored?"

"Our Bureau of Diplomatic Security agents formally requested an explanation from Interpol. The people at Interpol declined to provide any details, citing a confidential agreement with a 'third party.' The suggestion was made that the surveillance was merely a routine training drill and that Dalton was selected merely because he was a known foreign agent and would provide a challenging target. This entirely unsatisfactory reply seems to have ended the matter, as far as Miss Vale is concerned."

"You need to know who the third party was, don't you? Can't you insist, make a fuss? Go over her head?"

"Please recall that I am an operational nullity, my dear. I don't have that power. Do you have any other thoughts?"

"He made a cell-phone call?"

Cather nodded like an Easter Island statue, inclining slowly forward and then returning heavily to its base.

"The security camera shows it clearly."

"He has an Agency phone?"

"Yes," he said simply, offering no information.

"We would have picked up his calls. Incoming and outgoing. We always do that for CIA agents in the field. It's a security issue, a standing request from your agency. We'd have the voice packet. And his GPS. If we knew what he said on the phone, that would help us."

"It would if such a voice packet were available. Actually, to speed your plow a bit, none of Dalton's BlackBerry usage over the last twenty-four hours is now available to us. Miss Vale's report refers to the timing of Dalton's BlackBerry calls, but as to the *content* there seems to be no trace."

"But it's *automatic*. The Monitors *never* . . . We *must* have it."

"One would think. Sadly, no. Your Monitors have been commendably vigorous, but no trace of that call can be found."

"Then there'd be a log notation of the intercept—"

Cather shook his head, a thin smile playing on his lips.

Nikki stared at him for a while.

"It's been redacted?"

"A logical inference."

"By whom?"

"At this point, Miss Vale's name logically arises, but it is bootless to speculate. Naturally, the range of people in a position to effect such a thing is rather limited."

Nikki took in the implications, which were considerable.

"Okay. How about this? You say Dalton killed a man named Yusef Akhmediar at Veronika Miklas's flat?"

"A man named Yusef Akhmediar was found dead nearby. It does not automatically follow that Dalton killed him."

"And you also say that Dalton had thrown off the OSE surveillance unit?"

"Yes."

"Dalton's not an easy man to follow, is he?"

"*Res ipsa loquitur*. His record speaks for itself."

"How did Yusef Akhmediar know where Dalton was?"

Cather fell into what seemed to Nikki to be a satisfied and admiring silence, judging from the benevolence of his regard. He showed his teeth again and touched her hand with his fingertips.

"An excellent question . . . exactly the right question . . . As are all your other questions . . . And I will leave them with you."

"But you *can't* leave it there, sir. It looks as if Dalton found a bomb in the Saab and instead of simply running away he got inside the car and drove it clear of the crowds. He ought to get a medal—"

"Sadly, Miss Vale and the President, who has been strongly influenced by her arguments, have taken the view that Dalton killed Issadore Galan, wired his Saab to explode, and intended to drive it into Vienna and set the bomb off—"

"Why? For God's sake, what utter horse—"

"Miss Vale concedes that his motives do not speak as loudly as his actions. In her view, the arming mechanism failed him, and he narrowly escaped being blown up himself—"

"Sir, nothing in what you've told me supports that conclusion. And what about his cell-phone call records, his GPS data—all of it has *disappeared*? Disappeared because of whom? And why? And who disabled the main security camera? There should be video of the Saab arriving. The time? Who was driving it? It should on video *somewhere*. All of this is—"

"As I have said, all of this is very intriguing, and you are asking precisely the questions I would encourage you to ask. Do so repeatedly. Doggedly. Perhaps you may get your answers. Now, my dear, I really must let you go."

He raised his left hand, made a gesture toward the crew cuts, and stood up, weaving a little, his knees cracking audibly. Nikki started to get up, but he placed a leathery spotted claw on her shoulder, retrieving a long, thick navy blue envelope from an inside pocket of his suit jacket with his other hand. His escort stopped a few yards away and turned to look outward at what others would see as a playground park but to them was simply a perimeter. Cather handed the envelope to Nikki.

"I am about to place a great burden upon your lovely shoulders, Miss Turrin. There is a task I wish you to accomplish. You are of course at liberty to decline . . ."

"Am I, sir?"

Cather's smile did not alter very much, but now the effect was far less avuncular.

"Of course . . . Although I did refer to consequences if you continued to listen . . . Since you have done so, steps would have to be taken to ensure that what you have already heard here remains secure until the matter is resolved. You would go on a sort of holiday, someplace luxurious—palm trees, ocean breezes, complicated fruit drinks with paper umbrellas . . . However, I feel certain you will not refuse. I anticipate your steel, Miss Turrin. Your patriotism. This is why I am here. The envelope in your hand contains a valid passport in the name of Beatrice Gandolfo—"

"Beatrice Gandolfo? The wife of Amedeo Guillet? The Italian cavalry officer who fought the British in Abyssinia?"

Cather grinned, a broad, conspiratorial grimace, his face creasing and cracking into leathery deltas.

"I *knew* you would know these families. I thought Beatrice Gandolfo suited your style. She looked a little like you too."

"That is not surprising, sir; my family is connected to the Gandolfo family. We are all from the Savoy, from the Piedmont."

Cather smiled indulgently.

Did he know? Of course he did. That's why he chose the name. To charm her. Recruit her. To send her off on a mission, as he had sent off all the rest. And it is not possible that this "legend" could have been created in the last few hours; Cather had it ready with her in mind as part of a larger plan, perhaps weeks ago.

"Don't mistake me for a kindly old uncle."

And he had already told her enough to trap her, to leave her with no way out, unless she was willing to stunt her career forever, which a refusal would certainly do. And now he was closing the gates behind her. He had played her very well, played on her ego and her curiosity and her patriotism, even her sympathy for his apparent frailty. And now she was in his world.

Cather studied her face closely as if following her thoughts and then he sighed, perhaps with regret but probably not, and went on, adopting a more businesslike tone.

"Also in the envelope you will find a black American Express card in that name, along with other peripheral identifications—a Virginia driver's license, an ATM connected to an account in your name at First Dominion in Charlottesville, a Social Security card. The American Express card carries a credit line of something in the region of two hundred thousand dollars. Of course, references and phone numbers have been established and reliable people are standing by in case someone wishes to verify your credentials. From this moment forward, you are to speak of this assignment to no one other than personnel I myself may designate. Any breach of this order will have very unpleasant consequences, Miss Turrin, but I'm sure I don't need to make vulgar threats to a patriot such as yourself. You will also find my personal card in the envelope—my private cell phone is listed— you should not call unless your need is . . . pressing—"

A fully formed legend, designed specifically for her, with a support structure already in place, and created weeks ago.

Why?

"But, Mr. Cather, exactly what is it you want me to do?"

Cather's face hardened again.

"In Miss Vale's report, as you have correctly observed, she seems quite happy to conclude that Dalton murdered Issadore Galan for reasons of his own and has, in her lurid political terminology, 'gone dark.' Galan was ex-Mossad. The Mossad are an unforgiving organization. In her report, she mentions that the Mossad has offered their assistance in locating Micah Dalton. Given Dalton's aggressive nature, and his skills, any attempt on the part of the Mossad to detain and question him would effectively be a death sentence for everyone concerned. A violent confrontation between the Mossad and a CIA officer, however disavowed, would have a very destructive effect on our relations with our most critical ally in the Middle East at a time when Iran and her Russian proxies present a clear and present danger to both Israel and America. Dalton will need some help if he is to avoid a collision with their people. I have made arrangements with Clark Holden—"

"The Deputy Director? Of the NSA?"

"Yes. Clark's a good friend. He shares—privately—some of my concerns about the new administration. He has agreed to your being seconded to my . . . group . . . for a temporary research assignment."

"Your 'group'? Clandestine Services?"

"No. Not practical. I have been given some busywork to do, an operational history of covert operations conducted during the Cold War, to be used as a teaching document. Rather a convenient cover, actually. Silly of them to hand it to me. Your contribution would be to conduct field interviews with retired members of the intelligence community. Naturally, we both agreed that you should not be required to travel as a declared officer of the NSA or the CIA—too visible—so now you are a young political historian named Beatrice Gandolfo, working for a researcher named Kaelin Adair, connected with the University of Virginia in Charlottesville.

"But who am I supposed to interview?"

"You will begin with one man. I think you may know of him. He's a retired SAS soldier who worked with Dalton in Kosovo a few years ago and again last year in Indonesia and Singapore. You will of course recall his participation in the Chicago interdiction."

Nikki stared up at Cather, her eyes widening.

"You can't mean Ray Fyke? *THAT* Ray Fyke? Sir, with all due respect, Ray Fyke is . . . crazy. A killer. A drunk and a killer. There's an ICC warrant out for him. He's suspected in the beating death of a Singapore government official named Chong Kew Sak—"

"Yes, he is all those things. And, right now, he's exactly what Micah Dalton needs. And I have no one else. All of my Cleaners are being monitored. Our freelancers have deserted us. As I have remarked, my resources are limited."

Like hell they are, you scaly old basilisk.

This is a full-blown covert operation.

"Have you found the airline tickets yet, my dear?"

Nikki upturned the envelope and slid out a first-class ticket on United Airlines. She looked at the departure time.

"Tomorrow? *Tomorrow?* What about my job? My plants? My cats?"

"All necessary arrangements have been made."

"Look, sir, why don't you just go yourself? Find this Fyke person and . . . recruit him . . . yourself?"

"Mr. Fyke is a very cautious man. Our relations in the past have not been cordial. And I have little freedom of movement. It is an unlikely scenario. I would not be . . . allowed . . . to go. Such a meeting would inevitably draw the attention of Miss Vale and her acolytes. I think, knowing what I know of the man, that you will have far more success *recruiting* him than I."

She looked at the destination and then back at Cather.

"With due respect, sir, where the *hell* is Panama City?"

Cather had already turned away, signaling for his car. He came back, looked down at her, attempting to appear comforting and failing spectacularly. He looked like a vulture with a migraine.

"I'm not entirely sure," he said, his goal achieved, his little trap sprung, his reptile mind already moving on to new concerns. But then he paused and came back to her, putting a fatherly smile in place the way a doctor puts on a surgical mask.

"Oh yes, there was one last thing . . . I almost forgot. I have been advised to warn you about the alligator. Apparently, there's an alligator somewhere in the picture. So you *will* keep an eye out, won't you, my child? For the alligator?"

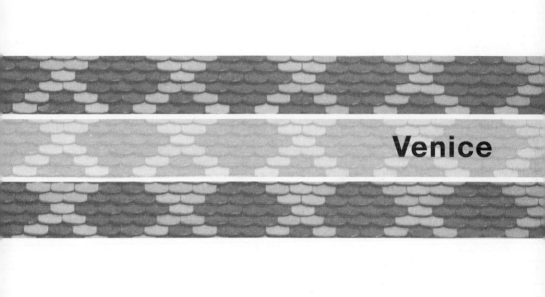

Venice

Dalton stopped the Benz in a pullout at the eastern end of the long
narrow bridge that connected the islands of Venice with the mainland
port of Mestre, killed the headlights. Veronika, in the shock-induced
fatigue state that always follows a shattering event, was deep in sleep.

He took his SIG out of the lockdown under the dash, did a press
check, shoved it into a shoulder holster, pulled a soft black wind-
breaker out of the backseat, along with a pair of black leather gloves,
locked the doors, and walked forward into the looming fog-shrouded
shadows of the Piazzale Roma.

The Piazzale Roma was the entry point for train and vehicle traffic
into Venice, but no cars or trucks got any farther than the Auto-Park
building on the south side of the plaza. After that, it was all water
taxis, vaporettos, tugs, barges, and delivery boats.

Dalton moved slowly through the terminal area, trying to see
through the floating sea mists. The entire city was wrapped in the
blanket of nighttime fog that often drifted in from the Adriatic at
this time of the year. He walked the whole area soundlessly, gliding
through the gray clouds, every sense alive, trying to pick up a tremor
of surveillance.

But there was nothing.

He stood for a while in the shadow of a doorway, opening his mind and stilling his ego, listening to the sounds of the night with his whole being.

Nothing. Not even a tremor.

He reached the boathouse beside the autobus station, unlocked the latch, pulled up the grating. Naumann's launch, a twenty-four-foot Riva, was riding gently on the rising tide. It was an elegant, handmade mahogany cruiser, lean as a lance, with a sharp destroyer bow. In the dim glow from the lights that lined the Rio Nuovo quay, she rocked gently on her spring lines, covered with a fitted shroud.

There was a thin coating of salt rime and stone dust on the shroud. He was reasonably confident that no one had touched the boat since he had tied it up here two weeks ago. He had hidden the key to the launch behind a loose stone in the supporting wall of the boathouse. It was still there.

He intended to use the launch to go north to the curve of the Grand Canal and follow it past the Canale di Cannaregio and on around until he reached the Campo San Marcuola. There was a small canal there, on the left bank, the Rio San Marcuola, that threaded north through the eastern edge of the Ghetto until it connected with a larger canal called the Rio della Misericordia.

Galan's villa was right on the embankment called the Fondamenta degli Ormesini, near Calle Turlona. Although the Ghetto was little more than a kilometer from the boathouse, taking the canals was better than trying to walk through the streets of the darkened city. The Ghetto was the most tangled and run-down quarter in Venice. Even residents sometimes got lost in its medieval alleys, dank passages, cloisters with iron gates and overhanging stone walls.

The canals were much simpler, much more direct. He pocketed the launch's keys and walked back through the parking lot to the Benz. Veronika was still asleep.

He slipped in beside her and sat quietly for a while in the dark thinking about tactics. Dalton had timed their arrival for the middle of the night. Even during high season, which was still several weeks away, Venice closed down shortly after midnight, after the ringing of the great bell in the Campanile. By two in the morning, the city would be sound asleep, wrapped in her ancient dreams. As she was tonight.

Dalton could hear a vaporetto out in the Tronchetto, the sound of her engines muffled by the dense fog, chugging and popping across the channel, making for the boathouses on the far side of the Giudecca.

The rest was hushed, and the clinging moisture of the fog coating the windshield, and from out of the fogbank the clanging of a marker buoy somewhere out in the lagoon.

He started the Benz, put it in gear—keeping the lights off—and rolled it slowly down the ramp toward the entrance to the Auto-Park. He eased the car into a slot, killed the engine, and looked across at Veronika, curled up under a soft white cotton blanket she had bought in Udine a few hours earlier.

The glow from the parking lamps cast a cold light on her cheekbones and made dark pools of her eyes. Her lips were slightly parted, her breathing deep and regular. She looked very young and very vulnerable, a fragile elfin thing, but she had killed a man last night.

People around me die.

Veronika, sensing that they had stopped moving, the engine suddenly stilled, woke up with a reflexive start, her face bone white, her eyes wild. Dalton touched her cheek, calmed her, comforted and reassured her, and, when she was more awake, handed her a thermos of coffee.

"Where are we?" she said, blinking into the dark.

"Venice. The Piazzale Roma. Near the Dorsoduro."

She looked around her, trying to shake off her confusion, the fog of deep sleep.

"What building are we in?"

"The Auto-Park. We have to leave the Benz here."

She sat up straighter, sipped at the coffee, her hair down over her face, her hands gripping the thermos tightly as the state of things came pressing back in.

"I had . . . such dreams."

"Yusef?"

She nodded, said nothing for a while. He thought about a cigarette but did not want to show a flame. She sipped at her coffee again and then straightened her back, set her shoulders.

"Okay. Enough of that. Let's get this over with. Do you still intend to try for Galan's flat?"

"We don't have much of a choice, Veronika."

"But is it *safe* to go there?"

"Probably not. We'll have to take the chance anyway. I checked the boathouse. Porter's launch is still there. There's heavy fog. That will muffle the sound of the engine. I know the canal system pretty well. As I said, if anyone is waiting for us, they'll be over in the San Marco District, around the hotel. How well do you know Venice?"

"I was here five years ago, part of a cruise we took on the Minoan Lines. Three days and nights in Venice. So, not very well."

Dalton didn't ask who had been with her. He didn't want to know. Her past, and her future, did not belong to him, aside from his commitment to seeing that she lived to have one. She drank some more coffee, set the thermos down. Laying her head back, she closed her eyes again.

"The news said a police officer was killed back there in Vienna and two others burned. They're saying it was a terrorist incident, Micah. How did we ever get across the Alps?"

"Great question. Right now, my money is on bureaucratic incompetence. We moved fast, and it's been my experience that cross-jurisdictional screwups happen all the time."

"Do you believe that? In this case?"

"Not entirely. But it's possible. It's harder to fix a border crossing than you think it is. No matter how well placed you are. Border guards are a cantankerous lot. I'm accepting it as a tactical reality."

"I hope you're right."

"We're about to find out. Before we do, check your laptop one more time. Maybe Jürgen got back to you."

"Can we get a signal here?"

"Yes. The Sole Spa over there has an unsecured connection."

Veronika took out her laptop, turned it on. The glow lit up the interior of the Benz with a bluish light. In a moment, the wireless icon blipped on, and she was at her incoming-mail site and a German carrier called *Quecksilber*.

She had about forty messages altogether, thirty-eight of which were from this same sender and contained the same message:

Zum Hauptquartier sofort unter Androhung der formalen Anklage

Dalton, looking over her shoulder, couldn't make it out.

"That looks like trouble."

"It is. It's an order from my boss, I am to report in to headquarters immediately, under penalty of formal charges."

She shrugged it off, hit DELETE, wiping out the entire list except for the other two messages.

> zuckerpupschen@quecksilber.au
>
> issadore.galan@discovolante.ita

Both messages had been sent within the last hour, long after midnight. Both had attachments. Veronika looked at the second one and then over at Dalton.

"The first one is from Jürgen. But this other one? This cannot be from your friend. And how could he have my private e-mail address?"

"It's not from him," said Dalton, his face hardening. "Save it and open the other one."

She did.

> Veronika meine Liebe, die ich für Sie das Video hier ist es merkwürdig, wo bist du? Sind Sie sicher? Bitte rufen Sie mich an meine grüne Telefon. jemand hier, ich muss gehen

"It's from him. He says he has the video, says it's a bit odd. He asks if I am safe and asks me to call him on his green line. Then he says somebody is there and he has to go. What does that mean, somebody is here? It was one in the morning when he sent this. Is he in trouble? Have I gotten him into trouble, Micah?"

Her eyes glittered in the laptop light, filling with moisture. She began to cry and then crushed it down, drawing in a long, shuddering breath.

"It had to be done, Veronika. We needed that video."

"I . . . I know."

"If it's the police, he won't resist. He'll be okay."

"And if it wasn't the police?"

"It was the police, Veronika. The bad guys don't knock or ring the doorbell. What's his 'green line'?"

"Jürgen likes to play spy. He has a cell phone he bought on the street. It is in someone else's name. Not traceable to him. He uses it to make horse-race bets. Also he orders—how do you say—*Kokain?*"

"Cocaine?"

"Yes. He uses it to stay awake on the job."

"Do you?"

She gave him a look that did not quite sear his cheek and did not quite convince him she wasn't lying.

"No. That is why we broke up. This cocaine drug."

"I have some SIM cards. If you want to call his green line, see if he's okay, we can switch out the SIM on your cell phone."

She considered him for a time, something elusive flickering in her eyes, a veiled look, and then she cleared.

"Maybe. Let's see the video."

She opened the attachment, an MPEG with a time stamp. The code stated that it was four minutes long. She copied it onto a separate flash drive and then hit PLAY.

The video quality was poor, a cheap record from a cheap analog source. The POV was limited, a view of the Leopoldsberg parking lot from the top of a post in the middle of the yard. The camera turned slowly on a base, sweeping erratically around the lot. The clock was running, starting at 0630.23. The lot was empty and the light very dim. At 0631.12 the camera caught a glow coming up the drive, then swiveled away, returning to that spot at 0632.15 just in time to catch a fleeting glimpse of the brown Saab driving across the deserted yard toward the far corner, where Dalton had found it later. The camera, turning, then showed them a view of the sky growing slightly less dark and then the circles of lamplight in the parking-lot gravel. It came around again at 0633.05, and there was a large hulk standing by the side of the Saab, slope-shouldered, his long ropy arms hanging loose at his sides, his face staring up at the camera as it swept by.

The face was a blur, but Dalton could make out the slash of a mouth, see the shine of scar tissue on the ruined face.

"Is that him?" asked Veronika. "The man you fought?"

"Yes. It is," said Dalton, watching the video. His face felt hot and his chest hurt. He thought that what he was feeling was fear. If this was true, it had to be driven down.

The question was how.

The camera moved away, showing them another maddening round of gravel, sky, gravel, stone wall, gravel, sky. And then, at 0641.06, it came back to the Saab and the apelike figure standing next to it.

The figure was naked, his pants in a heap around his ankles. He was holding his genitals out with one hand, his hips grinding, his other hand rhythmically busy, a simian leer on his slash of a mouth. Before the camera could move off, the man raised his left hand, pointed something dark at the camera. There was no sound, but they could see a narrow red laser beam coming from the thing in the man's hand. The video image disappeared in a burst of white lines. The MPEG ran for another few seconds and then ended. Veronika closed the screen and sat back into the seat.

"My God, Micah. He's a monster."

"Yes. He is. Have you got this on the flash drive as well?"

"I copied it all. To the hard drive also."

"Don't lose it. We'll need it before this is over. Open the other one. If you're up to it?"

She hesitated, and then clicked on the one from Issadore Galan's e-mail account. It opened with an attachment, a large file labeled JPEG. The message read:

> How this for slick slick got your bitches email off your own phone show the whore the picture maybe she see what kind of sick fuck she running with maybe she ask you about Podujevo see you soon slick
>
> your old friend.

"How did he get my e-mail?" asked Veronika, deeply shocked at how *close* this creature was getting.

"He says how he did it. The same way he got my GSP coordinates. Somebody has cracked my BlackBerry encryption. I found your e-mail on the InteliLink database. He has my records. It was right there."

"Somebody is . . . helping . . . him?"

"Somebody is *running* him, Veronika."

Veronika moved the cursor over the attachment, got the DOWN-LOAD box, and stopped.

"It's a picture, Micah. Do we really want to see a picture from this man?"

"Open it," said Dalton, his voice hoarse.

She clicked DOWNLOAD, and a moment later they were looking at a clear, crisp color photo of what looked like a burned-out building, stone, with heavy wooden beams that had fallen inward, bringing the walls down with them.

On the ground in front of the building lay a long row of dead bodies, all horribly charred, limbs twisted up into the fetal position as the fire had scorched their tendons. They lay on their backs, faces up to the cold clear sky, their mouths open, their blackened faces bloated and distorted.

But you could still tell that they were all women and children of varying ages: infants, toddlers, young girls, old women. They were displayed as if in a propaganda shot.

Two large men in black camos, their hair shaved into Mohawks and their faces streaked with camo paint, stood on either end of the row of dead people, one with an AK slung over his back and holding up a hand-painted sign, the other holding up what looked like a fragment of some sort of missile or rocket. On the fragment a row of letters could just be made out:

GBU 10 2089 I USAR

On the hand-painted sign, a scrawled phrase:

Подујеву

Амерички Убице ли овај

Dalton knew, in a detached, reptilian way, that his skin was getting hot. He could feel the burn on his forehead and along his chest. Interesting. Understandable, given the stimulus. So why was his belly full of ice? Never mind. It didn't matter, really. He knew what was going on. But thinking about his autonomic responses was a way to avoid thinking about that place in the picture for a few seconds.

And that was about all he got.

Veronika stared at the picture for a time. She was in an intelligence service, so pictures of atrocities did not shake her the way they would have shaken an ordinary civilian. Dalton could feel her thoughts, as she stared at the picture and the words. She knew this was something very serious, that it involved Dalton, and that if she asked him what it was he might tell her and then everything would change. Perhaps she wouldn't ask him.

"What . . . what do those words mean, Micah?"

"The first word is a place-name. In Serbian."

"Do you know what place?"

"Yes. It's called Podujevo."

"And where is Podujevo?"

"It's a village in northern Kosovo."

"It looks like a war is going on in that picture. Was it during the war there?"

"Yes. In 1999."

"Were you there, in 1999?"

"Officially, no."

There was a long pause.

"And what do the other words mean?"

"They mean 'American murderers did this.'"

More silence—this time a tight, pounding silence. Dalton listened to his own pulse thumping in his ears and to Veronika's shallow breathing.

She was no longer looking at the picture, not so much as looking away from it as looking at Dalton, the only other place to look. After a time she said in a soft voice, "You do not wish to talk about Podujevo, Micah?"

Dalton swallowed with difficulty, wishing for water.

"Yes, Veronika. I do not wish to talk about Podujevo."

More silence.

"Fine. Then we will not talk about Podujevo. Right now."

"Thank you."

"But what are we going to do about this Smoke person?"

"Find him. Find who's running him. Kill them both."

She looked at him as if from a distance.

"I thought you were not an assassin? If we find them, we should turn them over to the proper authorities."

He met her look with as blank an expression as he could manage, thinking, *You just killed a man by sticking a curling iron in his brain and now you want to go through proper channels?*

"Yes?" he said. "The proper authorities. Such as . . . ?"

She looked confused and then rallied.

"The UN has agencies. Interpol. The Criminal Court."

Dalton let it go. She was young. She was Austrian. She'd been to a modern university. You had to make allowances.

"At any rate, he's giving us a lot of help here."

"This . . . *Höhlentroll*. This . . . cave thing. How?"

"He's talking too much. He can't help himself. Every time he prods us, he gives something away. The things he knows—your e-mail, how to get to Galan, breaking my BlackBerry encryption . . . this thing about Podujevo—only a few people know all of those things. We follow the information, find the sources, and sooner or later we find somebody who knows who Smoke really is. Maybe even where. Then we find Smoke. And we kill him. And his people. It all ends. You're safe."

They sat together in silence for a while longer, and then Veronika put the laptop away. Dalton leaned forward, popped the latch on the gun locker under the dashboard, pulled out her pistol, checked that it was loaded, and handed it to her along with her spare magazine.

"You still want to come along on this?"

"Yes. We've already talked about it too much."

"Have you ever been in a real gunfight?"

"No. But every year we do two weeks of—what you Americans call CQB—close quarter?"

"Close quarter combat? You're in a *surveillance* unit, for Pete's sake!"

Mistake.

Dalton could almost hear her hackles rising.

"Sometimes, Micah, people object to being watched. Sometimes, like you, Micah, they are not so nice people. That's why they gave us the weapons. Loaded. So we can actually fire them. If you are going to fire a weapon in Vienna, they would like for you not to kill too many tourists. So we train. Okay?"

Dalton figured he wouldn't have to shave the Veronika side of his face for about a week. He nodded, took a breath.

"Okay. My apologies. You've got eight in the magazine," he said in a careful, businesslike tone, "and one in the chamber. They're Black Talon rounds, nine mil, just like I use in the SIG, so if you need some more I have them. The SIG has fifteen rounds in each mag. Black Talons will stay inside whatever they hit, and they hit *hard*. First rule of combat: Don't shoot your partner."

He managed a tight smile here as his equilibrium came slowly back. Podujevo had nothing to do with this woman, and they had a hard night ahead of them.

"You shoot me in the back, Veronika, I'm going to take it personally."

She gave him a brave, if slightly off-center, smile.

"I won't shoot you in the back. Unless you get in my way."

"I'll try not to do that. Keep cool. Remember. Keep cool. Don't spray the area. I know, I know," he said, seeing her expression, "but it happens, even to trained people. They get their blood up. They'll empty a mag in seven seconds. You know how to do a fast magazine exchange in a firefight?"

She nodded.

"We've practiced it. Empty, slide locks back, drop magazine out, load the second magazine, slide forward, you're ready to go."

"Good. You have a second mag, also with eight rounds. That's seventeen rounds in total. *Count your rounds.* Understand? Count your rounds. If things go bad and I'm not close, save one round. I mean that. If sixteen rounds out haven't settled the matter, nothing will. So you save one round. You follow me, Veronika? Hear me. Save one round."

She looked at him with a puzzled expression, and then her face set into harder lines.

"I understand. Save one round."

"One last thing. I get killed, you don't hang around. If we actually do get into a firefight, the *polizia* will come running. You reach them, ask for a Carabinieri major in town, his name is Allessio Brancati. He has an apartment in the Arsenale—that's along the Riva degli Schiavoni—a few bridges east of the Piazza San Marco. Get the *polizia* to take you to Brancati, tell him everything you know. He'll take care of you."

"Allessio Brancati. In the Arsenale. Okay."

"Okay. One last thing."

She sighed.

"I thought the *last* thing was the one last thing?"

Dalton grinned at her, a wolfish expression, his eyes pale in the lamplight, his lips thinned over white teeth.

"If we're dealing with Smoke and his people, I take one, a bad one, before you light out—"

"Don't leave you wounded? Put one in your head?"

"Yeah. Two, if you can spare them."

"Christ, Micah."

"I'd do it for you."

She smiled back at him, her breathing unsteady, leaned forward suddenly, and kissed him, open-mouthed, searching, hungry, pulling him into her, and then she broke away.

"Yes. You would. But you're a much nicer person than I am. So my advice to you . . . ?"

"Don't get shot?"

"Don't get shot."

THE sweeping northern arc of the Grand Canal, wide and smooth and empty as it curved around the southern edge of Cannaregio, was relatively easy to navigate, even in the fog that had settled in over the city, reducing visibility to less than twenty feet. At this hour the Grand Canal was deserted, the villas and shops along its banks closed down and lightless. Now and then, as they slipped quietly by a villa or a shop, a sliver of amber light showed through closed shutters or a few tinny notes of music would come drifting out of the mist. There were street-lamps and doorway torches all along the canal, but they were only luminous globes floating in the mist and shed no light on the canal, serving only to mark the outer limits of a cold gray water world.

The only warmth in that shapeless world was the blood-red glow of the Riva's instrument panels as it lit up the underside of Dalton's face, giving him a slightly satanic air.

Veronika, wrapped in a blanket, sat huddled in the stern, watching the shadowland of Venice pass by as if in a dream.

For the first time in many weeks, a single word was rising in the back of her troubled mind: *Kokain*. She pushed it down again with a shiver of apprehension, coming back reluctantly to the here and now. The launch was moving through the muddy water like a sea snake, its engines hardly a murmur, a bass-toned vibrato under the floorboards. Water lapped and rippled along her polished sides and curled whitely in her wake. Now and then a larger shape would loom up out of the fog—a tethered barge draped in canvas, a covered launch tugging at its moorings—but, in the main, there was only the slow unveiling of the middle distance beyond Dalton's tall shape, outlined in a red aura, and the field of gray water all around her, parting with a reptilian hiss as the launch's sharp-edged bow cut through it.

They had been running quietly for a half hour by Dalton's watch when he sensed rather than saw a flat space opening up on the northern bank, marked by two large boathouses jutting out into the water and an open park lit by a row of torches: the Campo San Marcuola. He slowed the launch and brought it in closer to the shore, barely making headway, looking for the blacker shadow that would be the opening of the Rio San Marcuola, the narrow canal running north for three hundred yards through the crowded, overhanging villas and stone-walled cloisters of Cannaregio until reaching a much larger canal, the Fondamenta degli Ormesini.

A left turn there, and Galan's villa was another three hundred yards farther along on their starboard side. Dalton eased the launch into the narrow opening, dead slow now, the gray shapes of boats and barges pressing in on both sides, the roofs looming above them in the fog, the eaves almost touching across the canal.

They drifted past an open door. Yellow light poured from it, tinting the fog around it golden. Soft music also came from the open door. Looking in, they saw a flight of polished wooden stairs leading up into the dark, and they heard cheerful talk flowing back down. They passed on in grim silence, a ghostly pair, a shadow disappearing into the fog. In a few minutes the golden glow was lost in a bend of the canal. A sharp pain in Dalton's right hand, a muscle cramp, made him realize that he was gripping the wheel of the Riva so tightly that he had cut off the flow of blood.

He straightened, took a breath, and turned to look at Veronika. Her face was an oval in the mist, her body covered in a blanket.

"Are you okay?" he said in a low whisper.

"I am," she said, "but I'm freezing. And Venice stinks."

Dalton smiled, took another breath. She was right.

Here in the smaller canals, the massive ebb and flow of the Adriatic was considerably restrained. As a result, Cannaregio tended to wallow in her own juices until the winds came up and the tides, such as they were, turned. The dank air was full of the scent of dead fish, wet stone, and raw sewage—not quite the romantic vision of Venice you got in the movies, he thought.

He saw a cluster of lights running across his course about twenty feet ahead. It was the opening to the Ormesini Canal.

He slowed to a crawl, made the turn left, swinging a little wide to clear a boat ramp. He quickly reached down and killed the engine, leaving the boat to drift slowly forward into the fogbank, water rippling softly along her bow and gurgling under the wooden keel. Veronika came forward and stood beside him, peering into the fog.

"What's wrong?" she whispered, leaning close.

Dalton took his SIG out.

"That bridge. Up ahead. I thought I saw . . ."

Veronika stared into the fog, straining to make out details.

"There's . . . There is *something*," she said in a whisper now so faint it was little more than a breath. "I can't quite make it out."

The launch moved forward on its own momentum, the darkened houses passing slowly by. A low stone bridge materialized out of the fog, arching over the canal. A few feet closer, and they could see a form, man-shaped, leaning on the railing of the bridge.

Dalton zeroed his pistol sights—all three green tritium dots in a row—on the center of the shape, his finger lightly resting on the trigger of the SIG. The shape stirred as their launch came out of the mist. It was a man. He leaned forward, calling down to them in a hoarse whisper: *"Micah, non fuoco. Sono Allessio."*

"Brancati?"

"Yes. Stop under the bridge."

Dalton lowered his weapon.

Veronika stepped back from the wheel. Dalton could see that she had her pistol out, holding it down at her side.

"No. It's the Carabinieri major I told you about. Brancati."

Veronika slid the weapon back into her belt holster, but her face was closed and wary. Dalton let the boat's momentum carry it slowly under the bridge, holding on to the stonework to keep the drift under control. The man dropped down from the bridge, landing in a crouch on the bow. Dalton reached out, the man took his hand and came awkwardly over the windshield and down into the cockpit, breathing heavily from the effort.

He took Dalton's shoulders in an *abbraccio*, pulled him in and smacked him on the back a couple of times and then pulled away, holding him at arm's length, grinning fiercely. He was a deeply tanned man with a strong, lined face, Dalton's height, solidly built, running a little to fat around the middle, with hooded Sicilian eyes and a large mustache shaped like a scimitar. He was in gray slacks, boat shoes, a light-colored shirt under a brown leather jacket that was open enough for Veronika to see the Beretta in a leather holster under his left arm. As he looked into Dalton's face, his grin—a white flash in the half-light—disappeared, and his expression changed.

"Galan? È vero?"

Dalton's face was a rock wall, his voice harsh and choked.

"È morto, Allessio. Un orrore. Mi duole."

Brancati held him a moment longer, his eyes shining. Dalton could feel the tremor in Brancati's powerful fingers.

He released Dalton with a sigh, stepped away, turning to face Veronika.

"Allora," he said in a soft baritone rumble, disarmingly gallant for a man who had literally dropped out of the fog. *"Questa è la signorina Veronika Miklas? Di cui sentiamo così tanto? Mi presento, con permiso? Sono Allessio Brancati, capo dei Carabinieri della Toscana."*

He bowed slightly as he spoke and offered his hand, his eyes careful, his expression polite but distant.

Veronika took it and smiled back.

"I am sorry—*mi dispiace*, Major Brancati—I have no Italian." Brancati's grin broke through his caution. Veronika was a stunner, and Brancati, although well married and the father of grown girls, was an aficionado of stunners.

"And I have no German, *mi dispiace*. But I have some English. You are okay, miss? This brute has not taken advantage of you? *No lei molestate?"*

Veronika smiled again, this time a little more easily.

"No. No molesting. He has been . . . a perfect gentleman."

Brancati flashed another broad grin and then turned back to Dalton, still speaking in a low, conspiratorial whisper.

"You are going to Galan's flat?"

"Yes."

Brancati nodded.

"Moor up for a moment, my friend. We must talk."

Using a boat hook, Dalton edged the Riva toward the quay, catching hold of a stone pillar and looping a spring line around it. Brancati took a seat across from Dalton, and Veronika sat down beside Dalton, leaning into him for warmth and comfort, thinking as she did so about another kind of comfort entirely: *Kokain.*

"Why are you going to Galan's villa?"

"How did you know I would?"

Brancati's smile flashed again, white against his dark skin.

"By now, after all this time, maybe I learn a few things about you, my friend. It would make sense if you wanted to know what had happened to Issadore to go to his house and see what there was to see. And if you were to come to Venice, you would come in the middle of the night while she is asleep. And you would not come by foot since you have this lovely Riva. So I left my people to watch your hotel and came up here to sit on the bridge and wait for you to arrive. And while I am here, I begin to see we have a problem. I am not alone in my thinking. Men are waiting for you, Micah. My men have identified four people in the area of the Savoia, all in a position to see the entrance, all hidden away. Up ahead, around Galan's villa, at least three. One is in an open boat by the door to Galan's villa. The other is across the canal in the little marina there. I think he is the perimeter watch, because he has a small assault weapon, it looks like a Heckler, perhaps the MP-55 with the silencer because the barrel is short and thick. The third I believe is inside the doorway to the villa or waiting up the stairwell. There may be more, but I do not think so. They have not seen me."

Dalton took it in, not really surprised by it.

"Thank you, Allessio. I guess I was expecting something like that. What do you want to do about . . . these people?"

"*Aspetta, aspetta.* Before we go further, if anything happens to you, I must know . . . about Galan."

Dalton glanced at Veronika and then came back at Brancati. In a few, economical words, he laid it out, from the surveillance in Vienna to the fight at Veronika's flat.

When he got to Galan's body, he tried to edit the details, but Brancati waved that off.

"Tell me. What was done. I wish to know."

Dalton told him.

Brancati took it with a stone-cold silence. And when Dalton was finished, he sat back, his face grim and set.

"This is not Italian. Not even Sicilian. Nor the *Camorra* of Napoli. They do not do the *sodomia* and then write letters about it. And it is not Arab. Their Sharia forbids such self-defilement. Intimate contact such as this with the body of an infidel Jew, a male, would require weeks of purification and would mark a Muslim fighter for the rest of his life with his own men. You and I both know who does this *infamia*, don't we?"

"Mexican *narcotraficantes*. The Colombians. The KLA used to do it. So did the Albanians. The Serbs."

"Yes. The Serbs again. *They* would do this. It is their way. And they have much to resent from Galan. And from us. And this scratching. On his own body. The number of his flat? You are certain?"

"Yes. I'm sure."

Brancati sighed heavily.

"They are saying it was you, Micah. You know this?"

Dalton's expression did not change, but Brancati could see he was deeply cut by the words.

"Who is saying this?"

He patted his pocket.

"I have a letter, on CIA letterhead, from a Mariah Vale. They disavow any connection with you. They offer no protection to you. The letter is not specific, but reading *tra le righe*, between the lines, it is clear that they believe you killed Galan, that you planted the car bomb, and that you were nearly killed by it—"

"*Planted* the bomb?" said Veronika, stung. "He saved lives! He got into the car and drove it out of the parking lot! We were both almost killed!"

Brancati lifted a palm, shaking his head.

"*Calma te, signorina. Sappiamo, sappiamo.* We know this. But there is more. The Austrians have issued an arrest warrant. You, Micah, are charged with terrorist acts, the murder of two policemen and a civilian named Yusef Akhmediar, and the kidnapping of an Austrian official,

Miss Miklas here. In the note, sent to the governments of Austria, of Italy, and of Israel——"

"Israel?" said Dalton. "Why Israel?"

"Galan was a Mossad agent. The Mossad have expressed an interest—these are *her* words, this Miss Vale—the Mossad has 'expressed an interest in assisting in the inquiry.' On a separate page—my agency had received a copy of an attachment which was also sent to Tel Aviv—is identified your *macchina*, the Mercedes, the plate numbers, and your last known position. As well as pictures and descriptions of both you and *la signorina*."

Brancati reached out and gripped Dalton by the knee.

"This is *un mandato di morte*, Micah. You have been offered up to the Mossad. By your own country."

Brancati sat back, finished his cigar, and tossed it in the water. He stood up, looking down at Dalton and Veronika.

"Allora," he said. "Now we begin to fight back, yes?"

"We?" said Dalton. "You're supposed to arrest me."

"Buono. Che cosa. If it pleases you, you may consider yourself arrested. Now, *per piacere, venite con me.*"

"Vengo con tu?" asked Dalton, off balance. *"Dove?"*

Brancati shrugged, lifted his hands in a very Italian gesture.

"I do not approve of *assassini* in my Venice. I have already told my men to move in and confront the people down at your hotel. They will be in custody very soon. You and I, we will go and take these men who are waiting by Galan's villa and we will put them to the question."

"No. You can't be involved in this, Allessio."

His face clouded and his body stiffened.

"I am *already* involved. This is *my* city. Issadore Galan was not only my friend, he was my security adviser and an official of the Carabinieri. I decide who will do what, my dear friend, stay or go, stand or run. Not you. And I will not allow foreign thugs to wander freely around my city. No. They will be taken in, and I believe the two of us are sufficient for the work."

Dalton, knowing the man, did not try to argue with him, but Veronika spoke up. "Oh no. *I'm* not staying behind."

"No," said Brancati. "Not left behind. We need you as a reserve. If anyone breaks this way, you'll have to stop them. Micah and I will go in. It's not an insult, *signorina*. Micah and I know the area. We have done this before. We need you here, with the boat."

"I don't believe you," she said, her expression tight. "And it feels like an insult. But I'll do it. And, Micah, you remember what I said."

Dalton smiled at her, kissed her cheek, drew back.

"I remember. 'Don't get shot.'"

"Yes," she said, her expression solemn. "Don't get shot."

YOU have three—at least three—enemy watchers contained in a small sector. Doctrine indicates that you take the outliers first, in this case starting with the rifleman in the little marina across the canal from Galan's villa. The marina itself was attached to an open area, a *campo*, with a *ristorante*, closed and shuttered. Wide wooden docks lined the edge of the quay. Perhaps fifty small launches and wooden dories were tethered there, tugging gently at their spring lines, bumping softly together in the mist. It had taken Dalton about fifteen minutes to work his way through the mazes and alleys of Cannaregio, feeling his way through the dark.

Now he was crouched behind a fence at the southern edge of the marina, listening so intently to the sounds of the night that he could hear his own blood singing in his ears. He held that position without moving a muscle for close to twenty more minutes, according to the luminous dial of his watch, his knees and thigh muscles burning and his chest tight, with no sign that anyone was waiting out there by the railing.

And then, the faintest whispery crackle of radio static and the sound of a man's voice, low, relaxed, almost bored, a sleepy exchange between the perimeter man and one of the other watchers.

The sound of it sent a jolt of adrenaline through Dalton's body. He inhaled and exhaled through his open mouth, deliberately slowing his heart rate, calming his body down.

He raised his head above the fence, staring into the fog in the direction that the sound had come from. The light was changing. Somewhere to the east, over Montenegro, a pale sun was rising above gray woolen cloudbanks. He saw a shape huddled up against the fence near the outside corner where the two canals met.

There was fifty feet of wide-open space between Dalton and the target, and he'd be a dead man if he made any sound at all as he covered that ground. And he couldn't use the pistol. The man had to be taken in silence. And alive, if possible.

An interesting situation, one more suited to cats than crocodiles, but, there being no other way to get it done, Dalton slipped over the railing and began to drift silently across the cobblestones toward the man, who, if his shape could be read properly in this fog, had his rifle braced on the railing in front of him, the muzzle aimed across the canal toward the doorway of Galan's villa.

Dalton moved slowly, picking his way through the square, setting each foot down carefully, his eyes fixed on the man in the corner. Twenty feet out, and the man stirred, groaning softly. Dalton tried to renegotiate his relationship with the cold wet stones under him. Fifteen feet still to cover, and the man swore softly, straightened himself, and began rising stiffly to his feet.

Turning to face the canal, the man tucked the rifle—from the silhouette, it was exactly what Brancati had guessed, an H&K MP-55—into the crook of his left arm. He then got into the sort of shoulder-hunching maneuvers that usually indicate an urgent response to nature's call. Dalton, no gentleman, allowed the man to get things well under way and then came swiftly up behind him, making no more noise than a leaf falling, got his left forearm across the man's throat. The man was a small but quick, his body jerking in an instinctive effort to turn around. But by then, Dalton had hooked his left hand around his right forearm and had his right hand gripping the back of the man's skull. Dalton squeezed hard, and almost a minute of silent struggle followed. The smaller man was very powerful but not fast enough, his gloved fingers clutched uselessly at Dalton's forearm. Dalton used his heavier weight to keep the man pinned against the railing, his kicking feet restricted by the balustrade. Dalton's choke hold was compressing the man's carotids, cutting off the flow of blood to the brain. His struggles weakened gradually, his hands dropped, and his body sagged heavily in Dalton's grip.

Dalton held the choke hold for another thirty seconds and then dragged the man's limp body backward into the park, bringing him to ground by an iron bench. In the growing light he could see the man was wearing black jeans, black rubber-soled combat boots, and a heavy black turtleneck. There were no official markings of any kind.

Flipping the man's body onto his belly, Dalton stripped off the boot laces. He ran a loop around the man's ankles and, bending his legs up toward his back, Dalton looped the cords around the man's wrists, jerking the laces tight and wrapping them around the man's belt.

As Dalton finished the job, the man started to come around. Dalton could feel the man's rapid inhalation as he got ready to shout some sort of warning. Dalton clubbed the man across the back of the skull with the barrel of the SIG. The man's face bounced off the stones, blood sprayed out from a broken nose, and he went flat again. Dalton did a quick search, found a tiny plastic, thimble-shaped object in the man's right ear with a pin-sized aerial.

Turning it in the half-light, he recognized it as a Collarset III, a wireless earphone system by TEA made in the U.S. Digging deeper into the man's clothes, he found the tiny microphone that went with it clipped to the man's jacket collar. And the PRESS-TO-TALK switch was in his right pocket. Dalton stripped the gear, along with two spare mags for the Heckler, and, sewn into the side of the man's pants, a narrow black leather scabbard holding a nasty-looking matte-black rib-gripped, double-edged blade tapering to a needle-sharp point—a Fairburn-Sykes fighting knife.

Well-armed little prick, aren't you? thought Dalton, a little out of breath. He then pulled out a spare cell phone borrowed from Brancati, hit SEND.

A hundred feet down, on the other side of the Ormesini Canal, Brancati's own cell phone, the ringer turned off, began to vibrate in his pocket. Brancati stepped out of a darkened archway on the north bank of the Ormesini and began to walk along the quay in the direction of Galan's villa, moving fast like a man with a serious purpose in mind.

As he neared the boat where he had first spotted the watcher, he saw a vaguely manlike shape rising up out of the craft.

Dalton, with the Collarset in his ear, heard a man's voice, a spidery rustle but clear enough, speaking English with a strong Boston accent. *Six and two, this is one. I have a male approaching.* Dalton did a double click on the transmitter, usually taken by security units to mean *Heard and understood,* but the voice said nothing.

Brancati was less than fifteen feet from the entrance to Galan's villa, doing everything he could to look like Micah Dalton would look in a heavy fog, when the figure stepped out of the boat and onto the quay, facing Brancati, raising a pistol as he did so.

There was a ghostlike flutter of rapid movement behind the man. A second figure appeared and seemed to melt silently into the first. There was a brief but vicious struggle, almost soundless. Brancati moved forward in time to jerk a small pistol from the man's grip as Dalton drove the man down to the stones.

Dalton delivered a sharp blow to the base of the man's skull. The man's body went boneless. Brancati, kneeling, cuffed the man and then began a quick body search while Dalton moved to the door of Galan's villa, keyed the transmitter, and said, in whisper, "Six and two, I got him."

A voice in his earpiece, female, saying, "Good, hold him." Thirty seconds later, a smaller figure, a woman, dressed like the other two, in boots, jeans, and turtleneck, pushed her way out of the entrance gate, saw Brancati kneeling beside a prone figure, made entirely the wrong assumption, and went slamming down hard onto her belly, with a knee across her neck and the blunt muzzle of an H&K MP-55 jammed very roughly into her left cheekbone.

"How many?" asked Dalton in a low, purring hiss.

"I'm an agent of the U.S. government," hissed the women, struggling, red-faced, outraged. "You're interfering with a Bureau of Diplomatic Security operation. You will be—"

But Brancati cut her off, sticking a large gold-plated, leather-backed badge in her face and saying in a low, grating tone and in English, "I am Major Brancati of the Venice Carabinieri. I have not been informed of any authorized BDS mission. You are undeclared and therefore *you* are illegal. *You* are under arrest. If you are wise, you will shut up now. *Capisce?*"

A quick search of her uniform revealed, among other things, a set of plastic wrist restraints that Dalton used to truss her up, along with the other man, who was coming around, still groggy. The woman, a whipcord-thin but wiry redhead with a sharp hawklike face, wisely seemed to have taken Brancati's advice and shut up, contenting herself with a glare that she fixed on Dalton, never wavering.

The other man, only semiconscious, was in no state to discuss anything for the moment. Dalton and Brancati lifted the two of them into a kneeling position, stuffed gloves into their mouths, and shoved them face-first against a stone wall.

Dalton left Brancati to cover them with the Heckler while he sprinted back across the bridge, returning a few minutes later with the body of the third man, now wide awake, draped over his shoulder. Dumping the man with a thud onto the cobbles next to the other two, Dalton looked up at Brancati.

"You should go get Veronika and the launch."

Brancati nodded, turned to go, stopped, hesitating.

"Micah . . ."

"They'll be fine. Go."

Brancati headed back down the quay toward the bridge where Veronika was waiting with the launch. As he walked away, the first man Dalton had taken, the one with the silenced Heckler, twisted himself around and started to say something to the woman. Dalton jerked his head backward until the man's face, covered with caked blood from his broken nose, was inches from Dalton's.

He had the Sykes blade pressed against the man's Adam's apple, drawing a thread of blood from the skin as he snarled into the man's sweating face. "Talk to me. Who the *fuck* are you?"

The man tried to move his neck away from the blade, but Dalton pressed it in harder, opening the flesh, the blood beginning to stream down the man's muscular neck.

"Jeez, man, stop! Stop—"

"I asked you a question. Who the fuck are you?"

"We're . . . We're Americans. Bureau of Diplomatic Security. Rome office. The female is Leah Trent. She's in charge—"

"Why are you here?"

The man's face paled and his mouth worked, and then he shook his head, glaring up defiantly at Dalton.

"Fuck you, asshole. You *know* why we're here."

Dalton shoved a glove into the man's mouth, cramming it down hard, and then whipped the blade tip in a shallow slashing cut right across the man's forehead. As blood sheeted into his eyes, the man began to thrash and struggle on the cobblestones, his screams muffled by the glove crammed into his mouth. Dalton stood up, kicked him hard in the stomach, and then dragged Leah Trent over, showing her the man curled up on the quay, face covered in blood. He pulled the glove from her mouth

"You're next. *Why* are you here?"

Her face went white, and she seemed unable to look away from the bloodied face of her agent. Dalton shook her and she came back, her breathing short and sharp.

"We're here to take you into custody."

"On whose orders?"

"The Justice Department. There's a warrant—"

"On what charges?"

She blinked up at him, clearly wondering how he could not know why they were here in Venice.

"Vienna. You killed a Mossad agent, left his body in a car wired to explode—"

"Why?"

She blinked, tried to swallow, her throat closing up.

"Why—"

"He was my friend. One of the best. Why the hell would I kill him? They give you a reason?"

"I . . . Look, I don't . . . This comes from your own boss. Pearson, the DD at Clandestine. Word is, you've gone outside—"

"Horseshit. I am being set up. I want to know by whom."

She stared up at him, a muscle in her left cheek twitching.

"Set up? Set up how?"

"Listen carefully. Try to remember this. The car bomb in Vienna was placed there by a burn-scarred man, ex-paramilitary, maybe a Serb or a Russian. He's on a videotape, delivering the Saab. I have that videotape. Now, hear me. I *did not set* that car bomb and I *did not kill* Issadore Galan. I am being set up by somebody who has access to U.S. covert security systems. That means somebody inside your own government. So if you're really BDS, if you're really a pro, get your head around that and do something about it. Now, tell me. Do you know anything about a program or an agency called *Verwandtschaft?*"

She blinked up at him, her mouth working like a gaffed fish. Dalton could smell her fear, her warm breath on his face, feel the heat coming off her body. But, above all that, he was very aware that he was fighting against the urge to let his red dog run, to *use* the knife in his hand, to punish America for this. How many years of uninterrupted combat, how many years of open and covert killing . . . and *this* was his reward? BDS agents in the night. The Mossad given a free hand to take him out. Left to die a squalid little death, branded a traitor, abandoned and condemned by his own agency? This was the *America* he was supposed to risk his life for?

Trent could see the rage moving in his face like something inhuman that lived under his skin and was trying to break through. If she was going to live through this encounter, she had to change the music. She swallowed, swallowed again, found her voice, and said in the kind of tone you would use to negotiate with a junkyard dog, "Mr. Dalton, I hear you. Maybe I even believe you. And I promise you that if what you're saying checks out, the BDS will do everything it can to make things right. About something called *Verwandtschaft* . . . is that what you said? Because I truly do not know what you're talking about."

Something in her tone penetrated the blood-red cloud that was filling his mind. He stared down at her, trying to regain his self-control. "You've never heard of *anything* called *Verwandtschaft?*"

"It's just a German word. I don't even speak German."

"You've never heard the name used by any U.S. agency?"

She shook her head, closed her eyes slowly, seemed to go away to a far better place, opened her eyes again, and he saw resignation, and the truth, in her face.

He released her, moving back a few feet, looking at her for a long, timeless interlude, while she blinked back at him, her chest heaving as she tried to get her panic under control. "What about my man? He's bleeding out."

"No. He's all right," he said, going inward and feeling himself quite distant from this place and these events. "He'll need some stitches. I just marked him."

"Why . . . Why did you do that?"

Dalton smiled at her, a sideways grimace. His head was a little light, and he felt slightly dizzy, as the anger that had flooded through him gradually receded.

"I was trying to get your attention."

"Well," she said, closing her eyes, "you surely did *that*. Clandestine warned us about you. We should have listened better."

A beam of light caught them. He looked up as Brancati and Veronika Miklas came up the walk. Brancati dropped the beam onto the huddled shapes at Dalton's feet, the light playing on the fresh blood on the cobblestones, on Leah Trent's white wet face as she stared wide-eyed back into the glare.

Brancati, seeing the man with what looked like a severe head trauma, started to come forward

"Micah—"

Dalton stood up, lifted a hand, palm out.

"He's okay, Allessio. He's okay. I didn't hurt him."

Brancati, giving him a hard glare, brushed by Dalton, kneeling down to check the man out for himself. Dalton, feeling suddenly weak, put a hand on the stone wall of Galan's villa, steadying himself.

He closed his eyes, trying to get some equilibrium again, stunned by the depth of his anger and what he had contemplated doing in the rush of it, what that was saying about his mental state. When he opened his eyes again, Veronika was standing in front of him, staring intently into his face. Her expression was remote. "You did . . . *this?*" she asked in a shaken tone.

Dalton looked around at the people on the ground. Leah Trent was sitting on the stones, her cord cuffs in pieces at her feet, her arms wrapped around herself, her face wet, her mouth a little open, slumping into herself, obviously sinking into shock.

"I do," he said, his face hardening in light of her disapproval, her chilly stare, "what is *necessary.*"

"Crocodile," she said in a whisper mostly to herself, cold judgment in her eyes. She went past him and knelt down beside Leah Trent, putting a hand on her shoulder and speaking in the low, soothing tone one would use with an injured animal.

Brancati came over to him, his face grave.

"We must deal with these people," he said. "They have no identification papers, but I think they are truly Bureau of Diplomatic Security. My men have taken another four, all dressed the same way, down at the Savoia. A total of seven men, according to the Trent woman. She admits that they are a covert team, sent in to take you without the problem of extradition. This does not surprise me. The CIA did much the same a few years ago on the streets of Milan. I have called for a police launch. My people will hold them in the Arsenale for a few days incommunicado. I will question them further. One will need *dei punti*—stitches—for his face. Also, he has a broken nose, and I think a *commozione cerebrale*—a concussion. And the woman, I think she is in going into shock. The third one did not receive . . . your attention . . . so much, so he is unhurt. The woman will need to be hospitalized"—here he gave Dalton a look of reproach, shaking his head—"but she will survive. *Allora.* It is done. What do you wish to do now?"

Find a bottle of scotch and climb inside, he was thinking. What he said was, "Finish this. That's what I wish to do, Allessio. Find out what's going on and finish it."

THE medieval door to Galan's flat had been taken from a ruined villa in San Sepulcro. Beside the silver plaque with 8B GALAN engraved on it, the door carried the signature images of that famous old Tuscan town—macabre skeletal figures carrying scythes and swords and axes, grinning masks of death dancing and prancing—carved into three-dimensional cartouches and surrounded by demons from the underworld—imps, dragons, spiders, scorpions, vipers coiled around bundles of bones. The skeletons glared down at them in the glow of the hallway lamps as Brancati fished around in the pocket of his coat, finally pulling out a ring with several large brass keys on it.

He was about to set the key into the lock—a brand-new dead bolt with DIEBOLD engraved on the face—when Dalton put a hand on his arm. Brancati stepped back and watched while Dalton ran a fingertip carefully up the jam and then across the top of the door. He brought his hand down and showed Brancati a single white hair, with a black root.

"I forgot," said Brancati. "From Cora."

"Cora?" asked Veronika, still distant but not quite as cold. Brancati glanced at Dalton and looked back at Veronika.

"Galan has a cat. He named her after Cora Vasari, a woman he much admired," said Brancati with a sidelong glance at Dalton. "He always takes from this cat a hair and sticks it somewhere around the door so he knows if somebody has been in the flat while he was out. The windows on the terrace are barred, so this is the only way in. Maybe we should take out our pistols anyway."

He slipped the key into the lock, pulling out his Beretta as he did so. The well-oiled tumblers clicked heavily, the latch gave way, and the door swung slowly open, revealing a darkened living room, and, beyond that, a kitchen and an open door leading to a bedroom and the terrace.

Galan's flat was a spare, monkish space, with two antique wooden chairs set across from a battered green leather couch with an old bronze reading lamp. There was a tiny wood-burning stove, stained with four hundred years of soot. On the walls were several very small but well-executed oils, scenes of the Chianti District, atmospheric studies of rolling golden hills marked with the slender spires of cypress trees, a study of the Amalfi Coast, and what looked like a watercolor of the Negev.

There was a heavy oak sideboard holding a Seabreeze record player, next to that a small bar with some dusty bottles of Chianti and an ice bucket. And there was a collection of photos—his long-gone wife and children, Dalton knew—as well as a new-looking and very striking silver-framed portrait of Cora Vasari sitting on a big bay horse, looking down with a playful smile at the camera, her long hair cascading over her shoulders, the quintessential Hussar in a trim military tunic that fit her lush body very well, jodhpurs, gleaming black boots with silver spurs.

Dalton registered shock, seeing this photo, and a red rush of guilt. Although she was cut off from him, being sheltered from his chaotic effect by her family in their seventeenth-century villa in Anacapri, she was still the last faint promise of a normal life beyond the Agency, beyond the life he was leading.

Past the sideboard, under a cork bulletin board filled with papers and notes, stood a plain wooden table with a very modern desktop Dell on it, and a wide-screen monitor, which was dark, the tower shut down.

To the right, a galley kitchen, spotless in the dim glow of a hallway sconce, dishes stacked neatly in a drying rack, a linen dishrag folded carefully in thirds and draped over the tap.

To the left was an open door into a tiny bedroom with a sloping wooden roof. There was a single bed with a table next to it, some hardcover books piled on the table, and on the far side of the bed a set of heavily barred leaded-glass doors leading out to the terrace. Through the translucent glass, they could see the lights of the Campo Novo Park on the other side of the Ormesini Canal. The flat smelled of tobacco smoke and coffee, dust and decay, and carried a whiff of the canals under that.

If a flat can be filled with *absence*, this one was.

As a precaution, Brancati went through the place while Dalton and Veronika waited in the living room. Dalton was feeling a searing sense of sadness welling up as he looked at what Galan's life had come down to: a nearly penniless, crippled old man surrounded by a few sticks of cheap furniture and some worthless souvenirs in a shabby little flat in shabby little Cannaregio, as cramped and gloomy as his homeland had been sun-filled and blue-sky open, the sun-warmed paradise he would never see again as a living man. And waiting for him at the far end of this life like a cobra under his pillow, a death more terrible than any nightmare, dying in agony, torn apart on a tin table, surrounded by hate. It occurred then to Dalton that since he was on the same road, he might be looking at his own future.

Brancati came back from the bedroom, putting his Beretta into his holster, his face showing as much sadness as Dalton was feeling.

He walked over to Galan's computer, pressed the ON button, and they waited for the machine to cycle up. The monitor opened up with a flaring light, showing them the ENTER PASSWORD bar. Brancati pulled a piece of paper out of his pocket, held it out at arm's length—his eyes were going—and punched in a series of letters, numbers, and special characters.

The screen flickered, and Galan's desktop came up, the screen saver a photo of Jerusalem taken under a full moon, the hills bathed in a silvery light.

Brancati sat down at the chair, touched the keys, and pulled up a list of documents. All of the document titles were in Italian and, according to Brancati, a duplication of the same working files Galan had carried on his office computer.

A quick look at the contents of the drive showed nothing else. Galan's relationship with computers did not extend to the Internet and, from the look of his file history, barely reached beyond e-mail and Word documents. There were no hidden files, no family photos, and, aside from the initial password, no serious attempt had been made to encrypt anything.

"We will go through them," said Brancati, "but I have already looked at his worksheet at the Arsenale and these are identical. As you can see, Galan did not keep very much on computers. He was an old-fashioned man and did not trust them. Most of his ongoing cases he kept in his head. I do not see very much here. And it is unlikely that if he had anything he wanted you to see that he'd put it on a computer that could be hacked into so easily. But there is this one file—"

He tapped the screen, indicating a title in a strange script.

סָאֵד דיא סֹאַוו

Brancati looked over his shoulder at Dalton and Veronika. "It looks like Yiddish. Can either of you read it?"

They both shook their heads, so Brancati hit OPEN.

The file contained only one thing, a photo of what looked like some sort of abstract artwork.

"*Perfetto,*" said Brancati with a note of frustration. "*Che cosa è questo?* What is this? Galan is buying paintings?"

Veronika, her curiosity overcoming the coldness she was feeling toward Dalton, leaned in, touched the Yiddish letters.

"You could cut and paste these into a translation program. If you want to, I can do it for you."

Brancati, thinking it over, stood up and offered her the chair. Ve-ronika sat down, hit a few keys, got a translation program up, cut and pasted the characters into it, asking with a nice sense of tact, thought Dalton, for a reply in Italian.

The program ticked over for a moment, and then she got:

סָאׅז דׅי אׅ סָאׅוו

che cosa è questo

Which, in spite of the violent confrontation they had just been through and its disturbing aftermath, made them all smile.

"Well, it must have meant *something*," said Brancati. "Issadore did not play games with his computer. This is there for a reason. We should have a copy."

Veronika asked Brancati if he had a flash drive.

"This is Venice," he said, puzzled. "We don't *drive* in Venice. For myself, I have a launch?"

"I think she means one of these," said Dalton, picking up a storage stick and inserting it into the computer's USB drive.

Veronika gave him a tentative smile, some of her former warmth returning.

"If you like, Micah," she said in a friendlier tone, "I'll see if I can copy all of his most recent e-mails. If there are any drafts, I'll copy them too."

"Yes," said Dalton, smiling back. "If you would, great."

Brancati seemed a little uneasy about letting a woman he knew nothing about have that kind of access to Galan's computer, but she went to work with such obvious speed and skill that he accepted it after a sidelong look at Dalton.

The two men stepped back, giving Veronika some room to work, and turned to consider the room.

"You're right," said Dalton. "Galan wouldn't have left anything important in the computer or anywhere else obvious. But he wanted me to come here. To his flat. So there must be something here. Something he wanted me to see."

"I agree," said Brancati, tugging out a cigar and firing it up. "But it will take us days to go through this place."

"Days I don't have," said Dalton, beginning to pace slowly around the main room, trying to put himself inside Galan's mind. Brancati walked over to the row of pictures and picked up Cora's portrait, turning it over to see if something was taped to the back. There was nothing. He checked the others as well but without much conviction.

"It must be on his computer," he said, frustrated and suddenly very tired. "There's no other logical place. Galan was a very *precise* man. Not a fanciful man. He usually meant exactly what he said."

Dalton stopped pacing, looked across at Brancati.

"And what exactly did he say?"

Brancati considered it.

"If you mean, what message did he leave, in his own flesh, it was two marks. The figure 8 and the letter *B*."

"Yes," said Dalton. "Exactly."

He walked over to the front door, pulled it open, and tapped on the silver plaque screwed into it.

"Eight B. Does Galan have a toolbox?"

That brought a wry smile from Brancati, his lined face creasing up, his eyes bright.

"You have never seen Galan trying to fix anything," he said, walking over to the plaque and studying the screws that held it in place. He pulled a small cigar-cutting tool out of his shirt pocket, used the edge of it to pry the plaque off the door.

The plaque popped away, leaving a rectangle of unpainted pine underneath it. Taped in the middle of the rectangle was a tiny microchip. Brancati pulled it carefully away from the wood, peeled the tape off it, and held it up in the light.

"Bravo, Micah," he said with a wry smile. "Well done."

THERE were three items on the microchip, which was neither encrypted nor password-protected. Two were Word files, and the third was a JPEG. Veronika opened the first Word file, titled simply DALTON ONE. It appeared to be a copy of a news report.

> BELGRADE (Reuters)—Four former paramilitaries were sentenced on Thursday by Serbia's war crimes court to prison terms ranging from 15 to 20 years for the killings of 14 Kosovo Albanians in 1999, a spokeswoman said. They were found guilty of participating in the murder of Kosovo Albanian women, men and children in Podujevo, northern Kosovo, on March 28, 1999,

court spokeswoman Ivana Ramic said. The youngest victim was a 21-month-old infant, and five children were wounded.

"Zeljko Djukic, Dragan Medic, and Dragan Borojevic were sentenced to 20 years in prison while Midrag Solaja was sentenced to 15 years in prison when the court determined he was under 18 when he committed the crime," Ramic said.

The men belonged to the notorious Skorpions paramilitary group. Some of its members have been convicted of killing Bosnian Muslim captives during the 1992–95 Bosnia war, and one was found guilty of killing ethnic Albanians in Kosovo. NATO began an air campaign against Serbian forces on March 24, 1999, to halt the killing of ethnic Albanian civilians in a two-year counterinsurgency war. The campaign ended in June 1999 when Serb forces withdrew from Kosovo.

"Podujevo," said Veronika with a wary glance at Dalton.

"Yes. And the Skorpions. I remember them."

"This is the place Micah won't talk about," she said with a warning tone. "The man he fought in my apartment, he has my e-mail address and he sent us a picture of this Podujevo."

Brancati wasn't following.

"You know about these Skorpions?"

"Yes," said Dalton. "I've gone up against a few."

"This Podujevo," said Brancati carefully, since he could see that the situation between Dalton and the Miklas woman was developing some stress fractures, "this village means something personal to you, Micah?"

Dalton sighed, and his light seemed to dim.

"Yes. Veronika got the e-mail from Galan's server. I think she's right, that it was sent to her by the man who killed Galan. There was a picture of a burned-out building, rows of charred bodies, and two men in black BDUs with KLA insignias, one holding a fragment of a Paveway missile—an American air-to-ground weapon—and the other one lifting up a sign in Serbian, roughly translated as 'American murderers did this.'"

No one spoke for a while, but the question was circling in the air above them like the Mariner's albatross.

"And *did* the Americans do it?" asked Brancati finally.

Dalton stared at the page for a time, his features hardening up. They began to think he wasn't going to answer, but he did. "Yes. We did that."

Veronika seemed to diminish, as if something tangible was leaving her body. She did not look at Dalton again for a while, but she listened to what he had to say and never forgot it.

"How?" asked Brancati.

Again, a very long and difficult silence.

Dalton let out a long breath and began in a low, flat tone as if reciting a line of dry statistics.

"Podujevo. It's in northern Kosovo. NATO was trying to stop the Serbs from massacring Albanian Muslims. I was part of that operation, just not a well-known part. We had Nighthawks overhead. There were a few Predators, but we weren't assigned one."

"Who was *we*?" asked Veronika in a soft voice.

"*We* were a Special Forces hunter-killer unit. We were boots on the ground, and we had air cover to take out targets we indicated. We worked all over northern Kosovo during the NATO bombing campaign, trying to protect Bosnian Muslims from the KLA extermination squads. My fire team had been inserted into the Podujevo area during the night, a HALO drop. The idea was to light up, use laser beams, to paint targets for the strike fighters upstairs. We had two F-117 Nighthawks committed to lay down GBUs—sorry—Paveways. They're a kind of precision laser-guided munition. They home in on a target identified by a laser beam, marking it. That morning, we lost a Nighthawk to a Serb SAM over Belgrade, so we knew we had a limited time frame to make a difference on the ground. We saw a large group of KLA holing up in this building, no markings on it. Turned out it was a mosque. So we set up a strike with the Forward Fire group, painted the building up with our lasers. The Nighthawk laid down some Paveways. We blew it to bits."

Here Dalton stopped, seeing again in his mind that huge swirling cloud of red-and-green fire, smoke rising up, the shattering roar of the strike. His own unit, five men, their black-painted faces lit up by the fires of the burning building, pulling back into the hills. A two-day hump to their extraction point. And the after action, the Damage Assessment Board verdict that they had just incinerated a mosque crowded with civilians.

Neither Brancati nor Veronika Miklas had anything to say. It was obvious to anyone watching that Dalton was in a very private hell and nothing they could say would relieve him. After a moment he came back to the surface, finished the story.

"Well . . . What we didn't know at the time was that a hundred and fifty-six men, women, and children had been herded into that mosque two days before and held there while the KLA lured us in. They had a tunnel dug in the basement. They made quite a show of going in and out for days. They knew we had a lot of eyes in the air and that we'd pay a lot of attention to that kind of concentration of troops—"

"But in the days before, you were not on the ground," said Brancati, "not when they did that. How could you know?"

"We should have checked out that mosque up close before we targeted it and we didn't. I got aggressive, and all those civilians died . . ."

"*La nebbia di guerra, Micah . . .*" said Brancati.

"Fog of war? Maybe. In the beginning, it tore me up. I couldn't cope with it. Got so bad, I had to pop an Ativan whenever I thought of it. So after a while I just . . . stopped thinking about it. I closed it off, sealed it shut, buried it deep. Nobody else wanted to talk about it either, sure as hell not the brass at CENTCOM or the Pentagon. So we didn't. Not ever."

"And what is there to say?" asked Brancati, who had his own demons in the cellar. "What is the use of raising the dead?"

"*Someone* has raised the dead," said Veronika, but not unkindly. "This Smoke person, do you think he could have been there at Podujevo?"

"Yes. In fact, I'm almost certain he was. But that doesn't explain how he knew I was there too. It was a black op. We were never officially there."

"You may have a traitor," said Brancati. "In your house."

"Yes."

"Do you think the man you fought in my apartment was one of these Skorpions?" asked Veronika.

"I think he probably was. We made a real project out of them. Killed and wounded fifty, sixty of them, in hot little engagements all around northern Kosovo."

"Did you take part in any of the war crimes investigations afterward?" asked Brancati.

"No. Not that any of the brass would have wanted me anywhere around those trials, not after what we did to the people in that mosque. Right after the Kosovo war, I got seconded to the CIA. My operational area shifted to London, and at that time our chief interest was in terror finance. I remember hearing something about a group of Skorpions being tried this year, but I wasn't paying a lot of attention. I didn't really like to think about the Kosovo war at all. I did do some work for the Agency in Pristina a while back, trying to deal with ex-KLA involved in the drugs-for-weapons trade."

"Are these Skorpions still *active*?" Veronika asked.

"Yes," put in Brancati. "Back in the late nineties, there were only a few, five hundred or less. But now—the war in Kosovo never really ended—much of the criminal enterprise in Italy is done by ex-Skorpions, Serbs and Croats working to fund the new KLA so they can take Kosovo back. Galan did a study for me last year. He reached an estimate of over a thousand current members of the Skorpions and related KLA—"

"A *thousand*?" asked Veronika.

"Galan did a study for you? Does it still exist?"

"Yes. I have a copy on file at the office."

"Did it include head shots of KLA people?"

"Yes. Hundreds of them. Galan was very thorough. And he had good contacts all over the Balkans."

"We need to look at those. Can you send us the file? You've got my e-mail?"

"I do. I will," he said, looking at his watch. "It's almost dawn. We should look at the other material."

Veronika opened the second file, another Word document, this one titled DALTON TWO:

Новини Керчі—KERCH NEWS
ENGLISH VERSION:

KERCH CHARTER CRAFT SEIZED
BY RUSSIAN GUNBOAT

Ukrainian officials have filed a formal protest with the Russian government this week after a private tour boat owned by a local Kerch man was boarded and seized in Ukrainian waters by a Russian patrol boat. The boat, called the *Blue Nile*, was carrying several Ukrainian couples on a sunset-and-dinner cruise around the coast of Kerch when the Russian boat gave chase and intercepted the *Blue Nile* within sight of Kerch harbor, according to Captain Bogdan Davit, Chief of the Kerch Constabulary. The passengers were forced to off-load into inflatable rafts and left to make their way to shore as the gunboat took the charter craft under tow and left Ukrainian waters.

The *Blue Nile* is a sixty-foot private craft valued at two million American dollars and was owned and operated as a charter cruise by a Kerch-based businessman named Dobri Levka.

So far the Russian authorities have refused to cooperate with the Ukrainians, saying only that Dobri Levka, a Croatian citizen, was arrested for "violations of Russian sovereignty" and that he is being held at an undisclosed location pending an official hearing.

Tensions between Russia and the Ukraine have increased dramatically since the natural-gas embargo imposed by Russia on the Ukraine a year ago, as well as the decision by the U.S. President to remove missile defense bases from Eastern Europe at the insistence of Putin.

"Dobri Levka," said Brancati. "I know that name."

"Yes, you do. Levka was a Croatian freelancer Mandy Pownall and I picked up last year on Santorini. The kid was working for the other side. The Russians had a cell operating out of an office building in Istanbul, their cover was trade and commerce. Levka was supposed to help take Mandy and me out of the picture. We changed his mind."

The hotel room in Fira, six hundred feet above the Aegean, at night, a storm rattling the windows, and Dalton with a pistol up against Levka's forehead, Levka waiting for the round, Dalton for some reason unwilling to pull the trigger, Levka's brazen offer: "Instead of kill me, you hire me!"

"Hire you?"

"I got no job here now. You hire me, I work for you. You man who kills much, got that look, no offendings. So maybe you make more bodies later. With handy service of Dobri Levka, you don't have to bust big fat dead men around place all by self, ruin good suit like you got."

Dalton had to smile at the memory.

The kid had real sand. Levka was the kind of knocked-around, hardscrabble roustabout you tended to find along the fringes of chronic war zones. Like a true mercenary, Levka was ready to take the round if he had to—the fortunes of war, and no hard feelings—but he had also been nimble and nervy enough to try to talk himself out of that bullet if given half a chance.

"Levka kept his word. He knew the people we were up against. He helped us out in Istanbul. Levka and I took Lujac's Riva away from the KGB and drove it all the way to Kerch, chasing the Russians. After Kerch, Mandy and I went to Langley to help Cather out of a fix, and Levka got Lujac's Riva."

"One more file," said Veronika. "Called Dalton Three."

"Open it," said Dalton.

It turned out to be a scanned-in note, in a rough scrawl, with a short typed message attached.

"Who's Piotr Kirikoff?" asked Veronika.

"He was the Russian FSB officer who was running the ring we took apart in Istanbul last winter. We nearly caught him in Kerch. He got out two hours before we got there. He murdered a Navy corpsman and a Latvian woman. We found their bodies in the basement of a clinic in Kerch. They had been beaten to death."

"So this was Galan's urgent message to you," said Brancati. "Why didn't he come to me first?"

"He said nothing to you?"

Brancati shook his head.

"No. He simply asked for a week's leave, said he was going to

Micah, this note came from my contact in Istanbul who received it by hand from a woman named Irina Kuldic. My contact confirmed that Irina Kuldic was listed among those who were forced off Dobri Levka's boat and that the woman he met was that same woman. I tried to contact Irina Kuldic through Captain Bogdan Davit in Kerch but believe I have only triggered some annoying attention from Kirikoff's people. Of course I am taking appropriate measures. As the warning is to you and the circumstances are urgent, I will deliver it in person in Vienna.

I leave these items by way of insurance in case things go amiss. Also here is attached a drawing which I have come across several times on a few KLA and Skorpion websites.

It means nothing to me but may mean something to you as a military man. Perhaps a Skorpion unit insignia of some kind?

I have not told Allessio of this contact yet since there is not very much useful to say but perhaps you will be able to enlighten us. I hope that if you are reading this melodramatic communication I am standing next to you and Allessio and we are having many glasses of vino bianco. But if not then I am not sorry to put down my tools for a nice long rest.

Your friend Issadore G.

Vienna on some business. He was a private man. I thought he might be meeting someone, a contact. He had a very strict sense of tradecraft, and, as he says, he did not like to talk unless he had something useful to talk about. His methods were his own. He was like an oyster, and I have never attempted to pry him open. And he said nothing about being 'watched.'"

"If he had, what would you have done?"

"I would have given him an escort, or even put him in the Arsenale, if the threat was serious."

"Either way, he wouldn't have been able to go to Vienna and talk to me."

Brancati's lined face looked suddenly much older.

"True. And he would also be alive. *Basta*. It is done. What will you do now?"

"Finish what Galan started. Find Irina Kuldic."

"How?" asked Veronika.

"I know the cop quoted in the article, Bogdan Davit. We'll start with him, see where it goes."

"But he's in *Kerch*, isn't he?"

Dalton caught the hesitation in her tone, saw the uncertainty in her expression, and was not at all surprised.

"You want to tell me something, Veronika."

She looked back and forth from Brancati to Dalton, her eyes filling. Then she looked down at her hands, her fingers twisting together so hard her knuckles were whitening.

Without looking up at either man, she said, "I don't want to just . . . desert you . . . I just . . . If you go to Kerch, isn't that what they—Kirikoff, these horrible Skorpions—will expect you to do? Won't they be waiting for you? For us?"

"Unlikely. They have no way of knowing what Galan left behind. The proof of that is that he carved it into his own flesh in the last minutes of his life, the one secret he managed to take with him. I'm certain they won't be expecting us in Kerch."

"But that's how we got into trouble in Vienna," she said with some heat. "You were *predictable*. Can't you just . . . let *somebody else* do this? For once? For *me*? Somebody from your government. This is *their* problem too, isn't it? They are always talking about fighting the big terror. Let them go fight this one without us! Why can't we just stay here, you and I? In Venice. Maybe Major Brancati can give us some protection while we figure out a safer way to . . . Micah, I *cannot* go to Kerch."

Dalton was not surprised. She was a brave young woman, but there was a limit to anyone's nerve.

"I understand. It's not like in the movies, is it? But if you don't go with me, Veronika, you'll have to stay with Brancati. Stay close. Until it's over. I can't operate if I'm worried about you all the time. You understand? Allessio, you can do this?"

"Yes," said Brancati with a formal bow. "The last time, with Cora Vasari, she insisted to move about the world and was therefore shot in the courtyard of the Uffizi. This I will not allow to happen again. You, Miss Miklas, may not move about in the world. On this, there can be no discussion. I have a guest suite in the Arsenale. Micah has stayed there himself. It is very secure. A fortress. With a pretty view across the lagoon to the Isola di San Michele. No one can reach you there. On this, I give my word. You remember these rooms, Micah?"

"I do," he said. "You'll be safe there, Veronika, if you do what Allessio asks. Will you promise to do that?"

Veronika was quiet for a while longer. She looked up at him, put out a hand, and he took it. It was cold as ice.

"Please, Micah . . . stay. Here. With me."

Dalton shook his head, a softer look in his eyes.

"I wish I could, Veronika. I wish that very much. I'm not sure you wish it as much as you think you do."

Podujevo, she was thinking. *All those children, burned alive, the women dying in torment, their hair streaming flames, the flesh blackening, cooking off the bones . . .*

Dalton watched her face for a time, seeing what was there and hating the burned man for showing it to her, even as he felt a strange combination of shame and burning resentment, some of it directed at Veronika. Judgment was easy. War was not.

"But if you stay, Veronika, there is something important you can do. Can you contact your friend Jürgen Stodt? See if he can find out anything about that name on the work file? Would you do that?"

"Yes, I will. Micah, I can help, even from here. I can contact Jürgen, and Nenia. Maybe I can find out what *Verwandtschaft* means. I'm so sorry, Micah. I wish I were more like you. But I'm not. It's all just too . . . ugly."

"I know," he said, kissing her on the cheek. "I know."

Florida

A blood-warm, coal-black ocean, sounding like rolling thunder under the starless sky, was crashing into the sand beaches that ran for hundreds of miles along Florida's Gulf Coast, every curving mile of beachfront lit up like a string of glowing pearls.

Tonight, in Panama City Beach, part of a two-hundred-mile-long coastal strip called the Redneck Riviera, the Spring Break crowd was out in full cry, supercharged on dope, meth, ecstasy, vodka coolers, beer, and raging hormones. Thousands and thousands of college kids were cruising back and forth along a meandering oceanside town full of run-down beach bars with names like Coyote Ugly and Dirty Dick's, neon-trimmed nightclubs called The Big Easy, Shalimar, Pineapple Willy's, bleached-out, wind-beaten fifties-era motels like Sea Haven, Malibu Shores, and The Flamingo, along with fifty or so tattoo parlors, T-shirt and bong shops, and, lately, rows and rows of brand-new pastel-colored condo towers.

The steamy, salt-scented air throbbed like a beaten drum with bass-heavy hip-hop, and, under that, the guttural snarl of Harleys, the muttering rumble of Escalades and Navigators and Cayennes, all of them stuffed to their moon roofs with red-faced yet pale-skinned tubular college boys with eyebrow piercings, trick facial hair, and shaved skulls, leaning out the windows of their SUVs and bellowing like hungry hogs at the ferret-faced little pop tarts who were stumbling along the sidewalks in stiletto heels and sprayed-on acid-colored sheath dresses. All the frat boys were getting for their efforts, as far as Nikki Turrin could make out, was a series of needle-tipped middle fingers. But, then, the night was still young.

In her rented Town Car, a gleaming black, turtle-shaped battering ram, Nikki was making approximately two miles an hour along Front Beach Road, trying to snake her way through the milling crowds and the migraine-inducing noise, her hands gripped tight on the padded steering wheel, nervously watching the neon lights playing like gasoline flames across the polished hood, the soundproof interior of the car vibrating to the massive bass beat coming from a black Jetta running alongside.

Nikki was also trying to avoid making eye contact with three beer-gutted and very drunk frat boys in baggy T-shirts on the other side of her tinted side window. They were close enough to the window that Nikki could only see the printing on two of their tees: DOES THIS SHIRT MAKE MY DICK LOOK TOO BIG? and I'M SORRY, YOU'LL HAVE TO BUY ME ANOTHER BEER BECAUSE YOU'RE STILL BUTT UGLY.

The boys were trying to get her to roll down the glass and relate and had started thumping on the roof with their fists, the better to emphasize their unique personal charms. Since she had flown into Panama City Airport as Beatrice Gandolfo and was therefore without her company-issued SIG and her NSA badge, she was about to resort to a needle-tipped middle finger of her own when the interior of her car lit up with blue-and-red flickering lights, and she heard the *whoop-whoop* of a police siren.

She stopped in the middle of the road and watched as three uniformed patrol cops—two hard-bodied black guys shaped like artillery shells and a tall, rangy blond woman in a flak vest—bulled into the hog-boy contingent, herding them off the road and out onto the beach dunes, jerking the beer cans out of their hands while backing them up against a hurricane fence.

The blond cop—by her bars, a captain—turned to Nikki, the cop's face a blend of controlled fury and concern. She came over and leaned down to knock on Nikki's driver's-side window.

As Nikki got the window down, the heat, the noise, and the smell of Panama City Beach—old sweat, fresh urine, sea salt, marijuana, and spilled beer—came rolling in like a wave, along with the cop's personal scent, a pleasant mixture of cigarette smoke and some sort of citrus-based cologne. The cop had wide-spaced light brown eyes, a turned-up nose, and the ruddy complexion of a surfer. She had to raise her voice to be heard above the din. Her accent was soft and had a lilting cadence, something in it of the Old Dominion.

"Sorry about that, miss. Piss-drunk little peckerwoods. My men will sort 'em out. You okay in there?"

"I am now," said Nikki, smiling. "Thank you, Captain."

The cop patted the window's sill a moment, seeing Nikki's luggage in the backseat, her laptop case beside it, and then giving Nikki a long, appraising look. "You don't look one little bit like these pestilential Spring Breakers, miss."

"No. Stupid of me. I should have phoned ahead."

"You didn't know about Spring Break?"

"No, believe it or not. Actually, I'm here on business. I'm looking for place called the Bali Hai Motel. I think it's on Front Beach Road?"

The cop's face changed, her smile slipping sideways.

"The 'Bali Hai'? You sure about the name?"

"Yes," said Nikki, shuffling through her purse for the note. She found it, tugged it out. "One-six-three-oh-one Front Beach Road. Panama City Beach."

"Are you *staying* there, miss?"

"No. I'm supposed to meet someone there. Business."

"Business? At the Bali Hai? During Spring Break?"

That was an excellent question, and one Nikki was having a hard time working out herself. In the end, she had simply wanted to get this meeting over with, so she had pushed ahead, never thinking about the lurid saturnalia she was going to step into down here.

"Yes. I guess I didn't think that through, did I?"

The cop looked at Nikki's clothes: a gauzy cotton sundress, light green, with a delicate pattern of interlaced golden flowers. A thin gold chain around her neck, complete with a tiny gold crucifix. Gold earrings with jade stones. Her olive skin was already deeply tanned, her long auburn hair pulled back in a shining wave behind her ears. The cop's smile went away entirely.

"Miss . . . Look, can you pull over for a second? There's a parking lot up there beside The Purple Haze. Please."

The *please* sounded a little imperious to Nikki's ear, but she did what the cop asked. The captain went back to her cruiser, killed the light bar, and followed Nikki's Town Car into a sandy parking lot behind a shuttered tiki bar with a CLOSED DUE TO LIQUOR VIOLATIONS sign on the doors. The cop parked the black-and-white, got out, locked it, and came around to the passenger side, opened it, and leaned into the car.

"Mind if I sit in with you for a second, miss? My AC's shot, and I'm about to boil."

Nikki, puzzled but unwilling to argue, nodded. The cop got inside with a leathery creak from her equipment belt, sighing as she got herself arranged. She took off her uniform cap and set it on her knee, staring out at the crowds moving past them. Nikki had the air-conditioning up on FULL, and the cop, her face moist and her hair a little damp, leaned into the flow of cool air for a moment, her eyes closed. Then she sat back and looked across at Nikki.

"Have I done something wrong, Captain?"

The cop shook her head.

THE SKORPION DIRECTIVE   163

"Nope. This is a rental, right? From the airport? You just flew in, am I right?"

"Yes, but—"

"You don't know Panama City Beach at all, do you?"

"I've never been here before, ma'am."

"'Ma'am'? You an Army brat? In the service yourself?"

"No—"

"Don't mean to pry, but could I see some ID, miss?"

Nikki didn't bother asking why. She just handed it over. The cop flipped through the license, the rental policy, seemed satisfied, handed it back.

"Okay. I guess I should let you know, Miss Gandolfo, you are not the type of woman who should be meeting *anyone* at the Bali Hai. What that place is, miss, is pretty much an outlaw-biker criminal enterprise retailing STDs and fitted out with the skankiest skanks who ever snorted up a line of coke. It's simply the very worst damned rat's-ass, running sore, piss-tank maggot ranch between here and Pensacola, and that's saying quite a bit. We keep a cruiser outside there twenty-four/seven. I can't imagine—"

Her radio erupted in a burst of cross talk. She reached up, said something into her shoulder mike in a low tone, and turned the radio down. She stuck out her hand, and Nikki shook it.

"My name's Marcy Cannon, by the way, Miss Gandolfo. Pleased ta meetcha. So, what I'm saying is, I can't imagine why you would want to be going to the Bali Hai Motel for *any* reason. Not even business. You mind saying what sorta *business* brings you down here, 'specially during Hell Week?"

"With respect, Captain, is it important that I tell you?"

The cop shook her head, her Sam Browne creaking with the motion. She gave Nikki a broad, gleaming smile.

"Nope. None of my damned business, Miss Gandolfo. I'm a big old nosey parker, for sure. But I'm also the top kick in these parts.

This is my beach, and I run it like an old-time marshal. Think of me as Wyatt Earp. So, I'm just askin' politely, now, because if you really gotta go to the Bali Hai I'm gonna send one of my guys along to see you get out of there okay, and I'd like him to know if the trip is worth his bitter salt tears."

Nikki said nothing for a time.

The cop, completely at ease with silence, said the same.

"Okay," said Nikki, "I'm on a research project for a professor at the University of Virginia—"

"No way! That's *my* old school. What's your cadre?"

Nikki was ready for that.

"The Purple Shadows."

The cop shook her head, going back into the memory.

"I was with the Tilkas. Lots of fun. You take a degree?"

At UV, students didn't "graduate," they "took a degree."

"No. Transferred to Georgetown. I was only there a year."

"Me neither. Went into criminal justice and finished up at Glynco. Still back the Cavaliers, though. For my sins. Anyway, you were saying . . . ?"

Nikki, feeling like a rat, gave her the cover story as it had been laid out in the notes Cather had included on the flash drive: a general history of the Cold War and various covert operations connected with it, a possible book on the subject, being prepared by a poli-sci professor at UV.

Captain Cannon listened with every appearance of belief, her broad, open face showing nothing but polite interest. Nikki finished the story with the name of the person she was in town to interview, an ex–SAS officer named Raymond Paget Fyke.

Cannon listened to the name, shook her head slowly.

"Okay, first off—and I mean no disrespect, miss—that story sounds like a load of utter horse poop. There is no doubt in my mind that you work for some three-letter government agency—IRS, FBI, maybe the PTA—and you are very sweetly twisting my tail. But, then, there's no law against shining on a beat cop. I got no right to a straight answer, and we do live in strange days. Concerning your Mr. Fyke, I don't know the fella. You'd think, if he's ex-SAS, in my town I'd of heard of a guy like that. Although, God knows, this coast is packed with ex-military of every patch and stripe. This the guy who's supposed to be staying at the Bali Hai . . . ?"

"That's my information."

"What's his description?"

"Six-three. Two hundred pounds. Very muscular. Has a salt-and-pepper beard, shaved close. Green eyes. He may have a drinking problem. Speaks with a slight Irish accent. I'm also told he likes to fight, and his nose has been broken several times so it's sort of . . . squashed."

Cannon was looking straight across at Nikki, her face settling into a look of pure, even carnivorous, delight.

"As I live and breathe. The things you tell me, my dear. And this gentleman lives at the Bali Hai? Pray tell, is he *expecting* you?"

"That was his last fixed address, ma'am. And, no, he isn't. He also may not be going by that name. He has apparently irritated some people on the International Criminal Court."

"Good for him! Buncha dipshit, left-wing busybodies."

"Yes, ma'am."

"Actually, Miss Gandolfo, the man you're describing sounds a lot like a guy I know. Works freelance at the Bali Hai, as a bouncer. But he doesn't *live* there. This maybe could be your guy?"

"Could be, ma'am."

Cannon gave her a broad, affectionate grin.

"*Ma'am* again. If you're not in the *gummint*, young lady, I'm Hillary Rodham Clinton," she said, opening her door and climbing out. Nikki, who was beginning to think her covert skills were deeply inadequate, thought—hoped—that Cannon was leaving. She was wrong. Cannon leaned back inside, raised her eyebrows.

"You coming along, Beatrice?"

"Me? With you? Where?"

"We're taking my ride. You just lock yours up right here. My guys will see to it."

Nikki didn't like the sound of that at all.

"Where are we going?"

Cannon gave her another one of those carnivorous grins.

"You just come along with me, my dear. Trust in the Good Lord, and all will be revealed."

WHAT the Good Lord had to reveal was a sharp left turn off Front Beach Road and into a narrow alley called Robin Lane that led north, away from the ocean, into the flatlands and marshes of the inland waters. Robin Lane ran between two high wooden fences: beyond the fences Nikki could make out the floodlit grounds of what looked like a very expensive gated community.

Captain Cannon had kept up a lighthearted banter all the way from Dirty Dick's, staying off the topic of Nikki's trip down to Panama City Beach and, although Nikki tried to open it up once, neatly avoiding saying anything more informative about their destination and what it had to do with Raymond Paget Fyke.

Halfway up the long curving lane, Cannon killed the headlights. A minute later, she brought the cruiser to a rolling stop beside a large wooden sign showing rolling waves crashing into a barrier mound covered in sea grass and announcing WINDWARD SHORES ESTATE HOMES.

The gates stood wide open. In the dim glow from the streetlights Nikki could see what looked like a very large black-water lagoon surrounded by expensive homes and bound on one side by a tennis court and a golfing range. At the far end of the massive lagoon, a crowd of people were gathered on a wide, lantern-lit dock, and the sound of reggae and happy, youthful chatter drifted across the water. The cop shut the car down, looked across at Nikki.

"What sorta shoes you got there, Bea? I can call you Bea?"

"Please. They're sandals."

"Gotta do. Now, you stay behind me, you folla? Come along, now, and mind you close the door real soft, okay?"

Nikki did as she was told, following in the wake of the cop, who was surprisingly light-footed for a woman of her size, down the sandy lane and onto the grassy verge of the lagoon. The water smelled of mud and salt and rotting weeds. Captain Cannon went a few yards into the darkness, stopped, held up a hand to keep Nikki behind her.

"Fitch," she said in a carrying whisper. "You out there?"

A low voice came out of the darkness, a man's voice, in a whisper, hoarse, deep, wary.

"Marcy? That you, Marcy?"

"It is. Safe to come up?"

"If you stay away from the water. She's *close*. I can hear her."

Cannon paused a moment, pulled out her Glock, turned around to Nikki. "You stay here a moment, would you, dear? And maybe you should step back from the water a little."

"Captain Cannon, what the heck is going on?"

"Aside from bouncing nimrods out of the Bali Hai, Fitch runs a water park up off Hutchinson, a tourist thing. Gators and sharks and such. He lost a cow gator a few days back. Name of Cloris Leachman. He's been looking for her ever since. We all figure she's in this lagoon."

"An *alligator*? How *big* an alligator?"

"Eight feet. Nine hundred pounds. Big enough to eat a German shepherd last week. 'Long with any number of cats and small dogs, all in this area. Fitch has the lagoon sealed off. And here he sits, every evening, waiting for her to come up for air. Stay here, and don't move around a lot, okay?"

Nikki, her head a little spinny, stepped back into the light from the laneway, thinking that the trip from Seven Oaks, Maryland, to Panama City Beach, Florida, involved much more than mileage.

Cannon, moving quietly, faded into the gloom along the edge of the water, leaving Nikki alone in the downlight, nervously listening to the roar and boom of the college crowds a few blocks south and to the delicate lap and ripple of wavelets on the grassy bank of the lagoon. The party at the far end of the inland lake rolled on, oblivious. And somewhere up on her bank, a lady cop and someone named Fitch were trying to catch an alligator. If she'd been in her own vehicle, she'd be six blocks away and accelerating.

Five long minutes passed, and then she heard a swirling of water, a loud splash, and two muffled reports, deep and low, rather like someone slamming a car door. Another minute, and she heard muted voices, getting closer, and the whisper of shoes in wet grass and a slithery sound, something large coming through the saw grass. Nikki was inside the cruiser by the time two figures appeared in the light from the lane: Captain Cannon, and, just behind her, barefoot and wearing faded jeans and a black T-shirt—no clever sayings, just a black tee—a large, slope-shouldered man with long black hair shoved behind his ears and a close-cut salt-and-pepper beard.

He had a big bolt-action rifle slung over his shoulder and was dragging a very unhappy alligator, trussed up like a Christmas parcel and hissing like the air brakes on a Freightliner. The light was dim, but Nikki was pretty certain the man was Ray Fyke.

Cannon came forward as Nikki got back out of the cruiser. Cannon's face was a little flushed. Something was humming in the air between the pair, and Nikki realized that Captain Cannon and this hard-looking man had more in common than alligator hunting.

"We got her," said Cannon a little redundantly, wiping her hands on the butt of her uniform slacks, her eyes a little wild.

"You shot her?" asked Nikki, staying well clear of the reptile, which was now twisting herself around inside a network of ropes and showing every sign of ripping her way clear.

"No, miss," said Fyke, coming forward into the light, his eyes squinting against the glare, his seamed and weather-beaten face cracking into a broad smile. "We just calmed her down with a tranq and hogged her up. We'll call a couple of my boyos with a pickup truck and take her back to the water park."

There was an uneasy pause as what was not being said became painfully obvious, so Marcy Cannon said it.

"Brendan," she said in the kind of warning tone all wise and attentive males learn to fear, "I'd like you to meet a *Miss Gandolfo*. She's flown all the way from Virginia just to meet *you*. Isn't that special? Beatrice, may I present the bottom-feeding slug known—to *me* anyway—as Brendan Fitch."

After a momentary hesitation, and a very wary glance at Marcy's face, Fyke stuck out a hand, took Nikki's hand in a gentle, dry-skinned grasp, held it for a moment as he smiled down on her with a less-than-fatherly look in his eyes, taking her in from hair to sandals and back again, pausing appreciatively at various points of interest along the way.

"Beatrice Gandolfo, is it?" he asked with a wry smile. "Well, you have a twin in the living world, Miss Gandolfo, although I know her only by her photograph. Do you by any chance know a young lady named Nicole Turrin at all?"

"I do," said Nikki. "And would you by any chance know a man named Raymond Paget Fyke? At all?"

Fyke smiled broadly, said nothing for a beat or two, while the alligator hissed and a wind off the Gulf stirred the sea grass.

Then, turning to Marcy and putting a hand on her left shoulder,

Fyke said, "Marcy, I believe I have some explaining to do. I propose that the three of us go for a drink."

"Or three," said Marcy Cannon, shrugging his hand away.

SINCE Cannon had to get her shift covered and Fyke had to get Cloris Leachman back to her tank, the drinks turned into a late-night dinner at an oceanside restaurant called The Sands, still busy at this hour but mercifully free of Spring Breakers. The restaurant ran for almost a half block along the barrier dunes, a rambling wooden structure made mostly of glass and square-cut timber, with accents of polished brass, hardwood floors, green glass lights hovering above the booths, and a panoramic view of what looked to Nikki like the edge of the universe, a perfect inky blackness that started just beyond the walkway lights and stretched all the way to infinity. White-curling waves unfolded along the shoreline, and far out to sea a tanker, yellow in the haze and glimmering like witch fire in a limitless void, crawled slowly into the east toward a distant oil rig, a grid of floodlit spires far out there on the edge of the night. The windows were wide open, and a cool breeze laden with salt and seaweed moved the candle flames and stirred the gold curtains. They sat in a semicircle around the comfortable booth, ordered up a bottle of pinot grigio for Marcy and Nikki. Fyke called for a double Jameson's, neat with a beer chaser. But Marcy, who knew her man—or, until tonight, thought she did—changed that to a glass of Chianti. A small one. Fyke, a wise man, let it stand.

Their drinks came, the willowy waiter wafted away on a shell-pink cloud, and a sudden and uneasy silence came down, taking a place at the table like an unwelcome guest.

Nikki broke it.

"Captain Cannon—"

"Marcy. Please."

"My name is not Beatrice Gandolfo. I apologize for the lie."

Marcy nodded, a little chill since she had seen Fyke admiring her fine points, but ready to be won back.

"Got good paperwork, I have to say," she said, trying for a smile. "I look at phony ID all the time, and your license is as real as mine. Which says that you're with the government. And I'd like to know which part, if you don't mind."

"My name is Nicole Turrin. My employer is the National Security Agency. I work in Fort Meade, Maryland. But I'm not here in any official capacity. I've been asked by a mutual friend to come down here and speak with Mr. Fyke about a matter that has to remain confidential."

Cannon grunted, sipped at her wine, set it down.

"Okay. I'll let that slide for now. How about, just as a courtesy between us girls, you tell me who the *hell* I've been sleeping next to for the last five months or so."

Fyke started to speak, but Marcy silenced him with a hand, never taking her eyes off Nikki's face, her fingers around the stem of her wineglass, her face flushed, real pain in her thin strained smile and flickering around the edges of her eyes. Nikki, who had just been blindsided by a man she thought she knew, understood Cannon perfectly and decided to tell her as much of the truth as she could manage. The woman deserved that much.

"This man's real name is Raymond Paget Fyke. He was a member of the British Special Air Service and was seconded to the CIA, at London Station, several years ago. His service record is impeccable—"

Fyke could not suppress a snort at that one.

Nikki rolled on over him.

"And he is now is an *honorably* retired agent of the Central Intelligence Agency—"

Cannon's eyes were filling with moisture, but she drove that down and steadied herself, her throat working.

"Horseshit. Nobody ever *retires* from the CIA. If he were actually *retired*, then I doubt you'd be here. And it doesn't cut a lot of ice with me to find out a man I thought was a dear friend is just another professional liar."

"Marcy . . ."

She rounded on him with some heat.

"Shut up, Brendan . . . Ray . . . whatever your name is. You and me, we'll sort this out later. Go on, Miss Turrin," she said, coming back. "You have got my full attention."

Nikki hesitated, took some wine, organizing her thoughts.

"Last winter, Mr. Fyke, along with other government agents, stopped a major terrorist attack on the Port of Chicago. I was part—a small part—of that operation—"

"What sort of terrorist attack?" asked Marcy, giving Fyke a look. Nikki gave her the A version, leaving in enough to lay out the risks taken and leaving out anything about Micah Dalton.

Marcy's expression softened considerably as Nikki unfolded Fyke's tangled career narrative. Nikki was putting a shine on Fyke's record, but the story was, Nikki realized as she was telling it, essentially an honest portrait of the man.

"You said earlier that Brendan—*Ray*—had gotten himself crossed up with the ICC. How'd he do that?"

Fyke stopped her there, and Marcy turned to look directly at him for the first time since they had all sat down at the table.

"I was on a ship, the *Mingo Dubai*, a gypsy tanker, a rust bucket. We were boarded by pirates at the eastern end of the Malacca Straits. They were Malays, Dyaks, working for a Serb named Branco Gospic. They killed most of us, and I killed some of them, and then, for health reasons, put myself overboard. A Singapore patrol boat fished me out of the water, and I got charged with sinking the ship, which wasn't sunk at all but was being reflagged for Gospic's people. A guy named Chong Kew Sak was the head of the Singaporean SID—sort of their CIA, Marcy. He was in on the deal, locked me in Changi Prison, and was in the process of having me beaten to death when a friend of mine—"

Nikki shook her head slightly.

Fyke got the message.

"Can't say who got me out of Changi. We did some things together in the South China Sea. Ended up in the Port of Chicago last fall, where I first heard of Miss Turrin here. We'd never met, but I saw her picture on the operations monitor. Anyway, when it was all over, well, having the likes of me around made the dons at Langley a tad uneasy. I might pee on the Bokhara or start humping a table leg. So they got the head reptile to walk me to the door, check my pockets for silverware, and kick me down the lane—"

Here he gave Nikki a look.

Cather, she realized.

"So, being at liberty, with a pittance in my pocket, I went back to Singapore to see about this Mr. Chong Kew Sak. Led me quite a chase, he did. Finally ran him down about six months ago, in Papua New Guinea, at a little village called Sogeri, upriver from Port Moresby, where we had what the House of Lords would call 'a frank exchange of views.' After that, things were a little warm in Southeast Asia. The ICC had a warrant out for me, and so did Singapore, so I picked up an old legend again and came out here because the U.S. doesn't recognize an ICC warrant. Yet. Here I met you, Marcy. Thought I was gonna live happily ever after until Miss Turrin shows up."

Fyke sat back, finished off his glass of Chianti, got the waiter's eye, and ordered up another. The silence came back, but now it seemed slightly more amiable. Marcy Cannon looked at her glass for a while, turning it in the glow from the lamp. Fyke watched her carefully, his green eyes bright in the table glow, a vulnerable look on his battered face. Cannon took the bottle, filled Nikki's glass, and then hers. She sat back with a sigh, took Fyke's left hand in her right, and looked across the table at Nikki.

"I guess now is where we find out why *you're* here, Nikki."

Nikki gathered herself, rode down her guilt, and went straight at it, addressing herself to Fyke.

"You heard about an explosion in Vienna two days ago?"

"I saw something on Fox about it," said Fyke warily. "A car bomb near a church? Terrorists, they said."

"It's a bit more complicated. An Israeli citizen was killed, along with two police officers. The Mossad is involved—"

"Oh Jeez. Nobody does revenge better than the Shin Bet."

"Yes. That's the problem. The man they're after—"

Fyke got there before she finished the sentence.

"Jesus, Mary, and Joseph," he said. "You're not talking about . . . about the *crocodile*, are you?"

"Yes."

"Who the hell is the crocodile?" asked Marcy, understandably confused. "Is that some sort of spook code name?"

"No," said Fyke. "Just a nickname. For an old friend. A lovely man. Is the Agency doing anything to help him at all?"

"No. Quite the reverse. The latest is, the Bureau of Diplomatic Security sent a covert unit to Venice last night, trying to arrest him."

"Did they," said Fyke with a glint in his green eyes. "And how did that work out for them?"

"Not well. The BDS now has five agents sitting in a prison block in Mestre and two more in a hospital—"

"*That's* my lad."

"And all without any papers. And the Carabinieri—"

"Brancati?"

"Yes. Major Brancati is threatening to send them all to a terrorist lockdown in Milan and hold them there indefinitely unless the U.S. government can explain—and also justify—why they violated stand-

ing protocols and formal undertakings in an attempt to kidnap someone who was enjoying the protection of the Italian authorities."

"Jesus, Mary, and Joseph. What a cluster . . . What a sorry fix it all
is. What's Langley doing about it?"

"They've denied any involvement. They say it was a BDS mission,
ordered out of the embassy in Rome—a State Department matter—
and they know nothing at all about it. As for our friend, they've effectively given the Mossad a free hand. They're staying well clear."

"Running for cover, now that there's a Special Prosecutor, is that
it? Like Pontius Pilate? Letting all their hard boys twist in the pre-
vailing wind that's blowing out of the President's arse? The Mossad
will do their sticky work, the clouds will all roll away, the golden lads
and lassies at Langley will climb into the sunlit uplands of prosecuto-
rial immunity, the President gets on *Oprah*, and everybody on the
wrong side of the blanket offers up a quiet novena for the late and
unlamented."

"Yes. Essentially. You know the old story about the scorpion and
the crocodile who meet at a river?"

"I do. I bloody well do. So poor bloody Mikey's out there on his
poor bloody own, is he?"

"No," said Nikki. "We're hoping he has you."

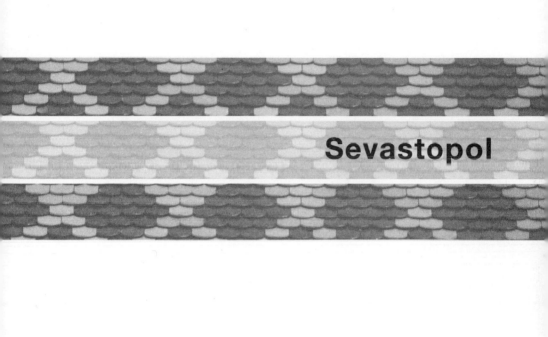

Sevastopol

THE SEVASTOPOL HOTEL, ARTBUHTA EMBANKMENT, EIGHT P.M. LOCAL TIME

Thirty-one hours and 1,756 kilometers later—290 from Venice to Zagreb, 390 from Zagreb to Belgrade, 450 from Belgrade to Bucharest, and another 626 from Bucharest to Sevastopol—and Dalton, who had somehow managed to sleep much of the way in spite of the five different planes involved in the journey, each one more rickety and bone-shaking than the last, was finally installed in a wicker chair on the shining-white pillared balcony of the Sevastopol Hotel's restaurant. In honor of a Free Ukraine, he was smoking a sky-blue, gold-tipped Sobranie Cocktail, nursing a G & T so cold it was hurting his fingertips, and watching the lights of Sevastopol Harbor come flickering on all around the shoreline. The broad bay, steely under a pinto sky, was studded here and there with the matte-gray spearheads of six Russian destroyers moored out in the offing, their amber running lights shimmering in the damp evening air. Because the eye-blink-brief tourist season was now under way, an armada of pleasure craft and tour boats was circling around the gunships like tropical fish darting around in a shark tank.

Sevastopol, shelled into ruins by the Brits during the Crimean War and halfheartedly repaired by czarist Russia, today nominally a Ukrainian holding, was still living under the shadow of the Russian Navy, which had a twenty-year lease on the port, granted in 1997 by the Ukrainians, a reluctant concession profoundly influenced by the guns of the Black Sea Fleet.

The town itself was pleasant enough to look at, full of lights and glitter, with many charming white limestone homes, blue-roofed town-house developments, gaily canopied seaside restaurants scattered along the embankment, dense, tree-shaded neighborhoods of apartments and town-house blocks rising up into in a cascading range of green hills, some neoclassical buildings dotted here and there about the town, and a large drum-shaped war museum set out on a hilltop, dominating the town and the harbor.

But to Micah Dalton, it looked, walked, talked, and smelled like a Russian satrap, which to him had always meant the dead-meat stink of totalitarian oppression and the mute, miasmic dread of a captive citizenry. Dalton had been here before. He had followed the progress of a Russian trawler through the Black Sea, a trawler that was suspected of carrying a shipment of missile-guidance systems to the Iranians. Dalton had found the place . . . unfriendly, having to leave by private boat under the cover of darkness just a few hundred yards ahead of a detachment of Russian naval security forces.

He was back now, checked into a nice suite of rooms under the name of Dylan Castle, an investment analyst working for a London-based private bank known to the fiscal set as Burke and Single. The Castle "legend," which had worked well enough to get him out of Venice and all the way to the Crimean, had been laid out by Porter Naumann under the cover of Burke and Single, a CIA false-front bank monitoring currency transactions around the world. It was only safe to use now because Naumann had firewalled the legend from Tony Crane and the people at London Station, mainly because he was afraid that one fine day he'd need it himself.

Along with a lot of other things Dalton had inherited from Naumann, the Dylan Castle cover was about the only ironclad thing he had left now that Mariah Vale and the CIA had shut down his bank accounts, his credit cards, published his picture and description all over the covert world, and taken initial steps to freeze his assets in London and Venice.

As Dylan Castle, he had a valid American passport, two credit cards—one from Barclay's and the other from the Banca Raiffeisen—and peripheral supporting cards. It was risky taking a legend that existed literally under the eaves of the CIA, but it had been his experience that the CIA, always obsessed with the big picture, often overlooked tiny details sitting on its doorstep.

Dalton checked his watch and looked seaward again for any sign of the Nordside ferry, which was now about fifteen minutes overdue. Yes. There it was, a small oblong of yellow light butting through the channel swells, carving a white curve through the darkening water. By the time it docked in the little harbor below his balcony, thumping into the concrete jetty with an audible crunch while the props boiled the water at her blunt stern, Dalton had called the waiter over and placed an order for a bottle of chilled Bollinger and two iced flutes, and made detailed arrangements for a large rack of lamb to follow.

A tall, long-legged and elegant woman in a charcoal knitted sheath dress under a long black coat, her black-and-silver hair flying in the wind, came striding down the gangplank, trailing a black leather rolling bag, one gray-gloved hand shading her eyes from the floodlights as she scanned the hotel balcony.

Dalton lifted a hand, and the woman waved back, crossing the jetty and disappearing under the trees.

Four minutes later, the glass doors behind him opened—he was, of course, now standing—as Mandy Pownall, listed in Burke's Peerage as Cynthia Magdalene deLacey Evans Pownall, late of London Station, now on a kind of tactical sabbatical, came through the doors with a broad smile on her fine patrician features, her gray eyes shining, the cashmere dress clinging to her graceful curves like a morning mist on the bend of a river.

She stepped lightly into Dalton and gave him a full-body hug, nose to toes, pressing herself into him so tightly he could feel her full breasts, her gently rounded belly, the heat of her hips, while her scent, White Linen, overloaded his senses, as she knew damned well. She kissed him full on the mouth, a lingering kiss, her red lips parted and her spicy breath blood warm on his burning cheek.

She stepped back, gave him a delighted assessment, taking in and approving of his light gray suit, his gray shirt, the gold silk tie, his black Allen Edmonds slip-ons.

"Well, for a desperado, you look very chic."

"I try to please, Mandy," he said, feeling his somber mood lighten as it always did when Mandy was around. "You do look splendid."

Mandy surveyed the crowded harbor as they sat down, sniffing at the usual Sevastopol smell of kerosene and diesel and seaweed but approving of the clear, tangy scent of the eucalyptus shrubs that ringed the balcony. She watched with a slight smile playing on her fine-boned, pale-skinned face as Dalton poured her a flute of Bollinger and held out his cigarette case, lined with fresh Cocktails, thinking, with an internal flinch, of Veronika Miklas back in Venice locked away in the Arsenale.

Mandy lifted her glass in a toast, they *ping*ed and sipped, and then she sat back in her chair, drew on her cigarette, turned her head to blow the smoke away, looking very much like the young Katharine Hepburn as she did. She then let her smile lose some wattage and gave him a considering glare.

"So. Did you screw her?"

"Screw who?" asked Dalton rather weakly.

"That little Austrian gumshoe. The one who latched onto you in Vienna. Vickie Mukluks or something like that?"

"Veronika Miklas?"

Mandy waved that away with a dismissive hand.

"Answer the question, you slithering toad."

"Do toads slither?"

"You do. Out with it. They say confession is good for the soul, although I've never tried it myself. Did you shag the girl?"

"No," said Dalton, summoning as much force as his guilty mind could muster and working heroically to keep his expression expressionless. "No. I did not."

Mandy lifted an eyebrow.

"On your sacred honor, as an officer and a gentleman?"

"On my sacred honor, as an officer and a gentleman."

She reached for her flute, put it to her full red lips, and studied him over the glittering crystal rim as though he were the remaining half of some crawling thing she had found in her salad. She set the flute down carefully, leaned over, and used his tie to pull him close enough for a hungry, searching kiss.

"You," she whispered in his ear, "are a lying shit."

"SETTING that aside," Mandy said, leaning back again, "what is our agenda here in this squalid Soviet sinkhole, Mr. Castle?"

Their rack of lamb—paired with asparagus, mint sauce, and tiny roasted potatoes—floated in on a large silver platter unsteadily piloted by a small mud-brown man with an absurd mustache and wearing a gravy-stained monkey suit that looked as if it zipped up the back and a bow tie that looked like it was made out of spray-painted cardboard. The lamb was, however, brilliant, and Dalton, suddenly ravenous, settled in for the long haul, as did Mandy, for whom all of the sensual appetites had irresistible charm. After a decent interval, the wreckage hauled away and the table duly whisked, Dalton poured out the last of the Bollinger, handed Mandy her flute along with a demitasse of thick espresso.

"Our agenda," he said softly, taking her in and thinking that his libido, which had once been MIA, seemed to have reasserted itself in force, "is to address the killing of Galan and, while we're at it, dig me out of a cesspit. How much do you know?"

Her face lost some of its cheer.

"I have most of it from Allessio. Poor Issadore. The Hessian gumshoe, that . . . hideous burned creature . . . you fought with in her flat. The car bomb at Leopoldsberg. The note from Dobri Levka. Is it true about the Mossad?"

Dalton, his face growing stonier, said yes.

"Oh my," said Mandy, a worried expression flickering across her face like the shadow of a swift. "Have you seen any sign? Not that one normally does until it's too late."

"None so far. And I've been looking."

"What will you do if they do take a run at you?"

"Try to reason with them," he said with a wry smile.

"In other words, strew their guts about the landscape in the usual Dalton style. That'll do *so* much for U.S.-Israeli relations."

"I think that's the idea," he said seriously.

"Kirikoff? You flatter the man. That's rather *too* clever for that fat gray slug, don't you think?"

"He led us quite a dance up and down the Bosphorus and across the Black Sea, Mandy. And then got clean away."

"With his pants flapping around his ankles and his great, wobbly plum pudding of an arse in the wind, I remind you. About this Mariah Vale creature, did I not warn you repeatedly about what was landing on our heads if Harvard Yard really took the town? Why do you think I went on leave?"

"Mandy, my darling, you went on leave because your daddy threatened to cut off your allowance and you couldn't finance the Sloane Square Fandango on a paycheck from Langley."

She made a moue and then smiled.

"Poppy's such a teapot. Iraq was giving him a migraine. And he *was* being an awful bugger about my stipend. But I'm glad to be out of it for a while. Really, I don't know how it will all end."

"No? I'm getting a rough idea."

"Yes," she said, frowning. "That's why I'm here."

"And I thank you for it. How did you manage it?"

"Getting here without Langley knowing? Poppy commandeered the Lear and billed it to Threadneedle Street. I wasn't even on the manifest. At this end, I was met by a lovely man who runs Poppy's mining interests in the central Ukraine. His name is Earl Ford. He's a cross between a Mafia hit man and the piano player in an upscale brothel. Quite well-off on his own. He keeps a pretty sloop in Bala-klava. Has a huge condo there too."

"Sounds like a good man to know."

"Poppy thinks so," she said quite seriously. "If all this goes south, I'd advise us to bear him in mind."

"We will."

Mandy stretched, sighed, gave him a coy and sleepy smile.

"So, Mr. Castle, dear boy, here I am, in the sinfully silky flesh. Tell me, are we leaving for Kerch right this *very* minute?"

Dalton shook his head.

"No. Too late in the day. It's two hundred and fifty klicks over-land, sixty from here to Simferopol—"

"God. That rathole—"

"Yes, and worse ratholes to follow. And a long, hard one hundred klicks over the spine and down to Feodosiya on the coast, and another one hundred klicks across some pretty bleak terrain to get into Kerch by the back door. Two-lane blacktop most of the way, but some of it could have worn down to dirt and gravel to within a hundred miles of Kerch. The hotel here has a fleet of Mitsubishi Lancers for rent. I've got one with an off-road upgrade, and I'm asking for extra tanks, a GPS, and some water bottles."

"What's our story? For the Russkies, I mean."

"You're my mistress. Locals love infidelity. It adds spice to their lives. You have pretensions to being a photographer and are simply on fire to document the entire Crimean Peninsula."

"God," she said, rolling her eyes. "Can't we just take Poppy's Lear? We could be there in a half hour."

"The idea is to come in low, look around, find Irina Kuldic and Bogdan Davit, see if we can get a handle on what Kirikoff is up to. I don't want to swan into town like Di and Dodi."

"Dead, you mean?" she said, blinking sweetly. "Poor Lady Di. Always wanted a halo around her head and all she got was a steering wheel. By the way, how are you fixed for funds?"

"Until you arrived, I figured that I had enough for a month. With you here, I'll be flat broke by Tuesday."

"Well, I have good news for both of us. Allessio had a package waiting for me at Stansted airfield. I have it in my bag."

"What is it?"

"Your *trousseau*, darling," she said, quite pleased with herself. "The one you had stashed away in the Savoia."

Dalton had kept a steel briefcase hidden at the back of a cleaner's closet in the Savoia Hotel. In it, he had twenty grand in mixed euros, another ten thousand in U.S. dollars, and a small Crown Royal bag filled with 99.9 percent pure Canadian gold wafers. Along with a Colt Anaconda and four boxes of .44 Magnums.

"Including the Colt?" said Dalton, since flying public airways as he just had meant leaving his SIG behind in Venice.

"God yes," she said, rolling her eyes. "Weighs a ton! Bloody great stainless-steel hand cannon with an eight-inch barrel. If I hadn't already seen you naked, I'd think you were compensating for a personal shortcoming."

"Anything for you?"

Mandy, taking another Cocktail and lighting it up with Dalton's gold Cartier, nodded through the smoke. "Yes. I have my cute little SIG. And some of those spare bullet-holder thingys."

"Magazines?"

"Whatever," she said, waving away the comment with the smoke cloud. Dalton was very impressed about the trousseau's unexpected arrival and said so.

"So was I," said Mandy. "I just adore a man with bags full of solid-gold wafers. May I have just a teeny one? As a keepsake?"

Dalton, who knew his Pownalls, said, "How many have you already lifted?"

"Only two," she replied with a sideways smile. "For mad money. So . . . we're staying the night . . . are we?"

"Yes. I've already booked you an adjacent suite."

"How very tactful. It follows that you already *have* a suite?"

"Yes."

"Well, Mr. Castle, as your designated harlot I'll be bunking with *you. In flagrante.* If only for the sake of the mission."

"Mandy . . . we need to keep this—"

She set her flute down, glaring at him through the smoke.

"Oh no you *don't*, you manky little git! I have *had* it with all this Hamlet hearts Ophelia stuff. Cora Vasari, a grown woman, on the flimsy excuse of a teensy-caliber bullet to the head, which she acquired only because she couldn't follow Pascal's simple instruction to sit quietly in her room, has allowed herself to be shut up in a tower like some dago Rapunzel, while *you*, my dear, have flirted with *me* as few men have and lived to tell the tale. Oh yes. I know. I let it slide after you stood me up in the middle of the Black Sea last winter. And if I were a cruel woman, I would call that the act of a sniveling eunuch. However, now that you've already boinked the Hessian Hussy, you will either stand and deliver tonight or die valiantly in the attempt. Are we clear on *that?*"

Tel Aviv

The Mediterranean side of Tel Aviv Boulevard looked a lot like Panama City Beach, as Nikki Turrin and Ray Fyke walked across the still-warm sand toward the squared-off, bunker-style building that housed Joko's Beach Bar. From the outside, at least, it was exactly the kind of migraine-inducing, rock-and-rolling stucco-walled beer joint that would have been packed with drunken kids from Ole Miss back on the Redneck Riviera. A few hard-nosed sago palms jutted up out of the grainy sand around Joko's like jagged green bomb bursts, and the waterside deck was trimmed in red-and-blue neon, pulsing in time to the music. But when you looked the other way, back across Tel Aviv Boulevard, it was another story entirely.

Then you were looking at South Beach in Miami or Santa Monica, row upon row of expensive and stylish houses and condos, Art Deco hotels, first-class dining, upscale shops. Tel Aviv had floodlights and neon and glittering marquees stretching for miles in either direction along a wide four-lane street lined with royal palms, softly waving in the gentle wind off the Med.

This warm spring evening, the beachside walks were crowded with families out for a stroll, dating couples, kids running wild on the sand, and even a few surfers, like seals in their black wet suits, trying out tonight's truly hopeless waves.

When she thought of Israel, Nikki had to admit, she pictured stony battlegrounds and ancient settlements: the Sinai and the Negev and the Golan Heights, battered but eternal Jerusalem, and the bleeding sores of Gaza and the West Bank. She did not think of the beaches and luxury hotels of Tel Aviv, of the river of SUVs and luxury sedans hissing past, the intricately laid stones of the walkway, the sparkling fountains, and the light off the wide Mediterranean floating above them like an aurora.

Ray Fyke, walking along beside her, almost but not quite taking her hand, seemed oblivious to the glamour. He was a looming presence in black slacks and a black polo, his muscular forearms and bulky chest stretching the material, his shaggy head moving from side to side as he studied the crowds swirling all around them, his easy loping stride covering the ground as she struggled to keep up with him in the deep sand.

They reached the entrance to Joko's, and Fyke put out a hand to get the door for her. He was quite gallant for a drunken Irish roustabout, thought Nikki, who was gradually getting used to traveling with him. It was rather like traveling with your own personal panther. Fyke paused and grinned at her, his green eyes alight in the glow of the entrance floods.

"Now, I don't have to remind you—"

"I know, I know. I'm just your biographer."

"Joko's a strange lad, Nikki. Looks like a fat old Kodiak bear, but he spent thirty years on the other side of the blanket . . . A real hard boy. I'm not sure which way this talk will go. If it goes badly, I want you to walk quickly away. And don't get—"

"I won't, Ray. Just relax. You look a little tense yourself."

"Do I?" he said, checking his reflection in the door glass.

"Yes. You look like you're going to your own wake. Try to smile more. When you smile, you're not as horrible to contemplate."

Fyke gave her a sardonic bow, took her arm, and shoulder-butted his way into the bar, the blare of easy-listening music assaulting their ears as soon as he got the glass doors open. Unlike Dirty Dick's in Panama City, Joko's place was crowded with reasonably well-dressed young people, very few backpacker types, and some sleek-looking older folks in Tommy Bahama and Banana Republic who had to be in on a cruise tour. The décor was a mix of *African Queen*, cargo cult, and *Pirates of the Caribbean*—twinkling pin lights in the fake thatch, bamboo walls, fiberglass spearfish and Styrofoam sharks caught in the ceiling nets—but the cooking smells coming from the kitchen were wonderful, and the entire glass front of the bar opened up onto the Mediterranean Sea, which was a shimmering field of deep blue under an opal sky.

A dazzling young waitress in a gauzy sarong that was struggling unsuccessfully to hold the line in the face of overwhelming pressures gave them a saucy smile and led them to a large booth overlooking the Med.

She took the stuffed parrot with the RESERVED sign in its beak off the table and seemed utterly thrilled to bring them a bottle of Perrier Jouët champagne and two iced glasses.

"And would you let Jacko know," said Fyke, touching the waitress's arm before she turned away, "that Ibis says hello?"

"'Ibis'?" she said, her expression faltering, and then she recovered. "Of course, Mr. . . . Ibis?"

"Yes," said Fyke with a piratical leer. "Ibis. Like the bird."

When she was gone, Nikki leaned into him, trying to make herself heard above Astrud Gilberto, who, Nikki felt, ought to be over the girl from Ipanema by now.

"Wasn't IBIS your operational ID in Kosovo?"

"That it was," said Fyke, watching a cluster of giggling young blondes bobble past their booth. "And Mikey was Shrike. That's how Joko knew us back in Pristina. It'll bring him running, if only to see who's pulling his . . . Who's playing a game with him."

In a few minutes, their champagne arrived, in a dripping silver bucket, along with two matching Art Nouveau flutes. The Sarong Girl wrung the bottle's neck like a Sunday chicken and poured out two fizzy servings, saying as she did so, "I spoke to Mr. Joko, sir. He's in his office now, but he'll be out in a moment."

"Thank you," said Fyke, trying manfully to keep his eyes up on her face. And then, breaking away with an almost audible snap, he lifted his flute in a toast to Nikki, who looked no less hypnotic in a light cotton sundress with a gold chain around her neck, her auburn hair pulled back and caught in a golden ribbon, the pin lights reflecting in her hazel eyes, and her already olive skin now tanned a rich milky chocolate with a satin sheen.

Fyke, taking a pull at his champagne, was thinking that if ever carnal temptation was made flesh, she was sitting across from him right now. It was going to take ten Hail Marys and possibly Divine Intervention to get him back to Marcy Cannon in a sinless state. Nikki, aware of his deep appreciation and grimly determined to keep him at bay—she'd had it with all men, forever, and was giving some idle thought to becoming either a lesbian or a nun—*ping*ed him back with a cheerful smile, touched her flute to her lips and then set it gently down, her attention shifting as a bulky and humanoid monster with a full black beard and tiny black eyes buried deep in a puffy roast-beef complexion emerged from the crowd to loom over their table.

Joko in the flesh, she presumed, wearing a hula shirt over a huge expanse of belly like a spinnaker, the shirttails draped over ragged cutoff jeans, and, to her practiced eye, carrying some sort of pistol in the waistband. The creature showed a set of large brown canine teeth to Nikki and then turned to look at Fyke, his smile fading into a puzzled frown.

"It is you. By God, it really is."

"So it is, Joko," said Fyke, smiling up at him, risking a paw and getting it back from Joko's punch-press grip without any permanent damage. "May I introduce you to my associate, Miss Beatrice Gandolfo?"

After a brief hesitation—most of the "associates" he met in his line of business were beefy, beetle-browed thugs from the local union halls—Joko sat down beside Nikki, giving her a detailed once-over with obvious approval.

"Miss Gandolfo, I'm Joko Levon," he said in a deep voice with a thick Israeli accent. "The ee-PON-ee-muss owner of this humble place."

"Lovely to meet you," she said, smiling and offering a hand she felt she could spare, getting it back safely, and giving the hulk some breathing room. Joko showed her his canines again and then turned to Fyke, laying his heavy forearms on the table.

"Ray. You Irish Mick prick. Sonia tells me Ibis. I say, What the fu . . . I say I do not believe her. You scare the latkes out of me. So. You look well fed, for a change. Not so much like a starving wolfhound. How goes it? You still with the Amis?"

"No," said Fyke with a thin, even a bitter, smile. "Got my watch and garters last year. Retired now."

Joko nodded as if confirming this.

"Yes. I make a call when I hear is maybe Ibis. Last we hear of you, you are in Port Moresby. Then you are not."

"Yes. Then I am not," said Fyke. "My business was done, no point hanging about waiting for the peelers to clap me in bilboes. And you? Still stranded on the Med like a beached beluga?"

Joko glanced at Nikki and then back at Fyke.

"The lady associate?"

"The lady associate knows you were once a member of the Mossad, which, last time I checked, is still a perfectly legal organization to belong to. Miss Gandolfo is also a very good friend of Israel, as I am, or I would not have brought her. She is traveling with me on a research project."

"I see," he said, his expression indicating that he saw nothing of the kind. "What sort of research project, miss?"

Nikki rooted around in her purse, came up with one of Cather's legend cards. "This man is a professor at the University of Virginia. I'm interviewing people who used to be active in the intelligence world. Sort of an archive work, an academic history, meant largely as an in-house training tool. Nothing that could affect the real world. If you like, you can call that number and verify—"

Joko waved the card away but not rudely.

"I always trust a pretty girl with hazel eyes. You think to learn something academic from me, Miss Gandolfo?"

"No," said Fyke. "She does not. I'm the specimen in her bottle, Joko. But since she's along for the ride, I thought it would be interesting for her to meet another old operator."

"Old? I am fifty-four only. You are, what, ninety-three?"

"Much older. It's the whisky preserves me. Look, Joko, time being fleet for both of us, and lovely as it is to banter with an old comrade, I got to be straight—"

"Hah! Straight like drain snake."

"I'm here to ask you to put in a word for an old friend—"

Joko's face hardened up.

"This have anything to do with what your *old friend* did a few days ago in Vienna?"

Fyke leaned back, laid his hands palm up on the table.

"Joko. My lad. I thought you were out of the game?"

"I am retired. Not deaf. You are Ibis, he was Shrike. You two are the famous Birdmen who did so much to make the Serbs and Croats unhappy in Pristina. Is it to be a coincidence when Ibis appears just as the name Shrike is on everybody's lips?"

"I guess not. Yes, it's about him—"

Joko held up a massive callused palm.

"I *knew* the man, you know. The dead man in the trunk of the Saab. He was my training officer. An old and valued friend. Also a patriot. A hero. His wife and kids, after he does not come back from the Negev and goes to Venice instead, we took care of his family. Whatever they needed—money, college, medical, dental, friendship—whatever was needed. For all those years. Took care also that they not ever know too much of what those Jordanian pigs did to him. You remember Ya'el Bar Zev?"

"Wiry. Looked like a starving ferret? Dark, brooding kid?"

Joko inclined his head, not taking his small eyes off Fyke, his voice a thick rumbling rasp deep in his throat.

"Yes. He and some others, they hunt down and punish every Jordanian officer what did this thing. Only Ya'el does not come back out of Jurf al-Darwish . . ." Joko shrugged, his shoulders lifting and falling with huge seismic shudders. "This is business, you know? Like with your people. You lose somebody you love, then somebody on the other side pays. Is the rule."

Fyke's smile was in place but now carried more threat than warmth. "Just as long as the *right* people pay."

Fyke leaned forward, speaking in a low, flat tone.

"Hear me, Joko. The boys should know—*you* should know—*it wasn't him*. The boys should back off. He and your friend, they were comrades. Fought a nasty little street war in Venice and then across the Adriatic in Kotor. In Trieste too. The man we're talking about, he did not do this."

Joko leaned in close to Fyke, inches apart.

"I know of this nasty little war. I also know when it is over. And

Shrike goes on killing Serbs in Venice anyway. Kills four men with his bare hands. Hunts an old man named Mirko Belajic through the streets, puts a bullet in his eye. Inside a Christian chapel! My friend says to him, 'You are crazy. Suicidal crazy. Get out of Venice.' Galan says to him, 'Get out of Venice and do not come back.'"

"Shrike did not kill Issadore Galan, Joko. He has been—"

"Set up? Hah. Proof, we have been given, Ray. Hard proof."

"No. Not possible. Faked."

"'Faked'?" said Joko in a growl. "Faked is Shrike's own voice? Your friends, the Amis, they have him on tape, from his cell phone, when he is in Vienna hunting Galan—"

"His cell-phone tape? How did *you* get it?"

"From his own people. The CIA. There is internal investigation of Shrike. For stealing Agency funds, for going crazy. Once he cut off a man's head with a hatchet and send it to some American cop, did you know that? There is picture of this. Did you know he owns a town house in London? On agent salary? Also apartment in Venice, also has a big boat? How does he do all that? I am a bar owner only, for which I still pay fat slug mortgage, and I am thirty years with the Mossad!"

"The house in London, far as I know, he inherited from—"

"Oh yes. From old maiden aunt. Ray, our friend is on tape threatening Galan. I myself have heard it. I know Shrike's voice—

"Joko, that's bullshit, and you know it."

"Yeah. What he says, and I have heard it. He is talking to some woman at Langley, she is not identified. He makes the call from the bar at the Regina Hotel in the Ring. On the tape he says, 'Galan's a problem, a nasty one. I need to take care of it.'"

That stopped Fyke for a moment.

Joko pressed his point.

"See. He says so himself. Galan is a problem. He needs to take care of it. And he does. He kills Galan, puts him in Saab—"

"Why, Joko? Ask yourself. Why would he do that?"

"Why? Because Galan chases him out of Venice. Maybe Galan also knows too much about his money, where he gets it. Time to shut up an inconvenient old Jew."

"So he *tortures* him to death, Joko?"

Joko shrugged that off with a flat look of cold dislike.

"Got to know what the old man knows."

Something seemed to leave Fyke then. He leaned back in the booth, looking at Joko as if seeing him for the first time.

"So you're not going to call the boys off?"

Joko shrugged, looked around the room as if he were expecting somebody, came back to Fyke.

"Ray, listen good. When I hear you are in the bar, I make a call."

"You shit. You called the Office."

"Yes. I did. They think you know where Micah Dalton is."

Fyke got up, put his hands on the table, leaned in close to Joko, who pulled back, lifting his hands up to ward off a blow.

"Here's a promise, then, Joko my old friend. You tell the lads when they get here that if they want to go to war with Mikey and me, we'll give them all the war they want. You follow?"

"I follow," said Joko, looking over Fyke's shoulder as three lean military-looking men in faded jeans and light summer jackets came in through the glass doors, already scanning the bar.

"But maybe you tell them yourself?"

Staryi Krim

Under a sky of Prussian blue, the central highlands of the Crimean Peninsula spread out in front of the Lancer like a patchwork cape. As they gained altitude, the lush farmlands slowly gave way to stony outcroppings and bare-bones ridgetops, the spring green and gold of the tilled lands fading into prairie foothills, relieved here and there by a darker green cloak of scrub forest. There wasn't much in the way of civilization up here, just a few cleared acres with squat little farmhouses tucked into lee corners out of the winter winds. Cruising at a steady eighty klicks on what was fairly good two-lane blacktop, they soon reached altitudes where the Crimean winter still lingered, a harsh, semidesert landscape dotted with weathered and deeply scored outcrops of rock rising above a sea of prairie grass, here and there a stand of stunted trees and a patch of plowed field, a few head of skinny cattle, mixed in with shaggy little goats, picking a scarce living out of the gorse. It was a sullen and wintry desolation that soon grew tiresome, which Mandy dealt with by fluffing a pillow behind her neck, reclining the passenger seat, and drifting off into quiet contemplation of the previous evening.

Dalton found a tape—an actual audiotape—stuffed into the glove compartment, turned it over in the light. Theme music from *Memoirs of a Geisha*, with Yo-Yo Ma. It seemed to fit the landscape. He looked over at Mandy, at the taut skin along the side of her neck and her face at rest in the pale light. She was not a young girl anymore, but every year she seemed to grow more lovely, as if, like Merlin, her beauty was traveling backward through time.

He reached over and pulled her cloak up around her shoulders. She sighed, said something he could not make out, and slipped back into her dreams.

Around noon, they broke out of the grasslands and crested a summit of the inland range, where they found a fair-sized town called Bilohirsk. It was a rickety collection of concrete storage sheds and transit yards, with some Soviet-era concrete housing blocks scattered around the terrain laid out in a distorted grid on the southern slopes of a razorback mountain.

Since he hadn't seen a gas station since Simferopol, Dalton turned off the road and pulled into a bleak little square lined with shabby shops and crowded vodka bars. He was hoping to find a trucking depot or a car lot where, if he was prepared to pay an outrageous markup, perhaps they'd sell him some gasoline that wouldn't immediately destroy the engine. The Lancer, by the local standards a vehicle roughly equivalent to a UFO materializing in a luminous green cloud, attracted a lot of sullen attention.

Dalton's fingernails' grip on the Slavic languages wasn't much help, but after getting a lot of blank stares and muttered rejections he was able to find a black-market stall on the eastern edge of the town and a grizzled old Kalmuck there willing to sell him some gas at about twice the going rate.

Dalton paid him in euros. The old man handled the crisp new bills as if they were pieces of the True Cross, smiling so broadly that his bright blue eyes disappeared in the folds of leathery skin around his eyes, the sunlight glinting off his silver tooth, which was also his only tooth. Mandy, who because of her father's mining interests in the region spoke Ukrainian and Russian fairly well, stayed asleep—or pretended to—throughout the entire exchange, a half smile playing on her slightly puffy lips.

A few miles on, and they were crossing a winding river valley filled with pine forests. Theirs was the only vehicle moving along a deteriorating road that snaked between low stepped hills, with roughly two hundred klicks between them and Kerch. Mandy sat up, looking off to the south, where she could see a faint brown object floating in midair along a forested slope. She used a pair of binoculars supplied by the hotel to take a closer look at the small beige dot.

"It's a helicopter. One of those ugly Russian things with the two stubby engines and all those propellers."

"You mean a Kamov. And I think they're called rotors."

Mandy took the binoculars away and pulled out the folded map that she had stuffed into the side pocket, unfolding it with some difficulty.

"Odd," she said, drawing a circle around the closest village, a place called Staryi Krim, "Nothing here but the ruins of a monastery and a museum for some writer named Alexander Grin. Even the Amosov heart clinic only runs in the summer. It's just a wide spot in the road, less than five thousand people, and there's nothing else in the region that would justify a helicopter. Unless they use them to herd the goats, which seems a tad excessive."

"Yes. Down in the farmlands, they use Kamovs as crop dusters. What's it doing up here?" he asked, straining to see the dot against the backdrop of green trees.

"Well," said Mandy, studying the chopper through the binoculars. "If I were in the espionage game, I'd say it was tracking us. It seems to be moving in a parallel line along the highway . . . he's keeping his distance . . . But it's definitely possible we've attracted somebody's attention. Any suggestions?"

"Yes. Look innocent."

Mandy put the glasses down, gave him an eyebrow.

"Too late for that, dear boy."

She studied the little brown dot for a time.

"Not trying very hard to avoid detection, are they?"

Dalton, who didn't like this development at all, was looking for some sort of cover anywhere up ahead just in case the chopper was hostile. "We just passed a little village back there . . ."

"Hrushivka," said Mandy, catching his tone. "But there was nothing there we could stick this truck in. Besides, the people around here don't seem all that friendly. Not a smile as we went through. Nothing but frowny faces, like a Young Republicans float in a Gay Pride parade. Anyway, it's too late for escape and evasion, I think."

"Why?"

"He's coming in for a closer look."

Dalton, craning his neck to look out the side window, saw the little brown dot getting bigger, turning into a stubby little ball with two fat attachments on the sides—the housings of its two piston engines. As he watched, the chopper tilted forward, its six rotors divided into two glittering disks, one above the other, sunlight reflecting off the machine's glass snout.

"A Kamov Two-Six," he said in a low tone, recalling the machine's capabilities. "Crew of two, can carry six passengers with the optional cargo box. Top speed around one-sixty, ceiling maxes out at nine thousand feet, range: four hundred and fifty klicks."

"Aren't you the little fountain of utterly useless data. He's coming in pretty fast. I'd suggest you do something clever."

Dalton, watching the chopper getting larger and larger, could see a white oval through the windshield, the face of the pilot, and another oval, a second man, beside him. The crackling mutter of the chopper's piston engines was getting louder. At about five hundred feet out, the chopper banked right, less than fifty feet off the pine canopy, and began to track the Lancer, matching its speed. As the chopper showed it angular profile—a lot like a dragonfly—Dalton could see that there was no passenger pod.

So, two people: a pilot and a spare.

"It looks like someone is pointing a camera at us," said Mandy. "Shall I wave?"

"Are you sure it's a camera?"

Mandy lifted the binoculars, studied the craft.

"Yes. No. Binoculars. What should we do?"

"It's their play," said Dalton. "Maybe they're just curious about the truck. And, yes, wave if you want."

Mandy, rolling the window down, gave them a gay flutter and a charming smile, and then rolled the glass back up. Nobody waved back. Dalton kept the truck steady, passing a sign:

STARYI KRIM 15 K

"If the pilot wants to do something snaky about us," said Mandy, "he's only got a few klicks left before we reach about five thousand witnesses."

"Yes," said Dalton, checking the rearview mirror, seeing nothing but a curve of eroding blacktop lined with dense pine forest. Up ahead, there was more of the same. "What's he doing?"

"He's . . . He's banking again. Coming our way."

"Okay. Put away anything loose and check your pistol."

Mandy shoved anything that was hard-edged or pointy into the glove and side compartments, got her SIG out and made sure there was a round in the chamber, checked her mag as well, her movements calm and steady as they always were when they had to be. Dalton kept his eye on the chopper, which was now on a course to cross the highway about a half klick in front of them, running very low, just skimming a tree line. As he flashed past the opening of a small side road on his right, barely a rutted track, he saw something brown and bulky out of the corner of his eye.

He checked his rearview mirror and saw a large mud-colored flat-bed truck pull out of the lane, jolting into the road behind him, and then accelerating quickly.

"Okay," he said, pulling the Anaconda out of its case on the rear seat, "now it begins. We have a truck behind us."

Mandy looked back, her face registering the truck and going a little whiter. "Not a coincidence, is it?"

"No. And look at the chopper."

The chopper had come to a hover just above the tree line at the edge of the highway. Painted a dull tan, it carried no registration numbers, no corporate or service markings of any kind, which was highly illegal even here in the Crimean.

They watched as it rotated around to face them, sliding sideways and down, rocking as the rotors kicked up a cloud of leaves and dust. It lowered, touched the pavement, settled into its struts, and now sat dead in the middle of their road about three hundred yards away. They were on a narrow stretch of deserted highway, scrub forest or prairie grass on either side, stony hills all around, with a chopper sitting on the road ahead and, behind them, down to a slow crawl, the flatbed truck, its motor chugging roughly. Two men were visible behind the dusty windshield.

"A neat little trap," said Mandy. "Any suggestions?"

"See the stand of forest up there on our left?"

Mandy nodded.

"I'm going to put us next to it. We'll have some cover there. Okay? One thing, Mandy. If it comes down to it with these guys, save yourself a round, Mandy. Save a round."

She smiled at him, nodding, but said nothing, not a tremor showing, her expression calm, although she was even more pale than usual

for an English rose. Dalton braced his arms on the wheel and accelerated, pushing the Lancer up through the gears, redlining the pedal,
getting some distance between them and the truck to their rear, trying
to get level with a small scrub forest about a hundred feet up the road.
He watched as the chopper rocked on its struts, the two side doors
popped open, and two men got out, both wearing rough farmhand
clothing: tan bib overalls, heavy boots, dark shirts. Both men were big
and hard-looking, and both were carrying AK-47s. One was an older
man with a grizzled Mohawk. The bald one on the right was Smoke,
his burn scars glistening in the light, his eyes two slits, his mouth a
rippled, distorted leer.

"Dear God. What a hideous *troll*. Is that—"

"Yes," said Dalton. "That's him."

Smoke lifted the AK, aimed it at the Lancer, sighting low. Dalton
hit the brakes and cranked the wheel to the left as the AK's muzzle
burst into a sparkle of blue-and-red fire. The grille of the Lancer took
three heavy rounds, from headlight to headlight, shuddering from
the impacts. A ricochet starred the windshield. Dalton fought the
Lancer to a grinding stop up against the stand of pines, cracked the
door, and said to Mandy, "Into the forest. Go in deep. Take a good
position and go to ground. Cover up. Stay hidden. Hide your muzzle
flash. Pick them off one by one. Go."

She was out of the Lancer and racing into the woods just as the
flatbed truck, air brakes hissing, shuddered to a stop a hundred feet
down the road. Dalton, his blood rising up, one image flooding his
mind—Galan's butchered corpse in the trunk of the Saab—stepped
out into the middle of the highway. Smoke and Mohawk were coming in at a dead run—now perhaps a hundred yards away—a very
long shot for his Colt. Smoke stopped and aimed his AK.

Dalton, not expecting a hit, just hoping to rattle these guys enough
to throw off their aim, fired three quick rounds, the Colt jumping in

his hands. Amazingly, both men went to the ground. Smoke, his rifle clattering away, rolled to his left, got to his feet, grabbed his AK off the tarmac, and stumbled into the prairie grass on Dalton's right.

A hit, thought Dalton. *A hit.*

Mohawk, still in the game, was up now in a firing crouch, his AK muzzle lighting up as Dalton watched. But his aim was too high, and heavy rounds hummed over Dalton's head and bounced off the roof of the truck behind him, the rest cracking into the pines a long way down the road. Dalton heard a shrill cry from someone inside the truck. Taking his time, he aimed three more rounds, and Mohawk flinched backward, falling flat to the pavement. Dalton pulled an autoloader out of his pocket, reloaded, snapped the cylinder shut, and turned to deal with the men in the flatbed truck.

He saw a brief flash, heard the solid crack of an AK, and flinched as a round hummed by his ear, smacking into a little pine tree by the side of the road and cutting it in two. Another wisp of muzzle smoke, more flashes, more thudding cracks.

At least one of the 7.62mm rounds, a slug as big as a lipstick tube, hummed by inches from his cheek. A second one passed so close to his neck that he could feel the heat of it on his skin and the slug plucking at his hair. The shooter, who was too damned good, was firing from the flatbed behind the cab, steadying his barrel on the cab's roof. Taking this guy out was a priority. Zeroing in on the patch of shadow in the middle of the truck's rear window, Dalton fired twice, the pistol bucking in his hands. The windshield shattered, and the shadow behind it fell away.

He heard a high-pitched shriek and saw a skinny figure tumble off the side of the flatbed, landing on the tarmac like a sack of meat. Another crack, another muzzle flash, this time from the side of the truck. Behind him, Dalton could hear the sound of a man running and turned to see how close he was. Still no sign of Smoke, but Mohawk was on his feet and coming in. With a good seventy feet to cover, his weapon at port arms as he lumbered down the road, he apparently was not confident enough about his shooting skills to take a shot at Dalton or was too worried about hitting the flatbed again. Dalton heard the man's breath chuffing, his boots thumping on the pavement, something metallic jingling at his belt. He had a few seconds.

Dalton came back to the flatbed truck, steadied his sights, and squeezed off three more rounds. They punched through the metal hood with an audible clang, paint chips and metal slivers flying up, with a distinct meaty impact as one of the rounds hit its target. A small man on the far side of the truck fender fell back and away, his rifle flying onto the rocks.

Time to deal with Mohawk.

Dalton spun sharply around on one heel and brought the Colt up just as Mohawk came skidding to a clumsy stop less than fifty feet away, freezing with his AK halfway up into a firing position.

No sign of Smoke. Had Dalton killed him? As easily as that? Not bloody likely. Mohawk, a barrel-bodied packet of bone and gristle with a squashed nose and scarred skin all around his eyes—maybe a boxer?—squinted into the muzzle of Dalton's Colt, the big revolver steady as a gravestone and aimed right at his forehead.

This usually gives one pause, as it did Mohawk. He saw two of his men near the flatbed truck, one lying in the ditch and very still, the other lying in the road in a fetal position and holding his belly, his legs kicking, whimpering. Wisps of gun smoke hung in the chilly, pine-scented air.

Mohawk looked around for his partner. Not a sign. He looked up. Nothing but Prussian blue. To either side of him, a wall of trees. Behind him, a chopper he did not know how to fly. And in front of him, a tall, rangy blond-haired man with a granite face and pale blue eyes holding a massive stainless-steel revolver.

"Put the weapon down and live," said Dalton in a low, carrying tone, icy calm, but very aware that he had only one round left in the Colt and that if the man had good eyes he'd know it too.

Mohawk's eyes flickered around the area as if he were hoping for Smoke to appear, for a shot out of the forest, to save him.

Then he came back to Dalton.

"You are Dalton?" he asked with a heavy Serbian accent.

"Put the weapon down."

He shook his head.

"No. I put weapon down, Vukov kill me."

"Is Vukov the man with the burned face?"

"Yes. You are *Krokodil*. You are the man who burns him."

"Glad to hear it. Now, put your weapon down."

"I . . . can't . . . Vukov, he don't like cowards."

"What's your name?"

"My name?" he repeated and then stiffened, his expression hardening. "I am Branislav Petrasevic. I fight in Kosovo, in Srebrenica, in Pristina. Kill all my enemies. I am . . . *Skorpioni*!"

"Vukov is the coward, Petrasevic. Not you. You stayed to fight. Like a soldier. Like a Skorpion. Good for you. But I will still kill you if you don't put the gun down."

Dalton said nothing more, concentrating on the forward sight of the Anaconda, which was zeroed on the man's forehead, thinking, *Where the hell is Vukov? One AK shot from the tall grass, and I'm through. Where the hell is he? Wounded? Dead?*

In the taut stillness, Dalton heard no movement from the little wood where he had last seen the man, no stealthy flanking approach coming through the long grass. Just silence, other than the soft breeze hissing in the grasses and the chuffing sound of the man's breathing, which was short and sharp, and getting shorter and sharper as his body reacted to the adrenaline racing through his body. Mohawk's eyes were fixed on Dalton's face, pale brown eyes with a gold fleck in them. His leathery skin was seamed, weather-beaten, scarred, and he had not shaved for a couple of days, the beard on his face showing ash gray against his sunken cheeks. Dalton could hear his mind working.

Fight or surrender?

Live or die?

Something changed in the air between them. The man's eyes widened, his knuckles whitened on the stock of his rifle, the muzzle began to move, and Dalton put a .44 Magnum round through the man's forehead. The round blew the back of the man's head apart, the crown of the skull spinning away like a saucer. What remained of Branislav Petrasevic went straight down, collapsing into itself, until the knees struck the ground. And then his body toppled forward, hitting the pavement face-first, no bounce. The jagged bowl of his exploded skull dumped blood and pink brains out in a lumpy arc across the tarmac.

DALTON, reloading, ran back to the flatbed truck, found the man with the belly wound lying at the side of it. He was a very young, very skinny kid with a wet white face and wild blue eyes, tears streaming down his cheeks. He was lying in a lake of blood, his lips blue, his hands clutching his belly, purple ropes of intestine bulging through his bloody fingers. His breathing was shallow and rapid.

He looked up as Dalton walked over. He opened his mouth, started to say something, Dalton had no idea what. Dalton leaned down, touched the muzzle to the kid's temple. The kid jerked his head backward, said, "Jesus no, Jesus," but Dalton put a round into his head anyway, shattering the kid's skull like a pumpkin..

Then he walked around the tailgate to the far side of the truck, found the other man sprawled in a ditch, his AK a few feet away. Another half-formed kid, barely in his teens.

Dalton's round had struck the boy in the throat, blowing it wide open. His head was almost completely severed from his neck, attached only by some stringy sinew and what was left of his spinal column. Dalton stared down at the ruins.

What were these clowns *thinking*?

And who was *training* them? Or failing to train them?

Raise them up on stupid hate, prattle on about glory, about the motherland, but teach them fuck-all about fire control or small-unit tactics and then stuff them into the grinder. Such a waste.

Dalton picked up the kid's AK, checked the magazine: seventeen rounds left. He stuffed the Colt into his belt, hefted the AK into patrol position, moved through the long grass and up into the little wood of twisted trees where he had last seen Vukov.

It was cool and shadowed inside the thicket, although sunlight dappled the rust-colored, needle-strewn ground, and beams stirred like golden straws in the rich green darkness. He moved as quietly as he could, which was very quietly indeed, slipping over the ground, stepping carefully across the deadfall and the broken branches of long-dead trees, breathing through his open mouth, listening with all of his mind and heart.

He saw something flit through a pillar of sunlight a hundred feet away, got a glimpse of a squat, bulky figure dragging an AK, limping badly. Dalton *had* hit him, at least once, but he was still covering the ground, moving very fast.

"Vukov!" he shouted.

The running figure stopped abruptly, a dun-colored shadow barely visible through the trees and the prairie grass like a lion on the veldt, and shouted back at him, "Kill all my boys with that fucking big gun? You pretty damned good, Slick. No matter. Next time coming. And the woman. I do her first, make you watch!"

"Talk, Vukov. Gutless talk. Come and finish it."

"Fuck you, Slick. Come and get me."

And then he was moving again, nimble, fast, darting through the grass and scrub trees, going up a slope,

Getting away.

Dalton, his blood up, started after him, got no farther than three steps, and then he realized that he couldn't leave Mandy alone. She would be waiting for him to come back or for Vukov to double around, find her, and kill her. Which was what would happen if he was stupid enough or angry enough to take the bait.

Protect your base of fire, the first principle of combat. Mandy was good, but Vukov was probably better. And Vukov wasn't the main point right now. The main point was reaching Kerch, finding Dobri Levka, trying to take this whole thing apart.

As a consolation, Dalton fired off a three-round burst. He saw Vukov in the distance dodge, tumble down into the long grass, get back up on his feet in a second, his tan figure melting into a stand of poplars. Dalton sent another long burst into the trees. The muzzle blast slammed and boomed and echoed in the stillness. The cocking bolt locked open, and the weapon was empty, the sounds of the gunshots dying away into a rumble. Slender showers of bark dust came drifting down through the shafts of sunlight all around him, the gun smoke curling inside them too, the cool air full of the coal oil and carbon reek of burnt cordite.

"Soon, Vukov," he shouted into the silence, his voice echoing off the hills all around him. "Soon!"

Dalton stood there for another minute, his heart rate slowing, his anger cooling, suddenly very tired, his unprotected ears ringing painfully from the gunfire, half deaf, in a muted, muffled world.

He sighed heavily, turned, walked out of the thicket, crossed the road, and went in again on the far side. The stand of trees here was dappled and silent as well, as if waiting for something to happen. He stood there for a long moment, listening.

"Mandy? It's Micah. Are you here?"

A rustle forty feet to his left, and Mandy, rising up out of a little hollow filled with dead leaves and pine needles, got to her feet, needles and leaf bits clinging to her hair, her jeans, and her leather jacket. "Yes, I'm bloody here."

Dalton walked over to her, started to help her brush the needles off, but she smacked his hand away, handed him the SIG, pulled the leather jacket off, and then her turtleneck sweater, Mandy frantically running her hands all over her body, swearing like a trooper.

"What's the matter?" he asked, picking her jacket up.

"Go to ground, you said." To his damaged hearing, her voice was sounding as if it were coming through cotton. "And didn't I just? Something was eating me! Something crawly and horrid. Can you see anything?" she said, turning around and brushing at herself.

"Yes, I can," he said, his voice too loud in his own skull, "And it's all quite lovely."

She stopped, gave him a look through her tousled hair.

"Bugs, I mean, you toad! God, I *hate* nature. We're not paving it nearly fast enough! Soon the whole bloody planet will be infested with bloody nature. 'Go to ground,' he says! *Chipmunks* go to ground, Micah. Next time, *you* go to ground and have crawly things climb up *your* bum. I'll be happy to stand around and shoot people. Have I got anything horrible crawling on me? Stop leering, you pervert. I mean it. Have I?"

"Nope. You're bug-free," said Dalton, keeping the grin under control as he shook out her sweater and her jacket, handing them back in the appropriate sequence. As her head popped up through her turtleneck, her hair in a state, she nodded toward the road.

"How did it go? I heard that hand cannon of yours. I trust you were of some practical use out there? I certainly wasn't."

Dalton was about to tell her what happened when they heard the sound of the chopper's engines beginning to whine.

"Dammit," he said. "Vukov!"

Dalton, followed closely by Mandy, ran back out to the edge of the highway, getting there in time to see the rotors spinning, smoke rising from the Kamov's exhaust. Even at two hundred yards, they could make out the face of Vukov through the windshield.

Dalton, dumping his empty magazine, ran back to the truck where the dead kid with the belly wound was lying, found a spare mag in his pocket, smacked it home, released the cocking lever, set the fire selector to single shot, got the butt up against his shoulder and his cheek on the stock, and started firing methodically at the chopper, taking his time, adjusting after each shot, the weapon kicking back into his shoulder. He was putting out aimed fire at a target that was right in the middle of the AK's effective combat range. And he was getting hits. Yellow ricochet sparks flickered off the fuselage of the Kamov as each round came in.

Armored, thought Dalton.

Now the rotors were at full speed, and the chopper was off the ground, banking hard to the left, showing the underbelly of the cockpit.

Dalton switched to full auto and put out another ten rounds, walking his fire onto the rear slope of the cockpit floor. He saw the airframe judder from hits, but Vukov tilted his machine forward, full military power, and clawed his way into the sky, gaining distance with every cycle, the prop wash shaking the tall grass and whipping the tips of the trees into a lashing blur.

Definitely armored.

Dalton, frustrated, angry with himself—*I should have chased him down*—emptied the rest of the magazine into the rotors, which ought to have been shredded by the rifle fire. But somehow the Kamov held steady, going straight northeast toward Staryi Krim, shrinking into a small brown dot that finally, after a flash of sunlight off the tail boom, disappeared into the blue.

Mandy walked over and stood beside him, looking around at the dead men on the ground, at the flatbed truck sitting in the middle of the road, its engine still ticking over, at the litter of spent shells scattered all over the highway.

"Christ, what an ungodly mess," she said. "What now? We sit here and wait for Triple A?"

Dalton looked across at the Lancer, jammed up against the pines, tilting crazily, both doors wide open.

"Can you see if the car will start? I'll police up the shells, dump the bodies in the truck, drive it back to that side road."

She looked down at the spray of blood and brains in the middle of the highway. "And . . . this ghastly stuff?"

Dalton looked down at it, gave her a haggard smile.

"Roadkill."

AFTER some fiddling with the wiring, the Lancer, to Mandy's delight, started on the third try, coughing to life, something metallic clanging loudly under the hood. She popped the fairing and jerked a piece of plastic grillwork out of the cooling-fan housing. The rounds had chewed up the headlights and the hood, and a large hole had been punched into the windshield-wiper tank. The engine block had a shiny groove carved into its side, but the slug had not come in at a direct enough angle to break through three inches of steel. This was a very lucky Lancer, she decided, putting the car in gear, backing it out into the highway, and heading back down to the side road after Dalton.

She found him standing by the driver's side of the car, his hands full of papers, some of them bloodstained. He looked up, his expression grim, as she pulled the Lancer into the cut.

He came over to get in on the passenger side and was still riffling through the papers as Mandy backed the Lancer out, turned east again, heading for Staryi Krim. The front suspension was unsteady, one of the headlight housings was clattering in the wind, and there was a large, crab-shaped bullet-star crack in the middle of the windshield, but the car was still working. And they were still alive. Mandy looked at the dashboard clock and was surprised to discover that the whole encounter had lasted about fifteen minutes.

"What have you got there?" she asked, keeping an eye out for the Kamov, half expecting it to pop up above the tree line.

Dalton looked up from the papers in his hands, smiled across at Mandy. Mandy thought he looked ill, sick at heart,

"They were kids. Back there. Poor, bloody kids. Look at this one," he said, holding out a black cardboard ID case with a color photo of a bony-faced, big-eared boy with a broad, snaggletoothed smile.

"His name was Giorgy Medic. If I can make out the language, he was seventeen. Makes you feel like a shit, killing kids. The one at the side of the truck, he was still alive when I got to him, but he'd been hit in the belly with a forty-four. A miserable death, unless he got medevaced out."

Mandy did not have to ask what Dalton had done. She would have done the same, or she hoped she would have. They drove on a while in silence, a mile later passing a faded sign:

STARYI KRIM 2 K

Dalton was still looking at the kid's ID.

"Interesting," he said, holding the card out. "He's from Sid. That's a little town near Belgrade. Sid is where most of the Skorpions came from. The Medic family had a lot of people in the Skorpions. Slobodan Medic was the one who ordered the massacre at Trnovo, in Srebrenica, in 1995. The Skorpions even made a video. Walked these Muslims into a little wooded clearing, shot them in the back with their AKs. Talking and smoking and laughing as if it were some kind of office picnic. See this?"

He touched the image in the upper right corner of the ID card, a black flag with red lettering in an arc above a bright green scorpion.

"That's the banner the Skorpions fought under in 1995. They were still using it at Podujevo in 1999. And they're *still* around."

"What does the other little flag mean?"

She tapped a small rectangle in the upper left-hand corner of the card. "Looks like some sort of symbol. Maybe a clenched fist?"

"It's on all their IDs—at least, the three bodies I searched. The Skorpion banner and this thing. I've seen it before. Galan had it on the computer at his flat. He said he was finding it on some KLA websites. He mentioned it in his note to me. He thought it was some sort of unit crest for the Skorpions."

"It means *something* to them if they're putting it on their military ID cards."

"I'm a little worried about how far ahead of us these guys are. They were waiting for us, had an ambush all laid out."

"You had to expect that."

"I expected them to make a move in Kerch. Not here in the middle of the damned peninsula."

"Even without Galan's attempt to reach Irina Kuldic, which is why they killed him, the Russians—"

"Kirikoff."

"Kirikoff. Yes, he had to know that once you found out about the Russians taking Levka and the *Subito* you'd come to Kerch anyway just to find out why. He'd got a snootful of your style last winter in Istanbul. He would *expect* you to come back at him, which, by the way, is exactly what you *are* doing, isn't it?"

"Yes. I know. Predictable as hell."

"I think someone in Sevastopol was put there to watch for you. You're quite memorable. If Kirikoff knew you were in Sevastopol, very likely headed for Kerch, it would make sense to set a trap for you out on a lonely road somewhere. What he *didn't* count on was you killing three of his men and chasing the fourth into the wild blue yonder with his arse shot full of buckshot. But he knew you'd be coming. It's your idiom, isn't it, dear boy?"

"Seems to be," he said, rubbing his cheeks with both hands and sighing. "But what else can I do? I'm all out of pixie dust. And God's not returning my calls."

"Mine neither," said Mandy with a smile. "But Satan keeps in touch."

"He would, wouldn't he?" said Dalton. "Since he's a relative. I keep thinking about the Kamov. Not very many of them around in the Crimea. Too expensive for this area. Can't be more than ten in the whole peninsula, and most of those would be down around the resort areas. Yalta, Sevastopol, Balaklava, Jasper Beach."

"So why keep one around here? In the middle of nowhere? Is that what you're thinking?"

"Yes. You'd have to have a damned good reason. It's not just the machine itself. Choppers need a lot of maintenance, as much as three hours for every hour of flying time. The operational range for a Kamov Two-Six is about three hundred miles. That's one-fifty out and one-fifty back home again, unless they have a FARP—"

"Micah, did we not agree on a no-acronyms policy?"

"Sorry. A forward area refueling post. Someplace at the other end where they could count on getting fuel. As we've seen, fuel is an issue around here. There'd have to be some sort of central support base, a supply depot, spare-parts warehouse, technicians to do the work, a hangar to keep it out of the weather."

They rounded a turn, and a few outbuildings started to appear in the prairie grass. "Welcome to Staryi Krim," Mandy said, shaking her head. "Christ, what a hole."

And it was, at least on the outskirts. As they rolled at high speed through the town—a bullet-pocked Lancer draws attention—they passed block after block of squat stucco-walled housing roofed in corrugated-tin sheets, with shabby wooden outhouses scattered about, packs of stray dogs and feral cats prowling through threadbare yards fenced in rusted chain link.

There were very few people out: a few peasant farmers pushing carts full of cordwood, more two-wheeled, rubber-tired carts pulled by undernourished oxen, here and there a run-down market stand, a vodka bar, sodden drunks littering the steps out front.

Things improved slightly when they got into the old part of the town, where the main street was lined with neoclassical buildings, white marble or painted to look like it, Doric and Corinthian columns holding up Greek temples, and, at the top of the stony street, a large drum-shaped church.

The area around the church was packed with locals waving colored banners. A balalaika quartet on a podium was playing something polka-ish, damsels in dirndls were flashing their petticoats, huddled villagers were clapping in time. It was a street party or celebration of some kind, which they dodged by taking a back lane and skirting the town center. Soon they were into the slums again. More butt-ugly

Stalinist housing and lots of Stone Age plumbing. Then Staryi Krim petered out like a drunkard's tale of woe, and they were back in the high-desert prairie again.

As they cleared a steep pass, the Crimean Peninsula opened up in front of them, and they saw in the hazy distance a cluster of office towers and apartment blocks beside an arc of glittering blue, the Black Sea port of Feodosiya, about twenty klicks away. On their extreme right, far away to the southwest, there was a jagged line of snowcapped peaks on the horizon, the Crimean Mountains.

"We're up pretty high now, aren't we?" asked Mandy.

Dalton gave her a sideways look.

"Yes, Mandy. We certainly are up pretty high."

"Sarcasm," she said, "is the last defense of the witless. What I meant was, I'll bet we can use the BlackBerry."

"I can't. I can't turn mine on. And I haven't had a chance to pick up a black cell anywhere. Why?"

"I have mine," she said, turning it on. "And I'm pretty sure nobody has my SIM card cloned. Look," she said, flipping the device faceup. "There's even a good signal."

"Is your GPS off?"

"Really, Micah," she said with a tone. "I was thinking about what you said, about the Kamov Two-Six needing a service base?"

"Yes? What have you got in mind?"

"Poppy's man in the Ukraine, Earl Ford? He has aerial photos of the entire peninsula. They take them to identify geological formations that might have coal, iron ore, bauxite seams in them. What if I call him and ask him to send us whatever photos he might have of this area? What was the operating distance of the Kamov?"

"A normal one, I'd say three hundred miles. The one we tangled with was armored, so that would bring it down to, let's say, two hundred miles. There and back again, if we assume no refueling depots on the perimeter, so they have to go back to home base before they run out of gas. That would still mean a radius of one hundred miles. Basically, if we're using here as the center, that's the entire Crimean, from Sevastopol to beyond Kerch."

"Worth a try, no?"

"Not really. Not without some way of narrowing the limits."

"Then narrow them, Micah. What else would isolate this particular chopper? You said it had armor. Anything else?"

Dalton gave it some thought.

"Markings. I didn't see any. No registration numbers. No corporate logo. Unmarked choppers would draw some attention, even here in the outback. The Ukraine's not some Third World backwater like Toronto. They have a very good civil-aviation authority. Just like everywhere else, each airframe has to carry a registration number. Sooner or later, someone would report an unmarked chopper."

"Maybe someone already has?"

That stopped him.

"This Ford guy, he got clearance for Poppy's Lear to land without the usual red tape, right? That means he has friends in the local government. Do you think he'd be willing to ask around, see if anyone knows anything about an unmarked brown Kamov Two-Six operating in the Staryi Krim region?"

"Yes. He would. *That's* worth a try, at least."

Mandy picked up the phone, tapped in a few numbers. Dalton watched the road unwind, bringing them down toward the sea again. Mandy got the receptionist, identified herself, and asked to speak to Big Bear. In a moment she was put through.

"Earl . . . Yes, everything's fine, sweetheart . . . No, really, just fine . . . Pardon? On the road near Staryi Krim . . . Yes, yes, it *is* a beastly little piss pot . . . Now, the thing is, Earl, I was wondering if you could do us a simply massive favor?"

She laid it out for him, described the Kamov in detail—dun brown, no markings at all, cargo box not fitted—leaving out the fresh bullet scars on the cockpit belly. She got a few clarifying questions, which she answered, and ended the call with, "Thanks, Big Bear. Do love you!"

She turned to Dalton, her face bright and happy.

"Finally I get to feel like something other than cargo."

"He'll do it?"

"Yes. He has a man at Simferopol Airport who has access to official records, incident reports, flight-path filings, airframe registrations. Earl says this man knows most of the Kamovs in the Crimean. He's going to call him and see what he can get."

"How long?"

"Minutes, he said. Hello, what is this?"

Her voice trailed off, and her face took on a look of puzzled concentration. She studied the screen for a time.

"Okay, this is interesting. I have the news feed for the BBC. It seems our old friend Ray Fyke has made the news."

"Ray? What the hell has Ray done now?"

"Apparently, he's gone to war with the Mossad."

"The Mossad? Show me."

"Pull over and read it," she said, handing Dalton the BlackBerry. He found a turnout near a bridge, pulled in, and parked.

BRIT SAILOR CLASHES WITH ISRAELI SECURITY TEAM IN TEL AVIV. REUTERS:

What was initially reported as fight in a beachside bar in Tel Aviv has taken on international significance after it was leaked that the three Israeli men who were injured in the incident were actually members of the Mossad, Israel's counterpart to the CIA. The confrontation, which took place at Joko's Beach Bar on Tel Aviv Boulevard yesterday evening, began when a British citizen, later identified as BRENDAN

FITCH, got into a loud disagreement with three unidentified males, two of whom then brandished firearms.

Fitch proceeded to overpower and disarm all three men. According to witnesses, Mr. Fitch, slightly injured in the affray, then left the bar in the company of a young woman and disappeared into the suburbs of Tel Aviv. So far, no arrests have been made.

The information that the three men were Mossad agents developed when an ER technician at Tel Aviv General Hospital, where the three men were taken after the assault, leaked the identity of the men to a local news reporter following the incident.

FITCH is described as being forty-one years old, about six feet two, weight two hundred and twenty pounds, with green eyes, a black, full-face beard cut short, and very muscular. The fact that FITCH was able to overcome and disarm three Mossad field agents seems to indicate some degree of military or martial-arts experience.

The owner of Joko's Beach Bar, Mr. Joachim Levon, who was also injured in the fight, has refused to comment on the incident, as has the Israeli government. The search for Fitch and his female companion, tentatively identified as BEATRICE GANDOLFO, a U.S. citizen, continues.

"What the—"

"My sentiments exactly," said Mandy, taking her BlackBerry back and hitting STORE to save the report. "By the way, does anybody outside hack journalism still use words like *brandished* and *affray*? I trust you brandished your hand cannon during the affray back there? Never mind. Merely rhetorical. What do you think this means? I mean, it *cannot* be a coincidence that you draw the wrath—totally unwarranted, I know—of the Mossad and shortly thereafter an old friend of yours shows up in Tel Aviv, the headquarters of the Mossad, where he proceeds to dismantle three of them and then saunters off into the night, can it?"

"Not with Joko Levon involved. I know the man. He's an old Mossad *katsa*, an intelligence operator. Fyke and I had some dealings with him when we were running the Birdman operation in Pristina. Fyke had a pretty good rapport with Joko; they both knew how to put away the Jim Beam. I can see him going to Tel Aviv if he wanted to make a back-channel contact with the Mossad."

"I think we can say with some degree of confidence that if this was Ray's intent, Fortune has not smiled upon his efforts. What I do wonder about is, how the hell would he know anything about your situation? I thought Cather booted him out the servant's entrance last year."

"No idea. Last I heard of him, he was back in the South China Sea—"

"Looking for Chong Kew Sak, as I recall? I haven't heard any more since I've been on my sabbatical."

Dalton smiled at her.

"He found him. In a village upriver from Port Moresby."

Mandy smiled back. Last year, Chong Kew Sak had done his very best to throw Mandy into Changi Prison in Singapore and keep her there for his personal amusement.

"I've always liked Ray. In theory. Any idea what he's up to?"

"I think we can assume that somebody inside Langley—"

"Maybe Sally Fordyce? She's always had a soft spot for footpads and scoundrels. She's very fond of *you*, I know."

"They've got Sally in lockdown. I asked her to look into the Vienna thing. She did, got out one e-mail to me—a warning—and then went dark. No. Somebody told Ray, but not Sally."

"Would your shiny new boss . . . What's his name? Something about dirt? Mud? Gravel? Pottery?"

"Clay," said Dalton, grinning at Mandy, who knew perfectly well who had replaced Deacon Cather as DD of Clandestine. "Clay Pearson. And, no, I think not. Now that Mariah Vale's got her fangs into my ankle, I'm more likely to get a French kiss from Nancy Pelosi than the time of day from him."

Mandy, shuddering, was about to say something withering when her BlackBerry kicked in with the first few bars of Mozart's *Dies Irae*. Mandy picked it up, saying to Dalton as she did so, "I know. Day of Wrath. I downloaded it last year when Poppy was always calling me up to scream about George Bush. Hello, Big Bear. That was quick . . . yes? Terrific . . . Hold on . . ." She waved her free hand at Dalton, making a handwriting gesture.

Dalton got a pen and the rental receipt for the Lancer.

"Okay . . . Yes, four-five degrees zero minutes two-point-eight-zero seconds north . . . Three-five degrees three minutes four-five-point-eight-five seconds east . . . Can you send me the JPEG? Right below the mountain . . . Three kilometers southwest . . . One road in . . . Take the last lane on the west end of town, turn south . . . Okay . . . No, I promise. We're just following up on a friend . . . Really, Big Bear . . . No risk at all. Anyway, I'm with a terribly competent fellow—" She looked over at Dalton, saying, "Big Bear says to tell you anything happens to me and he'll—" "Well, I'm not going to tell him *that*, sweetie. I'll just tell him you're worried, shall I? . . . Yes, I promise . . . Thanks so much! Bye, babe!"

She clicked off, turned to Dalton.

"I think we're going back to Staryi Krim."

.   .   .

THEY could see the upper levels of the compound from the outskirts of the village. It was sitting in a hollow below the tallest hill for miles around, a collection of white-painted outbuildings and one central structure, also white, with a long, peaked roof and a turret at the western side capped with red shingles.

It was only about two klicks away, as the crows flew, but for the Lancer it meant negotiating a long, curving track, little more than a gravel road, all the way around a lower slope and then working back along a narrow road running beside a little river and on into the hollow itself, some of it in plain sight of who or whatever was in that compound.

"Not an easy place to creep up on," said Dalton. "Let's see the JPEG again."

Mandy handed him her BlackBerry with the aerial photo of the compound taken by Earl Ford's consulting company. In the shot, according to the digital readout taken from five hundred feet, they could see the layout: the scattered outbuildings, the main structure, large and rectangular with a sharply peaked metal roof, a series of low tin-roofed sheds in a long row behind the main structure, and, on a cleared and paved area beside the structure, a landing pad, and, in the middle of the pad, the Kamov in its plain brown wrapper.

A few yards away, parked next to one of the outbuildings, was a large light brown flatbed truck and what looked like a long black sedan, almost a limousine, boxy, blunt-ended, shining like a polished stone in the lemon-colored winter light. The time stamp on the shot and the snow that lay everywhere around in it indicated that the shot was taken in early February of that year. Dalton handed the BlackBerry back, a look of resignation on his face, which Mandy correctly interpreted a few seconds later.

"Oh bloody hell. We have to walk?"

Dalton gave her a broad grin.

"We do."

And walk they did, following a dry riverbed that meandered down from the hills, their boots crunching on rock and dead brush, Mandy leading the way, her SIG in her hand and down at her side, and Dalton following a few yards behind with one of the AKs on a sling. For two and a half klicks, the bed ran along roughly the same path as the gravel road that led up to the compound. The road was built on a cleared track about eight feet higher than the riverbed, its bank giving them very good cover until, with less than a hundred yards to go to reach the compound, the river veered sharply away from the roadway.

If they wanted to cover the last one hundred yards, they'd have to do it in the open, across a stony field. Mandy stopped at the crest of the road and looked across the rising slope to the compound and then she slid back to the bottom of the riverbed in a little landslide of pea gravel.

"Can you smell that?" she asked, wrinkling her nose.

"I can," said Dalton. "I've been smelling it for almost half a klick. Haven't you?"

"I smoke more than you do," she said. "And a damned good thing. What is that vile stench?"

"Pigs," said Dalton, who had worked summers on a cattle ranch in Tucumcari only a few miles downwind of a large pig farm, which was not nearly far enough.

"Smell like that, you don't forget."

"I'll make a heroic effort."

Dalton was silent for a moment, listening hard. The wind had dropped as the day was dying down, and now they both could hear, faint and muted, a kind of guttural singsong tone—irregular, harsh, sustained—with a definite note of squealing desperation in it.

"What is that unholy sound?" asked Mandy, holding a very nice Liberty kerchief up to her nose.

"It's the pigs. They're in the sheds along the back, or at least that's where the sound is coming from. If I had to guess, I'd say they're hungry. Wait here a minute."

He worked his way around the bend of the road, got to within sixty yards of the compound. Even from that distance, he could see that the windows were closed and shuttered on the big house, and there were no vehicles in the lot, other than one rusted tractor and another tractor without wheels sitting on cement blocks.

The place looked—and felt—empty.

He came back around the bend to Mandy, took a knee, leaning on his AK. "I think they've bolted. Just like in Kerch."

Mandy gave him a look.

"What? You mean scarpered?"

"Looks it. One way to find out," he said, handing her the AK. Mandy stared at it as if he had just handed her a live flounder.

"Oh great. Is this the part where you say, 'Cover me, Tex, I'm a-goin' in'?"

Dalton gave her a quick kiss, turned away and went back to the curve, climbed to the top, his Colt out. He took careful aim. And he blew a large hole in the side of the main house, just beneath a small slit window that dominated the eastern side, right about where a sniper would be hiding if the house weren't really empty.

The sound of the gun rolled away into the hills and died. The large, splintered hole in the white-painted clapboard did not run with blood, and nobody opened up on him from another window. His experience with the people back down the road suggested that no one in the house would have the fire discipline to hold off after getting a round like that through the wall.

Empty. Had to be. One way to find out.

He got up and walked slowly across the field, his boots crunching down on the sliced-off stalks of corn freshly harvested. He reached the main gate, checked it for a trip wire or an IED, opened it, and walked slowly through the entire compound, looking for mines, explosives, traps, trying doors and shaking the shutters. He walked up to the back door of the big house, booted the glass to shards, and stepped inside. He was in some sort of mudroom, filthy boots caked with dried pig shit, coat hooks laden with farm smocks. Equally squalid, the rest of the interior rooms were in semidarkness.

The big house ticked slowly but steadily as the beams cooled in the gathering chill of sundown. Dalton did a quick walkabout through a large main room. Reeking of Russian cigarettes and spilled beer, it was set up like a military mess hall, with scruffy couches and mismatched chairs scattered about, a large stone fireplace, smoke still rising from the coals. There was a huge kitchen, and the trestle tables were bare and the cooking pots clean, but the smell of baked beans and boiled turnips still hung in the musty air.

The house was as empty as the yard, he decided. The noise from the pig sheds was getting louder and more shrill. Maybe they could sense someone was in the area. He went back outside, walked over to the helicopter pad, went out into the middle of it, pulled his gloves off, and got down on one knee to touch a fingertip in a pool of greenish liquid.

It was still warm.

Hydraulic fluid, leaking from the Kamov. He had hit the damned thing, all right. Vukov had flown it back here, patched it up somehow, maybe picked up another passenger . . .

Kirikoff?

And then he had taken off again.

Where to?

Kerch?

Or all the way back to Russia?

The grunting and squealing from the sheds was getting hysterical. So was the stench. He walked back to the gate.

"Mandy," he called out, his voice echoing back from the hill behind him. "It's okay. They're gone."

DALTON was using a crowbar to pry a lock off one of the shuttered outbuildings when Mandy reached him, looking nervously back across the yard toward the pig sheds.

"You're not going to let those little brutes out, are you? From the sound of it, they're ready to eat anything. Including us."

"Vukov and his people were growing corn out in the fields. For the pigs," said Dalton. "I think they've stored it in here."

The lock popped off, and the double doors swung slowly open. Inside the low, dimly lit barn was a huge mound of corncobs, along with some open feed bags and assorted bits of farming gear.

Dalton stood there for a moment, mulling it over, and then said to Mandy, "You might want to go inside. I checked the main house. It's empty, but they've left a lot of stuff behind. Do you feel like taking a look around?"

"What are you going to do?"

"Listen to those poor little guys," he said, grinning, looking at that moment more like a cowhand than a fixer for the CIA.

"I can't leave them to starve."

"I can," said Mandy. "Watch me."

A few minutes later, Dalton pushed his way out of a small stampede of hungry piglets—possibly fifty of them—gathered around the corncob mound, curly tails twitching, snouts buried in the pile. He walked back across the yard in the fading light, his shadow stretching out over the gravel, his boots kicking up stones as he looked up at the sky—*Cooling fast, rain or even snow soon*—and then he looked down at the house in front of him. Mandy was waiting at the door, the scarf at her nose again, her face bone white.

"The pigs getting to you?" he asked cheerfully.

In the golden light from the setting sun, her face was snow white, and her gray eyes misted. She looked at him over the silk cloth, took it away, and said, "This is where they killed Galan."

THEY did it in the basement, of course. These things are traditionally done in basements. Closer to Hell. Or just to kill the sounds. And if there's a dirt floor, as there was here, then that just makes it all the more convenient to bury the leftovers. As he and Mandy walked slowly down the rickety wooden stairs, the basement, reeking of mold, raw earth, old sweat, and other things less easily identified, opened up in front of them. It was a low, almost medieval, space, with massive wooden beams running the length of the open area and a dirt floor pounded flat by time and the hobnailed boots of heavy men walking back and forth.

The stone walls were lined with hooks for the storage of gear, and a few of them still had antique harnesses and oxen yokes hanging from them. There were no windows, and the light came from a row of new-looking clear bulbs hanging from wires looped around the beams. Along one wall there was a battered wooden table with a large television set on it and some VHS tapes piled up next to an old Panasonic VCR. Next to that table, set into the corner, was a marble slab set on two carved pillars, the slab draped in white-and-gold cloth with a Greek Orthodox cross set in the center and flanked by six tall gold candlesticks.

In front of the cross was a gold chalice, covered with a silver plate, the plate draped with a white linen cloth.

In other words, an altar for the Christian Mass.

On the far wall was a banner hanging from an old cavalry lance.

The banner was black silk cloth with the image of a large green scorpion in the middle.

And on a side wall, beneath a pair of crossed swords, was the clenched-fist image they had both seen before.

Under this fist banner someone had painted on the stones, in Serbian, three words:

крв и огањ

"Blood and fire," said Dalton in a flat, distant tone. "They used to spray it on the houses of people they had killed."

In the center of the room, looking like a cross between a butcher's block and an autopsy table, was a large trestle-style wooden table, maybe ten feet long, stained and gouged, with four large iron eyelet hooks bolted into it, two at each end. Hanging over the table was a green-shaded factory lamp, its large clear bulb protected by a wire cage. The interior of the shade was white yet unevenly spattered with streaks and drops of a dry brown substance. Next to the light was a video camera inside a glass-windowed box pointing straight down at the table. The window was also spattered with dried brown flecks. Dalton and Mandy stood there and took it in for a while. No imagination was necessary. The table spoke for itself, as did the room.

After a time, Dalton asked Mandy how she knew that this is where they had killed Galan. Standing close beside him, her arms folded under her breasts, she spoke without looking at him.

"There was a VHS tape with a label. Two words. *The Yid*."

Dalton looked over at the television set and the VCR.

"You looked?"

"I looked."

Prague

Spring had come late to Prague. The trees that lined the castle grounds had barely turned green, and the pale walls of the cathedral that constituted the eastern boundary of Vysehrad were streaked with damp. Rain hung in the air, a drifting mist, and the sounds of the old city all around were muted, muffled, as if heard through a fogbank. The huge bronze monuments that dominated the park—known simply as the Statues—rose up out of the mist like immense ghosts, silhouetted against a charcoal sky dense with clouds whose underbellies glowed pink from the lights of Prague.

Just inside the flat-topped stone arch that led from the cathedral close into the spare, sparsely treed park, on the middle of three very old benches, sat an aged and spidery man with tight gray skin, blue lips, a large black woolen coat, thin gray leather gloves, and a battered gray fedora. He was reading, apparently with close attention, a copy of *Prager Zeitung*, a German-language newspaper featuring all things *Praha* for expatriates from the old fatherland. His bony ankles, socked in dove gray wool and disappearing into large black brogues polished like marble slabs, were crossed rather primly, at least according to the watcher. The old man's entire aspect suggested precision, exactitude, a cold, dry, bloodless intelligence. He turned the pages with clockwork regularity, his sharp black eyes, huge behind thick wire-framed reading glasses, flicked over each new page like a crow hunting for prey, for gobbets of the kind of information this man fed on.

The man heard steps on the cobblestones coming closer, and he carefully creased the paper into a narrow rectangular strip, placing it on his bony knees and folding his long-fingered white hands, blue-veined and large-knuckled, on top of it. He moved slightly toward the left side of the bench as the man he was waiting for stopped in front of him, smiling carefully down.

"Gerhardt. Thank you for coming."

Kleinst considered the large man in front of him, his roast-beef face, his bright green eyes and the flicker of anarchic amusement around them, his heavy hands shoved into the pockets of his baggy camel-hair coat, under which were tailored jeans and brown cowboy boots. He had a general air of rowdiness with a touch of latent malice. They were not friends, but they were friendly on this occasion, inasmuch as their interests coincided.

Kleinst indicated the seat beside him, shifting to give Fyke room, which Fyke took, being careful not to touch Kleinst as he sat down. Kleinst, a fastidious man, intensely disliked being touched. They sat for a time in silence, both men staring out at but not quite seeing the low rolling parklands, the ancient oaks and lindens, haloed in a green mist. A rivulet of fog was moving along the base of a bronze statue of Siegfried, helm on his lap, broadsword at his booted heel, his cold eyes looking back to glorious ages lost.

"You . . ." Kleinst began, his dry rustle of a voice failing him. He swallowed with difficulty—his health was poor—and tried again. "You . . . have shaved your beard off."

"Yes. I needed a change."

"You made an impression in Tel Aviv, I see."

Fyke grinned, his gaze resting briefly on Kleinst, on his bony hands folded in his lap.

"That I did, Gerhardt."

"Yet, here you are."

"I never go into a place without having a couple of ways to get back out."

"In this case, you had a fast boat down the shoreline."

"Yes. How did you know?"

Kleinst made a dry, creaking sound, his version of laughter.

"You are the kind of man who always has a fast boat down the shoreline. The woman? This Gandolfo . . . legend, of whom I hear so much . . . This . . . Madonna . . . where is she?"

"In the car. A few blocks away."

"Am I to know who she really is?"

"Do you *need* to know?"

Kleinst considered it for a while.

"Information is always useful. But, perhaps, no. Your friend Joachim was not helpful, as I understand."

"No. The Israelis are convinced that Dalton killed Issadore Galan. They have been offered a proof of some kind."

"An audiotape?"

"Yes. On the tape, Dalton directly threatens Galan."

"Of course he does. Tapes are easily doctored. The Mossad are usually much harder to persuade."

Fyke made a face, rubbed his forehead.

"The new administration has tried damned hard to alienate their affections. Israel no longer feels that it has a . . . friend . . . in the White House. This is having an effect all along the chain."

"Yes," said Kleinst, who, although a Stalinist, was by birth, and even now in spirit, a Jew, and he retained a dream of Jerusalem even though he knew he would never see it himself. "For one thing, Raymond, it virtually assures that Israel will do something about Iran within a year. For Israel, Iran is an existential threat. They will not wait for this young Hamlet to wake up. Frankly, as he is not a reliable friend, why should they?"

"Hamlet will wake up when they hit those sites."

"By then, it will be too late. Total war will come to the Middle East and soon after engulf the West. Old Europe fails. Islam rises. The West . . . hesitates. We have seen all this before, in different disguises and under different flags. You wished to know something about this offensive against your friend?"

"Whatever you have, Gerhardt. We're at sea, I'm afraid."

"How is he, if I may ask?"

"I haven't seen him in months. Last time we were together was in Southeast Asia. He was . . . effective. A little . . . fey?"

"Pixielated?"

"Yes. Witchy. Like the fairies had got at him."

"This was the affair of Chong Kew Sak," he said, his lips working around the foreign words. "With whom you disagreed so forcefully in Papua New Guinea. Does Dalton still see ghosts?"

"Not when I was with him."

"He is . . . an anachronism, that young man. See these . . . warriors out here?" He indicated the statues for which the park was created, mythical gods and Valkyries, kings and heroes of the Old Norse tales, knights of the Nibelungen.

"He has visions, he engages in crusades and vendettas. In his heart, he seeks a good death, as these saints and kings and heroes did. As if there were such a thing. Still, I respect the man, and I am prepared to do what I can for him. Much good will it do. He is too good for the people he serves, you know? He carries this new scorpion king across the river because it is in his nature to do so, because he thinks it is the patriotic thing to do. He thinks he serves your country—"

"Not *mine*, Gerhardt. I cleave to the bosom of perfidious Albion. I'm backing the *man* here, not the scorpions he works for."

Kleinst sent him a wry look, a bright flicker of his old fire glimmering in his huge wet eyes.

"You cleave to *someone's* bosom, Raymond, that I do not doubt. You were always a rake. Well, enough of this. I will need a reciprocal gesture."

"Of course. Name it."

"You know I am not well."

"I know you always say so. You are always about to die, yet you go on. And on."

Kleinst led his head go forward slightly, showing his teeth, the skin around his cheekbones pulling tight. It was as if the skull beneath his flesh was trying to break through.

"Yes. I persist. Now, about Geli. Although I have struggled against it, acquiring wealth has not been a gift. I would like to leave something for Geli, other than my few shabby sticks of furniture."

"Where is she?"

Kleinst was quiet for a time.

"I do not know *exactly* where. Last I heard, in Hamburg. We do not speak."

Kleinst, a ex–Stasi intelligence officer, had fallen out with his daughter, Geli, over the matter of a large concrete wall that once ran down the middle of Berlin. Geli felt that it should come down. Kleinst disagreed with her. The wall in Berlin came down, and the wall between Geli and Kleinst went up.

"But I think, Raymond, that *you* can find her. I know she is not living very wisely, that she has fallen in with this 'social justice' crowd and spends her time organizing silly marches. They dress up like storm troopers of the Apocalypse and affront the police with plastic bags of urine and sacks filled with dog feces, for which intolerable impudence they are duly pepper-sprayed, perfunctorily beaten, and briefly arrested. Upon release, they scuttle back to their squalid little warrens, aflame with sanctimonious zeal, and there they copulate like dogs in a ditch. I find it grimly amusing that we fell out over a wall that separated two forms of governance, socialism and democracy, and now that she has her . . . *democracy*"—he pronounced the word with evident distaste—"she busies herself in futile efforts to undermine it."

"My father used to say that one of civilization's biggest challenges was seeing that it didn't get ruined by the political fantasies of its children. I have resources, Gerhardt. I'll find her, see that she's on solid ground."

"Thank you. If you have time, one other matter. I understand she has taken up with an unsuitable boy and that he beats her. I would like this boy to be chastised and sent on his way."

"I'd be delighted to chastise the boy. You have my word."

Kleinst, nodding, took a small white handkerchief out of his coat pocket, dabbed at his blue lips, folded it and put it away. A flurry of crows erupted from a stand of alders and whirled into the darkening sky, their harsh cries echoing off the cathedral walls. Kleinst and Fyke stared at the alders for a time with fixed intensity. And then they gradually relaxed.

"I know this about our Dalton: he has a lot of enemies. The fee for the surveillance in Vienna? It was paid to a file the OSE called *Verwandtschaft*. In German, this word means 'kinship' or 'family.' It is a highly classified OSE term for NATO."

"The surveillance was NATO's idea?"

"It was *billed* to NATO, but my informant believes that the request originated in D.C. My informant suspects that it came from within the CIA itself."

"Is that what you think?"

"My informant is in a position to know these things, but that does not mean that this particular item of information is correct."

"Spoken like a Jesuit, Gerhardt. Your guy have any idea who might have done this . . . in the CIA?"

"We all know the list of people who could make such a thing happen is short. Beyond that, we cannot help you. Are you aware of a Russian operative named Piotr Kirikoff?"

"Yes. By reputation. Intelligent. Looks a bit like a garden slug. Likes the ladies. And the lads. A deep-background player, not a field-man. Skilled. Dangerous. He ran a honey-trap operation against an NSA code breaker last year using a Montenegrin field agent. Damned near worked. Dalton broke it up."

"Yes. Kirikoff has decided to make an example of Dalton. In this effort, I believe he has enjoyed the perhaps inadvertent assistance of people highly placed in the CIA or the NSA, inasmuch as he has managed to intercept and decrypt Dalton's BlackBerry and GPS data, which, as you know, is impossible without prime-number algorithms from the encrypting agency. As well, there are some tectonic shifts within the Agency. People are being punished for . . . a lack of re-forming zeal, let us say."

"Goddamned Special Prosecutor," huffed Fyke.

Kleinst lifted a calming hand, swallowed drily, and went on.

"All of this is merely inferential. My observations follow naturally from the events. However, you may rest upon it, Kirikoff is not oper-ating without the full consent of his Russian masters. Putin would not allow the weight of his intelligence arms to be brought down upon the head of one lone CIA agent no matter how troublesome. Kirikoff's operation is directed toward an endgame, a result that suits Putin's purposes, the nature of which must be well worth the risk involved. I do not know what this endgame may be, although one can infer from the effort and coin being expended that it is . . . *significant.*"

Here, he turned his magnified myopic glare on Fyke, driving his observation home, his blue lips tight and his expression cold.

"I hear you, Gerhardt," said Fyke, "I'm listening."

"Good. In some obscure way, I feel that I am betraying the cause. But *Germany* was my cause, not Vladimir Putin's febrile hegemonic obsessions. Well, I do have information concerning what sort of people have been recruited by Kirikoff. You're familiar, I know, with the Serb Skorpions."

"Too bloody familiar," said Fyke.

"In Kerch—this is a port city in the Ukraine, something of a lawless frontier outpost full of mercenaries and soldiers of fortune, the flotsam and jetsam of various wars—Kirikoff got in touch with an ex–Skorpion paramilitary leader with direct ties to Ratko Mladic. As you know, Mladic is wanted by the ICC for war crimes committed in the Kosovo wars. He is thought to be hiding in Serb provinces, protected by a cadre of the KLA. Mladic had a unit commander named Milan Babic. Babic's XO, his executive officer, was one Aleksandr Vukov. A very able man, he had been trained by the Spetsnaz as a sort of KLA commando. In 1999, in the town of Podujevo, while fighting alongside the KLA, he was assaulted by a group of captives in a mosque, Bosnian Muslims. As he struggled to get away, a U.S. Special Forces unit that had been observing Skorpion activity in and around the mosque for two days, unaware of the presence of captives inside, painted it for an aerial strike. A Nighthawk put two Paveways into the mosque, incinerating the captive Muslims, over a hundred and fifty women, children—"

"A setup. Christ. Jesus Christ."

Kleinst turned and smiled at him, a death's-head grin.

"Alas, Christ was a nonparticipant, as He usually is. Yes. The idea was to be able to portray the Americans as careless and barbaric. Vukov had managed to travel partway through an escape tunnel. When the Paveways hit, he was effectively roasted alive in this tunnel. He lived—

these sorts of creatures often do. Perhaps the Devil sees to his own children. He was taken to Belgrade, hideously burned, a monster, and underwent several years of reconstructive surgery, which was not very effective. Although now physically quite repulsive, he was, from the reports before the flames reached him, a very handsome young man and much caressed by the ladies. However, his gruesome war wounds have given him a mythic stature with the Serbs and Croats, the Macedonians, who cannot forget their long centuries of torment under the Turks and the Albanians. They burn with the shame of their *dhimmitude*, their forced submission to the daily humiliations of life as infidels under the boot of Islam. Now they repay this brutality in kind. Babic and Vukov have lately emerged as the charismatic leaders of a resurgent KLA underground. Their area of operations is, of course, the Balkans—drugs and guns, kidnap, rape, extortion—working, I am told, out of a farm his family owns in the central Crimean highlands. Vukov especially has conceived a great hatred of NATO, and in particular the United States, a Christian nation that in Bosnia took the side of the hated Muslims and made war against its own Christian brothers. Kirikoff made contact, I believe at a bar called The Double Eagle on the Kerch waterfront, with Vukov and his cadre, perhaps with Milan Babic himself, and has placed them at the head of this operation against Dalton. Shall I tell you why Vukov took the job?"

"Dalton was the SFO man on the ground in Podujevo."

Kleinst looked at Fyke. "He told you?"

"No. But it follows. Dalton was in the area at that time. I don't believe in coincidences. What I'd like to know is—"

"Who told Kirikoff? Exactly. Trace that information, and you will find the spider at the center of this entire web. Another line of inquiry would take you to Athens, my friend."

"What's in Athens?"

"Kirikoff draws his operating expenses through a corporate entity known as Arc Light Engineering. This firm does extensive business throughout the Mediterranean, from Spain all the way down to sub-Saharan Africa. It is a legitimate construction-and-design firm, specializing in large civil-works projects in developing nations, as well as privately funded construction in wealthy Arab nations such as the Emirates, Saudi Arabia, Morocco. It is an umbrella corporation with many subsidiaries, some quite recently acquired. One of these recently acquired subsidiaries is indirectly controlled by a Moscow-based oligarch by the name of Yevgeny Korchoy. Korchoy, a friend and supporter of Vladimir Putin, is, in the Tolstoyan labyrinth of Russian familial kinships, distantly related to Piotr Kirikoff."

"Do you know the name of this subsidiary?"

"I believe it is called Cobalt Hydraulic Systems."

"What's Kirikoff's official title?"

"Assistant Director. His mandate is unclear, his duties nonexistent, but his draws from the company funds are substantial. The company maintains a large motor yacht for his personal use called *Dansante*. He berths it at the Flisvos Marina. I suggest that it may be useful to take a closer look at Cobalt Hydraulic Systems."

"Based in Athens."

"Their HQ is not there, but that is where Kirikoff is alleged to maintain a sort of branch office. I have not been able to discover the precise location. However, he is also an investor in a seaside restaurant called Serenitas, on the Flisvos Marina. He was seen dining there last week but has not appeared . . . since . . ."

Kleinst sighed heavily, slumping a little into himself.

"Other than this . . ." Kleinst went on almost in a whisper, "I have only one thing to add. As I have said, this is not merely a vendetta. I was a satrap of the Soviet Empire for many years. I truly believed in the Socialist cause as the last best hope for humanity to have lasting peace. Thus, I justified its . . . excesses. History has demonstrated that I was grossly in error. For my sins, I am now an exile. I once thought the Russian Empire was in the dust, but it rises, Raymond, it rises. It senses weakness, indecision, in the West. Already it has made inroads. What inference should the people here in Prague, and the Poles, draw from America's craven consent to the removal of a missile shield, a groveling appeasement which got them only mockery from the Kremlin and the contempt of America's allies . . . ?" He lifted his hands, let them fall.

Fyke stood up, offered his hand. Kleinst, after a moment's hesitation, took it.

"Can I offer you a lift somewhere, Gerhardt?"

"No, Raymond. I am happy to sit here for a while with the monuments. See to Geli, that will be enough. And to her unsuitable boy. Will you go to Athens?"

"Yes. We'll go tonight."

"You and the . . . Italian legend?"

"Yes."

"Is she very beautiful?"

"Yes. Heartbreaking."

"You are lovers?"

"No."

"Why not? You are not old, life is short, the road is fraught . . ."

"I'm trying . . . to be faithful."

"You are? To what?"

Fyke looked away into the gathering darkness, sighed, and came back. "To myself, Gerhardt."

Kleinst dabbed at his blue lips, settled into his voluminous coat like a turtle, pulling it tight around him, his breath misting the chilly air, the shadows drawing in. Prague hummed and boomed and clattered in the distance: electric, vital, remote, oblivious.

"To yourself, is it? How brave. I tried that, Raymond, a long while ago, with Geli's mother. Before I knew that I had lost myself in the places in between, like water slipping through a grate."

"'In between'? In between what?"

"There are *spaces*, Raymond. Gaps. You are walking on railroad ties, across a trestle, above a deep gorge. Watch your step amidst the spaces. Now, go. Do your work. We will meet again."

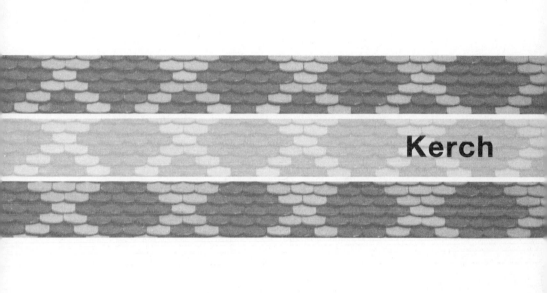

Kerch

Captain Bogdan Davit, prefect of the Kerch Constabulary, head of the
port police, inspector of customs, commander of the Coast Guard, and
the unofficial boss of pretty much anything else worth bossing in the
little port town of Kerch, was waiting for them in the third-floor corner office of a slab-sided, bilious-looking concrete bunker across the
road from Kerch's industrial waterfront.

Dalton and Mandy Pownall, ushered into Captain Davit's bare-
bones office by his secretary—a round, cheerful peach-colored young
girl, her hair pulled tight in a stern official bun—got a broad, wel-
coming smile from Davit. He was a tall, well-muscled blond with eyes
the color of glacier ice, wearing his tailor-made sky-blue uniform very
well and, although young for the job, carrying the competent air of
an infantry captain in a beleaguered outpost. He had, as Dalton recalled, despite his boyish manner, a core of toughness coupled with
a sly dark humor, a pragmatic willingness to take events on the fly and
people as they came.

His office had a wall of windows that overlooked the waterfront
and the port itself—admittedly, a dreary industrial morass, red-brick
silos, tin-roofed warehouses, rust-streaked derricks rising up out of
the mist, heaps of coal and iron ore, slag piles steaming in the damp,

squalid gypsy freighters and oil tankers slouching by the crumbling quayside, a pall of smoke and rain and coal dust hanging low over it all, and, beyond this grim scene, across the muddy shark-tooth chop of the Kerch Strait, the dun-colored and moody forward slopes of fog-shrouded Russia.

Davit, still grinning broadly, came around his desk—a short trip, since it was basically a card table—took Mandy's hand in both of his and kissed her on both cheeks, breathing her in as he did so, then stepping back and smiling down at her with warm appreciation, before turning to Dalton and offering a strong, dry hand.

"You are both well, I find. I am happy to have you back in my city. Marika"—he turned to the peach-colored girl still hovering at the door—"may we have . . . You will both take tea, I hope? Yes? Perfect! . . . Marika, would you be so good . . . Thank you. Now," he said, pulling two hard wooden chairs out from against the wall and setting them in front of his desk, "now will you sit, please? And before we talk about what is in front of us—Dobri Levka and his boat, of which I have no news, sadly—and of our own homegrown spy . . . No, no, tea first . . . You must tell me . . . Miss Pownall, if I may, allow me to say you are *exquisite* today. My men still speak of you with great admiration, and of that terrible night, those poor people in the clinic . . ."

They talked amiably for a time about the chase the KGB had led them on last winter, from Istanbul across the Black Sea to Kerch, what they had found there, with Captain Davit's help, in the basement of a clinic. Dalton told Davit what he could of the story, leaving out a few critical details, which Davit understood and did not in any way resent. He himself lived near the cave of the Russian Bear and felt its great bulk looming over everything he cherished.

"But it ended well, I hope," he said, still beaming at Mandy, running a sharp cavalier's eye over her body, from her black boots and tight jeans to her turtleneck and her fine leather jacket.

"Actually," said Mandy, smiling back—she loved to be admired, especially by chiseled young Nordic officers in well-cut uniforms— "I think we ought not to say that it has *ended* at all."

Dalton, setting his cup down on a small side table—he loathed tea, but this was the East, and tea was the inevitable drink—leaned forward, folded his hands. Davit, setting his tea down too, sat back quietly in his chair, tenting his fingers, watching Dalton's face, his expression calm, interested, watchful.

"I assume, Captain Davit—"

"Please. I am Bogdan."

"Bogdan. That you've checked into my situation."

Davit smiled—a thin, careful smile.

"Oh yes," he said, lifting his hands as if to ward off an evil spirit, smiling broadly. "Be warned! I am on my guard. I have been told to watch out for you, the American servant of Satan himself. That you are . . . a wanted man, an evil rogue, like—what is his name?—Austin Powers, the International Man of Mystery."

"You're not taking the warning very seriously," said Mandy.

Davit lifted his tea, sipped it, set it down, his smile fading.

"I think for myself, Miss Pownall. I have good experience of Mr. Dalton, and of you, so I am not inclined to leap at squeakings of some little mice, am I? I hear from the Israelis that I am to do this or to do that or else rue the day. Kiev also has blustered at me. But Kiev is seven hundred kilometers away. I am here. For me, I dislike being blustered at."

He made a gesture at the window, invoking the port, the harbor, the Strait, and what lay beyond.

"They—over there—the bully Russians, they bluster too and stamp their heavy boots. Last winter, we all froze here in Kerch because *they* wished to play ducks and drakes with our natural gas. So. Look around my office. Empty as a barn. We burn all our furniture. Keep warm. Russians starve. Ukrainians go on a diet. We survive. No, I will do what is good for Kerch and the Ukraine, not for the Mossad or even for Kiev. The Russians came into *my* waters and hijacked a boat belonging to one of our townsmen, Mr. Dobri Levka. Your friend, Mr. Dalton, and a fine, generous man, although perhaps not so sober as he could be. They force people from Kerch into rubber boats and tell them to row for their lives. Old people, women, kids. A father has a heart attack, an old woman dies of fear. Now they deny everything and blame it on Dobri. I mention maybe our homegrown spy?"

"Yes," said Dalton. "What did you mean?"

"I mean exactly that. One of our own. A corporal. His name is Pavel Zelov. He is in Kiev now under arrest. I am afraid he is the cause of Mr. Galan's death. After they took the *Blue Nile*, I received a call from Mr. Galan, from Venice. He mentioned you as an associate. He was asking for Irina Kuldic—"

"Is she all right?" asked Mandy, by now quite ready for terrible news. "Nothing happened to her?"

"No," said Davit. "She is safe. After we found out about Pavel, we put her in a safe place so nothing could come to her. Do you wish to see her? She is only a few hours away."

"No," said Dalton. "Tell us about this spy."

"Yes. Pavel," he said, his mood darkening. "As I say, I am afraid that he is the cause of Mr. Galan's death. After I heard about what had happened to Galan—in Vienna?—I required an . . . *audit*? A security audit. A process of elimination, of checking personnel logs, e-mail lists, the timing of events . . . We arrested Pavel Zelov a few days later. After some . . . difficulties . . . he admitted he was hired by some Serbian person, he did not know who. But the nature of the contacts are consistent with the way Mr. Kirikoff works . . ." His voice trailed away, and his face lost some light as he went inward. "But there it lies. Zelov is in Kiev, Irina Kuldic is safe, but Mr. Galan is brutally dead, and you are here to avenge. As for me, I am angry. I too am ready to do something about all this whether or not Kiev says okay. So, you—how do you say it—you show me mine and I'll show you yours?"

"Something like that," said Mandy, smiling at Dalton.

Dalton, still leaning on his forearms, looking into Davit's eyes. Holding his attention now, he told him about the death of Issadore Galan, the manner of it, the attack on the highway from Sevastopol. Davit began to write rapidly on a notepad as Dalton described the Kamov and the men he had fought, what they found at the compound in Staryi Krim.

"You will excuse a call," he said, picking up the phone, waiting a moment, his long fingers drumming on the card-table top. Then there was a rush of Ukrainian, delivered with quiet force. He set the phone down, lifted his hands in an apologetic gesture.

"Forgive me. You have been badly treated in the Ukraine. I have sent men to . . . *mop up?* To Staryi Krim, and to the road beyond it. This Kamov you mention. I have seen it go over—"

"When?" asked Dalton sharply.

"Two hours ago. A little less. No markings, brown. It flew slowly over the city and the harbor. I thought it was looking for something. For your car, I now think. It flew over the harbor and hovered low. I was having my lunchtime tea on the roof deck. Then it rose up and went east into Russia, the impudent fellow. There was no way to stop it. We do not have helicopters in Kerch."

"Is there any way to find out where it went?"

Davit smiled broadly, a sharklike grin, drumming his fingertips, a happy little rattle on the tabletop. "But we *know* where it went. This is a shipping port. Kerch, The City of Industry. We have excellent radar equipment, even a big dish up on the mountain behind us. The coastal hills here are low, the sea flat and wide. When it appeared, without markings, I called over to the harbormaster and asked her to track the flight. I have her chart right here," he said, holding up a sheet of plotting paper. "It went east southeast for about eighty kilometers and then dropped below our radar screens. We believe it landed here."

He laid the paper out in front of Mandy and Dalton, held it flat with his left hand, set his teacup on a corner, and touched a point on the southern coastline of the Russian mainland.

"This is Anapa. It is a little seaside town, a resort. Many Russians go there for the beaches, the clinics, the mud baths—"

"Clinics?" asked Mandy, "Like the one Kirikoff was running here in Kerch?"

"Yes," said Davit, losing some of his lightness. "Just like. In Anapa, there are many of these sanatoriums, on the beaches and in the town. Many for drunks—Russians drink almost as much as we do—for people recovering from cancer, even for plastic surgery."

"Can you . . . Do you have any access to the business records of those clinics? Any kind of description."

Davit was looking at Mandy, but his mind was clearly deep in the question. "There are so many. But, yes, there would be—what you call *samizdat*?"

"Pamphlets?" asked Mandy. "Brochures?"

"Yes, we would have those." He tapped a button on the wall. A heartbeat later, Marika appeared at the door, her cheeks a little red. Dalton realized that she had probably been listening and hoped that Davit noticed it too. "Marika, those clinics in Anapa . . . Can you find some material on all of them? Brochures?"

She bobbed, turned away, and then reappeared in the doorway, looking uncertain, as if afraid to raise a delicate topic. Davit apparently recognized the look.

"Yes, Marika, what is it?"

"Corporal Zelov, sir—"

"Yes?"

"He was drinker, remember?"

"God yes," said Davit, not in any way delighted to have the matter aired in front of Dalton and Miss Pownall. "And . . . ?"

She plucked at her hair and then at her uniform blouse. Dalton wondered how close she had been to Corporal Zelov.

"I . . . I was *listening*, sir," she said, her face flaring into scarlet, setting her eyes alight by contrast. "You did not close the door—"

"We *burned* it. Last February, Marika. Remember?"

"Oh yes. So we did. I am sorry. But Pavel—Corporal Zelov—went to a clinic in Anapa. For drunkards. He was there six weeks."

"I thought he was seeing his sick mother in Kiev."

Marika went from red to snow white, her lower lip trembling, her cornflower blue eyes welling up.

"Yes. Well, sir, he was afraid you would—"

Davit, now as pale as Marika, began to erupt in Ukrainian, and Dalton, if only to get the kid out from under Davit's acid rebuke, cut in, asking her if she knew the name of the clinic. She turned to him with obvious relief, her voice rising into a squeak.

"No, sir. But Corporal Zelov said it was very big and had a bright red roof. His room even had a view of the water. It was all by itself, far out on the sand. Nothing else for many, many meters."

Dalton stood up, glanced out at the harbor, turned back to the girl: "Thank you, Marika. Bogdan, you have patrol craft? Fast cruisers? I recall one that met us after the fishing boat we were chasing last year blew up. Long, steel gray, a big fifty on the bow?"

"Yes. The *Velosia*. She is there," he said, pointing to a ninety-foot-long slate-gray cruiser moored at the quayside studded with swivel guns, a huge radar array, and flying the Ukrainian flag.

"How fast is she?"

Davit looked reflexively out at the water—flat and steel gray, under a lowering charcoal sky, rain drifting downward in curtains.

"She will do forty knots," he said, realization opening in his face, his eyes widening. "You think Dobri Levka is in Anapa?"

"Yes," said Dalton. "But not for long."

BY twilight, they were lying a half klick off the Russian coast, well within her territorial waters and therefore illegal as hell. All her running lights out, the *Velosia* was dark, her sharp destroyer bow slicing with a sibilant hiss through the surface chop hidden inside a bank of fog that had spread itself out across the Russian coastline. To the north, off their starboard bow, the yellow lights of Anapa glimmering faintly through the mist.

Directly abeam, set out on an isolated sandspit, there was a low, rambling structure, the Bospor Clinik Spa. It was world famous, according to the clumsy translation of the online brochure that Dalton had found on the Internet, "for the certain resurrection of big drunkards and the putting of their feet to the solid ground." Its sloping red roof was just discernible in the fading light. A few yard lights twinkled in the haze, and a light glowed on the front deck. Other than that, the place looked shuttered and deserted.

He and Mandy and Davit had studied the floor plan of the place, laid out for their convenience on the website. There was a large parlor, spreading across the entire front of the house, full of comfortable chairs, and a large dining hall on the north side next to a communal kitchen with showers and a bathroom next to it.

On the second floor, running along the beach side of the spa, were the guest rooms, fifteen of them in a row, each with a little fenced-in balcony overlooking the ocean. Behind the guest rooms, accessed by an internal hallway, was a clinic and some private rooms where patients could consult with their therapists.

A phone call to the spa, placed by Marika using Mandy's Black-Berry to disguise the local number, found that the spa was "closed for renovations" and had been for two weeks. The speaker, she reported, was a male, who spoke fluent Russian "but with a strange accent and a lisp. And his voice sounded funny, like he was whispering."

"Vukov," said Dalton.

DAVIT was standing beside Dalton, both men in jeans and black sweaters, booted and gloved. Both men were staring out at the coastline, Dalton quiet and withdrawn, thinking about what might be happening to Dobri Levka right now or what might already have happened, Davit, vividly alert, humming with energy and a kind of gleeful anticipation like a gundog on a chase.

"I have three of our patrol boats out there," he said, indicating the darkening seas. "They have radar. They will stop and search any boat coming out of Anapa. Our own radar tells us that no helicopter or other aircraft has left Anapa since we steamed out of Kerch. We are *blockading* Holy Mother Russia," he finished with a flourish, spreading his arms out wide. "Isn't it *wonderful*?"

"They'll have radar too. In Anapa."

Davit made a dismissive gesture, grinning at Dalton.

"But *they* are not military. They are a tourist town. Even if they see us, they will think we are trawlers, poaching their fish in the Kumani Canyon. It is right underneath us. They would never think we Ukrainians would be so crazy as to sail a fleet into their waters."

Dalton nodded, distracted, troubled.

Worried sick, images of Issadore Galan's body flickering on the screen at the back of his skull.

"They may have taken him inland," he said.

Davit nodded, put a comforting hand on Dalton's shoulder.

"This is true," he admitted. "But we can do nothing about that. Come. Be cheerful. We are doing what there is for us to do. I have six men ready. Or do you still insist to go ashore alone?"

"Is it a big town?"

"No. A few thousand people, spread out along the coast. It is early for the tourists, so most of the beach places will be boarded up. This business here, the Bospor Clinik Spa, it is set apart from the main town. I think you will be okay to approach it. Please. You will take my men?"

Here he gave Dalton a sidelong look, smiling carefully.

"Or maybe . . . just me?"

Dalton turned to look at the young man.

"If you got caught on shore, what would happen to you?"

Davit's face hardened.

"Maybe better ask what would happen to men who try to catch me. I am sick at heart to rest on my ass and let Russians push us around. Anyway, you know what, my friend? I *decide*, I am captain of this boat. *You* are not going at all if you are going in alone. No offense to America and the CIA."

"None taken," said Dalton, smiling into the gathering darkness, his heart lifting at the idea of doing something—anything—to strike back at these people. "Okay. Just us two, then."

"Good," said Davit, whistling to one of his sailors, giving him a quick instruction in Ukrainian. The man lumbered into the darkness, and Dalton could hear an electric pulley begin to whine, a boat being lowered into the water. Davit came back to stand beside him, but this time he was holding a large pistol. He press-checked it and stuffed it into a holster on his belt. He straightened his shoulders, chuffed out a breath, stopped for a moment.

"Miss Pownall . . . If we do not come back, what would you wish to be done for her?"

"Mandy knows what to do. She has a video proving that I did not kill Issadore Galan. And another video of the parking lot at Leopoldsberg showing Vukov dropping off Galan's Saab in the early morning. When they see those, the Mossad will be very happy to come after Kirikoff and Vukov themselves. Mandy knows enough to help the Mossad deal with them. Where is she?"

"In the officers' wardroom, drinking vodka, charming all my boys. Do you wish to say go inside and say good-bye to her?"

"No," said Dalton in a soft voice. "We don't do farewells."

THE boat, a gray lap-strake cutter with a powerful and virtually silent electric motor, slipped away from the *Velosia*, the towering bulk of the cruiser fading quickly into the fog. Davit twisted the throttle, and the cutter shot forward, the sharp bow rising, seawater hissing and curling along her wooden sides, a gurgling sound coming up through the slanting floorboards.

Davit sat on a bench at the rear, the control stick in one hand, his pistol, a Polish P-64 he had probably retained from the Russian occupation, in the other. Dalton, in the bow, watching the shadow of the beach come slowly closer, had his Anaconda, three autoloaders and a slender, double-edged fighting knife he had taken from the BDS agent back in Venice.

The air closer to the mainland smelled of seaweed, mud, and salt. The twilight had passed into night, the amber lights of Anapa shimmering in the north, ahead of them only the glow from the Bospor Clinik Spa, and a few faint halos from the yard lights.

In a few minutes, the cutter—long and narrow, high-peaked bow—hissed lightly over a sandbar, grating along the keel, broke free into a tidal lagoon close to shore, skimmed across it, and ran up onto the beach, crunching gently into the gravel. Dalton was out over the bow before it settled, jumping onto the coarse sand and tugging the boat ashore. Davit clambered up the centerboard and stepped off the peak, carrying a thin rope with a mushroom anchor on the end of it.

He walked a few yards up the beach and set the anchor into a dune, driving it in with his boot. In a crouch, he turned and looked back at Dalton, tugged his watch cap low over his head, and led the way up the slope. There was a wooden barrier, and a set of stairs and a walkway that rose up and over the barrier dune. At the top of the walkway, less than fifty feet from the front steps of the spa, they saw a wide wrought-iron fence blocking the path. Dalton came forward, set himself, vaulted it, landing lightly on the other side.

He walked a little way up toward the house, watching it, hearing Davit's soft footfalls coming up behind him.

"What do you suggest?" he whispered, close enough for Dalton to smell the little shot of vodka Davit had taken just as they stepped into the cutter.

"Check the perimeter, and then cover the back. Stop anyone who tries to leave. Bogdan, listen, don't close in with Vukov. Don't go anywhere near him. Stay well back and shoot him where he stands. Shoot him a lot. Head shots. Then reload and shoot him some more. If you hear gunfire from inside, kick in the door and come fast. Watch out for trip wires, anything like that. Okay?"

"Okay," said Davit, a flash of white teeth as he smiled. And then he was gone, slipping away over the dunes and disappearing into the darkness.

Dalton came slowly up to the front steps, pistol up, studying the approach. No motion detectors visible. No pressure plates that he could see. From the house itself, silence.

He tucked the Anaconda into his belt, gripped one of the porch pillars, and climbed rapidly up it. Reaching the edge of the upper deck, he lifted himself up by his hands, trying very hard not to make the boards creak with his weight, and kicked up his leg.

He got his toes wedged on the outer lip of the deck, eased himself up and over the railing and down onto the deck itself. He was in a small, fenced-off area with two slatted chairs and a small round table. The chairs and the table were thick with salt rime, and the decking half covered with dried leaves and beach grass.

There was a large glass door, a sliding panel. He ran his fingers all around its rim and lower lip looking for an alarm. Nothing. He stepped in close, put his ear up against the glass. The glass was cold to his skin.

He listened carefully, breathing shallow. A low, murmuring vibration, more felt than heard. Voices, coming from some distance away. Not inside this room but near. Toward the rear of the second floor, very likely in the clinic.

He got a grip on the handle of the door and put his other hand flat against the upper portion of the slider. He lifted up, the door moved slightly, making a faint grinding sound as the aluminum frame lifted from the track. He strained under the weight, going slowly, hardly breathing, first an inch, then another. There was a hiss and a click, and the glass door came free in his hands.

It weighed more than he thought, and he almost dropped it as he shifted it out of its track. A rush of stale air poured out through the open frame: smoke and burned coffee, household cleaners. He placed the sliding door gently against the fence separating this unit from the one next door, stepped back, and pulled the pistol out of his belt again.

The window curtains were lifting in the sea wind, and he brushed them out of his face as he stepped into the dark, chilly little room, his boots brushing softly across the hardwood floor. He could just make out a single bed to his left, a low dresser beside it, a lamp with a small shade, and, beyond, a door, hooks in the door, a robe hanging from one of the hooks.

The room smelled stale and unused. He ran his glove across the surface of the dresser, held it up in the faint light coming from the yard lights below. A thin streak of dust.

He crossed to the door, stood there for a while, letting his eyes adjust to the changing light. He touched the door. It was warm, heated from the hallway on the other side. He recalled the floor plan, guessing that he was about halfway along the upper hallway. If he opened this door, the entrance to the clinic—a large, central complex with a reception desk, a waiting area, and some treatment rooms behind it—would be about fifteen feet to his left.

He put a gloved hand onto the knob, turned it slowly, felt a click. The door opened a crack, and a shaft of light cut through the gloom, along with a waft of warm air, smelling of floor polish and something medicinal—rubbing alcohol or some other antiseptic.

He eased the door open, blinking as the light grew, leaned out into the hallway. It was a long corridor carpeted in beige, with light green walls and harshly lit with overhead fluorescent squares running in rows down the full length. Music was coming faintly from behind the frosted-glass walls of the clinic, a few feet down the hallway.

Dalton stepped out into the hall and padded softly along it until he was near the clinic. The main door was closed, but he could see faint light coming from somewhere beyond the darkened reception area.

Here, the music was louder. And the murmur of voices that he had heard earlier was louder as well. It was a radio playing. Some sort of Russian soap opera? No, more urgent. Staccato, hectoring, urgent. A newscaster was delivering the latest word from Moscow in that shouting, cadenced manner that Dalton had come to think of as the Blitzer Bark. From down the hall behind him, there was the sound of a toilet flushing, a door being jerked open,

Dalton spun around, lifting his Colt with his right hand. Vukov stepped out into the hallway about thirty feet away. Booted, in faded jeans, a white T-shirt stretched across his chest, massive pectorals sliding like steel plates underneath, the shiny, ridged burn scars rippling over his forearm muscles and his biceps swelling out as he tugged at his zipper, looking down as he straightened his belt, he heard the solid metallic click as Dalton thumbed the Colt's hammer back. He looked up, saw Dalton standing in the hallway, and stretched his lips wide.

"Slick," he said in a thick Serbian accent, his voice a rasping whisper. "How's tricks?"

Dalton had a steady sight on a point between Vukov's bulging pectoral plates. The trigger, incised with grooves for good contact, felt dry and cool under Dalton's finger, the wooden grip solid in his hand. He felt . . . nothing . . . just a great soothing calm spreading through his chest and belly.

Kill him, said a voice, not his own, down in his lizard brain.

Kill him now.

No.

We need what he knows.

He won't talk. No matter what you do. Kill him.

"On your knees," Dalton said.

Vukov stretched his leathery lips, showing a set of yellow teeth, and shook his round, earless head, his lidless eyes two narrow slits, a bright black glitter inside them.

"Can't," he said, slapping his left thigh, where Dalton could see a large bulge under the jeans. "Nearly broke my thighbone with that fucking cannon. One hundred fucking meters, not possible. You hit me anyway. No, to kneel is . . . No. I can't—"

Dalton shifted the muzzle a tick, pulled the trigger, the blast a deafening explosion in the narrow hallway. Vukov jerked backward, going into a low crouch, his hands up in front of him reflexively as if to ward off the incoming slug. For the first time, a flicker of fear in these eyes? He put a hand up and felt the side of his skull, touching the raw furrow the round had carved along his temple as it hurtled past to bury itself in the wall at the end of the hall.

Behind him, Dalton heard a shrill shout, a woman calling out. "Aleks!" The sound of glass sliding on glass. "Aleks!" At the same time, a muffled shot from the back of the house, two heavy thuds, wood shattering. "Aleks!" Dalton had the muzzle centered on Vukov's face. Vukov was still in a low crouch, his hands out on either side, palms up. His eyes suddenly flicked to a point just beyond Dalton's left shoulder. Dalton pivoted, saw a shadowy figure, a girl wearing some sort of a nurse's uniform. She was aiming a small stainless pistol at him. Dalton and the woman fired at the same second. Dalton's round struck her in the hollow of the throat. He felt a heavy blow to his hip bone. In the girl's throat, a huge red flower opened. She gaped at him, falling. He spun around. Vukov was charging straight at him, but too slow, a stumbling lurch with his damaged leg. He was still ten feet away when Dalton lifted his pistol, sighting on Vukov's ruined face, Vukov skidded to halt, lifted his stumpy hands in the air.

"Okay. Okay. No shoot. Okay?"

"Down," said Dalton through gritted teeth. "Now."

Vukov dropped to his knees, put his hands out, and flattened face-first on the floor, spreading his arms and legs out wide. Dalton stood over him, aimed the Anaconda at the back of his bald, distorted head, his finger tightening on the trigger.

Kill him.

He heard a voice behind him, weak but steady.

"Don't shoot him yet, boss. Please."

Dalton, without turning his head away, keeping the pistol fixed on the back of Vukov's skull, said, "Dobri?"

"Yes. Is me. Good to see you, boss."

"You sound like shit. They hurt you?"

"Not . . . not so much."

Heavy boots on the staircase, and Davit slammed through a door at the far end of the hallway, his pistol out, his face a slab of pale rock. He took in the picture. A large, apelike man spread-eagled on the ground. Dalton, blood running down the front of his jeans, standing over the prone man with a pistol zeroed on the back of the man's skull. Dobri Levka, a few feet behind Dalton, in striped pajamas and paper slippers, shackled, his ankle cuffs attached to some kind of long silver chain, his face a black-and-blue horror, one eye battered shut, his lips caked in dried blood. And a dead girl in a bloody heap in front of the clinic doors.

"Hey, Bogdan," said Dobri, smiling through dry lips. "Got vodka?"

"Dobri," said Dalton in a flat, hard voice, the pain from the wound in his hip starting to make itself known, his chest filling up with cold fire, "Tell me why I can't kill this . . . thing."

"My boat," said Levka, coming to stand at Dalton's shoulder. "The *Blue Nile*. They put it on big cargo ship ten days ago. I think they going to do something terrible with it."

"What?"

"I don't know," he said, blinking down at Vukov through one puffed-and-purple eye. "But maybe this thing does."

DALTON held the gun on Vukov as Levka—rail-thin and haggard, unshaven, his thick hair matted and filthy—used his own shackles to cuff Vukov up and bind his ankles while Davit radioed for a Zodiac and a shore party. When Levka was done, Dalton reached down, grasped Vukov by the back of his jeans, and jerked him to his feet. As Vukov stood upright, he looked down at what was left of the girl in the doorway and then grinned at Dalton.

"You put nice big hole in Maya, Slick. Maybe you should fuck it while is still warm."

Bogdan Davit stepped in across Dalton and slammed Vukov on the side of the skull with his pistol, knocking him back down to his knees. He put a boot on Vukov's chest and shoved him backward onto the floor. Two of his sailors appeared at the top of the stairs. He said something short and direct to them in Ukrainian, held up a hand, making them wait for a moment longer, stepped in again and kicked Vukov hard in the crotch, hard enough to move him back a full yard. Vukov made no sound, but he turned slowly onto his right side and folded into himself as much as he could, his breathing going short and sharp.

Davit sighed, nodded to his men, who stepped in and gathered Vukov up like a sack and hauled him down the stairwell. Davit turned with a satisfied air to Dalton and Levka.

"Okay. Daring midnight raid. Prisoner rescued. Shots fired. Dead girl on the floor. One CIA agent with bullet in his hip. Lights coming on in the town. The Gulag opens up before us. I hereby declare this invasion of Holy Mother Russia officially over. Yes?"

BACK on the *Velosia*, steaming for home, Dalton, his hip bone aching and a hole in his flesh where the ship's doctor had plucked out a .22 slug, hobbled down to the supply room to have a talk with Vukov. He found him sitting on a metal chair, the chair chained to a ringbolt in the bulkhead, Vukov chained to the chair by a waist belt and ankle shackles.

Vukov looked up as Dalton opened the door, tilted his head back, and stared up at the overhead light inside his wire cage, laughed softly to himself, and then lowered his eyes and fixed them on Dalton as he pulled up a box and set it down in front of Vukov.

Dalton pulled out a pack of Sobranies, lit up a pink one, inhaling the smoke, staring back at Vukov.

"Cigarette?" he asked, lifting up the pack.

"Yeah. I like cigarette. Even faggot cigarette."

Dalton stuck one into Vukov's mouth, lit it, sat back, and watched as Vukov sucked the smoke in and expelled it through his nostril slits. The effect was demonic. Smoke rose up between them.

"So. Slick. Time we have nice chat, eh?"

"Your man, Branislav Petrasevic. The man I killed—"

"Kill three, Slick, but who is counting?"

"The other two were boys. Half trained."

His troll's leer appeared again and his yellow teeth. He spoke around the cigarette, holding it in his teeth.

"I like to work with troubled youth. Like Boy Scout leader. Hey. You bring that big gun? *Fucking* good gun. You damned good shot. One hundred meters. Right in fucking leg. Surprise shit out of me. Maybe one day, I buy one too. What kind is?"

"Colt Anaconda. Forty-four caliber. Two thousand euros, retail . . . Petrasevic said I was the one who burned you."

Vukov nodded, his heavy skull rocking forward, his lipless mouth stretching wide.

"Yes. Is you."

"Where?"

"In Podujevo. You know Podujevo, Slick? Is where you barbecue all those people. In Podujevo."

"You were there?"

Vukov rolled his head around on his thick neck, lifted his shoulders in a shrug, his muscles sliding under his T-shirt. His hands were folded together against the chain waist belt, his fingers curled slightly. He was breathing slowly and steadily, a machine.

"I was in mosque."

"In the mosque. Bad decision. Not bright."

He laughed.

"No. Not bright. In come rocket. I am in tunnel. Pow! Flames come and eat me all up. Now I am monster. You do this, Slick. Girls. I bet all girls like you, Slick. Pretty boy like you. I was pretty boy too. Girls, they all love me. Now not so much. Now I want girl, I pay or I just take. So. What happen to the Miklas whore? I not see her. Got new bitch now? Very fine. I would do her with big grin. Maybe some day, she get real dick, yeah? The Miklas girl, she not like you so much after she find out about Podujevo?"

"No. Not so much. How did you know I was in Podujevo?"

Vukov showed his teeth.

"Is for me to know."

Dalton suddenly made the connection.

Colin Dale, the retired U.S. Army officer, the KGB mole that he and Mandy had hounded into the light last winter.

"Kirikoff's mole. Colin Dale. He would have known. He told Kirikoff. Before he died. Kirikoff used it to recruit you."

Vukov shrugged it off.

"Maybe. So what? Dale is dead. You execute him. Right on beach. All this means shit to me. Is politics. I am fighter."

Dalton looked at Vukov for a while in silence.

"You were a Skorpion."

His eyes grew wide and his skin changed.

"I *am* Skorpion."

Dalton shook his head, a sideways, mocking smile.

"Not to us. We called you the Whack-a-Moles. It was like hunting gophers. You pop up, we take off your head. It was fun."

Vukov sucked on the cigarette, shaking his head slowly.

"You believe in God, Slick?"

"I try. Doesn't always work."

"Believe in Jesus Christ, who die for our sins? Who gives us eternal life in Heaven? You believe in Him?"

"I'm a Christian."

Vukov leaned forward into the haze of his own smoke, his great round head seeming to float inside the cloud, bodiless.

"Then you should kill *Muslims*. Not Christians. *This* is the big war, Slick. This is true crusade. There is no peace with Islam. *They* know this. Soon, or late, one day they know we will all go back under the boot. Is in their Koran. You know what *Dhimmi* is?"

"Yes."

"No. You do *not* know *Dhimmi*. You never live under *Dhimmi* law. My people, *my* people, *we* live under that law. The Turks. The Moors. Six hundred years, we live under the boot. Since first battle of Kosovo. In Ottoman Empire, if you are infidel, there is no talking back to anyone Islam who insult you. No fight in court against anyone Islam. Wear *markings* to show you are *dhimmi*. Look away in street. No riding horses. Donkeys only. Islam man want your woman, he take her. You say nothing. Islam man want your house, he take it. You got business, Islam man want it, you say yes and look down at ground. Islam man strike you, you kneel and beg him stop. Islam man kill you, you die, say thank you. What is *dhimmi*? Fear is *dhimmi*. Fear is on the face of every man and child of my people. What nation are you? Who are your people?"

"My family came from Norway."

Vukov smiled as if confirmed in a theory.

"Vikings. Good. Vikings never live under Islam boot. Macedonians, Serbs did. We were once rulers of earth. Alexander was Macedonian. Listen, Slick, you think there is peace with Islam? Only difference between al-Qaeda and ordinary Islam man? Al-Qaeda impatient. Ordinary Islam man, he can wait. They will *never* have peace with infidels. With Christians. Everywhere on earth where Islam man live near infidel is blood. It is in their book. Their Koran. Just like Hitler put his word in *Mein Kampf.* Is there for all to read. No peace until we kneel or die."

Vukov sat back, breathing a little hard. He spat the cigarette out onto the floor, shaking his head at the madness of it.

"Then in Kosovo," he continued, "where it all start, after six hundred years finally we Christians put fear on the faces of *their* wives, *their* children, *their* old men, *their* fathers and sons. *That* is what a Skorpion is. *That* is what I am. You. What are you, Slick?"

"What am I?" repeated Dalton. "I face men in combat. I don't rape and torture crippled old Jews. I don't run from a firefight and leave young boys to die. Branislav Petrasevic didn't run. He faced me in the middle of the road. Neither did the Medic kid or his friend. Only one man ran from that fight, Vukov. You did. And that is what you are."

Vukov looked down and became still.

"I did not run. It was . . ."

"Necessary?"

Vukov looked up, his skin rippling as the muscles under his cheek worked, his eyes bright and black.

"Yes. For the mission."

"So you say . . ." said Dalton, leaning back, lighting up another Sobranie and blowing the smoke toward Vukov. "*Of course* I couldn't stay. The *mission* was too important. I had to run away to save the mission. It's all about the mission. Horseshit, Vukov, just plain horse-shit. There is no mission. You're a petty thief, a criminal, a junkyard dog. Captain Davit will put you in his jail, and stronger men will use you like you used Galan. Because, you know, when it comes down to it, Vukov, you run. But when you run in a prison, you don't get far. Sooner or later, they'll corner you in a cellar or in the laundry, and you'll do whatever it takes to stay alive. That will be *your* story. Vukov. The man who ran."

Vukov had gone somewhere else. His body was motionless, and he was not breathing. The scored wound on his temple, where Dalton's bullet had glanced across the bone, had opened up and blood was running down the side of his face, a gleaming red snake under the overhead light. It was the only thing moving on the man.

Dalton stood up, brushing the ashes off his jeans, staring down at Vukov, his expression one of disgust, dismissal.

"The mission?" he said, smiling. "There is no mission."

He turned to go, but Vukov stirred, pulling at his chains, his boots scraping on the steel floor. He looked up at Dalton.

"I need toilet."

"So piss yourself."

"No. Is not to piss, okay. Look. I give you something. You let me go to toilet. Is okay to bring guards. But I must to go."

"Give me something and you can go to the toilet."

Vukov was struggling with it.

Dalton waited, still, patient.

"You know Kirikoff?"

"What about him?" said Dalton, his hand on the latch.

"We are to do something . . . something big."

"The mission?"

"Yes. The mission."

"What is this mission, Vukov?"

"I don't know. Kirikoff keep it close. But I know where is Kirikoff."

"Good. Where is Kirikoff?"

"I can go to toilet, I tell you?"

"Yes."

"Honor as soldier?"

"I don't give my honor to people who run."

"I do not run! Is for mission!"

"I still need you to give me something."

"Okay. Piotr Kirikoff. He is in Athens."

DALTON called in three hard-looking sailors and told them that Vukov needed to go to the toilet.

"Don't take the shackles off. Just enough for him to get his business done. And you *stay* with him, follow? He is never alone."

The oldest man there, a petty officer with lean, grizzled cheeks and tobacco-stained teeth, grinned at Dalton.

"Uri here can wipe his ass. Right, Uri?"

Uri shuffled his feet, his face reddening.

They gathered around Vukov while the petty officer keyed the lock holding the chain to the ringbolt. Dalton cleared the door as the chain gang shuffled down the narrow corridor toward the heads. He went back into the little storeroom, sat down on the bench, put his feet on Vukov's chair, and lit another Sobranie, feeling reasonably pleased with himself. Military pride was a tender thing, even with a man like Vukov. Three minutes passed in this pleasant way. After five minutes, Dalton, suddenly feeling uneasy, got up and walked down the hallway to the head, where he opened the door and found three dead men. They searched the entire ship, from truck to kelson. They were sixteen klicks out of Kerch Harbor, in the middle of a night as dark as a dragon's colon, the hull slicing through muddy chop, two white wings curling away from the cutwater, and Aleksandr Vukov had gone over the side. Dalton leaned on the taffrail for thirty minutes as Davit's men played searchlights on the surging waves. Mandy stood nearby, intending to comfort but knowing there was none to be had. Finally he pushed himself upright and walked back into the cabin with Mandy, no longer feeling quite so pleased with himself.

Athens

If spring had come late to Prague, it was long gone in Athens. The
sprawling white city, terra-cotta-roofed, spread itself out across the
huge valley, from the mountains to the sea, in a crazy maze of circular
streets, hexagonal blocks, squares, grids, arches, highways, byways, alleys, dead ends, all piled up around the limestone Acropolis and Par-
thenon, with fluttering palms along the coast and cypress spikes
marching down the hillsides. Today, Athens was baking and shimmering under a noonday sun that blazed down from a sky so light it looked
like glass. A single contrail moved slowly across the blue, the jet itself
a diamond sparkle at the tip, trailing a line of snow-white lace, like the
blade of a glass cutter moving over a crystal bowl, catching the sun and
glowing like pale fire even as it spread slowly out and faded away into
wisps of cloud.

Nikki, shading her eyes from the knife-edged glitter off the sea,
watched the contrail as it cut its path slowly into the west. She thought
briefly of her home in Seven Oaks, her cats and her plants, and—this
thought, uncalled, unwelcome, breaking through her defenses—of
Hank Brocius, in the early winter of last year, on a roof deck overlooking the parking lot at Crypto City, the winter light shining on the

unscarred side of his face, his gentle eyes on her as she wrapped a gold-and-blue scarf around his neck and kissed him on the lips for the first time.

The memory stung, bit deep, brought down all her defenses, and the Flisvos Marina in Athens dissolved at once into a blur of white and blue and yellow limestone. Her throat closing up, her chest tight, she looked down at her hands, a watery blur, folded around the stem of a glass of chilled white wine. She picked up a pink linen napkin, lifted her sunglasses, and dabbed at her eyes. There was someone at her shoulder, a soft male voice, warm, caring. "Miss Gandolfo, are you okay?"

She set her sunglasses back in place, adjusted them, and only then turned to smile brightly up at the lean brown boy in the crisp white mess jacket and creased black slacks who was hovering over her, his handsome face full of concern.

"I am fine, Tomás," she said, "just the glare off the water."

"Let me fix the umbrella," he said, leaning in to move the shaft, swinging the heavy shade around to shield her from the reflections in the harbor. As he did so, he cut her off from the long window of the Serenitas Restaurant. There, alone at a table for four, Piotr Kirikoff sat, all in baggy, shapeless white, with a large bib spread over his spinnaker belly. He was leaning forward and ripping a large lobster apart with his bare hands, stuffing gobbets and bits into his mouth, his greasy purple lips working, juices dripping from his sausage fingers, oblivious to the nauseated stares of a tourist party across the aisle.

Nikki thanked Tomás and, when he was gone, shifted her chair to the left to regain her view. It had taken a while for Kirikoff to surface, and her station here at the Serenitas, after a full day, an evening, and the morning of the second day, was becoming obvious, if only to Tomás, who was sure this stunning Italian girl was falling madly for . . . him. But of course. How could she not?

But Kirikoff had finally made an appearance, less than an hour ago, arriving on a long gleaming-white motor yacht that proceeded into Flisvos Marina like a swan. It glided regally past rows and rows of other equally magnificent yachts, many of them larger, all of them just as sleek, finally making a ponderous swing into a berth halfway up the mole. The yacht, the *Dansante*, would have been a sensation in Bar Harbor or Newport. Here among the riches of Athens it was, if not ordinary, then at least unremarkable.

Tomás, watching it arrive, informed Nikki in a careful aside that the yacht was owned by some large corporation. Many of the yachts at Flisvos were corporate. But as they watched the mountainous fig-ure of Piotr Kirikoff waddle along the quay toward them, Tomás's expression altered into one of guarded hostility, and he pulled back into his more formal pose as the solicitous waiter. Kirikoff rumbled past the table, his small hooded eyes fixed on the glass doors, his thighs shaking under the thin linen of his pleated slacks, his leather flip-flops shuffling across the tiles, his great dimpled ass visibly vibrat-ing with every step.

"Peter Christian," said Tomás in an over-the-shoulder whisper as he stepped briskly over to open the door for Kirikoff, "he is part owner of this place." Kirikoff sailed past Tomás without so much as a sideways glance and disappeared into the cool shadows behind the tinted glass, only to emerge a few seconds later and take his place at the table where he now sat, dismembering a crustacean with the fixed attention of a seasoned glutton.

Nikki went back to her lunch, a wonderful tomato-and-olive salad that had suddenly become dust and ashes. She pushed the plate away, calmed herself, and dialed a number on her cell phone. The line rang three times, and then Fyke picked up.

"He's there?"

"About an hour," she said, speaking softly, very aware of the tour-ists that were gradually filling up the tables all around her, all talking cheerfully in several different languages—Greek, German, Italian,

Swiss—their voices combining into one goose-and-gander barnyard gabble, getting louder by the second.

"You see a car?"

"No. he came in a boat. Eighty-foot at least. Called *Dansante*. He's going by the name of Peter Christian."

"What's he look like?"

"Moby-Dick in a leisure suit."

"You're sure it's him?"

"It's him. Micah Dalton found a video of him on the *Subito*. There can't be two of him in the world. The planet would tip over. Where are you?"

"I'm over in Piraeus. The harbor—"

As if to validate this, Nikki heard a huge, blaring blast from Fyke's end of the line, one of the cruise ships casting off. A moment later, the sound of it came across the water and echoed off the hills to the south.

"As you can hear," said Fyke after the deep bass tones had died away, "I'm at the harbor. I'm supposed to be interested in renting a warehouse. I've got a list of businesses operating down here. There's no Cobalt Hydraulic Systems listed anywhere in Athens—anywhere in Greece, for that matter—but there is a warehouse on Kondyli, right across from the main wharf, leased to a company called Northstar Container Logistics, which is a subsidiary of Arc Light Engineering. They own a fleet of cargo tankers, a worldwide outfit. Own something like forty hulls, tankers, containerships, even a couple of yacht trans-porters—"

"What's a yacht transporter?"

"It's special hull that can sink below the waterline. They have a big gate at the rear. The owners just drive their yachts through the gate, like entering a lock, then the transporter rises up again under the yacht, and off they go. They used a huge one on the USS *Cole*. Any-way, something interesting in the records here. Guess what investment bank has a stake in both Northstar Logistics and Cobalt Hydraulic Systems?"

"Ray. Please."

"Okay. Hold on to your garters, my child. Burke and Single."

"Burke and Single? That's . . ."

"A CIA front, started up by Porter Naumann ten years ago. Still in operation, run out of London. Mikey used to work directly for them, along with Mandy Pownall. Mandy Pownall and Porter Naumann used to be an item."

"I . . . I don't think I understand any of this. Is Kirikoff a double? Is he working for both sides? It makes no sense."

"Not yet. But it will. I'm standing down the street from their warehouse right now, and there's a large tanker truck parked outside with the name Cobalt Hydraulic Systems on the side. So I'd say we're in the right neighborhood anyway."

Nikki looked up as Kirikoff pushed his plate away and lifted a large pink flipper that he waved at someone out of sight.

"I think our man has company—"

"Is it Vukov?"

"No . . . I can't see . . . Wait a minute . . ."

She watched as a tall, tanned well-groomed man walked into the dining area. He was gray-haired with a trimmed gray beard, slender, dressed in a lightweight tan suit. He extended a hand and allowed it to be enveloped in Kirikoff's greasy flipper with a shiver of distaste.

"Someone I don't know. Looks Middle Eastern. They're ordering . . . coffee. How do you want to handle this?"

"Has Kirikoff ever seen you?"

"Not that I know of."

"Can you get any closer?"

"I can. There are tables inside. But I've already had lunch. I'm going to stand out, won't I?"

"I don't want you to sit anywhere near them, but if you can get a cell-phone shot of them together maybe we can figure out who the guy is. Could be totally unrelated, but it's worth it. But, Nikki, please don't get caught."

"I just love it when you're stunningly obvious, Ray."

FYKE flipped the cell phone shut, stepped out of the crowded side lane where he had been standing, and walked across the large concourse toward the wharf area. The entire harbor, the third-largest port in Europe, was lined with freighters and tankers and containerships, all either taking on or off-loading cargo, derricks whining in the diesel haze. The tarmac under his feet was soft and sticky. Pushcarts and trolleys and forklifts hummed around the ships. Thousands of people—some tourists but mainly locals with jobs at the port—milled around, some with purpose, some without, no one showing any interest in the large sunburned man with long black hair and green eyes who was moving through the crowded docklands.

He took a position across the deck from the entrance to Northstar Container Logistics, where he could see the door and keep an eye on the tanker truck. It was a large stainless-steel tube, glittering and brand-new, with COBALT HYDRAULIC SYSTEMS on the side. He stepped back into the shadows again and lit up a cigarette. Five minutes later, his cell phone buzzed in his shirt pocket.

UNKNOWN NUMBER

"Nikki . . . ?"
"Ray?"
"Joko?"

"Yeah. Joko. Where the fuck are you?"

"Well, I'm not in Tel Aviv."

"Good fucking thing. You break my ear bone with fucking champagne bottle. Still can't hear right. The boys send you kiss."

"They out of the hospital?"

"Jona is but can't walk yet because his balls all swollen up like cantaloupes. Levi still has to get pins put in, and his collarbone is not so good. Daniel is okay, but he wants his tooth back."

"Found it stuck in my knuckle, Joko. Dropped it on the beach somewhere. To what do I owe—"

"Parcel service drops a box off at Mossad HQ downtown this morning. Inside is this videotape. Not fun to watch."

"Jesus. Not Mikey?"

"No. Galan. Is long tape, my friend. They cut out some bits. Not so much fun, dull stuff. Just Galan dying. But most is here."

"You see any faces?"

"Yeah. Four of them. Two guys, sort of young-looking, wearing black uniforms. They looking pale, and one is sick in corner. Big laugh. Another guy with a Mohawk, older, also in black uniform. But one guy, very bad burns all over his upper body, no face left, only slits, he has his shirt off—big, strong guy—he is doing something to Galan I do not want to talk about. On wall behind him is black flag with green scorpion on it."

"Serbs."

"Yes."

"So it wasn't Mikey, then?"

A long pause.

"Doesn't look like it. Tape was faked, we think,"

"You guys aren't usually so gullible."

"Us guys aren't usually getting fucked over by old comrades either. CIA all of a sudden is cold to us. U.S. is cold. Sucks up to Arabs, bleeds for Palestine, sign statement endorsing Goldstone Report that we commit war crimes in Gaza. Even join fucking Human Rights panel at UN. We feel the cold, we resent this. Makes us cranky. But about Micah, yes, I am sorry. I was wrong. I should have known better."

"Okay. Penance. A Rosary and the Stations of the Cross."

"I am a Jew, Ray."

"So was Jesus. Roll with it. Any idea who sent the video?"

"Yeah. Come from a Captain Bogdan Davit. I think is a policeman, in Kerch, on the Crimean across from Russia. Had a note with the package. I read it to you?"

The cell beeped in his hand.

He looked down at the screen.

CALL WAITING

"Yeah. Please."

"'Dear Mr. Dagan . . . I have the duty to present you with very disturbing evidence of the murder of one of your countrymen. I vouch for integrity of these difficult images and I express my deepest condolences that such barbarity took place in my country. Three of the men you see in this picture were found dead in a truck a few kilometers from a town called Staryi Krim. The third man, the scarred one, his name is Aleksandr Vukov, a Serbian national and a leader of a paramilitary group known as the Skorpions. His whereabouts not known. He may be drowned off Kerch. I am under the news that your organization has suspected an American CIA agent of this atrocity. I warrant to you that he is innocent of this thing. I offer my services in any capacity to help you in your investigation of the murder of your Mr. Issadore Galan . . .' He goes on, gives his phone and e-mail numbers. Meir Dagan has already called him—"

"Any mention of . . ."

CALL WAITING

". . . Micah Dalton?"

"No. But we know who he is talking about."

"Does Meir Dagan buy it?"

Another pause.

"Yes. We all do. Pretty hard to argue with."

"So Mikey's off the hook?"

"With us, yes. With the Russkies, no. Dagan did some digging and found out that Dalton made a midnight run on a Russian coastal town called Anapa. Girl was killed. Somebody else kidnapped. He might have had the help of the Ukrainians. Big international incident, if that comes out . . ."

CALL WAITING

"Look, Joko, I got a caller . . ."

"Okay. But I got to say something."

"Shoot."

"We were out of line. No hard feelings, okay?"

"No . . . And thanks . . ."

"No. Is more. You going after this Aleksandr Vukov guy?"

"Yes."

"So are we. You want in?"

"I *am* in. I own it. *You're* the guy who wants in."

"Okay. You own it. We want in. How about it?"

"Who have you got?"

"Me. And Daniel. He still wants his tooth back."

"Declared? Flying the flag?"

"No. Not declared. But we got some backing, if we need."

Fyke was silent for a moment, thinking it through.

"Okay. Just you two. And I'm running it."

"Good. Okay. Where are you?"

"In Athens. At the docklands in Piraeus. When do you leave?"

"We are in air already. Dagan gave us a jet. Meet us at Ellinikon Airport in . . . three hours. Okay?"

"Done."

Fyke clicked off, hit CALL, and heard Nikki's line beeping, his chest suddenly cold. *Answer please, Nikki, answer . . .*

"Ray, I've been ringing and ringing."

"Where are you?"

"In a cab, on . . . Poseidon . . . We're going by a big football stadium . . . I'm following Kirikoff . . . They're in a white Mercedes, a two-seater of some kind . . . He's with the guy he met at lunch."

"You get a shot of them?"

"Yes. That's why I was calling. I went on our Greatest Hits page— all known terrorists on the watch list?"

How does she have access to that? he thought.

"Okay. And . . . ?"

"I think the guy with him is Milan Babic. He was Ratko Mladic's second-in-command."

"Kleinst said he was involved. And here he is. If you have access to that database, then you have access to Deacon Cather too, don't you?"

"Yes. Indirectly."

"Then send him a flash about Babic. Where are you now?"

"We just merged with a big street . . . Piraeus something . . ."

"You're headed to the docklands. Don't get too close."

"I won't. We're already falling back. Where are you?"

"Where you're going to be in about five minutes."

FYKE was still in the shadows across the road when a white Mercedes SL550 roadster came gliding down the wharf, weaving in and out of the carts and forklifts, pulling up in front of the door to Northstar Logistics. The door pulled back—electric—and Fyke was treated to the prolonged spectacle of a sweating, writhing, red-faced Piotr Kirikoff struggling to extricate his bulging bulk from a car not specifically designed for bipedal belugas.

Fyke was aware of Nikki walking down the wharf toward him, having dumped her taxi a block back, but he found it impossible to look away as Kirikoff, wrapping his fat flippers around the door trim, managed to give birth to himself. It was like watching a giant pink crab leave home and waddle off down the shoreline without his shell.

His passenger, Milan Babic, a whipcord type, tall, slender but muscular, with a trim gray beard, stood by the entrance to the warehouse and pretended to be fascinated by his BlackBerry. Nikki reached Fyke just as Kirikoff came free with an audible *pop*, his pink face dripping wet and his linen shirt already hanging limp.

"Dear God," she said softly.

"Yes. They'll have to bury him in installments. That your Serbian lad with him? Babic?"

"Yes. Kleinst thinks Babic is next in line if Mladic ever gets caught. He's taking quite a chance walking around in Athens. Every security agency in the West wants him."

"You hear back from Cather?"

"No. Early in Langley."

"He'd still be in his crypt, then, sleeping on a bed of his native soil and dreaming of nubile young Carpathians?"

"Transylvanians."

"He really behind this . . . whatever this is we're doing?"

"He's paying for it anyway."

"How'd he talk you into it?"

"It was more trick than talk. By the time I had finished listening to him, I was already wrapped up in spider silk and hanging out to cure. Why are you here, Ray?"

"Mikey."

"Simple as that."

"Not simple at all. By the way, one of us is going to have to go along to Ellinikon Airport in . . . about an hour and a half."

"Why?"

Fyke told her.

"Dear God."

"Is that relief or horror?"

"I didn't like Joko very much. And you knocked out that poor boy's teeth. What was his name?"

"Daniel. You hit Joko with the champagne bottle."

"I did not. I merely handed it to you."

"What did you think I was going to do with it? Stick a flower in it?"

"Do they still think Micah killed Galan?"

Fyke shook his head, his smile fading.

"What is it, Ray? You look strange."

"You remember a cop named Bogdan Davit, in Kerch?"

"I heard good things, but I never met him. I never got to Kerch."

"Seems he has . . . acquired . . . a video of Galan being killed. It clears Dalton. That's why the Mossad want to help. We're after the same people now."

"'Acquired'? That sounds like Micah Dalton."

"Yeah. Has Mikey written all over it, especially since there now seems to be a good chance that Russia and the Ukraine are going to war. He's an active lad, is Mikey."

"I'd like to know what he knows. There's a good chance we've got hold of both ends of the same tail."

"If we do, I hope he's got the end closest to the tiger's ass. There's one way we can get in touch with him."

"What's that?"

"Set fire to this end of the tail. He'll hear about it. I'll bet he already knows about Tel Aviv."

"Everybody does. We made the BBC, Ray."

"Yeah. Good point. Then be patient, Nikki. He'll turn up."

Nikki looked across the wharf, watching as Kirikoff and Babic circled around the big stainless-steel tanker truck. Kirikoff was leaning in close to Babic to make himself heard over the din of the port, Babic running a loving hand over the gleaming surface of the tanker's body.

"What is this?" asked Fyke. "Is Kirikoff trying to sell the damned thing to Babic?"

"I don't know," said Nikki. "But we better not lose sight of this thing. Whatever's going on, that tanker has something to do with it. I'd love to know what's in it."

"I can tell you that," said Fyke. "Nothing. That tanker's bone-dry. You can tell by the tires and the height off the ground. A full tanker, one that size, would be squatting down over its shocks like a beetle with a brick on its back, tires all bulged out."

"So it's empty? That tanker?"

"Empty as my pockets, Nikki, dear heart."

"Well, this is too deep for me. I guess I better get going."

"Ellinikon. You know it? It's down the coast from here, about ten klicks."

"I know it."

"You'll recognize them, then, will you, my darling?"

"Yes, Ray. I think so. They'll be the grumpy ones in the blood-stained bandages."

Airborne

Dalton watched the city of Istanbul glide by underneath the starboard wing of Poppy Pownall's corporate Learjet. The Sultan Mehmet Bridge was almost directly below, noonday traffic streaming across it, hundreds of gypsy freighters dragging their white wakes up the Bosphorus to the Black Sea, through the Kerch Strait and into the Sea of Azov and the gritty Russian coal and iron ports or down to the Sea of Marmora through the Dardanelles and out into the Aegean. A pall of smoke and haze lay over the low, crowded slopes of Istanbul, the spear tips of a hundred minarets lancing up out of the smog, facets of sunlight bouncing off the dome of Hagia Sophia.

He checked his watch, checked their airspeed indicator, made a rough calculation that they'd be on the ground in Athens by three in the afternoon. He sipped at his G & T and shifted his weight in the wide leather chair, easing the pressure on the wound in his hip, which was painful as hell. Mandy, sitting opposite, gave him an up-from-under smile, crossing her long legs as she did to great effect, since she was wearing a tight blue skirt and a crisp white blouse, sleek black stilettos with bright scarlet soles. She looked, as always, shatteringly and untouchably beautiful.

For his part, Dalton, although shaved and showered and turned out in a very fine blue pinstripe over a fresh white shirt, felt like a low-rent fur ball. He smiled back at Mandy, sipped at his G & T, and asked about Dobri Levka, who, after getting some medical attention and a couple of stiff vodkas, had gone limping off to sleep at the rear of the jet.

"Levka's a tough lad," said Mandy. "He just needs some sleep. How are you doing?"

"Vukov. I can't get over it."

"Well, try," said Mandy, holding her wineglass out for Dalton to fill, "Whiners bore me."

"I'm not whining."

"Not yet. But you're circling the drain. Anyway, what's left of him is probably working its way through some creature's alimentary canal right now. We were sixteen miles out at sea. You really think he could swim sixteen miles, in water that cold?"

"I think Vukov is hard to kill."

"So's my sense of humor, but you're managing. What do you want to do when we get on the ground in Athens?"

"How's your math?"

"I don't do math. I have people for that. How's yours?"

"The Russians intercepted Levka's boat three weeks ago, towed it to Anapa. Two days later, he watched as a yacht transporter took the *Subito* aboard, lashed it down under a tarp, and steamed out into the Black Sea. According to Earl Ford, Turkish authorities had cleared a Kerch-bound yacht transporter to transit the Bosphorus seven days before. There aren't many yacht transporters going into the Black Sea. None in over a month. This transporter was called the *Novotny Ocean,* owned by a shipping conglomerate with offices in Athens, Marseilles, Bremen—"

"Northstar Logistics. Fast-forward, Micah, dear boy."

"The Turks passed it back *down* the Bosphorus fifteen days ago. No record was kept of the load. According to Lloyd's, the *Novotny*

Ocean is over three hundred feet long, has two Wartsila Vasa diesel engines, and can cruise at fifteen knots with a full load, faster with only one boat on board. It's eight hundred and fourteen klicks from Kerch to Istanbul—"

"Dear God, I need a drink—"

"You've got one."

"I need a *real* drink."

Dalton mixed her up a G & T, handed it over. She took a sip, shivered, set it down, leaned back, and artfully recrossed her legs, giving him an eyebrow as she did.

"That's not going to work," said Dalton, his face a little hot.

"Not immediately. Please, *do* go on. I'm utterly transfixed."

"Another five hundred and forty-one from Istanbul to Athens. It cleared Greek customs and was logged into Piraeus Harbor twelve days ago. It was refueled and resupplied by the dock crew and left the next evening, declaring a course for Gibraltar. It's roughly twenty-six hundred klicks from Athens to Gibraltar—"

"We Brits just call it Gib—"

"Thank you for that, Mandy. At fifteen—"

"You're welcome."

"At fifteen knots per hour—"

"Do I get a prize if I guess this right?"

"Yes. At fifteen knots—"

"What sort of prize?"

"A kiss on any body part you care to name. At fifteen—"

Mandy named one.

Dalton took some time to refocus, but, being a trained professional, he managed. Mandy sipped at her G & T and felt rather good about her flirting skills. They were not in any way declining.

"At fifteen knots an hour," said Dalton, beginning again, "the *Novotny Ocean* would reach Gib in eight days. Am I right?"

"Actually, no, since a knot is a nautical mile, and a mile is longer than a kilometer. Say, to be safe, seven days. But what if this *Novotny* thingy wasn't really going to Gib?"

"The IMO keeps a geostationary satellite over the Med. I don't think there's a body of water in the world, other than the Indian Ocean, where ships get tracked as carefully as in the Med. I think we can assume the *Novotny* was going to Gibraltar—"

"Since it left Piraeus Harbor roughly ten days ago, we can assume it's already *in* Gibraltar. We just don't—"

"Know *why?*"

"Yes," he said, picking up his glass. "We don't know why."

The bathroom door at the back of the Lear cracked open, and Levka, showered and shaved and wearing jeans, cowboy boots, a black T-shirt, and a black leather jacket that he had borrowed from one of Captain Davit's sailors, came down the aisle, stopping at the bar to pour himself a large vodka. He wasn't moving very well, but he wasn't dead either. He came along to their seating area, sat down—carefully—beside Dalton, and lifted his glass to Mandy.

"You come to get me, Miss Mandy. I wish to say thank you! And to you, boss, I *hope* you will. But, even so, I never think I leave that place alive."

"How are you feeling?" asked Mandy, looking at his bruised and battered face, at his general pastiness. Levka, when properly fed, had developed a kind black Lab aura, solid, friendly, a bit of a scoundrel but an honest scoundrel. She was sorry to see him looking so downcast.

"I am okay, Miss Mandy. I am not happy to lose boat. Was my business. My new life. Now is gone."

"Did the ship have one of those embedded GPS things?" asked Mandy. "The ones they hide in the hull somewhere?"

Levka looked a little shamefaced.

"Yes. But battery was dead, and I not getting around to fixing.

Battery cost three hundred euros," he added by way of an explanation, looking down at his hands. "I am idiot. Boat gone."

"Maybe not. We have a rough idea where it is," said Dalton.

Levka brightened.

"Is true? How?"

Dalton nodded to Mandy.

"My father has a friend in Yalta," she said. "We were able to identify the boat that came to get the *Subito*. The *Blue Nile*. Shipping records show it on a course for Gibraltar. We think it may be there now."

"In Gibraltar? But why?"

"Good question," said Dalton, offering him a Sobranie, which he lit and carefully placed between his battered lips, drawing the smoke in. From up in the cockpit came a female voice, gently chiding, "Please, sir, there's no smoking on this jet."

Levka sighed, stubbed it out, looked out the window.

"Speak of no smoking," he said, "I hope they pumping out engine compartment every day."

"Why?"

"Sump is malfunction. Fumes always building up in engine area. Make you pretty sick, you go down there."

"Isn't that a fire hazard?" asked Dalton.

"No. Everything, all the electrics, are shielded. Fuses, breakers, wiring—all shielded good. No. No hazard there. But if you go down with cigarette in mouth, you come back up pretty fast. Only in little pieces. Along with rest of boat."

"Maintenance, Dobri," said Dalton, giving Levka a look. "You ever get it back, you need to take better care of that boat."

Levka sighed again, nodded.

"Sure will, boss. If I ever see it again. Where are we now?"

"Over the Dardanelles," said Dalton. "We'll be in Athens soon."

"What we going to do in Athens, boss?"

Dalton told him about Northstar Logistics, about their warehouse in Piraeus. "Vukov said Kirikoff was in Athens. If he is, that's where to start looking for him."

"You believe him? This Vukov?"

"It's the only lead we've got. And the *Novotny Ocean* logged in there twelve days ago. So it's a good place to start."

"Okay, boss. Work for me."

"I have a question," said Mandy. Levka drank some vodka, wincing as the alcohol stung his lips. "Please, miss."

"Why are you alive, Dobri? Why didn't Vukov kill you?"

Levka shrugged, pulled his lips down—a very Italian gesture.

"I am not knowing. I am glad. But not knowing."

"He beat you pretty badly. What was that for?"

"He want to know about boss," he said, looking over at Dalton and then back to Mandy. "Where he live. His work. How me and the boss got into work together. He know about Istanbul, about Mr. Galan . . . Sorry about him, boss . . . Anyway, I say I know nothing. He beat me. I pass out. He wake me up. We start again. After time, I forget who I am . . ."

"But he kept you alive," said Dalton. "He must have needed you for something. Needed you alive, at any rate."

"Yes," said Mandy. "And they needed his boat."

"Yes," said Levka. "My boat . . ."

He fell silent, staring out at the water.

"I forget a lot while with Vukov. But it come back a little. Anybody see cell phone in that place? In Anapa? Red Motorola Krzr? MP3 player? Very nice."

"We didn't look that hard," said Dalton. "But I'd say no. It wasn't with what was left of your clothes, and they'd all been shredded to bits. We gathered what we could, but people were coming. We left in a hurry. Just got off the beach when a cop car pulled up at the back of the place."

"No Krzr phone?"

"No."

"Then maybe is not dream. When Russians show up—two patrol boats, sirens going—we are to stop engines and be boarded. I try to call out on ship radio but only get static. They jam the radio, I think. Boss, you remember engine room in Istanbul where we find Kissmyass, the KGB guy?"

"Yes. In the pilot's cabin, there's trapdoor in the deck that leads down to the engine compartment. He was hiding there."

"Yes. He had cell phone, remember? So do I. I think, Okay, hide in engine compartment like Kissmyass, make call to Bogdan, tell him what is happening. This I do. I go down in engine room, close hatch. I making call when hatch open up. Sailors are there, Russkies. I fight. I think I drop the phone in engine room. I think may still be there."

"Did that phone have a GPS function?" asked Dalton.

"Yes. Maybe if we—"

"More than three weeks ago," said Mandy. "The battery would have died after a couple of days."

"No. I set to shut down if not using. Shut off time sixty minutes."

"Dobri," said Dalton, letting him down easy, "The GPS function wouldn't work if the cell phone is turned off."

Levka's face went slack, and then he rallied.

"Can we turn back on? From remote?"

"It was a Krzr?" asked Dalton. "A Motorola?"

"Yes. Very fine."

Dalton worked that through, found a trace memory.

"Motorola phones can't be totally powered down unless you remove the battery. It's . . . I have heard that it may be possible to download software that might . . . *might* . . . allow you to turn the phone back on. I know the FBI figured out how to turn a cell-phone *mike* on even when the unit wasn't being used. They used that trick on the Genovese family. And I know the NSA have been refining that stunt for years. Yes. If the battery isn't totally flat, you *might* be able to do that."

"And that would tell us where the *Subito* is?" asked Mandy.

"As long as it's in a covered area, down to the nearest tower."

That was a comforting thought, and they drank to it again, then fell into a weary silence. The Lear hurtled through the deep blue, and the gentle rise and fall of the jet put them all to sleep.

They woke a while later as the Lear began a slow bank, six sunlit ovals sliding across the cabin bulkhead, the liquid in their glasses slanting a couple of degrees.

The pilot's voice came on the radio, another soft feminine voice. Apparently, all of Poppy's pilots were female.

"We're beginning our approach to Ellinikon Airport in Athens, Miss Pownall," she said with a crisp British accent. "Would your guests mind getting ready to land?"

DESCENDING in a smooth glide through the afternoon smog of coastal Athens, the Learjet touched down at Ellinikon at a few minutes after three, being redirected by Traffic Control to that part of the seaside airport reserved for private corporate jets. The Lear slowly taxied past a row of other small jets—a Gulfstream, another Lear, a Cessna. They rolled past a small, sleek number with the blue-and-white flag of Israel on her tail. Dalton took note, stiffening.

The plane rocked to a stop, the hatch popped open, and they sat there for a while as the heat of Athens poured into the cabin, carrying with it the salty tang of the sea and the reek of jet fuel and diesel fumes. A customs official checked their passports, not very carefully, bored to tears, and welcomed them all to Athens. Technically, he welcomed Mandy Pownall's breasts to Athens, since that was where he was looking as he said this. He then was gone, his boots clanking down the aluminum steps, the papers on his clipboard fluttering in a hot wind off the Aegean Sea.

Mandy and Dalton, with Levka trailing them, falling back into his role as their majordomo, insisting on carrying all the luggage, walked across the tarmac toward the cab stands. Mandy was fighting to keep her skirt under some sort of control. Dalton was staring rather intently at a small party of three that was walking more or less in the same direction: a slender, deeply tanned young man in slacks and a sports shirt, a large, bearlike man in jeans and a loud parrot-print shirt, and an attractive young woman with auburn hair, also having trouble with her skirt.

Dalton stopped, went back to Levka. He reached into his luggage and pulled out the Colt Anaconda, held it down at his side.

"Mandy," he said, stepping in front of her, "that's Joko Levon over there. He's Mossad."

Mandy looked over, saw the large man in the parrot shirt. He was now looking right at them. And the smaller man with him had stopped as well. The auburn-haired woman walked on, not yet noticing the developing confrontation. Dalton watched as Joko stepped forward. Joko seemed to be reaching into his belt. Dalton lifted the Colt. He heard someone shouting, a woman's voice, from across the landing strip.

"Micah, no. Don't—"

Dalton had his sight zeroed in on Joko's belly. The younger man with him had drawn a small pistol. Joko had his arms straight out at his sides, shaking his big shaggy head. Mandy put her hand on his gun arm, pulling it gently down.

"Micah, no. That's Nikki Turrin."

Dalton shifted his eyes, took in the young Italian woman now rushing toward him across the tarmac, her hair flying, holding up a hand, calling to him . . . It *was* Nikki Turrin.

He looked back at Joko Levon over a range of fifty yards.

Joko looked back at him, dropping his arms to his sides, shaking his massive head. The young man standing beside him, holding his pistol up and aiming it at Dalton, slowly, reluctantly, let it fall away.

"Jesus Christ," said Joko, shouting to make his voice heard over the wind, outrage in every aspect. "Jesus H. Christ, Micah. It's me. Joko."

Dalton, the wind rippling his suit jacket, his long blond hair flying out, walked slowly across the airstrip, stopping a few feet away. Joko stepped forward, held out his hand.

"Micah. All is forgive. You shake?"

Dalton looked at his hand and then up at Joko's face.

"What happened to you?" he asked, shaking Joko's hand.

Joko's smile opened up in his bearded face, creasing his eyes.

"Ray Fyke. He broke a champagne bottle on my skull."

"Did he?" said Dalton, grinning back. "Well, you're big enough. Maybe he thought you were a ship."

"I am Daniel Roth," said the smaller man at Joko's side. He had an intense, hawkish face, sharp brown eyes, weathered skin, some gray in his blue-black hair. Dalton saw that he had a tooth missing right in the front: "Ray do that too?"

"Yes," said Roth. "He owes me a tooth."

Nikki Turrin stepped in, windblown, nervous, memorable.

"I'm Nikki Turrin, Mr. Dalton," she said, offering her hand and a charming smile. "We've never met. But I know *you* very well."

"Made a *study*, have you, dear?" said Mandy as she walked up, Levka trailing with the bags. "Come to any conclusions?"

Something passed between Nikki and Mandy that might have been the kissing hiss of steel on steel. All the men missed it completely. Nikki was thinking of a way to reply without giving too much ground when her cell phone rang, Happy to have a deflection, she picked it up.

"Ray?"

"Yeah. You get Joko?"

"I did. And I got Micah Dalton."

"Mikey's there? Perfect! Can I talk to him?"

Nikki handed her phone over Dalton.

"Ray?"

"Jesus, Mary, and Joseph. It's the crocodile. Mikey, your timing could not be better. Nikki tell you what we've been doing? We've been dogging Piotr Kirikoff—"

"So have I—"

"We've been doing a better job. He's here, in Athens. He's gone to ground in Piraeus. He and a guy named Milan Babic—"

"Ratko Mladic's guy. Christ. Are you sure?"

"I'm sure. Point is, Nikki and I, we got them both in a warehouse here. Been on them since around noon. Kirikoff's car is parked right out front. Next to a big tanker. But then I get that . . . sick . . . feeling. So I decide, go inside the building, check it out—"

"Let me guess. The place is empty. Just a front."

"Worse. There was a camera inside the door. I walked right into it, looked up. Flash! I'm burned. Probably Nikki's burned. Maybe we're *all* burned. Kirikoff waltzed us in and waltzed us back out. Warehouse is all shut down. And Piotr Kirikoff is in the wind."

Gibraltar

The Rock loomed high above them in the warm Mediterranean night,
an overwhelming presence, invisible in the velvet darkness, its shark-
finned bulk defined only by the blinking strobes of the radar masts and
communications towers that rode along its razorlike, ridged-back spine.
Through the windows of the port captain's office, Dalton and Mandy
Pownall could see the harbor and the marinas laid out in front of them,
the quays and docks crowded with ships, floodlit and full of activity,
even at this late hour. In the marina, the flying bridges of private yachts
and the masts of barques and schooners dipped and rocked, beads of
lights strung along their rigging. Beyond the harbor lights, the Atlantic Ocean was a negation, a blank nothingness, out of which came a
long, withdrawing roar as the tide ebbed away. Twilight was gone, but
there were no stars. Gibraltar stood at the brink of a limitless void, a
single point of light, of human presence, here at the outermost edge of
the Old World.

The man running the GPA, the Gibraltar Port Authority, was a
leathery, windburned middle-aged man named Dugald Woodside.
Clearly a sailor, he had a full head of snow-white hair, cut a little long,
a trim regimental mustache, and careful blue eyes with deep creases

around them. He was wearing the uniform of a Royal Navy captain, the tunic neatly hung on a wooden hanger at the side of his office.

He was smoking a pipe, a Peterson Bent, its bowl full of rich Virginia Flake. He had asked permission before lighting up and seemed delighted that both Mandy Pownall and the tall, rather grim-looking American took the opportunity to light up their Balkan Sobranies. The Brotherhood of the Habit established itself at once. Soon his wood-paneled office was hazy with smoke, which drifted through the glow of his green-shaded desk lamp. They all contemplated the clouds with obvious satisfaction until Woodside, recalling himself to the matter in front of them, tapped the printout on his desk.

"This is the Gibraltar Movement Summary for the last week. We track every commercial and private vessel that comes in and out of the GPA zone. By 'we,' I mean the Royal Navy, although we work in close association with the civilian authorities."

Here, he ran a tobacco-stained fingertip down the page, stopping halfway.

"Yes. The *Novotny Ocean*. A yacht transporter. Length: one-sixty meters. Beam: thirty-one meters. Tonnage: nineteen thousand. Captain: Nick Maloutsis. Crew of eight, mainly Serbs and Croats . . . We get a lot of these in Gib flagged Panama. Don't like those Panamanian registries, Miss Pownall. But we've seen this ship and this crew before, she's a regular. Arrived from Athens with papers for Gibraltar, here to pick up some of our local yachts and ferry them back to the Aegean and the Adriatic for the summer season. Fifteen hundred nautical miles is a long run for these private owners. She came in empty. She's still moored at the quayside. She's been taking on yachts, and weighs tomorrow."

Mandy, British gentry, with her entries in Debrett's and Burke's Peerage, was the natural choice to lead this inquiry, which for Dalton might not have gotten much past the *commissionaire*'s desk in the central hall. She leaned forward to look at the sheet.

"She came in empty, Captain Woodside? I suppose there can be no mistake?"

He shook his large head, his expression regretful.

"None at all, Miss Pownall. Ships are tracked by radar in the approaches, and we have Royal Navy ships out in Gibraltar roads all the time. She radioed in from a hundred miles out and was logged into the arrivals process right away. She declared herself empty and was confirmed to be when she came under the Rock. This boat she was carrying . . . ?"

"The *Blue Nile*. A Riva. White-over-blue. Sixty feet."

"The *Blue Nile*. Absent any bills of lading, it's quite possible that the *Novotny Ocean* put in at some other port. Anywhere along the Med, possibly quite legitimately, possibly not. But with a submersible hull, they could have heaved to practically anywhere in the western Med, even out in open water. Filled the tanks, lowered the deck underwater. As soon as your boat floated off the supports, she'd back out of the gate, and, from there, merrily off into the deep blue Mediterranean."

"How many private craft of that size would clear Gib on the average day?"

Woodside leaned back with a creak in his leather chair, tapped his bowl on its arm, looking into the middle distance while he worked out his estimate.

"Now, in the beginning of the cruising season . . . I imagine you'd see upward of a hundred a day . . . potting back and forth between the Pillars. This is very popular cruising ground . . . ports like Cádiz, the Algarve, Tangier—"

"No way to track them, sir?" put in Dalton, who here was simply Dylan Castle, Mandy Pownall's American friend. No mention had been made of Nikki Turrin, Ray Fyke, Dobri Levka, and the two Mossad agents, all of whom were currently dining at a seaside café that Dalton could see from the captain's office window.

Woodside, idly wondering where this interesting young American had acquired what looked very much like a bullet wound on his cheekbone, sucked on his pipe and shook his head once more. "There are *some* ways. Is the matter so urgent?"

"Not urgent," said Mandy with an engaging smile. "Just a minor mystery. The boat was stolen by some port rowdies in Yalta. My father, who has mining interests in the area, was asked to help in the search. Since I was at liberty, he asked me to see if it had turned up in Gib."

"There was some reason to believe it was on the *Novotny Ocean,* then?"

"Nothing solid. Poppy looked into the shipping records, and there was some indication that the *Novotny Ocean* had been in the vicinity of Yalta around the time the yacht was stolen. It's just as likely—even more so—that the boat was sailed over to the Russian side and sold on the black market. That happens all the time."

"Do you suspect Captain Maloutsis of complicity in this?"

"Not at all. We're told that any boat taken aboard a transport has only to show her ownership and insurance papers. Since these papers were on the boat when it was stolen, there's no reason for Captain—Maloutsis?—to be under any suspicion."

Mandy leaned back, conveying careless resignation.

"No, Captain, it was just a whim. Dylan and I were in Athens. The *Novotny* had docked there a few days before, then departed for Gib. Poppy loaned us the Lear, and we flew out here. More of a lark, really. A touch of intrigue in our dull lives."

Captain Woodside thought but did not say that there was a lot more to all of this than this lovely woman was suggesting, but Alistair Pownall, Mandy's poppy, a man of some influence at the Admiralty, was not unknown to him.

He decided to push things just a touch more.

"Miss Pownall, you and Mr. Castle asked about means of tracing private hulls. Most motor cruisers of the size you describe would have been equipped with an embedded GPS identifier. By that, I don't mean simply the EPIRB beacon, which activates only when it comes in contact with water. The maker you cite, Riva, does this sort of thing as a matter of course. The GPS beacon is buried deep in the hull, runs on a long-life battery that has to be changed only every couple of years. These beacons are usually put in locations known to the ship's owner alone. I take it the *Blue Nile* was not fitted with such a device? Or was it deactivated? And if it was deactivated, its silence should have been a warning signal to Captain Maloutsis, since the entire idea of such a device is to prevent the very kind of theft you describe. Does your father have information that such a device was not present?"

Mandy was not rattled.

"Our understanding is that the embedded GPS was somehow switched off. Would Captain Maloutsis have realized this?"

"Certainly. I imagine he would scan every yacht he takes on, if only for his insurance people, to make sure it carried a working GPS identifier. If he actually did bring this boat, the *Blue Nile*, into the western Med under the circumstances you have proposed, then as a matter of course and in line with my duties as port captain of Gibraltar I could discuss the matter with him. In fact, I think I *should*. Would you like me to?"

AN hour later, at the table in the seaside café, Fyke, Nikki Turrin, and the others listened to the story, the two Mossad members with growing concern. Joko Levon let Dalton finish and then laid his heavy hands on the table in front of him.

"We're not *declared*, Dalton. If this Navy guy wants to call for the

Lear manifest, he'll see that we came in with you. He'll want to know who we are. And what if he digs into you? Will the Castle cover stand up?"

"To a cursory search, yes. And if *you're* not declared, you have plausible ID."

"Yes. Of course. That's not the point. If it comes to it, Tel Aviv will let us declare, but then we'll have to share this whole damned thing with the Royal Navy. The last thing I want is Kirikoff and Milan Babic, let alone this Vukov guy if he's still alive, sitting in a brig in Gibraltar while we try to get Her Majesty to let us extradite them."

"The idea," said Roth, calmer but no less intense, "is to either take them back to Tel Aviv or leave them all dead. We don't do due process in Tel Aviv. The other risk here is that Woodside will turn up something about the *Blue Nile* that we weren't counting on. Or something about either of you two."

Nikki shook her head.

"I think they did the right thing, Mr. Roth," she said, holding her own pretty well in this sort of company. "The idea is to find the *Blue Nile*. That's the only thing we have that connects to Kirikoff. If the seven of us spent the rest of the summer combing every port in the western Med—"

"Or up and down the African coast," said Mandy.

"Or the Atlantic," Nikki said with a grateful glance at Mandy. "We'd never find that boat. But the Royal Navy, if *they* get interested, has access to the satellite, ships in every port, literally thousands of contacts—"

"What good will that do us if the guys we want end up in somebody else's jail?" asked Joko, scowling into his beer.

"A British jail," said Fyke with some heat, "is a good jail. Where would you rather have them?"

"Look, Ray—" Joko began, but Dalton cut in.

"We're committed now, Joko. No point arguing about it after the fact. Woodside will grill Maloutsis in the morning. Maybe he'll get something out of him. Personally, I doubt it. All Maloutsis has to do is play dumb."

"So what's the upside?" asked Roth, cooler but still unhappy.

"The upside is, Maloutsis—who is in this up to his shorts, by the way, along with his entire crew of Serbs and Croats— gets his cage rattled hard enough to make him call for instructions. Who's he going to call?"

"Kirikoff," said Roth. "Or Babic."

"Yes," said Dalton, nailing it down. "Or Vukov, if he's still in the mix. If we get all of Maloutsis's communications lines monitored, maybe we can get a line on Kirikoff."

"Nice trick," said Roth. He looked at Nikki, who, as they all knew by now, had a line directly to Deacon Cather. "Will your guy do that? Can he get the NSA to do that?"

Nikki shook her head.

"I don't think so. They've got him pretty isolated. Micah tried to get some help from . . . What was her name, Micah?"

"Sally Fordyce."

"Sally Fordyce. She was senior aide at Langley. She disappeared right after Micah called her—"

"And nobody has heard from her since," said Dalton. "We can't ask Cather for anything. He's done what he could, with Nikki and Ray. Mandy's not in the game anymore, not officially. That leaves you two."

Joko and Roth exchanged looks.

"We're not up to that. It would take . . ."

Fyke was getting a little red around the edges.

"You *wanted* in, Joko. Now that you're here, so far you're just cargo. You said Dagan would give you some help. Nobody taps a line better than the Mossad. You could get that done in an hour."

Joko leaned back, leaving it up to Roth, who was still on active duty. Roth fingered his swollen upper lip absently while staring at Fyke not at all lovingly.

"Okay," he said, getting up. "I'll see about it. What's the guy's full name?"

"Nickolu Maloutsis," said Mandy, who had gotten the data from Captain Woodside. She pulled a sheet of paper out of her case, handed it to Roth. "It's all there. Ship registry, her call sign, even Maloutsis's cell-phone number. Woodside said he'd contact Maloutsis as soon as the GPA office opened in the morning. That gives you—what?— six hours to get his electronics into the system. Do you need a warrant?"

Roth showed his teeth, a bloody gap right in the upper front.

"No. We leave that crap to you Americans. You guys would have to wake up Carl Levin, see if he was okay with it. Wait here. I'll be back."

Roth turned away, striding across the half-empty dining room, pushing his way out the glass doors and into the night. After he was gone, a silence fell over the table, mostly fatigue, frustration. Some free-floating blame looking for a place to land.

Dobri Levka, so far silent, leaned into the circle of light.

"Excuse, but there was also *other* way to find boat. No?"

"The cell phone?" asked Dalton.

"What cell phone?" asked Joko. Dalton nodded to Levka, who filled Joko in—and Fyke and Nikki Turrin as well—on the possibility that his Motorola cell phone *might* still be on the *Blue Nile* and *might* be remotely turned on and that *might* . . .

"Jesus, Dobri," said Joko, blinking across the table at Levka. "That's a lot of *might*s. I'm gonna start calling you Mighty Mouse."

Nikki, who was an NSA agent, spoke up after a pause.

"Don't laugh. It could work."

She had the full attention of the table.

"Dobri, do you know the model number of the phone?"

"Yes. Is K1M. Motorola Krzr. With MP3 player. Phone number is three-eight-zero-six-five-six-one"—Nikki was scribbling on a napkin—"three-two-nine-four-nine."

Nikki looked at her watch: a little after midnight.

"What time is it in Maryland right now?"

"Around seven in the evening," said Dalton.

Nikki got up, pulled out her BlackBerry, started hitting buttons as she walked away. "Give me an hour."

"Well," said Mandy, picking up her champagne and looking around the table, "that leaves us five. Anyone for poker?"

"Not yet," said Dalton. "Here comes Roth."

"Oh dear," said Mandy, watching the intense young man striding across the floor. "He does not look happy."

"I'm not," said Roth as he reached the table, looking back to the entrance and then scanning the room as he took a chair. "I've been talking to Tel Aviv— "

"Do we get the tap?" asked Dalton.

"They said yes, but that's not the point. We also monitor marine communications along the Med. What was the name of the port captain you spoke to . . . Was it Woodside?"

"Yes," said Mandy. "Dugal Woodside. What's the problem?"

"Well, he's just filed a formal notification with the IMO that he's decided to seize the *Novotny Ocean*. Under suspicion of smuggling stolen yachts. In the filing, he says he already had some problems with the Panama registration. And he has the authority to commence a formal investigation. He's already got a guard on the wharf, and he's quarantined the entire crew on board. Including Captain Maloutsis."

"We thought he might do that," said Dalton. "We *hoped* he would. Why so worked up?"

"According to the bulletin, he intends to stage this inquiry here at

Gibraltar. And he's going to call for anyone connected with the matter to come in and make a formal deposition."

"Oh . . . bloody hell," said Dalton.

"I'd have put it stronger than that," said Roth. "That means he's going to want to talk to you and Mandy. He's already left an official notice at the hotel requiring you not to leave Gibraltar until you come in and provide an affidavit. Mandy's credentials will stand up, of course, but how about yours, Micah? I think not. They'll hold you and start digging. None of which we have the time for. We have to *find* that boat. Where's Nikki Turrin?"

"Outside. She's on the line to somebody in Maryland," said Fyke. "About Levka's cell phone."

Roth got up, looked around the table at a series of shocked expressions he found quite impressive, particularly for range and impact. "I warned you about this. I suggest we go find her—"

"And get the hell out of Gib," said Mandy, rising.

"*You* can stay, if you want—"

"Like hell," said Mandy.

"Then, let's go," said Roth. "Dagan's having them fly the Legacy in from Athens. It'll be on the ground at Boukhalef field in Tangier. If we can get there."

"Yes. And how *are* we supposed to get to Tangier? The Lear's definitely out," said Mandy. "We can't avoid a Royal Navy inquiry by buggering off in Poppy's jet. He'd have a fit."

"A pox on Poppy," said Fyke, looking down at the darkened marina, at the cruisers moored there, hundreds of shapes and sizes, a sea of masts and flying bridges, rocking gently in the changing tides. "Anyone up for a little piracy?"

IT was sixty klicks across the strait to Tangier. The motor yacht, a classic wooden Chris-Craft about fifty feet long, which was chosen by

Fyke for its primitive electronics, making it easy to jump-start, and approved by Dalton on the possibility that it wouldn't have any modern GPS gear, which it didn't, covered the sixty klicks in five hours, with no sign of pursuit either from the sky or from some naval patrol boat out of Gibraltar.

A long, narrow, sharp-bowed, spear-shaped boat without a flying bridge, the Chris-Craft also had a wooden hull and low superstructure that made it a good choice if you were hoping to avoid radar detection. It was not a good choice if any of the passengers were prone to seasickness. A long, narrow hull in open water tends to pitch and yaw with every roller. So although the boat covered the sixty klicks in five hours, for some of the more delicate passengers, such as the two Mossad agents and Ray Fyke, these were not happy hours.

Levka, at the wheel of the boat—she was called *Tropical Dancer*—and back in his element, seemed content just to be driving a big cruiser again even if it was likely to result in a lengthy jail sentence in some North African hellhole. It had occurred to Levka that staring Third World prisons in the face made up a large part of his daily duties when in Micah Dalton's employ.

Dalton, standing beside him, listening to the chatter on the marine radio, smoking a Sobranie, and staring out at the lights of Tangier as they started to spread out across the black horizon, was thinking about the size, shape, and dimensions of the problem that was also spreading itself out on his own black horizon.

Down in the lounge, all teak and brass and mahogany, with a lovely stainless-steel galley and a cozy little stateroom in the bow, Mandy was reclining on a leather couch, watching Nikki Turrin set about making chicken soup. It was about the only thing the men had been able to keep down, but even that not for very long.

Ray Fyke, Joko Levon, and Danny Roth were out on the fantail under the open sky, a place with easy and frequent access to the ocean from all three sides. Perhaps in honor of Fyke, whose sainted mother was from County Clare, all three men were green. Although he had spent a lot of time at sea with the SAS, and later during a turn as first mate on a gypsy tanker in the South Seas, this bouncy little voyage across the straits in what he felt was little better than a high-toned canoe was just too damned much.

Behind the flat stern of the boat, far off in the east, the light was beginning to change, the sky turning from a featureless void to a pinkish gray. In the cabin, Levka, still on the question of staring prison in the face, drained his coffee cup, set it down in the gimbal ring, and glanced sideways at Dalton.

"So, boss, no offendings, but what are we going to do when we get into Tangier?"

Dalton's hard face creased in the dim light, the red glow from the instrument panel giving his smile a sardonic cast.

"Mandy met me in Sevastopol with, among other useful things, a bag of gold wafers. I'm told they like gold in Tangier."

Levka found this comforting, but he followed the line of inquiry awhile longer.

"You got any idea what is all about? Kidnap me, take my boat, set you up for killing Mr. Galan?"

"I'm beginning to. We've been following the *Blue Nile* all the way from Kerch to Gibraltar. And I've left a paper trail all the way along the line. Vienna. Venice. Kerch. Istanbul. Athens. Gibraltar. If they manage to use your boat for something spectacular, I'll be the one most closely associated with it. And you? I think that was why they kept you alive. The idea was, after . . . whatever it is . . . they'd find your body in the boat. Mine too, and Mandy's as well, if the trap on the road to Staryi Krim had worked a little better. I have no idea how they managed to get Burke and Single on the owners' list of Northstar Logistics—"

"That your company in London?"

"Not mine. But it's a CIA front. That's another marker. If you could see it how the authorities would see it, Galan has a contact with you through Irina Kuldic, he turns up dead, and I'm the guy in the Leopoldsberg parking-lot video, so you and I are connected, we own the boat. The boat turns up at some disaster. They could make a case against us that would hold up in the court of world opinion, if not in a real court."

"A—what you call—propaganda?"

"Yes. Something like that. Embarrass England and the U.S. Implicate the CIA in some atrocity. Ramp up the tensions between us and Israel. Not to mention further inflame the Muslim world against the Great Shaitan. Typical Russian ploy. The part I can't figure out is . . . where."

"But Bogdan, he know the truth."

"Killing Bogdan Davit wouldn't faze them. The only witness to what happened in Leopoldsberg is an Austrian OSE agent. Brancati's got her in the Arsenale. I don't think they can get to her. But all she has is what she saw. And that can be picked apart."

"But, where they do this . . . propaganda?"

"It has to be at this end of the Med, or why waltz us all the way out here in the first place?"

"So. To know this, we *need* find boat."

"Yes. Wherever your boat is, that's where it will happen."

"Where *what* will happen?" asked Mandy, coming up from the lounge with two cups of soup in her hands. She looked out at the stern and saw what looked like three dead men sprawled along the benches back there. No, not dead. One of them was up and over the stern again. "Dear God. You'd think they'd be empty by now."

She turned and handed a cup to Levka and kept the other one for herself, delicately sipping at the rim, steam rising up.

"Where what will happen?" she asked again.

Dalton laid it out for her. She listened in silence, nodding from time to time. When he was finished, she said, "Let's get Nikki up here. She's the one with friends at the NSA."

Nikki came up the stairs carrying a cup of coffee for Dalton, looking a little drawn. Going from a sunny spring afternoon in Seven Oaks to hunting gators in the Florida Panhandle to a midnight race across the Straits of Gibraltar to Tangier is the kind of thing that sounds better than it lives.

She looked out the windshield, saw Tangier filling up their future, the scattered lights of the Medina piling crazily up the sides of the hill, the radio masts on the top of Cape Spartel blinking in the dark, the sky turning from black to gray behind them, and wished she found the sight wonderfully romantic. As it was, she needed a shower, she was hungry, she was homesick, and she was scared. Mandy looked at her for a while, feeling a strange emotion for her . . . Sympathy? Compassion? Affection?

"Sit, Nikki," she said, pushing her over to the copilot chair and putting a sweater over her shoulders. It was chilly out on the water, the dampness working its way into the bones. Mandy stepped back, looked at Nikki, reached out to brush a strand of hair out of her eyes. The girl *was* very beautiful, if you liked those dusky Mediterranean odalisques like Isabella Rossellini or Juliette Binoche. Mandy supposed some men did.

God knew why.

"We've reached a dead end, Nikki," she said, folding her arms across her chest, cocking her head sideways. "These two berks haven't a clue. It's down to you and that trick with the cell phone. Were you able to get anywhere with that?"

Nikki sighed, looked up at Mandy.

What a simple question, and the answer was a killer.

"Yes. I managed. I ended up calling Hank Brocius."

"The AD of RA," said Dalton. "The Marine with the IED burns. I heard he was on leave."

"Yes. He's in Garrison, Upstate New York. With Briony Keating."

Mandy and Dalton exchanged a charged look.

"With?" asked Mandy, who knew something of their history. "Or *with*?"

"I have no idea which," she said, hardening up. "And I don't really care. What's important is, he said he'd put a tech on it and get back to me."

She lifted up her BlackBerry, turned it in the red glow of the instrument panel. "That was . . . hours ago. So far, nothing."

They heard a low moan and the sound of heavy feet dragging across the decking, turned and saw Daniel Roth making unsteady progress toward the gangway that led down to the head. He looked about as bad as a man can look and not be on an autopsy table. "I need," he said, swallowing carefully, "to visit the facilities. You might wish to stand clear in case I do not make it."

He got level with the pilot chair, stopped to stare out at Tangier, surprised to see how close it was.

"God be praised. Dry land. I may yet live. Is that Tangier?"

"It had better be," said Dalton. "If it's not, Levka goes overboard."

"And I will go with him. Gladly. But if it *is* Tangier, before we dock, radio the port, ask for a man named Tariq Ibn Zuliman. He's one of the harbor police. A secret Hebrew. If I am dead, tell him that Daniel Roth said *Shālōm*. Do we have money at all?"

"Better," said Levka. "We have gold."

"Good," said Roth, weaving. His hawkish face suddenly took on an abstracted glaze, and his color altered for the worse.

"You will . . . excuse . . ."

"Dear God," said Mandy. "Go!"

Roth went stumbling down the stairs. Mandy leaned down and called after him, "Mind, you make it all the way to the head. If you don't, you're the one who mops it up."

She straightened up, registered the disapproving looks.

"I am not well suited," she said with dignity, "to the caring professions. Sick people make me angry. I want to smack them."

"She doesn't approve of blood either," said Dalton.

"Fine on the inside," said Mandy, "where it belongs. But people who get some minor flesh wound and then go tottering about the terrain, moaning and wailing, spouting and gouting, ruining the rugs and draperies, well, they're just . . ."

"Inconsiderate?" suggested Nikki.

"Exactly," said Mandy with a thin but approving smile.

DAWN light was slowly rising up the crowded slopes of the Medina, and already hundreds of people were out in the streets and swarming the crowded, dumpy little harbor. A small, neat brown man, in a starched tan uniform, a Sam Browne harness, and gleaming riding boots, was standing on the mole, watching with an amused smile, as their boat cruised slowly along the quayside.

He bowed as they came level, tipped his kepi when he saw Mandy and Nikki in the pilot cabin, adroitly caught a line from Ray Fyke, pulling briskly on the rope until their port-side bumpers rolled, squealing, up against the wooden dock.

"Mr. Roth is with you?"

Dalton stepped up to the taffrail.

"Mr. Roth is . . . unwell. Are you Ibn Zuliman?"

A cavalier bow, a sardonic half smile, eyes bright.

"I am he. We received your radio message. Are you intending to disembark? There will of course be . . . *formalities . . .*"

"Yes," said Dalton. "We have the 'formalities' in hand. May I introduce Miss Mandy Pownall and Miss Nicole Turrin, both of America. And the large unshaven gentleman with the lime-green skin is Raymond Fyke, a British national. We have some tea brewed. Will you step down and join us?"

"Tea? Tea would be wonderful!" he said, stepping lightly through the gate and down onto the teak decking, He looked around at the boat with an experienced eye and then came back to Dalton.

"A very fine craft, Mr. . . . ?"

"Dalton. Micah Dalton. Yes, she is."

"But perhaps a little narrow in the beam to cross such waters. She would toss about a bit if the swells set in."

"She tossed about more than a bloody bit," said Roth, stumbling up from the lounge deck like an undead corpse rising from a crypt, shirtless, his face wet, a damp towel around his neck. He was holding on to the bulkhead and weaving, but less than usual. "She tried to kill us all, Tariq. I'm very glad to have lived to see you again."

The officer's dark face broke into a broad, teasing grin.

"I have always said you are no sailor, Daniel. Welcome to Tangier. Welcome, all of you," he said as Joko and Levka climbed up to the pilot deck. "And your . . . *borrowed* . . . boat."

"You know this boat?" asked Dalton.

"Oh my yes. A most famous boat, here in Tangier. We see her all the time. A Chris-Craft, built in 1967. A classic. She belongs to Margaret Llewellyn Woodside—"

"Woodside?" Roth asked. "As in—"

"As in Captain Dugald Woodside. I take it she is a friend?"

"Oh my yes," said Mandy with a dazzling smile. "For-simply-ever. We were Head Girls together at Queen Ethelburga's. Such happy times. I wonder, Major Zuliman, if you would consider keeping her lovely boat safe here in Tangier. I'm sure dear, darling Maggie will be along very shortly."

Dalton sent Mandy a quick sideways look.

Maggie?

Queen Ethelburga's?

Mandy ignored him, turning her powers of enchantment loose on the dapper little major, who crumbled before them as men usually did.

"It will be an honor, Miss Pownall. An *honor*. But please, you are not staying in Tangier? I would love to invite you—invite *all* of you—for a luncheon. The café there, close by the sea. The lovely aspect. Tea, perhaps something pale and sparkling, a *priorato*? We have, fresh from the Levant . . ."

"Sadly, no," said Mandy, looking over at Roth. "I do so wish we could. But . . . I'm afraid . . ."

"There's a jet waiting for us at Boukhalef," said Roth.

The major managed to tear his attention away from Mandy, visibly disappointed. Nikki Turrin, apparently invisible, sighed.

"Then we must not delay," said the major. "I can lend you our Mercedes and driver. You must be away! So let us quickly conclude the . . . formalities . . ."

Dalton handed over the . . . formalities.

Two were required.

IN a battered and overcrowded antique Mercedes, as they were speeding along the rue Ibn Zaidoun, the green peak of Cape Spartel dominating the northern horizon, about ten klicks from Boukhalef airfield and the waiting Israeli Legacy, Nikki Turrin's BlackBerry finally rang. She picked it up, listened intently for a while, and then made that universal handwriting gesture meaning *I need a pen and paper*. Fyke, on whose lap she was sitting, after a pleasant interlude that involved some incidental contact with Nikki's thighs while he ransacked his pockets for a pen, finally found one in his coat pocket, and Dalton handed back one of the limo driver's business cards. Nikki, head down, her long auburn hair blowing in the hot wind coming in the open window, wrote furiously for about two minutes. She finished writing, saying something low and intense that no one could make out over the rush of wind and the rumble of the tires on the uneven blacktop, and ended the call.

She looked around at the faces, all of which were staring back at her with varying expressions.

"Yes," she said. "He got it. But not—"

"Not here," said Roth, agreeing completely.

Casablanca

Roth and Joko Levon were up front with the pilots, engaged in a low-level but heated discussion with their people back at Tel Aviv, trying to give them a plausible reason for asking the Moroccan authorities to allow a Mossad plane to land at Anfa and not be placed immediately in quarantine while the two governments worked out the ramifications over the following weeks and months.

Dalton, on the starboard side, was watching the coastline of Morocco unwind beneath the silver wing, an undulating ribbon of sand and rock, the long rollers of the Atlantic looking like lacy white ribbons as they crashed into the coast five thousand feet below him. There were boats in the water—tankers, stubby little trawlers, a large schooner far out beyond the sandbars in the deep blue, heeled over hard, trailing a widening V of wake a half mile long. Small craft, motorboats, what looked like a Zodiac. But nothing that looked like the *Blue Nile*.

He was aware of Mandy at his shoulder, craning to see the water through the small round porthole. Her face was set and tense.

"Anything?"

"Not a thing."

"I'm not seeing any marinas," she said, shading her eyes from the glare off the wing and the glare fracturing the water.

"No. Fort Meade had the location of the boat—"

"Or of Levka's cell phone anyway—"

"Or Levka's cell phone, at 33 degrees 36 minutes north and 7 degrees 36 minutes west. That's basically in the middle of those dockyards coming up right underneath us. If the boat is there, it's underneath one of those corrugated-tin shelters."

He checked Mandy's BlackBerry, still not using his own, and saw that they were approaching the sector very fast: they'd be over it in thirty seconds. In the cabin behind them, Fyke and Levka were pressed up against the porthole doing pretty much the same thing: looking for any sign of the *Blue Nile*.

Nikki Turrin was sitting on the opposite side, looking down at Casablanca. A flat, meandering city, streets and lanes laid out in no particular order, it looked to her like an aerial shot of Gary, Indiana. So much for Bogart and Bergman.

She felt the jet banking, and her coffee tilted. She heard the crackling voice of the copilot up front.

"We have been denied permission to land at Anfa. We are to leave Moroccan airspace at once. If you care to look out the port-side windows, you'll see how serious they are about this."

Everyone went to the port side. Everyone except Dalton, who was suddenly riveted by something that was passing below them right now. He could hear Fyke's low growl from across the aisle. "Jesus, Mary, and Joseph, Mikey, they've scrambled a fucking Mirage. He's sitting right off our wing."

"Give him a wave," said Dalton as the Legacy did a slow bank to starboard. Dalton's attention was fixed on something large and rectangular, set out on what looked like landfill, right on the rim of the coast. It was some sort of palace or public building, with a blue roof, a square tower. The grounds around it were a complex pattern of inlaid stone. He picked up Mandy's BlackBerry.

"Mandy, does this thing have a camera?" he asked.

"Yes. A good one."

"Thanks."

He held the BlackBerry up, found the trigger, and snapped a picture just as the coast fell away and they were passing over the muddled maze of downtown Casablanca.

He held the screen up for Mandy.

"Look at this."

She studied the image in the little screen.

"Bloody hell," she said, her gray eyes widening. "That's the Hassan II Mosque. It's the largest mosque in the world, I think. They've been working on it for years. Where's that card?"

She started ruffling through the pockets of her leather jacket, emerging with one of the ID cards Dalton had taken from the bodies of the men he had killed on the road to Staryi Krim.

She held the card up, tapped the symbol they had assumed was a Serbian unit badge . . .

"This is what they're going at. The mosque. It has to be. They put it right out there on the Web too. Like a piece of a puzzle. So they could brag about it later. The sods. What bloody cheek."

Dalton, his face paling as the enormity of the thing went home, stood up, slipped by Mandy, who was still staring down at the ID card, shocked, stunned, silent.

"Danny. Joko," he said, standing at the door to the cockpit.

Roth and Levon turned around.

"Come back into the cabin. Both of you. There's something you need to see."

ROTH slammed the microphone back on the cradle, stared out at the desert below. The harsh, arid terrain was slowly rising into a chain of ancient mountains, ground down to rocky slopes by a hundred million years of wind and sand.

"Fucking Moroccans," said Roth. "They don't believe us."

"Then screw 'em," said Levon. "We did what we could."

"What about Vukov and the rest? What about Galan?"

Roth looked at Joko and then around the cabin at the rest of them, everyone looking either angry or depressed or both.

"They've pulled the Mirage off. But you can bet they're watching us on the radar. If we do anything but leave Moroccan airspace, they'll force us down. Everyone in this cabin will end up in a Moroccan prison. Joko, you and I know what will happen to us. We're not only Jews, we're Mossad. Look, everybody, it was one chance in Hell that these dumb-ass carpet jockeys could see past their hatreds even to save their own fucking mosque. They can't. So I'm going back to Tel Aviv. I'm sorry about Galan, but you all know what these people do to captured Israeli soldiers. I'm not up for being tortured to death in Meknes Prison."

"Or being handed over to Hezbollah or Hamas," said Dalton. "No. You two have to get out of this now. But I'm staying."

Roth and Joko looked across at Dalton.

"Lovely," said Joko. "What are you going to do? Open the door and step out, hope you land on a camel?"

Dalton pointed to the four-lane blacktop running north along the coast. "Put me down on the A3. Touch and go, I'll manage from there."

Roth and Joko stared down at the tiny ribbon snaking along the coast, a perfect picture of bloody nowhere.

"You, my friend—and I say this with the greatest respect—are totally fucking nuts," said Levon with nonetheless a touch of reverent awe in his voice. "Totally, utterly, completely bat shit. And the pilots would never agree to it. It's a rat fuck from the get-go."

"Yes it is. Ask them anyway."

Roth looked at Dalton for a while, shaking his head.

"Fine. You're nuts. But I will. And I know what they'll say."

Roth was wrong.

THE pilot turned out to be an ex–fighter pilot from the IDF. Grinning like a loon, he pulled a hard left bank, dropping down through the heat haze like a falcon diving on a wren, lining up on the A3, choosing a straightaway and heading right at it.

"I crash this thing," said the pilot over the intercom, "I'm sending the bill to Langley."

He didn't. He touched down, bounced twice, taxied to a stop. Dalton, grabbing a leather bag full of borrowed guns and ammo, along with his own Anaconda and his gold, popped the latch. The door swung upward, a hot blast of desert air and grit flowing into the cool of the cabin. He turned around in the doorway and saw Mandy, Levka, Fyke, and Nikki all up and getting ready to go.

"No," he said, hardening up. "This is no—"

"Dear God," said Mandy, brushing past him and jumping to the pavement. "This is no time to stand in the door and pose for the *Oath of the Horatii*. Hand me my bag, Dobri."

Fyke was on the ground a second later, and then Levka. Nikki was about to step off when Dalton put a hand on her shoulder. "No, Nikki. I'm sorry. One of us has to stay."

She shot him a ferocious look, but he pressed his point.

"Nikki, listen. It *has* to be one of *us*. You know everything we know, Nikki. If we don't pull this off, you're the only one who can do anything for us back in D.C. I know you want to go—"

"No! I'm not going to end up as a . . . goddamned REMF!"

Dalton, in spite of himself, had to grin at that.

"Where'd you get that phrase?"

"Hank. He used it all the time."

"Where is he? Where is Hank right now?"

Her face changed, softened a bit.

"He's on his way down to Fort Meade."

"Good. What about Briony?"

"She's . . . staying . . . in Garrison."

"Then go see him, Nikki. Tell him everything that went on. If anyone can find the other end of this crazy tangle, it's him."

She was still in the door, struggling with it.

"Truck coming," said Fyke from the ground.

Nikki looked at Dalton for a moment longer, her eyes hot and her breathing short and sharp. Then she reached out, put her hand behind his neck, pulled him in, and kissed him hard on the mouth. She broke off, shoved him out the door, slammed it down, and the engines began to spool up immediately.

They all stepped back out of the Legacy's wash and watched as it gained speed and rose into the air only a hundred feet in front of a large tractor trailer, which plowed into the shoulder and shuddered to a stop in a cloud of dust. As the jet climbed, it became a glint of steel in the sunlight, a booming roar that shook the sky. And then it was gone, and they were left on the ground in the grit and heat of the desert, the pavement smelling of tar and kerosene.

"How sweetly romantic, a farewell kiss from a devoted fan," said Mandy, shouldering her bag. "Remind me, if we ever meet again, to put something truly horrid in her tea."

They watched as the truck jerked and stalled and then started up again, a column of smoke belching from its stacks.

"Here he comes," said Fyke. "What do you think? Should I show some leg?"

"No," said Dalton, pulling out a couple of gold bars. They glowed in the sunlight, little slabs of heat and fire. "This is prettier."

THE night had come down on Casablanca by the time they reached the center of town. The trucker, a Sephardic Jew who had noted the Israeli flag on the Legacy's tail, grinned and swore that God was smiling on their enterprises, whatever they were, since not only had they survived a landing on a crumbling highway, but the first person to come along was a Jew, not some Moroccan thug with a cell phone. In exchange for three "formalities"—Dalton's Crown Royal bag was getting lighter—he happily drove them all the way into the center of Casablanca and then out along the Boulevard Sidi Mohammed ben Abdallah, circling the roundabout and pulling to a halt about a quarter mile from the Hassan II Mosque. It was, he explained, adopting a solemn, professorial tone, "the largest mosque in the world, capable of accommodating twenty-five thousand worshippers inside and another eighty thousand on the grounds. It was seven epic years in the making, the most awesome wonder of the Islamic world. Whatever you are doing here, I trust that it will meet with the favor of whatever gods you follow. In your case, Mr. Blondie, I suspect he is Thor or perhaps Odin. Good-bye to you all. And know that you have made an old man happy today."

He gazed down upon them, a wizened, leathery old scoundrel with a silver tooth, grinning hugely, jiggling his little bag with three solid-gold wafers in it—he had just collected thirty thousand dollars. He slammed his door, shoved the gearshift forward. There was a clash of gears, a burst of compressed air from his brakes, and the truck jerked forward, lumbering away into the rush and clamor of the streaming traffic, the smoke from its stacks rising up and spreading out and losing itself in the generalized yellow haze of smog and coal dust and sea-salt mist that hung in the humid air.

Dalton turned and considered the mosque itself, set on its landfill delta projecting like a broad square shelf out into the Atlantic Ocean. The old driver was right, even if as a Sephardic Jew who was in no way a valued fragment of the Casablanca mosaic he was being grimly sardonic.

The building, still open to worshippers at this hour, *was* a timeless Moorish classic, with a slender square minaret three hundred feet tall that to Dalton looked like the Campanile in the Piazza San Marco. Down here at street level, bathed in the glow of floodlights, standing out massively against the twilight sky behind it, a laser beam at the top of the minaret lancing out toward Mecca, the ocean booming in the dark, the immense structure breathed of the divine, of the infinite. It looked eternal, untouchable, serene, impregnable. Dalton knew it wasn't.

"Okay, boss," said Levka. "What is plan?"

Fire and blood, he was thinking. *Fire and blood.*

Dalton gave Fyke and Levka a considered appraisal. Levka, still battered and sporting a very black eye, had gone without shaving since bruises and cuts presented obstacles. Fyke, although he had shaved his beard between Tel Aviv and Prague, now had a three-day growth.

"We need two people inside the mosque. I don't look Muslim, and Mandy isn't going to put on a burqa anytime soon . . . Or are you, Mandy?"

"Soon as you do, dear boy," she said with a sweet smile.

"So you two are it. Don't try praying, you'll just blow it. Wander. Look dazzled. Look for any bad guys. And, while you're at it, see if you can get an idea of how fireproof this place is. They have the boat here for a reason. My guess is, they're planning to use it to put a couple of incendiary rounds into the mosque—"

"That wouldn't bring this place down," said Fyke. "It might scorch the front porch a bit. Look at it. It's bigger than Saint Peter's. You couldn't bring that structure down with anything short of an air strike."

"I know. So they've got something else in mind. Maybe you can figure out what it is. Mandy and I will go over to the docklands, see what we can do about the *Blue Nile.*"

"Works for me," said Fyke. "Keep your cells on. We'll be in touch. Let's go, Dobri."

Levka, a worried expression on his face, looked like a man eyeing possible exits and not finding any.

"Okay. Boss, if you can, save my boat, okay?"

"I'll do my best, Dobri."

IT was about a mile, going east along the causeway, to the docklands. Mandy and Dalton covered it like strolling tourists, passing unnoticed through the milling crowds around the mosque, mainly hairy and pointless young men. *Loitering with intent,* thought Dalton. They watched Mandy as she passed by them with a mixture of hunger and scorn. Mandy felt it must be very difficult to be a Muslim man. There were just so damned many things to find both deeply offensive and achingly desirable. How *did* they manage it?

The docklands, when they got there, were like any other port in the world. Freighters lined up at the moles, derricks ready to work. Although not this evening, Friday, and the closing for the Muslim holy day. A lot of tankers and barges were moored out along the roads, waiting for workers to come back again in the morning. A pall of smoke and haze was hanging over it all, set aglow by rows of harsh-blue floodlights lighting up the train tracks and the container yards.

There was a guardhouse at the gate. The gate was open and the house was closed. They strolled through unchallenged and walked down a set of concrete steps to the dockside deck. The corrugated-tin shelters that Dalton had noticed from five thousand feet up ran for a hundred yards along the eastern mole.

When they reached the entrance and looked inside, they saw several hundred small boats—private cruisers, some sailboats, a couple of houseboats—all of them tied up along a battered dock. They were protected from the elements by the roof of the shed but were bobbing in the ebb tide, gently bumping into one another, their bows rising and falling like horses feeding in a stable.

They went inside, walked along about fifty feet, and were just in time to hear the growling mutter of a boat engine and see the *Blue Nile* backing out of her slip a hundred feet away. A heavyset man on the bow was coiling a line, and someone was inside the cabin, a large round-headed shadow, apelike in silhouette, with a troll-like slope to the skull. *Vukov!* Visible in the dim light of the pilot cabin.

The *Nile*'s navy blue hull was streaked and filthy, her white superstructure coated in dust and grime. A tattered American flag was hanging limply from her sternpost.

Mandy got on the cell as Dalton began to jog along the wharfside, revolver out, looking for a way to jump onto the bow. He saw a fishing boat, tarped, rocking in the boiling wake of the *Nile* as she backed out, ripples flaring away, white water churning at her stern. Forty feet away, thirty, Dalton in a dead run. The man on the bow coiling the rope looked up and saw a blond man racing toward the boat, his pale blue eyes fixed on it. The crewman dropped the rope, shouted something to Vukov, who hit the throttle, widening the gap of greasy black water between wharf and bow, beginning to turn seaward. Dalton got to the bow and vaulted up onto the tarp. The tarp was slick and oily, and he slipped and went down. The man on the bow of the *Blue Nile* opened up on him with an automatic weapon, the muzzle a flare of fire, the noise deafening under the corrugated-tin roof. Rounds chewed up the wood near Dalton's head. He rolled back and away, off the fishing boat and onto the wharf. Three more rounds, and he felt something hum past his cheek. Then the shooting stopped abruptly.

The *Blue Nile* had her bow around and pointed toward the open sea. Vukov shoved the throttles down, and the stern buried itself in white water, the engines rumbling and growling. Dalton got to his feet just in time to watch her powering out of the shed, water curling away from her sharp destroyer bow, the brass letters on her stern dull, tarnished, but still readable:

THE BLUE NILE
KERCH, UKRAINE

Mandy reached him, and they stood there, watching the white superstructure, showing no lights of any kind, getting dimmer and dimmer, the U.S. flag whipping in the wind, a patch of red, white, and blue, fading into a dim fluttering shape as the boat cruised out into the starless night, now fading, a wisp only, then gone.

Dalton checked himself for wounds, found nothing other than a skinned palm and a large wooden splinter sticking in his left forearm. He looked at Mandy, who was still staring out into the blackness. If anyone around the docklands had heard the shooting—how could they not?—no one had bothered to come to check it out. They were alone inside the shed. Mandy looked up at him.

"I got in touch with Ray. They're inside the mosque."

"What did you say?"

"I said whatever's happening, it's happening right now."

INSIDE the mosque, which Fyke and Levka entered through the base of the tower, everything was aglow. A golden light, muted, seeming to come from everywhere, filling the great open spaces under the towering onion-shaped arches. Each archway defined a separate space topped by a coffered ceiling supported by elegant square columns of sandstone, their bases covered in green mosaics. Each archway lined up with the following one—nine great arches in all—leading the eye down the length of the mosque into a soft amber infinity, the air hazy with incense, all the way to the far end, which opened onto the Atlantic.

Every surface gleamed with green and gold in intricate patterns covering the interiors of the great arches or glimmering in the dimness of side chambers and hallways, the entire space humming with the murmur of voices, a rhythmic rumbling sound that made the entire mosque vibrate like a hive of bees.

In the entrance, a space had been set aside, large and orderly, where men could leave their shoes and walk in paper sandals provided for the purpose across the shining inlaid floor to the prayer halls.

Fyke, his mind busy with Mandy's news—*Whatever's happening, it's happening right now*—did the same, putting on the paper slippers, Levka even bowing to the nut-brown little man behind the desk and saying *Salaam alaikum* while leaving a euro on the tray. They headed back out into the hushed but amiable atmospherics of the mosque, a more relaxed and informal environment now that the hour for *Salah*, for prayer, was over.

Although Dalton was right that Fyke and Levka never could have passed for Muslims here—there were thirty distinct errors in the performance of the *Salat* that were specifically forbidden by the Prophet Himself, such as counting your *tasbeeh*, your ritual prayer beads, with your left hand—as a pair of visitors they attracted little attention as they moved through the echoing interior.

Levka was trying not to gawk. And Fyke, the onetime first mate on a tanker and therefore responsible for its safety and security, was looking around the great hall, seeing it as a vessel and not a building, trying to see how the engineering laid out.

"One thing, Dobri," he said in a hoarse whisper. "They don't have any sprinkler piping up there." He pointed to the ceiling vaults. "Must have another kind of system, a Micro Mist or Halon."

They walked into a smaller side chamber. It looked like an anteroom where the faithful might meet about the business of the mosque. They passed through this room into another anteroom, and soon they found themselves in a narrow hallway. From an open door could be heard the sound of running water, and there was a sign in several languages, including French and English, that indicated the presence of *Facilities*, as it was so delicately expressed.

Fyke, a seasoned campaigner, never passed up a chance to hit the head, and Levka followed him into the huge white-tiled area, harshly lit by a bank of fluorescent tubes. One wall, also tiled, tilted slightly back, and water flowed down it in a cascading sheet, where Fyke stood and delivered, looking around him at the mosaic-covered tiles as he did so. Levka, wandering a bit, came across a storeroom at the rear of the facility, opened it, and found himself looking at a floor plan of the entire mosque.

"Ray, come see."

Fyke, at the sinks, tidied up and came over. Running a stubby fingertip over the plan, he tapped a section marked off in red.

"That's their maintenance hub. Heating, cooling, electrics, water systems. On this side of the structure, if I'm not turned around, should be a flight of stairs or an elevator—" They heard footfalls and the soft murmur of voices. Levka closed the door, and they both crossed back to the sinks, watching in the mirrors as two small bearded men in the clothing of imams and another man came into the room.

They bowed slightly to Fyke and Levka, who returned the greeting, *Salaam alaikum.* The two imams went into stalls at the back, the other man, youngish, without a beard, dressed in expensive Western clothing, with fine gold-rimmed glasses and clear green eyes, paused on his way to the water wall, looking at Levka.

He came over, a look of concern on his face, his eyes narrowing. He said something to Levka in a language neither Fyke nor Levka understood, smiled, lifted a hand, indicated Levka's black eye. It was no longer black but, rather, a lovely apple green with purple highlights.

"I am . . . a doctor," the man said in accented English. "This eye is not so good. Have you seen an ophthalmologist? There may be some bleeding. Do you experience darkness, my son?"

Levka, steadying, smiled and said yes, he did have some darkness. The man blinked at him, stepped away.

"There is a clinic in the mosque. If you wish, we can have that looked at now. But I must ask, you are not of Islam, are you?"

"No," said Fyke from the sinks. "But we meant no offense."

"Perhaps not. It was your trousers, sir. It is forbidden to attend prayer with trouser cuffs flopping about below your ankles. No devout Muslim would do such a thing. But I do not think you mean to give offense. However, this is a holy place, and this is the evening for prayers and not meant for unbelievers. Tours are available during certain hours.

"So," he said, smiling, light glinting off his lenses as he nodded toward the doors, "you will please go?"

"Yes," said Levka. "No offendings, please. And for my eye, I will go see an . . ."

"Ophthalmologist," he said, bowing. "I would advise it."

He turned away to attend to his business. The two imams came back into the main room, talking between themselves. They bowed again, politely, to Fyke and Levka, said something in Arabic to the young doctor and swept out, footfalls whispering into silence.

"Sir," said Fyke as the young doctor was walking toward the water wall. "May I ask you something?"

The man stopped, looked at Fyke, his expression open but not unfriendly. The mosque was magnificent. Sometimes curiosity got the better of people. "Yes?" he said in his soft, French-tinged voice.

"You say there is a clinic in the mosque, sir. Are you associated with it?"

"I attend there, several nights during the month. For the poor. They do not eat well. Their vision suffers."

"You're on the staff, then?"

"Yes," he said, a shorter answer.

"Then you have heard about the threat against the mosque?"

The doctor blinked at Fyke, his expression altering. He reached into his clothing and took out a small silver pistol, holding it in his hand but loosely, not aiming it at anyone . . . yet.

"We are all armed this evening," he said. "All of the staff, the imams as well, and of course there is added security. As a result of this silly rumor. We are told the Israelis played at some . . . Hebrew game."

"Sir, my name is Raymond Fyke. I'm a British soldier, a member of the Special Air Service. I'm a Christian, not an Israeli. I give you my word of honor, as a British soldier, that the threat is real, that my friend and I are actively trying to prevent an attack on this mosque, and that this attack is happening right now."

The young doctor stepped back, leveled the pistol at Fyke, putting his other hand in a pocket.

Pressing a silent alarm, thought Fyke.

"What sort of threat?"

Fyke shook his shaggy head, his green eyes bright in the hard-blue glare. "I don't know. We believe it has to do with fire."

"Fire? This building is impervious to fire. I am aware of the emergency plan. All imams are instructed in it. Every modern—"

They heard the sounds of boots on stone, a rumble of voices, and two large men in tan uniforms and red berets walked into the room, weapons out, their faces hard and angry.

"Father," said the older man, a dark-skinned, beak-nosed hard case with wary black eyes and a British regimental mustache, "there is trouble?"

"These two Christians, Hamid," said the doctor-imam in a calm tone, "believe the mosque is in danger."

Hamid turned his gunsight glare on Fyke.

"Explain," he barked, his voice echoing off the tiles.

"Your fire system?" asked Fyke, cutting through the bluster in a flat, icy tone. "Was it installed by Arc Light Engineering?"

This took Hamid aback, a visible ripple.

"No. But Arc Light is the general-construction firm. How—"

"Have you heard of Cobalt Hydraulic Systems?"

"Yes," he said, his face losing some of its aggression. "They installed and maintain our fire-suppression systems."

The muzzle of his pistol remained steady, but his manner was softening. "Where do you get your information?"

"I'm SAS. We've been chasing a group of Serbs across the Med. They're connected to a company called Cobalt Hydraulic Systems. Has Cobalt made *any* changes to your system lately?"

"Yes," he said, the muzzle dropping down. "They have upgraded us to what is called a microdroplet system. There are pressurized tanks located all over the mosque. Two of their men are in the control hub right now monitoring the—"

"Take us there now. Please. And get this mosque emptied."

MANDY and Micah were coming in the main gate of the mosque when the doors at the base of the tower opened up with a loud crack and men began to spread out into the courtyard and the cloisters along the perimeter walls, their voices harsh and urgent and tinged with panic and alarm. One running boy, his eyes glancing over at Mandy's uncovered hair, stopped Dalton and said, "Sir, you cannot go in, there is a fire alarm," but Dalton brushed by him, Mandy close behind.

Inside the mosque, as they fought their way through the crush, they saw two guards, weapons at the ready, standing in the central hall. The guards both reacted as soon as they saw Dalton's blond hair, one of them stepping forward quickly.

"You are Captain Dalton of the U.S. Army?"

"Yes—"

"We are to take you to the control—"

They all jumped at the sound of gunfire, distant, muffled, but unmistakable. They heard men shouting orders, then more gunfire. Then Dalton's cell phone rang.

"Fyke?" he inquired.

"We're in the control hub. Two bad guys down. Levka's hit. This place is under control, but they've got pressurized tanks all over the place. Supposed to be a fire-suppression system. They're all filled with ethylene oxide—"

Dalton got it in one take.

"Christ. An FAE?"

"Yeah. A fuel-air explosion. They have the tanks wired with computer-controlled triggers. I think we've got most of them shut down here at the hub. But if even one of those tanks lets go, the whole place will be misted up with the stuff. One spark—it's like a barn full of hay—this entire building and everybody in it are gonna go way up high and come back down as pink rain—"

"Where do you want us?"

"The boat, Mikey. Out on the water side. Stop that boat."

Dalton shut the phone off, turned to the guard.

"This mosque, part of it's over the water, right?"

"Yes, sir. The prayer hall extends right out over the ocean. It has a glass floor. You can see the water below."

"Show me!"

Four of them—two guards, Dalton and Mandy—went down through the archways at a flat run, one of the guards blowing a shrill whistle and shouting at people in French and Arabic. Although the place was clearing out fast, there were still hundreds of men—confused, frightened, or angry—milling about the huge central hall. As the four cleared the third archway, something popped on the far side of the hall, and a cloud of white mist began to fill the area, hissing like a pit full of vipers.

"Don't breathe in," said Dalton to the others as they ran past it. "Don't get near it. Even if it doesn't go off, it'll kill you."

Another tank in a far corner, concealed behind a carved wooden screen, popped and began to hiss. One of the guards stopped, pulling out his pistol.

"No guns!" said Dalton. "No radios. No spark of any kind!"

They reached the final arch and ran out into a wide, soaring space filled with a rippling blue-and-green light. The glimmer of waves rolling under the floor, illuminated by floodlights, reflected up through thick glass panes set into the mosaic floor and turned the entire space into an underwater cave.

"There," said the guard, pointing to an arched, onion-shaped gate with a large carved doorway that was open to the sea.

Beyond the open door, a faint shadow floated on the water. It was lit only by the lights shining on the walls of the mosque. It was a long, slender boat, its windshield reflecting the lights of the mosque as it cruised slowly past the façade. The *Blue Nile*, running dark.

Dalton, followed by the two guards and Mandy, ran through the doorway and out onto a wide stone terrace built over a wall of barrier rock. The ocean was crashing up against the wall, spray flying up, the night air filled with the immense roar of the sea.

The *Blue Nile* was drifting about fifty yards off the shore, and in the glow from the mosque they could see a figure on the bow, steadying some sort of long weapon with a fat, spear-shaped tip. It was an RPG. The wind ripped at Dalton's coat as he lifted the Anaconda, aiming at the figure on the bow. He heard a faint electronic beeping, and then there was a red flash from somewhere inside the boat. The boat seemed to lift up out of the water, riding a billowing red-and-gold flower of light and fire, cracking like an eggshell, pieces of boat went flying off into the night. Then they heard and felt the thudding concussion of the explosion. It hit them all like a physical blow, heat flaring on their faces and hands. They saw a big man, in the water, on fire, struggling in the oil-covered sea. Pieces of the boat and crew began to fall back to earth, flaming splinters, metal, chunks of meat, landing with a hiss on the roiling surface of the water, setting alight the diesel-and-oil slick spreading out from the explosion. A large roller covered with a sheet of flaming fuel picked the man in the water up, driving him toward the shore. Already soaked in fuel, now he was literally a human torch in a lake of fire. His upper body was a molten mass of flames, his mouth a round hole inside a billowing globe of fire. They could hear him screaming—a thin, agonized gull's cry—almost drowned out by the crashing roar of the ocean, the thunder of the surf on the rocks.

They watched the man burn for a while. There was nothing to be done for him. And nothing that *should* have been done either. Aleksandr Vukov was going back to the death that should have taken him in Podujevo, a self-inflicted execution by fire that was long overdue. They continued to watch in silence, grimly fixed on the sight, each person alone with the vision.

It took quite a long time before Vukov, a large man, finally burned down into a small, fiery ball, sinking into the water like a small sun setting, a tongue of fire flaring up at the end. Then he was gone, and there was only the yellow flames rippling across the black seas and a few sticks of smoldering wood bobbing in the surf.

Dalton turned to Mandy, staring out at the ruins of the *Blue Nile*, her face set in hard lines, as she watched what was left of it drifting on the petroleum-soaked waves. She was holding her cell phone in her left hand, down at her side, the way someone holds a weapon.

She moved closer, looked up at him, put her hand on his arm.

"I remembered it," she said with a shaky smile. "Levka's cell phone. In the engine room. He said there was a problem with the gas fumes building up. I guess he was right."

"You took a chance. We all ran through that mist."

"We were outside. All I had was the phone. I thought it was worth a try. Next time, I'll make sure I have a gun."

Dalton and Mandy turned and looked back out at the water.

"Poor Dobri," said Mandy. "I killed his boat."

New York State

LONG ROCK ISLAND, SAINT LAWRENCE RIVER,
UPSTATE NEW YORK,
TEN P.M. LOCAL TIME

The great Saint Lawrence River flowed majestically into the east under a starlit sky. The last traces of an indigo twilight were fading into night, the pink veil of the Milky Way stretching out across the pine-covered islands and rocky shoals of Thousand Islands country. Across the broad back of the river, to the north, the mainland of Canada showed as a wall of forest broken here and there by the lights of a cottage or a small village. The air was cold and clear, the water rippling in silvery curls around this scattered archipelago, around literally hundreds of islands ranging in size from bare rocky outcrops less than a yard across to huge, shaggy green mounds, granite rimmed, with one, two, sometimes three private cottages or estates set out on high points or on cleared land down at the waterside.

Old Money lived on these islands, Old Money came from the mainland on sleek Art Deco motor cruisers or sailing yachts, and Old Money sat warming itself by crackling wood fires, sipping single malts, while the northern night rose up and covered it all with silence, peace, comfort, certitude.

At the little supply village of Clayton, on the U.S. shore, a whippet-thin, sharp-featured woman of indeterminate age with a *Damn Yan-*

kees air of cranky self-confidence about her, her hair a shining bell of blue-black hanging down, cast off the ropes of her motor launch and turned around to speak to the harbor mate.

"I've got enough for a week, Simon," she said in a carrying voice, glaring at Simon, a young man with a round pasty face and darting, nervous eyes. "See to it I'm left alone. You sure Gabe had the wood-shed filled up and the generator checked?"

"He did, ma'am. I loaded the gas cans up myself. Gabe checked the house, opened it up. Being shut all winter, it needed an airing. But everything's fine. You might have a squirrel in the mudroom. But, other than that, it's all ready for you."

The woman nodded, unsmiling, already staring out at the water between her and the island where her great-grandfather had built his home one hundred and three years ago.

Although she knew these waters as well as she knew her own face, she had been delayed for two hours down at the 69 interchange, a tractor trailer accident. She'd had to take a side road damned near all the way to Oswego and hadn't gotten back on to 81 until after Watertown.

So it was dark, dark as a pit, out on the river. And though she was an experienced waterwoman, the cruise down current to Long Rock Island involved some tricky shoal water. And the river was running fast tonight, a deep, cold rushing surge you could feel through the hull of the boat, a thrumming vibration in the ribs.

Well, this timid stuff wasn't going to get her home. She hit the starter, and the little Grew coughed to life. Simon cast off her stern line as the bow came around into the current. She caught it with her left hand and flaked it neatly at her feet. In a moment, the lights of Clayton were falling back behind the stern, and the huge shapes of the islands out in the great river were looming up like freighters all around her.

She followed the navigation lights, steering past all the old familiar landmarks—Pine, Gull, Little Round, Big Round. Basswood Island was coming up. Looked like the Garlands had opened their place up early, lights all over the grounds. Looks like a damned lunar landing. So much for starlight and moonlight. The council had already sent letters to all the islanders, asking them to shut down their dock lights and floodlights so people could enjoy the stars and, every now and then, the northern lights. She heard a high, mournful cry—a loon—on the Canadian side. Closer in came a comical, blatting honk from a solitary Canada goose. Canada geese—a feathery, farting, crapping plague. They ought to shoot them all and feed them to the homeless.

She came slowly around and set a careful course between Basswood and Woronoco islands. She could hear the river current hissing along the granite edges of Woronoco. Little Basswood went by, a mound in the night. She edged the boat to port a little, aiming for the docks on the north side of Long Rock Island, her private island, freehold and clear title and riparian rights for over a hundred years. A rock in uncertain times.

The big house was dark except for the porch lights, and a single orange lamp marked her dock. Executing a practiced curling turn, she threaded back through the current and slipped in smoothly between the swing booms, gliding to a muttering coast in the moorings, finally bumping up against the deck, quickly stepping off with a line in her hand and snaking it in a running reef around the iron stanchion.

She looked down at the bags of food piled in the stern, sighed. She had wanted to be alone, had *insisted* on being alone, after these frustrating weeks, after all the *recriminations*, and so she was alone. She would have to make a couple of trips up to the house. She decided to take the scotch and the perishables first.

It was a long walk up a rocky slope to the side door. The house rose up before her, black against the stars, walls made of granite from the Canadian Shield, with leaded windows and peaked dormers.

Hardly a *cottage*, she thought, more like a hunting lodge for a merchant prince. Which it had been. But that's what they still called it, at least on her side of the family.

She punched the code into the security pad, the automatic interior light came on and the heavy side door slid open. She carried her bags into the mudroom, breathing in the smell of old pines, long-ago wood fires, her father's pipe smoke . . . And something else? A darker scent, some sort of aromatic smoke? Gabe, she was thinking as she set the bags down and came down the hall to the main living area, still in the dark. If he'd been sitting in the big room smoking one of those cigars, she'd have his legs cut off at the . . .

There was a hard-looking young man sitting in a leather wingback next to the fireplace and facing the hallway entrance. A single reading lamp was burning at his shoulder, his long blond hair shining with amber highlights, his rocky face in darkness, a large revolver shining in his right hand, the muzzle aimed at her. "Miss Vale," said Dalton, not rising. "You're late."

Mariah Vale turned, stepped to a hallway table, jerked the drawer open.

"Your little Smith is on the mantle," said Dalton, standing in the doorway, smiling down at her. "Unloaded. I hope you don't mind, but I made myself a drink. Would you like one?"

Vale turned around and glared at him, fear in her eyes and in the lines around them. Fear and something else. But she was fighting it. Dalton watched as she literally wrapped herself in an invisible cloak of federal authority. She even seemed to get a little larger.

"Yes. I'll have a drink," she said, stepping past him, sweeping with immense dignity into the great room and flicking on a table lamp. Yellow light flared out, revealing a stone-walled room with low wooden beams, a massive granite fireplace, lots of warm plaids in all the colors of autumn, and a large green-leather sofa. Vale got to the long bar by the wall of windows, started clattering crystal, her hands shaking as she did.

Dalton walked over to the coffee table—a single slab of maple— picked up a bottle of Laphroiag and a glass, poured her a stiff one, set it down on a side table by one of the plaid armchairs. He picked up two ice cubes and dropped them gently into her glass and stepped away, the revolver sloping down, then took a seat in the wingback again.

Mariah Vale came over—vibrating still but mastering herself with effort—sat down, straightened the crease of her navy blue slacks, plucked at her starched white blouse, picked up her scotch, and looked at him, her face settling into a magistrate's cold judgmental regard. She had learned this intimidating look from her grandfather, a famous jurist and a senior lecturer in law at Cornell.

"How did you get on my island in the first place, Mr. Dalton? Some secret covert-ops trickery?"

"Yes. I hired a boat. Don't tell anyone. It's a trade secret."

"I'm at a loss to understand why you are here. You have been re-instated. Allegations quietly dropped. Your contribution to the prevention of an atrocity in Morocco has been recognized . . ."

"It's also been classified and sealed. And the Moroccan authorities are still calling it a Jewish plot foiled by the Brits."

"I am not responsible for what those people manage to convince themselves of," she said. "And the Israelis can take care of themselves. Regarding your achievements, there are stars on the wall at Langley. Many of those stars record acts that have also been sealed and the details classified. No one finds that demeaning."

Dalton nodded.

"I get that. I'm fine with it."

She sipped at her drink, seeming to relax into herself, feeling more like the judge than the prisoner now.

"And yet here you are, effectively throwing it all away. And why? So you could throw a fright into a person you dislike?"

"I don't dislike you, Miss Vale. I *disagree* with you."

"You're thinking of the role my committee plays in righting some of the Agency's past wrongs? Mr. Dalton, we are attempting to redress grievous excesses, acts of prolonged savagery, that have stained our national honor."

"I'm not recording this, Mariah. You can hold the Patrick Henry stuff. I'm not even here to try to set you straight. I think, in the main, you're doing what you really think is the right thing to do. I don't even think you're an evil person. You're sort of accidentally dangerous. You can't help yourself."

He shrugged, took a sip of the scotch, went on in a low, amiable rumble, his expression calm.

"I think you may be a little too . . . fastidious . . . for the job. And I'm puzzled why it's okay with you that we stand off at twenty thousand feet and launch Hellfires and Paveways into crowded villages in Yemen and Waziristan, knowing with absolute certainty we're going to kill and maim at least a few innocent women and kids in order to take out a couple of jihadists and a donkey but it's not okay to rough up a prisoner who might know which train station or airport his buddies are going to blow up."

"The first is war, but the second is not. It's a violation of the Geneva Convention."

"So's embedding your fighters in the middle of a crowded village packed with innocent civilians, like Hamas did in Gaza, knowing they're going to die and being happy to use their deaths as propaganda."

"The world can be dark," she said. "We are the light. We remain true to what is American by *never* compromising our sacred principles in exchange for some fleeting sense of security. America shines through the darkness *because* of those principles."

Dalton pulled at his scotch, set it down again.

"Fine, ringing words," said Dalton." We'll see how that all works out for you. We'll see if the American people are ready to lose sons and daughters so you and your crowd can feel really good about yourselves. I find it's risky to preen at funerals. Anyway, this is not really why I came. This is between you and me. It's personal."

Her face paled slightly, and she reached for her glass.

"Fine," she said. "It's personal, I'm tired. I'd like to go to bed. Make your point, say your say, and then get out and swim for it."

Dalton reached into his coat pocket, pulled out a piece of paper, walked it over to her. She put on a pair of gold reading glasses and held it up to the glow of the table lamp. Dalton noticed that the sheet of paper was vibrating very slightly.

CLASSIFIED UMBRA EYES DIAL
INTERNAL AUDIT COMMITTEE
File 92r: DALTON, MICAH
Service ID: REDACTED

Security cameras outside the Westbahnhof station Auto-Park in Vienna confirm that DALTON and MIKLAS arrived there at 0821 hours and that it appeared from their actions that some sort of physical intimacy had taken place, which is common in hostage situations if rape is a component.

Although the main security camera at Leopoldsberg malfunctioned, peripheral cameras confirm that DALTON and MIKLAS were next seen in the parking lot of the castle at 0917 hours, just prior to the explosion of a brown Saab.

In the confusion of the blast, which killed one and injured two police officers, the authorities lost track of the pair, and their current location or direction remains unknown.

MOSSAD confirms that the body found in the trunk of the Saab was that of GALAN, ISSADORE—a former MOSSAD agent currently in the employ of the Italian Carabinieri in Venice. BDS officers from

*the Vienna Station have been dispatched to Venice to interview the
local officials.*

*As GALAN, ISSADORE, was an Israeli citizen, the MOSSAD have
expressed a desire to assist us in our inquiries into this matter. As a
courtesy and at the request of the Consulate, we have notified the
MOSSAD of DALTON's last known GPS coordinates, as well as a
description of his vehicle.*

*Actions considered this time/date after consultation with Commander
PEARSON, DD of Clandestine Services, and his Adviser Pro Tem,
D. CATHER, former DD of Clandestine, with the DNI in attendance,
include but are not limited to the possibility of an official Joint Task
Force Liaison with elements of the FBI, the BDS, and the Justice
Department, under the aegis of the Audit Committee's Official
Mandate: (op cit: Presidential Finding F2391).*

*No conclusion has as yet been reached, pending final decisions from
POTUS/DNI.*

LEGAL IMPLICATIONS:

*The Secretariat, having consulted with General Counsel Dir/CIA
Justice and DNI, takes note that new POTUS Intelligence ROE Policy
mandates that, since all subsequent events that occurred in the early
hours of the following morning had their predicate cause in DALTON's
aggressive response to the possibility of surveillance by Parties Unknown
to him, Presidential Finding F2391 requires that legal responsibility
for these outcomes must devolve upon DALTON and not upon this
Agency or the U.S. Government, since DALTON was not acting in
any official capacity as a CIA employee but as a private citizen.*

CONCLUSION:

We bear no legal responsibility for and offer no protection to *DALTON, MICAH, in this matter. This is the* official position *of the United States Government and as such will be communicated to the relevant authorities in Vienna, the UN, Tel Aviv, INTERPOL, and the ICC officials in Bonn. No statement will be issued to the media or the press concerning this matter until it has been resolved by the investigating authorities or by external events.*

MARIAH VALE/OD/DD/EXECUTIVE SECRETARIAT

Vale read the page without comment. Only a very slight tremor in her hands and a certain fixed look in her eyes gave anything away. She set the page down, looked at him over the rims of her reading glasses, her mouth a little prim.

"First, this is a highly classified document. How did you obtain it?"

"Fell off a truck. Tough read, isn't it? More of an indictment than a report."

"This was how the events were interpreted," she said, looking away and then coming back. "The report is a reasonable inference from the facts on the ground, as they were—"

"That passive voice . . . it always gets me. I'll bet Pilate used it in his official report to Rome. 'After due deliberation, a decision was reached to crucify the subject according to accepted practice. A regulation cross of recycled wood was obtained from on-site inventory and nails procured from local suppliers after a competitive and open-bidding process, subject to appeal. Regulation hammers were then deployed as per the manual.'"

"Please. You're hardly Jesus Christ."

"True enough. Anyway, what I'm getting at is that middle part, where you write you have notified the Mossad of my last known GPS

coordinates as well as a description of my vehicle. I found that interesting. I mean, aside from how happy you were to feed me to the
Mossad. But the bit about the GPS data, I wondered about that, since
part of the indictment against me was that I deliberately shut down
my BlackBerry to avoid any kind of tracing operation and that after
the fact none of my BlackBerry voice recordings were available."

"That's hardly conclusive—"

"No. Just suggestive. But then there's this . . ."

He held up a small digital recorder.

"Couple of guys in the Mossad got me this little sound bite. Care
to hear it?"

She nodded, her eyes fixed on the machine.

Dalton clicked the button. A tinny voice came out but recogniz
ably his own.

"Galan's a problem, a nasty one. I need to take care of it."

"Pretty damning, isn't it, Mariah? Turned out not to be quite accurate. The Mossad worked the tape over and determined that it had
been doctored. A slice of the digital recording had been taken out.
By somebody good. It was an important slice. I managed to get hold
of the original. It was when I was talking to a woman named Sally
Fordyce, in Clay Pearson's office. Another one of those voice records
that dropped off the grid after I got out of Vienna. Lend an ear,
Mariah."

He held the machine up again, clicked the button.

*"Galan's got a problem, a nasty one. I need to meet him, take
care of it."*

He reversed it, hit the button again.

"Galan's a problem, a nasty one. I need to take care of it."

There was a silence. Dalton put the recorder away.

"Well," said Vale. "It's obviously been doctored."

"Obviously."

"In an attempt to . . . *incriminate* you."

He smiled at her, nodding, pulled out a pack of Sobranies.

"Care for one?"

She looked at the pack for a time.

"Yes. I think I would."

Dalton leaned across, the pack open. She took a turquoise one, and Dalton lit it for her. She inhaled, started to cough, mastered it.

"Sorry. I don't smoke," she said through a cloud, her face reddening, her eyes watering. "Or at least, I didn't."

"Couple other things," said Dalton, lighting one for himself. "A woman named Veronika Miklas was able to get a video of the main surveillance camera at Leopoldsberg. It showed a man we subsequently identified as Aleksandr Vukov, in the early morning hours, delivering a brown Saab to the Leopoldsberg parking lot. This tape, which clearly shows that at the very least I had an accomplice, was supposed to have gone missing. The kid who obtained it, a young man named Jürgen Stodt, a member of the Austrian OSE, was later found floating facedown in the Danube. He had been beaten to death."

"How terrible!"

"Yes. Veronika Miklas was shattered by it."

"I would imagine so. Where is she now?"

"In Venice. Under the protection of the Carabinieri."

"Do you have a copy of that video fragment?"

"I sent it to the Audit Committee. You didn't get a copy?"

"I'm . . . temporarily on leave from the Secretariat. For administrative . . . realignment. Clay Pearson will step into the chair until the process works through."

"Really? You're being hung out to dry, then, for failing to nail me to the door of Clandestine Services?"

"Micah, I have willingly shouldered much of the blame for the procedural errors that led to your . . . situation. Concerning these . . ."

"Procedural errors?"

"These tapes, that doctored voice clip—"

"Are you familiar with the term *Verwandtschaft?*"

She looked genuinely puzzled.

"No. It's obviously German, but—"

"It's an OSE code for NATO. It was on the original order authorizing a surveillance operation to be started as soon as I got to the top of the Schottentor trolley station in Vienna. Ray Fyke talked to a source in Prague, ex-Stasi, who confirmed that although the *Verwandtschaft* tag stood for NATO, the actual request came from Langley. From your office in Langley, to be specific."

"I did . . . no such thing. I made no such call. The phone log—it must have been . . . doctored . . . to make me look like a traitor! And I am accused by some anonymous ex Stasi criminal. I didn't make that call. Why would I?"

"Great question. I have another one. My BlackBerry codes got broken by Piotr Kirikoff. Because he had the codes, he could read my GPS. He sent people to Veronika Miklas's flat to kill her and lay it on me. This was part of a general plot to set me up, to set America up, for an attack on a mosque in Casablanca. It almost worked. If it had, my history in the NATO operation in Podujevo where my mistakes cost the lives of innocent Muslims would have been . . . leaked . . . to support the idea that I was some sort of Christian terrorist on a crusade against Muslims. If it had worked, and it could have, it would have made the Danish cartoons thing look like a fistfight at a Legion Hall. My question, how did Kirikoff get the keys to break my Black-Berry?"

"I don't know. How *could* I know?"

"Maybe he got them from you?"

"What . . . ? I would communicate secret code to a Russian agent? Codes I have no access to in the first place—"

"Would you like to hear my read on it? How it looks?"

"I don't know. Actually, probably not."

"Some recent history. You knew Colin Dale. You fought our investigation of Dale every step of the way. He got exposed as a long-time mole anyway. Even then, you refused to allow charges to go forward—"

"Colin Dale is dead. He committed suicide in Florida—"

"Since then, you've done everything you could do to break Clandestine Services. You've succeeded in crippling our HumInt operations, and you've got half the field agents in Clandestine lawyering up and hiding under their desks. We're losing allies, the Russians are making moves all over the world, the Iranians think we're a farce, and in the meantime you're busy burning down our own intelligence services. That's what moles do."

"You . . . You think *I'm* a mole?"

Dalton sat back, stubbed his cigarette out.

"No," he said after some thought. "You're not a mole. You could be. You *might* be. Hell, if you look at all the damage you're doing, you might as well be. But no, I don't believe you're a mole. I do believe you're a danger to yourself and others, and that something has to be done about you. You need to be stopped. You don't belong in the CIA. You should be running a B and B in Rockport, or maybe an earnest little NGO for the United Nations."

"But . . . But I'm *not*. I'm not a . . . mole! I . . . You know this. You agree, then? I'm being framed. Someone is working to ruin me. We need to find out. You can help me. It must be someone inside the—"

"Don't tell me. Inside the Agency. Isn't that what happened to me, Mariah? I said so, and nobody believed me. Why should anyone believe you?"

Dalton got up, drained his glass, picked up a cell phone and dialed a number, hit SEND, and looked at the screen.

ON THE WAY

"Anyway, I think I can make a good enough case," he said, ending the call.

"What? A case where? With who?"

"That you're a mole. With whoever will listen."

"But that's not what you actually believe?"

"Nope. Actually, I think we both have a pretty good idea who gave Kirikoff my BlackBerry codes. *Cui bono,* is the phrase. No, I don't think it really was you, but I'm going to work real hard at selling the idea anyway, because if I can, then you'll be gone—out of the game entirely—and the CIA will be a better place . . ."

"You'll . . . You'll *destroy* me. The allegation is enough. The press *never* covers a retraction the way it features an *allegation.* Even if I can *prove* my innocence, it would take months, years. In the meantime, I'll never get another responsible position . . . I'll be out of the Agency, out of public service. Out of public life. My family name . . ."

She looked around the house, at the solid political power and the family forces that had built it up and held it all together for over a hundred years, the connections it represented, the money and influence and prestige. "Dalton . . . Micah. Please. You can't do this."

"Why the hell not? Only fair. You did everything you could to drive me out. Now it's your turn. That Audit report you put together, that . . . *Skorpion directive* . . . it was meant to get me killed. Didn't work, but no thanks to you. You did that to *me,* so why shouldn't I return the favor?"

"Because . . . Because I'm *innocent.* I did not do the things you're accusing me of doing. I am not a traitor, Micah. I'm a *patriot.*"

The sound of a boat, muttering in the dark, coming closer.

"Yeah?" he asked, tossing his cigarette into the fire. "So was I."

PERSONNEL NOTES:
general distribution

The Executive Committee, after reviewing the files and consulting with POTUS and DNI confirms that Commander Clay Pearson will take over the office of Inspector General, with all related duties and responsibilities, effective immediately.

Commander Pearson expressed his deep sadness at the passing of Mariah Vale, who was tragically drowned in a boating accident last month while vacationing at her family home in Upstate New York. Commander Pearson's duties at Clandestine will be taken over by Deacon Cather, who, in spite of health concerns, has reluctantly consented to resume his old role as the steady hand on the tiller of the National Clandestine Service.

The Director and his staff wish to express their deep appreciation of the efforts of both Commander Clay Pearson and Mr. Cather to assist the Agency in the difficult period after the tragic passing of Mariah Vale, whose unceasing work at the Audit Committee, the Secretariat, and later at the Inspector General's Office, did so much to make the Central Intelligence Agency what it is today.

Debra Black, Chief of Human Resources

Central Intelligence Agency